Beaumont reined in  one arm, the index direction.

'That scum,' Beau... said, slowly but clearly, 'is a murderer and a rapist, whom I personally brought to justice and sentenced to death. It was he who was responsible for the foul murder of Sir John Seagrave's daughter. I had thought him hanged for his villainy. I ask again, what ill-fate allows him to be still with us, and apparently roaming free?'

'The same thing that brings us all here.' It was the voice of a nobleman, speaking in calm and measured but nonetheless firm tones. 'The service of His Majesty the King.'

Daniel Hall is in his twenties. He graduated in history from the University of Leicester, where he was elected deputy president of the students' union, and he now works for South Gloucestershire Council. *Kemp: The Road to Crécy* is the first novel in the series.

By the same author

Kemp: Passage at Arms

KEMP
THE ROAD TO CRÉCY

Daniel Hall

ORION

An Orion Paperback
First published in Great Britain by Orion in 1996
This paperback edition published in 1997 by
Orion Books Ltd,
Orion House, 5 Upper St Martin's Lane,
London WC2H 9EA

A CIP catalogue record for this book
is available from the British Library.

ISBN 0 75281 080 4

Typeset at The Spartan Press Ltd,
Lymington, Hants
Printed in Great Britain by
Clays Ltd, St Ives plc.

For my parents

ACKNOWLEDGEMENTS

Thanks to the following people, without whom this book would not have been:

Michael Curtiz, Errol Flynn, Olivia de Havilland, Basil Rathbone, Claude Raines *et al* for exciting my interest in the Middle Ages at an early age; Terry Gilliam and Terry Jones for showing me what the Middle Ages were *really* like; Norman Housley for encouraging my interest at an academic level; the late Alfred Burne, whose book *The Crécy War* inspired me to write about the Hundred Years War in particular; Jonathan Sumption, Michael Packe, R. J. Barber and H. J. Hewitt (along with countless others) for their scholarship; Tony Harcourt for technical advice about longbow archery and many other aspects of the medieval life; Duncan Cloud for his scholarship in medieval ecclesiastical Latin; and James Hale for advice, support, encouragement and, most important of all, faith.

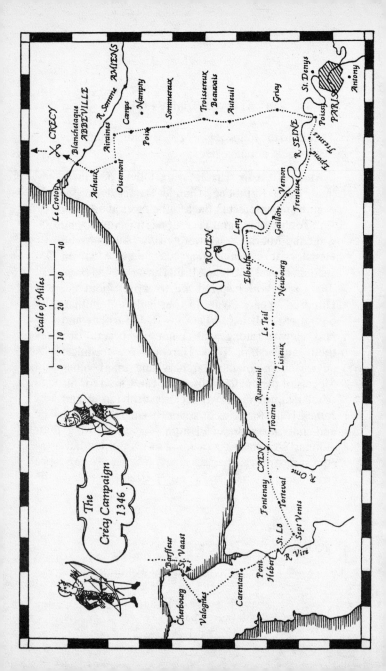

The Crécy Campaign 1346

Scale of Miles
0 5 10 20 30 40

CRECY

AMIENS
ABBEVILLE
R. Somme
Blanchetaque
Le Crotoy
Airaines
Acheux
Oisemont
Camps
Poix
Nampty
Sommeraux
Troissereux
Beauvais
Auteuil
Grisy
St. Denys
PARIS
Antony
Poissy
Yvrans
Epon
R. SEINE
Freneuse
Vernon
Gaillon
Lery
Elbeuf
ROUEN
Neuburg
Rumesnil
Le Teil
Lisieux
Troarne
CAEN
Fontenay
Torteval
Sept Vents
St. Lô
Pont Hebert
R. Vire
Carentan
Valognes
Cherbourg
Barfleur
St. Vaast
R. Orne

CHAPTER ONE

The hart paused by a pool in the middle of the glade and turned its head this way and that, its snout twitching. It was a magnificent beast, fully-grown with ten tines on its antlers, only now beginning to run to fat in preparation for the approaching winter and the time of rut. Its chestnut coat matched the reddish-brown leaves that carpeted the ground beneath the trees. A thin blanket of mist hung a few feet above the ground; the landscape was silent save for a steady drip of condensation falling from the branches of trees, the air rank with the dank smell of decaying leaves. Satisfied that there was no immediate danger, the hart dipped its head to drink from the pool.

A twig snapped a short distance away. The hart raised its head abruptly, standing motionless as it stared through the trees, its hind legs tensed ready to spring. After a few moments it saw figures moving slowly towards it, three green-clad riders seated astride horses, allowing their mounts to crop at the occasional tufts of grass that grew amongst the trees as they advanced. Then it saw two more figures, a man being led by a dog on a leash snuffling at the ground before it.

It was the smell that decided the hart; the hunters had made the mistake of approaching from up-wind. Reacting at once, the hart leapt over the stream and bounded away from them. One of the riders turned to the huntsman on foot who held the leash of the scenting hound, 'Sound the *chasse*!'

The huntsman had already lifted his horn, which hung

from one shoulder by a baldrick, to his lips, and now he sounded the warbling fanfare to announce the chase. A hundred yards behind the three riders, more huntsmen unleashed their tawny-brown alaunts, swift and tenacious hunting dogs that would take over where the scenting-lymer left off and bring the hart to bay. The three riders spurred their mounts into a canter, riding as swiftly as they dared through the trees, but they were soon overtaken by the baying alaunts.

The hart had moved swiftly but, as the whole wood came alive with the sound of horns, baying dogs, and hunters urging the dogs on, it realised that this would be a lengthy pursuit, a race of endurance.

More alaunts were bounding out of the trees to the right, released by their handlers as the hart passed the relay points the huntsmen had planned in advance; it was now being driven. Crazy with panic at the tumult in its wake, driven on by fresh relays of alaunts, the hart crashed through the undergrowth, heedless of the trail it was leaving in its wake.

Half a mile further on, a spread-out line of green-clad archers waited amongst the trees. They had heard the sounding of the *chasse*, and now their ears picked up the distant but approaching crash of horses, dogs and men blundering through the bracken. They each took an arrow from the soft cloth quivers they wore at their belts and laid them across their elmwood bows, callused fingers finding grey goose-feather flights, nocking them to hempen bowstrings. They then stood waiting, motionless, even their breath no longer rasping from their lips to form clouds of condensation in the chill autumnal air. It took immense strength just to draw those massive bows, but these men were skilled and experienced archers. They were English yeomen, destined to make a name for themselves as the deadliest killers in Christendom.

Approaching the line of archers from up-wind, the hart could not smell them, and in its panicky flight it was too busy to look out for fresh dangers ahead. It burst out of the trees into a broad clearing, realised it had made a mistake in breaking cover, but did not check its flight for an instant, bounding over the grass and heading for the trees on the other side. It was less than ten yards away when the arrow took it full in the chest. It never saw its killer, for the young man who loosed the fatal shaft stood in front of a tree, his torn green coat and dirty face blending with the lichen-covered trunk. The barbed arrowhead tore effortlessly through flesh, and the hart stumbled, its long, powerful haunches crumpling suddenly beneath it, so that it was dead before it hit the ground, the paler fur of its chest now spotted with blood that steamed in the cold air.

The archers emerged from their concealment in the released tension of the moment after the kill, and gathered in a circle around the dead hart.

'It's . . . it's dead,' one man pronounced plaintively.

'Aye and like.' Only the youngest of the archers seemed unperturbed, crouching over the dead hart to tease his arrow free of the bloody wound. Although perhaps no more than sixteen years of age, he was tall, and possessed shoulders broadened from a decade of pushing a plough. His green coat was of coarse cloth, worn over a fustian tunic, woollen leggings, and wooden clogs. He wore a round, broad-brimmed ploughman's cap over a torn hood, rags for mittens, and a bracer of hardened leather on his left wrist polished by years of use. A pair of dark, blue-grey eyes were set in a face that was tanned from a lifetime spent out in the open, and a tousled thatch of pale-blond hair spilled out from under his hood.

'Dear heart alive!' The speaker, though four years older, had the looks of the youth in coarser detail. 'You've killed it, Martin!'

3

'Aye.' Having finally freed the barbed arrowhead from the hart's flesh, Martin Kemp inspected it intently before cleaning it with a rag, as if more interested in the condition of the arrowhead than anything his brother had to say – which, Thomas Croft reflected wryly, was probably the case. Croft was the reeve of the village of Knighton, as responsible for conveying Sir John Beaumont's demands to his villeins and tenants as he was for being the villagers' representative to the lord of Stone Gate Manor. Croft was in his late thirties, a freeman who had been selected for the post of reeve by the tithing, the village's governing body, an appointment which had to be approved by Beaumont. It was customary for the post of reeve to be reappointed each year at the end of September, but since both Beaumont and the villagers found the current incumbent honest and competent in his work, he had been reeve for several years now, and had already been re-elected for the coming agricultural year.

'We were only supposed to wound it, to make it easier to catch,' Croft pointed out. 'The honour of the kill was supposed to go to Sir John.'

A member of the Leicestershire squirearchy, Sir John Beaumont was not a wealthy man; at least, not by the standards of the nobility. He could not afford enough dogs and men to hunt *par force des chiens*, as was the preferred manner on the continent, so instead he had to use the old style of 'bow and stable' hunting, using village bondsmen as archers, in return giving them half a day off from the boon-work that they owed him as his villeins. It was hardly befitting a man of noble birth, so he tried to combine this economy of manpower with the nobility of the chivalrous *par force des chiens*, riding after his quarry on horseback.

'Then he should learn to catch his own venison,' Martin asserted sullenly. Croft admired Martin Kemp's spirit but did not approve of it; spirit was a quality villeins could

4

well do without. Martin's had always stood him in good stead in fights and football matches with the boys from the neighbouring village of Oadby, but with it came a rebellious streak that chafed against the three days' boon-work he was required to work on Beaumont's demesne each week. Croft had always suspected that one day it would lead him into a head-on clash with his superiors.

Beaumont's squire, Richard Stamford, rode into the clearing on a roan courser even as the baying packs of alaunts streamed out of the undergrowth. Stamford was a handsome lad in his mid-teens, with bright blue eyes and curly blond hair hanging in a thick, waved bob, dressed in a close-fitting cote-hardie of emerald velvet that barely covered his crotch, a pair of tight-fitting hose, and a furred cloak with dagged hems fastened on his right shoulder with four silver buttons. Seeing the six peasants standing around the hart's dead body he reined in abruptly, staring down his nose at them. Then he turned his attention to the slain quarry, and saw it was just as noble a beast as the chief huntsman had promised him. 'Who slew the hart?' he demanded coldly. He might be younger even than Martin Kemp, but he had all the years of the ancestors he could trace back to the time of the Norman Conquest to give him authority.

At first no one said anything; they shuffled their feet, unable to meet Stamford's harsh glare.

'Who slew . . .' Stamford began again.

'I did,' Martin interrupted, meeting Stamford's glare defiantly.

Stamford's courser was prancing skittishly amongst the alaunts, and he had to tug on its reins so that he could continue to meet Martin's gaze. 'You were told not to kill the beast, man! You were to wound it, to bring it to bay so that I or my master could deal the death-stroke.'

5

Martin shrugged. 'I'm a poor shot,' he lied. Despite his youth, he was the best archer in the village, and the others could not suppress their sniggering.

Stamford suspected that he was being mocked, and knew he could not allow the insult to go unpunished. He glared at Martin for a moment, then dismounted, handing the bridle of his courser to another peasant before slapping Martin savagely. Martin took the blow without retaliating but without flinching from it, either, even though it drew a trickle of blood from the corner of his mouth. That only infuriated Stamford more. He knocked Martin's hat from his head and, swinging wildly at him, caught him on the temple with a powerful blow that made the youth stagger. 'Doff your hat when you address me, churl!' he snapped.

'Aye, Master Stamford,' Martin replied sullenly, turning around and bending over to retrieve his hat from the ground. In a final venting of his frustration, Stamford kicked him in the backside, sending him sprawling on his face in the mud. Martin lay there for moment with the alaunts running all around, and then something within him snapped and he pushed himself back on to his feet. Before he even realised what he was doing, he had struck Stamford.

Despite Martin's size it was not a powerful blow, being guided more by anger than by skill. But it caught Stamford so off-guard that he stumbled, tripping over a dog to land on his backside in the mud. He stared up at Martin in numbed disbelief. 'How . . . how dare you? How *dare* you?'

The other peasants were looking on in horrified disbelief, knowing Martin had overstepped the mark.

Stamford quickly pushed himself to his feet and swung at Martin again. The squire had trained for warfare since childhood, and was skilled with both sword and lance; but fist-fighting was for peasants. Martin ducked the blow, caught Stamford by the wrist, and twisted his arm up into the small of his back. Stamford gasped in pain.

'Don't you touch me!' Martin snarled in his ear. Then he pushed Stamford forward so that he fell on his face as Martin had done a few moments earlier. The scene would have been comic had it been a fellow churl Martin had been fighting and not his lord's squire.

'Dear Heaven!' protested Michael. 'For all loves, Martin, what do you think you're doing?' He tried to grab his youngest brother by the arm, but Martin shrugged him off angrily.

Then Stamford was pushing himself to his feet, his face suffused with rage. Tugging his hunting sword from the scabbard that hung at his belt he lunged at Kemp.

'Look out, lad!' cried Simkin Sewell, the oldest of the six peasants, a grizzled ancient who was too old to care whether or not he earned the displeasure of his betters.

Martin turned and barely managed to dodge the thrust. He clamped his hand over Stamford's wrist, and the two of them wrestled for possession of the sword until Croft decided that it was time to intervene, interposing himself between the two combatants. Taking their lead from the reeve, the other peasants lent a hand, pulling Martin and Stamford apart, and at that moment Sir John Beaumont rode into the clearing on his chestnut courser, followed by his daughter Beatrice astride a white jennet.

Beaumont was a tall, well-built man in his late thirties, the hood of his brown cote-hardie pulled back to reveal dark hair, his green cloak thrown back across his left shoulder.

Beatrice was dressed in a close-fitting green and auburn gown, her burnished-copper hair completely hidden from view by her coif. She was in her mid teens, small and delicate of stature, a sickly child who had defied the odds simply by living so long. With her pale, angular face and her large blue eyes with long dark lashes, she was the very

7

image of her mother, who had died giving birth to her. But whereas her mother had been soft-spoken and demure, there was a wilful streak in Beatrice of which her father ill-approved. Yet he knew he had only himself to blame: deprived of the young wife he had loved so dearly, he had doted on his only child, denying her nothing.

The chief huntsman emerged behind them, a burly man with thick black brows and a bushy beard.

'God's love!' exclaimed Beaumont. 'What is going on here? How came you to this pass, Dickon?'

The peasants holding Stamford hurriedly released him, and the squire returned his sword to its scabbard, straightening his clothing with as much dignity as he could muster. 'This churl dared to raise his hand to me, Sir John,' he said, indicating Martin with an arrogant toss of his head.

Beaumont turned his attention to where Martin stood between the two peasants still holding him. 'Well, boy? Is it true? Did you raise your hand to Master Stamford?'

Martin, who had been staring up at Beatrice, turned now to meet Beaumont's gaze. 'Aye, Sir John, but . . .' he began.

'Silence! There is no excuse. You shall be punished for your impudence, churl.' As lord of the manor, Beaumont's powers over his bondsmen barely stopped short of life and death. 'Take him, Wade,' he added to the huntsman.

Martin said nothing, knowing it was useless to argue, but he glared malevolently at Beaumont as Wade grasped him firmly by the upper left arm. Beaumont had already turned his attention to where the body of the hart lay. 'Who slew the hart?'

'He did.' Having climbed back into the saddle of his courser, Stamford indicated Martin. 'That's how we came to blows. He disobeyed our instructions.'

'Should we unmake the hart?' asked Wade. 'Unmaking' was the final ritual of hunting, the flaying and butchering of the hart's carcass, and rewarding the dogs with the choicest giblets.

'There seems little purpose in it now,' muttered Beaumont. But the dogs had at least played their part and deserved their reward. Beaumont dismounted from his courser, rolling back his sleeves. With Stamford's aid, he turned the carcass on its back and slit its throat up the length of the neck, pulling back the skin in flaps and cutting through the flesh down to the neck bone. Still holding on to Kemp with his right hand, Wade lifted his hunting horn to his lips and blew the 'death'. The dogs were briefly allowed to run in and tear at the raw flesh with their teeth for a few moments, before the finest morsels were cut from the hart. The tenderest muscles were all destined for Beaumont's dinner table, but the alaunts were rewarded with the rest of the meat, the lymer being given the heart. Black carrion crows circled in the sky above.

'A pity that that peasant's stupidity should rob us of our sport,' grumbled Stamford while he rode at a slow walk to the manor house with Beaumont and Beatrice, followed by the huntsmen, dog-handlers, dogs and peasants. 'It might have been a fine chase otherwise.'

'I would rather be chasing Frenchmen,' replied Beaumont, clenching his fist around the hilt of the broadsword that hung in its scabbard from his jewelled baldrick. 'It is three years since I last drew my sword in battle.'

Stamford drew his own sword and leaned from the saddle of his courser to slash listlessly at a few stalks of wheat. 'You at least have had the chance to prove yourself in battle, Sir John,' he said, with an arrogant toss of his head.

'I'm certain there will be other campaigns,' said

Beaumont's daughter, smiling. It always amused her to hear men talk of fighting as if it were their whole *raison d'être*.

'Aye, and like as not my lord of Derby will not ask us on those campaigns, either!' said Beaumont. Only three months earlier Henry of Derby had sailed to the king's fiefdom of Gascony to campaign against the armies of Philip of Valois, the man who sat – unrightfully, in the opinion of all loyal Englishmen – on the throne of France.

'Oh, come now, Father!' teased Beatrice. 'Do not be so childish! Why not swallow your pride and volunteer your services?'

'I have nothing to prove,' he replied stoically. 'I've already fought for his Majesty in the fields of France. If he should need my services again, he knows where I may be found.'

Beatrice turned to Stamford, who rode alongside her, attentive as ever. 'And what about you, Dickon? I've often heard you talk of war, yet it seems to me you have much to prove before you can win your spurs. Will you offer your services to the king? Or simply grow old waiting for an invitation?'

'My lady, I would fain ride alone against all the men the usurper Valois can muster, if you should but command it,' Stamford replied gallantly, falling almost unconsciously into the formalised, exaggerated idiom of the court.

She laughed merrily. 'How ridiculous you are!'

Stamford scowled. Ever since he and Beatrice were children, there had been a tacit agreement between their parents that they would one day be married. Yet Beatrice coquettishly persisted in spurning his romantic overtures, and he was reluctant to press the issue until he had proved himself worthy by winning his spurs in battle. For her part, Beatrice did not truly care whether or not a man had proved himself in combat, but she knew of Stamford's obsession with winning glory in battle, and it amused her to tease him.

They had reached the fortified house of Stone Gate Manor. It had been built in Norman times, and the land had been in the possession of the Beaumont family for the past ten generations. The high-gabled stone house had neither doors nor windows in its two outer walls; the inner walls faced across a courtyard enclosed by a high stone wall. Inside the courtyard stood a chapel adjoining the house, and some small wooden buildings that comprised the kitchens, servants' quarters, the stables, the kennels, and the mews and the falconer's hut. There were also three beehives and a large dovecot. At the centre stood a drawing well, surrounding by a low stone wall and topped off with a roof and winch. The dog-handlers returned the lymer and the alaunts back to the kennels, and Beaumont, Stamford and Beatrice dismounted, handing the bridles of their horses to waiting grooms.

'What should I do with this one?' asked Wade, indicating Martin.

Beaumont had almost forgotten the insolent churl. 'Flog him, of course. A dozen lashes.'

All the servants at the manor house came out to watch in numb silence. Floggings were rare there; they happened just often enough to make sure that everyone knew the consequences of displeasing Beaumont. Martin had never seen a flogging before, let alone been subjected to one; otherwise, as he reflected afterwards, he might have struggled more as he was dragged across to the cart that stood by the stables and tied by his wrists to the tailgate. Simkin Sewell helped Wade tie Martin's hands, then took the leather sheath for his dagger and pressed it against Martin's lips. 'Bite on this, lad,' he murmured. 'Don't give the whoresons the satisfaction of hearing you scream.'

Martin nodded, clamping his teeth over the sheath.

Sewell stepped back, and Wade pulled off Martin's hood before ripping open his coat and tunic to expose his back. Then he fetched the whip from the stables, uncoiling it. The huntsman glanced across to where Beaumont stood at the top of the wooden steps leading to the first-floor entrance of the house with Stamford and Beatrice, perhaps hoping that the knight would reprieve Martin, but Beaumont merely nodded curtly.

Martin breathed in sharply around the sheath in his mouth as the first lash raised its bloody welt across his back, shuddering at the burning agony. His whole body flinched as each stroke lashed him, heaping pain upon the pain until he thought he must faint. But he clung tenaciously to consciousness, determined not to let Beaumont see that he was hurting him. After the first few lashes his whole back felt as if it was aflame, and he was panting raggedly through gritted teeth, his fists clenched until his nails drew blood from his palms, his face crimson with the effort of suppressing the sobs that rose within him.

'Stop it!' Beatrice screamed suddenly. 'For pity's sake, stop it at once! Can't you see he's suffered enough?'

Hearing her, Wade paused, glancing at Beaumont. The knight nodded, and Wade gratefully took that as a signal that the punishment should cease. 'Get him out of my sight,' Beaumont said quietly, his voice carrying clearly across the courtyard. Then he and Stamford turned, disappearing inside the house, and Beatrice descended the steps and crossed to where Sewell and Michael were unfastening Martin's bonds. As soon as he was released, Martin sank to his knees, spitting out the sheath and sobbing air into his lungs. The ropes had chafed his wrists cruelly, but he felt only the agony of his bleeding back. Sewell and Michael supported him between them.

'Will he be all right?' asked Beatrice.

Sewell nodded curtly, not meeting her gaze. He hated Beaumont for what he had done to young Martin, and Beatrice was Beaumont's own flesh and blood. He and Michael helped Martin walk towards the gateway and out of the courtyard, the rest of the peasants following behind them, subdued by what they had seen. The six of them walked the three-quarters of a mile back to Knighton in silence.

Knighton was a small village of about thirty cottages or so just over two miles south of Leicester town, nestling in the lee of the ridge above the Washbrook, where the water-mill and the old Norman church of Saint Mary Magdalen stood on its north bank. Pigs snuffled in the muddy lane, and hens picked their way fastidiously through the vegetable patches that stood outside every cottage. As Sewell and Michael walked Martin back to his father's cottage, the villagers began to emerge from their homes to stare in silent astonishment at the sight. Little Jankin Petling stopped playing with his toy bow and arrows and ran down the street to announce the circumstances of Martin's return.

Like most of the houses in the village, the Kemps' cruck-framed thatched cottage was roughly thirty feet by eighteen, and was constructed of a timber frame with wattle-and-daub panels built on a low, stone foundation wall. By the time they reached it, John Kemp was standing by the midden outside the door with his burly arms folded across his barrel chest, his expression grim. He was a tall, heavily built man in his late forties, with blond hair and a face like tanned leather. Behind him, his wife Margery and his second son, Nicholas, peered out of the doorway. As soon as Sewell and Michael reached the door with Martin, Kemp stepped silently aside to allow them to enter. Inside, they had to pause momentarily while their eyes adjusted to the gloom of the windowless cottage.

The cottage was divided into two rooms: the hall, where the animals were kept, and the smaller bower at the back, where the family slept. Kemp followed Sewell and Michael through to the bower where they laid Martin face-down on the huge bed that the family shared.

'What happened?' Kemp demanded brusquely, addressing himself to Sewell.

'Sir John had him flogged,' Sewell replied grimly.

'He was asking for it,' added Michael. 'He struck Master Stamford.'

'There's some might say as how young Dickon had it coming to him,' Kemp replied with a humourless smile. 'Who struck the first blow?'

'Stamford,' explained Sewell. 'He struck the first several blows, as it happened. I didn't think young Martin had so much patience in him.'

'Did he take his punishment bravely?' demanded Kemp.

Sewell nodded. 'Without a murmur.'

Kemp nodded, and dismissed Sewell with a wave. The two men had been friends too long for Sewell to need any expression of thanks from Kemp; he knew that Kemp was grateful.

Kemp and his eldest son made their way into the main room of the cottage, where Kemp turned to his second son. 'Nicholay,' fetch Mistress Withcote,' he ordered. Mistress Withcote was the village midwife, reputed to be a witch by some, but indispensable because of her cures for various maladies and wounds.

'She's already on her way,' protested Nicholas. He was in his late teens, dark-haired, pale-faced and intense.

'You know better than to argue with your father, my duck,' Margery Kemp told her son softly. Nicholas nodded and slipped outside. 'Michael, you go with him.'

As soon as the two young men had left, Kemp turned to his wife with a questioning glance, knowing that she had sent the boys away because she wanted to talk to him in private. 'I blame Simkin,' she said bitterly.

Her husband regarded her with some surprise. 'How is it his fault?'

'He's the one that's always filled Martin's head with all those stories about King Arthur. Is it any wonder that the boy wants to be like one of the Knights of the Round Table, his head filled with daft ideas of honour and chivalry?'

'There's nothing wrong with a love of honour,' asserted Kemp.

'Jankin Kemp! You stand there and tell me that, while our youngest son lies in the next room, his back torn to ribbons, because he thought he was just as good a man as Master Stamford?'

'Our Martin's a better man than Dickon Stamford will ever be.'

'Perhaps, but he's still just a villein. It's a pity that you and Simkin couldn't have taught him his station in life at the same time you taught him all that nonsense about chivalry. You of all men should know better. Where are you going?' she added, seeing that her husband was pulling on his cloak.

'I've something to attend to,' he replied gruffly.

'Don't you do anything we might all have cause to regret!' Margery called after him, her voice tense with fear.

He shook his head. 'What I go to do should have been done a long time ago.'

It was afternoon by the time John Kemp reached Stone Gate Manor House, and he marched through the gateway into the courtyard unchallenged. As he mounted the flight of wooden steps leading to the door of the house, Beaumont's steward, Treroose, emerged.

'Good afternoon, Kemp. Can I help you?'

Kemp brushed past him. Treroose wheeled and tried to seize him by the arm.

'Sir John is not to be disturbed. If there is a matter you wish to bring to his attention, I suggest you do it through Master Croft, or else present your plea at the manorial court next Thursday . . .'

Kemp shrugged him off brusquely and burst into the hall, where Beaumont sat at the table, listening as Stamford plucked at the strings of a gittern. The two noblemen glanced up as Kemp entered, followed by Treroose. 'I tried to stop him, Sir John . . .'

Beaumont made a dismissive gesture. 'We can all see where Kemp's youngest whelp learns his manners,' he said coldly.

'I didn't come here to discuss manners!' Kemp snarled angrily. 'What makes you think you've the right to flog my son without a fair hearing?'

'There were no disputed facts to the case,' Beaumont said mildly. 'Your son admitted to striking my squire . . .'

'If Martin struck Master Dickon, it was because he was provoked! What true man of spirit would not retaliate under such circumstances?'

'I have already discussed the matter with Richard.' Beaumont's tone had grown cold. 'Your son disobeyed his instructions. Furthermore, when asked to explain himself, he was insolent.'

'He's a fifteen-year-old boy! Can he help it if he is spirited at that age?'

'Then he must learn to curb his spirit. Perhaps today's flogging will have taught him to do so in future. Now I suggest you leave, Kemp, before your impertinence pushes my patience too far. You have not grown so old that I would shrink from having you likewise flogged.'

'Have me flogged!' Kemp's face was puce with apoplexy. 'You God-damned ungrateful whoreson!' he roared. 'After all I have done for you, now you talk of flogging me! Damn you, Beaumont! Sometimes I think it would have been better had I let that Scotchman slay you at Dupplin Moor!'

Beaumont leapt angrily to his feet. 'God's passion, Kemp, you try my patience!' he snarled. 'Am I to feel indebted to you for the rest of my life?'

'Indebted! I never asked you a favour in my life, Sir John!' Kemp was trembling with rage. 'I've served you loyally on battlefields and wheat fields alike, and this is how you repay that loyalty!'

'You insolent dog! You're just like that whelp of a son of yours! By God's bones . . .' He broke off, frowning. Kemp was trying to speak, but it was as if his rage was choking him. He clutched at his upper left arm, his face screwed up in pain, then gasped, sinking to his knees. Beaumont stepped back hurriedly, upsetting a table with a flagon of wine on it so that the wine spilled in a broad red puddle across the white flagstones. 'Kemp?'

Kemp fell forward to lie on his face, motionless. After a few moments of stunned silence, Treroose ran forward and felt for a pulse in his throat.

'I never touched him!' Beaumont had blanched. 'You saw, didn't you, boy?' he asked Dickon. 'I never laid a finger on him!'

'He's had some kind of seizure,' Treroose observed grimly.

'Is he all right?'

Rising slowly to his feet, Treroose shook his head. 'He's dead.'

The church of Saint Mary Magdalen at Knighton was too small to warrant a priest of its own, so arrangements for John Kemp's funeral had to wait until the following Sunday when the curate came down from Saint Margaret's church in Leicester. The bier was placed at the

17

entrance to the chancel with brass altar candlesticks on the floor at its four corners, and that evening the villagers stood in the nave while the curate performed the *Placebo Domino in regione vivorum*, the Office of the Dead.

Early the following morning, Martin attended the penitential matins and lauds in the church with the rest of his family, while the curate prepared the ground for Kemp's grave. It was the first time Martin had left the house since his flogging. He was still unsteady on his feet, but he refused the various offers of support he received, the paleness of his face emphasising his grim expression. After the mass of requiem, the curate led them in communion. He went through the liturgy mechanically, reciting the words without understanding, for he was as ignorant of Latin as he was of God; not that anyone in the village was any the wiser, except perhaps Nicholas.

After the mass had been sung, the curate led them in prayers. There were prayers for the dead to be said, not only John Kemp but also the Earl of Leicester. Then the curate led them in a prayer for the health and well-being of the earl's son, Henry of Derby, who was campaigning against the French beyond the seas and was as yet unaware of the death of his father. The prayer seemed a spontaneous addition by the curate; there was no indication that he was acting under the orders of the priest of Saint Margaret, handed down to him by the Bishop of Lincoln, who had received the orders from the Archbiship of Canterbury, who in turn had been encouraged to spread anti-French propaganda by the king. Similar prayers were said in every church and cathedral in the land that month.

After the prayers, the curate removed his chasuble and put on his cope, sprinkling the body with holy water and then censing it. Then the altar party and mourners formed into a procession, singing the antiphon *In paradisum* as they marched out into the churchyard where Sewell, in his

18

capacity as church sexton, had finished digging the shallow grave. There the curate asperged and incensed the body again, and the shrouded corpse was laid in the grave, the curate placing a cross of stamped lead on its breast.

Leaning on his spade, Sewell watched the faces of the Kemps as the body was asperged and incensed a third time. Martin's expression was blank and unreadable, while Michael glared at his younger brother with undisguised hatred, as if blaming him for the death of their father. Margery Kemp's eyes were fixed on the body of her husband for the last time, while beside her Nicholas stood with his hands clasped in a gesture of rapt piety.

Nicholas had been the runt of the litter, and his parents had been surprised that, unlike his two sisters, he had survived the first year of life. But it had always been obvious that he would never make a good farmer. Nicholas lacked his brothers' strength, and had always been fastidious, not liking to get his hands dirty. Lazy, Sewell called it. John Kemp had raised no serious objections when Margery suggested that Nicholas be allowed to attend the local almonry school in Leicester town. He might be a poor prospect as a farmer, but at least if he gained an education he might be able to supplement the family's meagre income by going into a lettered profession. Beaumont had already given him permission to leave the manor to study theology at Oxford as soon as the harvest was in. His departure would mean another mouth less to feed, and he had never been much use with a plough, scythe or flail; 'too busy dreaming about what he reads in them there books of his,' his father had always scoffed disapprovingly.

Another psalm was recited, followed by more prayers, and the curate spaded the first few clods of earth on to the corpse in the form of a cross. Then the burial party returned to the church singing the seven penitential psalms, leaving Sewell behind to finish filling in the grave.

The villagers spent the rest of the day in the fields, men and women alike, for the following Thursday would be Michaelmas, and the harvest had to be brought in before the weather turned against them. John Kemp might be dead, but life went on in the village, and there was always work to be done. Martin was hacking at a swathe of corn, wincing at each stroke of the scythe from the pain of his back; but he was too proud to ask for a rest from his labours, and knew that Beaumont would have refused if he had.

Thomas Croft, overseeing the work, sidled up to him. 'I'm sorry about your father, Martin.'

'So am I.' Concentrating on his work, Martin did not meet the reeve's eyes.

'Your father and I were good friends.'

'I know.'

'You understand that your father's death was a mischance, don't you? That he died of a seizure. It might as easily have happened to him working here in the fields as it did when he was up at the manor house, talking to Sir John.'

'All I understand is that my father went to see Sir John about my being flogged, and the next thing I knew he was dead.'

'Sir John regrets your father's death as much as any man . . .'

'That I very much doubt,' sneered Martin.

'You cannot blame him for what happened.'

Martin stopped reaping to meet Croft's gaze coolly. 'Can't I? If the likes of Sir John reckon they can do as they please just because they can trace their father's fathers to the Conquest, they've got another think coming.' Martin, who had practically been raised on the stories of King Arthur and the Knights of the Round

Table, found it hard to reconcile that image of chivalry with the real nobility he occasionally encountered. 'They reckon they own us.'

'You're a villein, Martin,' Croft reminded him bluntly. 'One of Sir John's bondsmen. He *does* own you – and you'd be well advised to bear that in mind, if you would avoid another flogging.'

'We'll see,' was all Martin would say, returning to his work.

Margery Kemp was in no state to prepare supper that night, pottering about the cottage as if she could block out her grief by burying herself in housework, repeatedly sweeping the same patch of beaten earth floor over and over again; the meal was left to Nicholas, who had often helped his mother about the house while his brothers were out working in the fields. The four of them sat down to their usual meagre supper of a mess of vegetables and oatmeal pottage, served with dark bread, all of them painfully aware of the empty place at the head of the table. No one spoke.

On Michaelmas Eve, the third day after the funeral, when the last sheaves of wheat had been carted into storage for winnowing, the Kemps made their way to the church to attend the solemn mass for the soul of the departed. The words '*Heri et hodie ipse et in specula*' were carved in the stone arch over the side door of the church. Martin could not read English, let alone Latin, but Nicholas had already translated the meaning of the words to him: 'The same yesterday, today and for ever.'

To Martin, those words always seemed to sum up the futile monotony of the peasant's life, and in the wake of his father's death they were given an added poignancy. John Kemp had spent his whole life working on the land, Martin reflected bitterly, struggling hard to scrape a meagre living from the soil for himself and his family, and in the end it had killed him. Was such to be Martin's own fate? It filled him with a sense of rage and frustration. All year long they struggled to make ends meet, telling themselves that they had only to wait until the harvest was in, and then everything would be all right. When the harvest was finally gathered in, it was never as plentiful as it should be. In a life lived on the knife-edge between hunger and starvation, it did not take much to tip the balance: a blight on the crops; not enough rain; too much. And the various taxes – from the tithe paid to Beaumont to the Peter's Pence collected by the ecclesiastical author-ities – were not reduced in times of hardship. Beaumont cared no more than the Pope whether or not the people of Knighton starved.

Martin hated and envied the nobility at the same time. He dreamed of being a member of their ranks, never having to worry about whether he had enough food to see him through the winter. There was only one way he could aspire to join those ranks. If he became a soldier and took service with the king, he might win booty at the very least. He was about old enough, if his parents had kept an accurate account of the years. If the harvest was rich enough that year, he would feel no qualms about leaving the village and setting out into the world beyond to seek his fortune as a soldier. If it was not, then he would have to stay another year, until the family was well set up enough for him to be able to make the break. Except there would always be something else to hold him back, another poor harvest, something to ensure that his dreams were never realised but remained just that: dreams.

At noon on Michaelmas Day, the villagers gathered outside Joan Cradock's alehouse for a meal of cheese and bread, provided at Beaumont's expense, before the harvest thanksgiving ceremony to be held in the church that afternoon. The Kemp brothers found themselves sharing one of the old oak tables with Sewell. The old man was generally shunned, and Michael and Nicholas tried to ignore him as politely as they could, but Martin never tired of the veteran's reminiscences of his long military career. Sewell was always happy to recount the numerous battles in which he had fought against the Scots, and it always pleased Martin to hear that villeins could acquit themselves in battle as nobly as any Knight of the Round Table.

The villagers were still eating, drinking and talking in front of the alehouse when Beaumont rode past with his family and retinue on their way to the church to join in the thanksgiving mass. The completion of the harvest was as important to him as it was to his villeins, for although he was the least likely of all the manor's residents to starve, a good harvest meant more money for him. Apart from exchanging a few curt words with Croft, he barely acknowledged the villagers; but Stamford spotted Martin, and shot him a look of unreserved hatred.

The arrival of Beaumont and his family was the signal for the villagers to drain their pots of ale and follow him down to the church. Beaumont and his household were seated on the single pew at the front of the nave, while everyone else stood on the rush-strewn flagstone floor. The sevice was led by Beaumont's chaplain, a stocky little man with a hooked nose and a bald head. Like the curate, he had only the weakest grasp of the basic tenets of Christianity. Most of the villagers lost interest during the sermon and started to talk amongst themselves, while Beaumont, trying to pretend an interest in the chaplain's words, struggled to control his temper towards his ill-mannered villeins.

When the service was over, the congregation filed out after Beaumont and his family. By the time the Kemp brothers emerged from the lych-gate, Beaumont, Stamford and Beatrice were mounting their horses. Martin found himself staring at Beatrice as she rode past and – as

23

if feeling his eyes upon her – she twisted in her saddle and saw him. Their eyes locked, and she momentarily smiled with amusement before spurring her jennet on after the rest of her family.

'She's not for you, lad,' a voice murmured in Martin's ear. 'Her kind are far above the reach of the likes of us.'

Martin turned and saw Sewell standing there, baring his toothless gums in a wicked grin. 'I . . . I weren't thinking that at all,' he stammered.

'You're a rotten liar, young Martin. Just remember: a cat may look at a queen, but don't torture yoursen by thinking you could ever do more than just look.'

'I wouldn't want to do more than just look at a stuck-up little girl like that anyhow,' scoffed Martin, trying to convince himself that he meant it.

Simkin chuckled. 'That's some little girl,' he drawled.

Martin chose to ignore him, hurrying on to catch up with his brothers while the grizzled veteran stood cackling in his wake, shaking his head sadly.

Nicholas departed for Oxford a few days later, and with both him and father gone the tiny, two-room cottage seemed empty. Margery seemed to retreat within herself, while Michael and Martin rarely exchanged words except to argue, but then it had always been like that between them. Nothing had really changed in the village, but then nothing ever did, except the usual seasonal variations. Autumn gave way to winter. The months between Michaelmas and Candlemas were the lean months, when the whole village attained a state close to hibernation. With the soil too frozen to be tilled and often blanketed with snow, there was little work to be done apart from repairing buildings and fences, or sitting inside mending old tools or fashioning new ones. In the long winter evenings the villagers would huddle around the fireplace in the alehouse, supping pots of ale while listening to Simkin's tales. The stories were mangled versions of the

Arthurian legends he had learned from his grandfather, or his own reminiscences of the wars against the Scots. It was hard to say which tales were more mythical in their content, but Simkin had enough military experience to imbue his stories with a convincing degree of detail, whether he was talking of jousting knights, or of archers holding off charges of wild Scotsmen.

Yuletide came, its celebrations a welcome break in the yearly round. The peasants decorated the interiors of their homes with evergreen to provide a cheery contrast with the stark world of white and black outside. On Christmas Eve they went wassailing in the alehouse; in a life of suffering and misery, drinking and festivity provided a welcome relief.

The trees were bare when Stamford and Beatrice went out riding in Knighton Woods one day early the following January, their trunks and branches black against the white patina of snow that lay across the landscape. Breath billowed in clouds of condensation from the mouths of humans and horses alike in the crisp winter air.

Conversation between the two was stilted. They lived in the same house and saw each other over breakfast, dinner and supper. It was always difficult for Stamford to find new topics of conversation to discuss with her. 'They say the king will lead an army to join Henry of Derby in Gascony this year,' he remarked after they had ridden in silence for some time. 'Perhaps I will have my chance to fight in battle before the year is out.'

Beatrice nodded absently. She listened to the same *chansons des gestes* as Stamford and took the same pleasure from the feats of arms of the men of olden times, men like King Arthur and the Knights of the Round Table, Charlemagne and his twelve peers; but she suspected that the reality of war was very different from those stylised, poetic adventures. 'Is that all you ever think of? War?' she teased him.

He shrugged, puzzled by the question. 'What else is there? If I were a churchman I could think of God; if I were a peasant I could worry about the crops. But I am the son of a nobleman: born for war, trained for war. I would not have it any other way.'

'And what of love?' she asked, smiling.

'I love you, of course, my lady, and hope that one day I shall have the chance to prove my love by wearing your favour into battle.'

Removing her gloves, Beatrice contrived to drop one on the forest floor. 'Oh! My glove! Pick that up for me, would you?'

Stamford dismounted unhesitatingly, but as he stooped to retrieve the fallen glove Beatrice dug her spurs into the flanks of her mare jennet and galloped off, laughing. He cursed under his breath and vaulted nimbly back into the saddle, urging his palfrey to give chase.

She rode at such a breakneck pace through the trees that he was hard-pressed to keep her in sight, and he feared not only for her safety, but also for his own. Just when he thought he had lost track of her, he caught sight of the jennet tied to a tree at the edge of a small clearing. He rode into the clearing and dismounted, trampling across the dead leaves to where the jennet stood. There was no sign of . . .

'What kept you?'

He looked up. She was perched on one of the lower boughs of an oak tree, her green and auburn gown blending with the lichen-covered trunk. She smiled down at him.

'Were you trying to get us both killed?' he demanded angrily.

'No one asked you to follow me,' she replied, pushing herself from the bough to land nimbly on the balls of her feet before him, still smiling. 'Besides, faint heart never won fair maid.'

He was panting slightly, both from the exertion of the ride and from his lust for her. He could see her small but well-rounded breasts clearly outlined through the fabric of her gown. She stood with her arms akimbo, her hands on her hips, as if taunting him, goading him. Suddenly he found himself encircling her narrow waist with his arms, drawing her roughly against him, bringing his mouth down on hers. She neither resisted nor responded, letting her arms fall so that they hung loosely at her sides. After a few moments she relaxed her jaw enough to allow his probing tongue into her mouth. He slid his hands down the small of her back, smoothing his palms over her buttocks, pulling her hips hard against him. She brought up her hands and placed them on either side of his head, pulling his face down against hers for a few moments. Then she traced her bony fingers down the sides of his neck until her palms rested against his chest.

He broke off the kiss to come up for air. 'I want you,' he rasped urgently.

She smiled, and suddenly pushed him away from her. Caught unawares, he struggled momentarily to keep his balance, and stared at her in bewilderment.

She laughed at his puzzlement. 'I'll not grant you the gift of mercy before you've won your spurs, remember?' she teased. 'You have to prove yourself worthy first.' She unfastened the jennet's halter and was in the act of swinging herself into the saddle when something flew out of the trees, and the jennet reared wildly, throwing her to the ground. She lay there dazed for a moment, the breath knocked out of her body, while the jennet keeled over to lie on its side.

Stamford ran to where she lay, crouching down beside her. 'Are you injured, my lady?' he asked, taking one of her hands in both of his own.

She sat up and clung to him momentarily, needing to feel the touch of another human being to reassure herself that she was still alive.

She managed to smile at him. The boy could be so kind and gentle when he wanted to be . . . he really was rather dull, just like every other young squire she had ever met, desperately trying to be the very epitome of chivalry. How she longed for a man who would treat her as a woman, rather than as if she were a delicate piece of glassware. 'I am not hurt,' she assured him. 'Merely winded, that is all.'

'You know I would rather suffer the fires of Hell for eternity than see the slightest injury befall you.'

'How kind you are.' How full of the formulaic graces of the court, rendered meaningless by the very strength of their hyperbole. She struggled to suppress a yawn.

He realised that the jennet had not risen after its fall, and glancing across to where it lay he saw its pelt flecked with blood where the shaft of an arrow had pierced its chest. He frowned, reaching for the hilt of his sword, and was about to speak when three men ran into the clearing. One of them carried a longbow; the other two were armed with ancient, rusty swords.

Stamford pushed himself to his feet to face them. 'You damned careless jackasses! Don't you look where you shoot? Someone might have been killed!'

'Someone may yet be killed, if you don't hold your tongue and stand still!' The leader of the three rogues levelled the tip of his sword at Stamford's throat. 'I've a dozen more archers hidden in the woods, the shafts of their arrows aimed at your heart.'

Stamford froze. 'What do you want?' he demanded harshly.

'Your gold will do to start with.' The leader indicated the bulging purse that hung from Stamford's belt.

Stamford's face flushed with anger. 'Do you know who I am?'

'No, and nor do I care. All I know is that my men and I haven't eaten in a week, and that gold should keep us fed for at least a month.'

'You'll not get away with this,' snarled Stamford, unfastening his purse and tossing it at the leader's feet. 'I'll hunt you down and . . .'

He broke off as Beatrice screamed, and they turned to see her struggling with the man armed with a longbow. 'She's a spirited one, this,' he said. 'We can have some fun with . . . arrgghhh!' He staggered back, one hand to his cheek, while blood seeped between his fingers. Beatrice stood there, panting heavily, her dagger in her hand, its blade ruddy with the man's blood.

'How dare you touch me!' she demanded.

The leader laughed. 'There's little we'll not dare. We're outlaws – we've naught to lose.' He nodded at the third man, who had been circling around behind Beatrice, and the man suddenly leapt forward, catching her by the wrist. He twisted her arm up into the small of her back until she cried out in pain and dropped the dagger, and then caught her, struggling, around the waist.

'Unhand her!' commanded Stamford.

The leader laughed. 'You're in no position to give orders, my fine peacock.'

'You heard the man,' growled a new voice. 'Unhand her!'

CHAPTER TWO

Stamford, Beatrice and the three robbers turned to see Martin Kemp standing at the edge of the clearing, an arrow nocked to the string of his drawn longbow. It was aimed at the leader's heart.

'Put down your bow, boy,' growled the leader of the outlaws. 'I've another six men hidden in the woods, their bows aimed at you.'

Martin shook his head, grinning nervously. 'That might fool these two gentlefolk, but it won't fool me.'

The leader scowled. 'Begone, boy. This is no concern of yours . . .'

Stamford seized his chance, drawing his broadsword from its scabbard and striking the leader down from behind, before turning on the man with the bow and driving the tip of his sword into his heart. He had never killed before in his life, and he was astonished how easily it came to him, a lifetime of training guiding his instincts.

Still holding on to Beatrice, the third man backed away, the edge of his sword at her throat. 'Drop the sword, young master!' he ordered, his face pale, his voice trembling.

'Unhand her!' snapped Stamford, refusing to relinquish his sword.

'Do as I say, or I'll slit her throat!'

Martin loosed his bow, and the arrow pierced the man's right shoulder. He dropped the sword with a gasp, releasing Beatrice and staggering back. Stamford moved in for the kill, stabbing the man in the throat with a grunt, while Martin ran into the clearing to catch Beatrice before she fainted. 'Are you all right, my lady?' he asked her. She nodded, her face pale and taut.

Stamford finished cleaning the blade of his sword on one of the dead men's cloaks, and turned to see Beatrice in Martin's arms. 'Unhand her, damn you!'

'It's all right, Dickon,' said Beatrice as Martin released her. 'He was merely supporting me. It was fortunate he came by when he did.'

'Aye, and fortunate for us that he just happened to have his bow with him when he did so,' sneered Stamford. 'Do you always carry your bow with you when you go for a walk in the woods?' he asked Martin.

Martin grinned insouciantly. 'Of course. You never know what dangers the woods may hold.'

'Aye – nor what game they might offer a poacher's pot. You should know it is against the laws of the forest to carry any arrows but blunt ones. I should tell Sir John . . .'

'Enough, Dickon!' protested Beatrice. 'No more accusations. You should rather reward this man for saving us. Had he only been carrying blunts, it might have been the worse for us.'

Stamford retrieved his purse from where it lay. He was about to toss a coin at Martin's feet when the churl stopped him. 'Keep your money. I wouldn't have bothered hadn't her ladyship been in peril.'

Scowling, Stamford turned to where his palfrey cropped the grass at one side of the clearing and took it by the bridle, leading it across to Beatrice and holding it while she climbed into the saddle. But her attention was on Martin. 'You are the churl my father had flogged for striking Dickon, are you not?' He nodded. 'Tell me, do you always come to the rescue of damsels in distress?'

Flushing hotly, Martin tried to shrug nonchalantly. Dressed in her fine robes and with her scrubbed face artfully painted, Beatrice was the most beautiful thing he had ever seen, and it was awe rather than lust that tied his tongue. 'When I must, your ladyship,' he managed to stammer.

'What is your name?'

'Kemp, your ladyship. Martin Kemp.'

'A warrior's name,' observed Beatrice, smiling. Saint Martin was the patron of soldiers, and 'kempe' was a Middle English word meaning 'champion' or 'soldier'. 'Martin is an unusual name – how did you come by it?'

'I was born on the Feast of Saint Martin,' explained Martin.

'Perhaps you should be my champion and wear my favour into battle, as did Sir Lancelot when he defended Queen Guinevere's honour.'

Martin did not know that Beatrice was speaking more to tease Stamford than to praise him. 'I'd be honoured,' he managed to stammer.

'It was I who slew the three outlaws,' grumbled Stamford.

'But you could not have done so had it not been for the assistance of my Lancelot here,' said Beatrice. 'It seems to me that Master Kemp apes the style of a knight. Was it not the churlish Sir Kay who mocked the unknown Beaumains, little thinking him to be destined to be one of the noblest knights in Christendom?'

'Beaumains was the son of Sir Lancelot,' argued Stamford. 'Kemp is a churl, the son of a churl, and doubtless destined to be the father of countless churlish bastards.'

'He was the King of Orkney's son,' blurted Martin.

Beatrice turned to Martin with renewed interest. 'I beg your pardon?'

'Beaumains. He was really Sir Gareth, the King of Orkney's son. Master Stamford is thinking of Sir Galahad.'

32

Beatrice smiled. 'He is right, Dickon. It seems my churlish champion knows more of the deeds of Arthur's knights than you do.' She chucked the palfrey's reins. 'Come on, Dickon. Father will be wondering what has happened to us.' As she rode out of the clearing, she cast one final glance over her shoulder at Martin. 'Farewell, my Lancelot. Perhaps another day will give you a chance to defend my honour.'

To his own astonishment, Martin found himself hoping it were true.

'Wade tells me you and Master Dickon had an adventure today,' said Beatrice's maid Edith as she brushed her mistress's hair that evening. Edith was in her early thirties, a handsome, full-bodied woman with strawberry-blonde hair and bright green eyes. She had been Beatrice's nursemaid when she was born, and had remained in Beaumont's service as his daughter's maid after she had grown up, becoming the young woman's only confidante.

Beatrice nodded. 'We were set upon by three outlaws. I dread to think what might have happened had not Martin chanced upon the scene.'

'Martin?'

Beatrice nodded again. 'Martin Kemp. You remember – the churl that father had flogged for striking Dickon last September. He's really quite gentle.'

'I did not think that you were on first-name terms with anyone from the village,' Edith remarked with amusement, and Beatrice flushed. 'What about Dickon? Was he not there to defend your honour?'

'He did his best,' admitted Beatrice.

'Master Wade tells me that he slew all three outlaws.'

'He could not have done so had not Kemp intervened,' said Beatrice, taking care to use Martin's surname this time.

'You sound quite taken with him.'

33

Beatrice smiled. 'He is certainly fair of face.'

Edith wrinkled her nose in an expression of distaste. 'Fie on you, for speaking so of a churl! They all stink of dung!'

Beatrice pouted. 'I think he would look quite presentable, if he were given a bath and some clean clothes.'

'You can't make a silk purse out of a sow's ear. Now, young Dickon, on the other hand . . .'

Beatrice frowned. 'He's sweet enough . . .'

'He's better-looking than any churl. Has he proposed to you yet?'

'Not yet. He says he wants to win his spurs first, so he may be worthy of me.'

'And why should he not?'

'Should I love him any better, knowing he has fought well in France?'

'You should be more proud of him, knowing that he has proved his courage in battle.'

'And if I did not love him at all?'

'That is not important. You will marry whoever your father chooses.'

'I shall marry who I please!' Beatrice protested indignantly.

Edith shook her head. 'Your father has been patient with you, but you cannot rely on his tolerance for ever. If you do not accept Dickon, he may well choose another man for you, one who is older and uglier.'

Beatrice grimaced at the prospect. 'We'll see.'

The following Monday was the first Monday after the sixth of January, called Plough Monday because it was the day on which tillage was traditionally resumed. Even though it meant a return to labour, it was a cause for rejoicing. The fact that the soil was no longer too frozen to be tilled signified that the worst cruelties of winter were behind them, and the approach of spring could not be far away.

Michael and Martin joined their fellow villagers working in the west field, which had lain fallow during the previous year to allow the soil to regain its fertility. Three days a week they were all compelled to do boon-work on Sir John Beaumont's demesne. Every seventh day they would rest from their labours to attend mass at the church, afterwards sharpening their arrows on the church walls before strolling across to the village green for archery practice. Today the same as tomorrow and for ever.

Martin noticed one change, however. Now the curate would end his services by preaching a sermon against the French. He would speak of how King Edward was the rightful king of France, and how the French usurper, Philip of Valois, was rejecting all attempts at reconciliation and inciting the Scots to fight the English in direct contravention of the Truce of Malestroit.

Martin could recall hearing of French attacks on Portsmouth and the Isle of Wight when he was a young boy; distant, exotic places he only ever dreamed of visiting, but still part of the Kingdom of England for all that. The County of Leicester had never been in danger from either the French or the Scots as far as he was aware, but the French had nevertheless been the bogeymen of his childhood with which his mother had tried to threaten him when he was unruly. 'If you don't go to bed this instant, the French will come and get you!' she had often warned him. He had always pictured the French as demons with horns, tails, and cloven hooves for feet. 'I'm not afraid of the French!' he had finally begun to protest when he had grown a little older. 'I'll fight them with my sword and my bow, just like Uncle Simkin used to fight the Scots!' And he had brandished his wooden sword, and the toy bow with which he shot squirrels and birds, while his mother threw up her hands in despair and his father chuckled approvingly . . .

Martin suddenly jerked out of his reverie, and realised that once again he had almost nodded off during the curate's sermon. The curate was reiterating that the French held the English in contempt and were determined to subjugate them. He said that the French intended to invade Kent that year, and that once the whole of England had fallen to them, they would stamp out the English language and force everyone to speak French. The French needed to be taught a lesson. Not for the first time, Martin found himself envying the men who had gone with Henry of Derby to fight the French in Gascony.

He did not even glimpse Beatrice again for the next few months, although it was not for want of trying. In his few moments of daylit spare time, he found himself loitering as close to the lane leading to the manor house as he dared without being too obvious. He continued to see her in his dreams, though; dreams in which he won a knighthood for courage on the field of battle, and thus made himself eligible for her hand. He was well aware that such things were extremely rare, but they did happen: it was only seven years since the famous John Chandos, born a commoner, had been knighted for valour while campaigning in France. Chandos had been a freeman rather than a villein, but the jump from villein to freeman was not impossible, either. If one such step could be made, why not both? He knew, deep within his heart, that if any man were capable of such a feat it was himself. But in the meantime there was work to be done, fields to be ploughed and sown, and during that time he became even more taciturn than usual.

The months passed slowly, even by rural standards. Easter came and went. The villagers continued the work of ploughing and sowing in the fields. Then came May Day, signifying the beginning of summer. It was the one day of the year when Beaumont's villeins automatically had his permission to leave the manor, so that they could attend the festivities at Leicester town. May Day fell on a Monday that year, so they were all given a day off from their labours.

The sun was shining in a bright blue sky, promising a long, hot summer. The villagers hitched up the communal cart, decorated with May boughs and flowers, to the team of oxen, and walked alongside it, laughing and joking as they made their way north along the Welford road to the town, the men carrying bows and arrows. May Day was a day of competitions, in which men sought to prove their skill or stamina in various contests of athletics and other sporting events. There was running, jumping, bowling, shot-putting and quoits, but the most popular contest was always archery. Much to his own surprise, Martin had been one of the runners-up in last year's competition. Now that he knew he had the first prize within his grasp, he had been practising hard all year.

Leicester was a large, walled town on the east bank of the River Soar. The houses there were larger than anything Knighton had to offer, and many of them were made of stone. Their doors had been decorated with May wreaths of oak and hawthorn, while a tall maypole had been erected on the common to the east of the town, just outside the walls, where children performed the traditional May Day dances. A troupe of mummers had set up a stage before an enthusiastic crowd, while stalls provided a variety of entertainments, from fortune-telling to puppet shows. There were games of skill and games of chance, minstrels who played love songs on psalteries, rebecs, lutes, dulcimers and pipes, and *gestours* who recited epic poetry, such as the 'Song of Roland' or – more popular with the commoners – the various ballads of Earl Ranulf of Chester and Robin Hood. There were jugglers who skilfully tossed burning brands back and forth, and tumblers who formed human pyramids and catapulted one another from see-saws. The tumblers were extremely popular, as some of them were women, and their art required that they wear skimpy costumes for agility, or so they claimed.

This was Martin's favourite day of the year. Any rest from the eternal labour of the land was welcome, but May Day was one of the few times when his own world was extended beyond the narrow confines of Knighton and the surrounding fields. In the small village, where everyone seemed to know everyone else's business, Martin felt as if he was permanently under scrutiny. At least here, in the crowds of the town, he could escape all that and lose himself in the comforting anonymity of the multitude.

The villagers of Knighton strolled amongst the stalls and tents in a loose gaggle, taking in all the sights, sounds and smells of the festival. Alison Forester – a young woman from the village who had in vain been trying to gain Martin's attention for the past few months – pointed to where a row of archery butts had been set up against the east wall of the town. 'Look, Martin! That's where they're having the archery contest. Aren't you going to have a go?'

Martin waved her to silence; his attention had been attracted by a *gestour* who was telling a small but growing audience of peasants and townsfolk the latest news of Henry of Derby's campaign in Gascony. Apparently a place called Aiguillon, held by Lord Ralph Stafford and Sir Hugh Menil – a Leicester knight – was being besieged by a French army commanded by Philip of Valois' eldest son, Duke John of Normandy. Gascony, Aiguillon, Normandy – exotic-sounding, far-off places where a courageous man could win honours and riches on the field of battle. Martin found himself wishing that he could be at the siege, if only to prove himself as worthy as any so-called nobleman.

The *gestour* turned his attention to other matters of less interest to Martin, who turned back to Alison. 'I'm sorry, lass. What were you trying to tell me?'

'The archery contest,' she reiterated, pointing. 'You are going to take part, aren't you?'

He grinned, showing her the longbow he had brought with him all the way from Knighton in its woollen bow-bag. 'I didn't bring this as a walking stick.'

'Go on, Martin,' Sewell urged him. 'We need a Knighton lad to show them how it's done.'

Accompanied by the other villagers, Martin grinned wryly and shuffled up to the short queue of men waiting to prove their skill with the bow. While he was waiting, he strapped his leather bracer to his left wrist and slipped the bow-bag off his elmwood bowstave. It was almost six feet in length, as tall as he was. He took out his hemp bowstring, tying one end to the lower horn of the bow and wedging it against the inside of his foot, bending the stave so he could loop the other end of the string over the upper horn. He plucked it experimentally to check the tension.

Glancing up, he saw Alison watching nearby with his mother and brother, and Sewell. She waved at him enthusiastically, and he waved back rather more shyly. He turned his attention to the men who were already shooting at the butts. Their skill was fair, but Martin knew he could do better, and that knowledge gave him confidence.

'Next!' called one of the marshals. The next man up was a tall, lean individual with lank, dark hair and a long, equine face. He obviously had not heard the marshal, for he continued his conversation with the slatternly dressed wench who stood beside him.

'Come on, we haven't got all day!' the marshal called irritably. When the horse-faced man still did not show any sign of having heard, the marshal signalled for Martin to step up to the mark. Martin had taken two steps forward when a hand landed on his shoulder and jerked him roughly back, catching him off-balance.

'Oi! Where in Christ's name d'you reckon you're going?' The horse-faced man pulled him roughly aside, winking at the wench, who giggled. '*I'm* next.'

'Then why don't you get on with it?' demanded Martin, offended by the man's blasphemy and angry at being handled so roughly.

The man waved a dirty finger in front of Martin's nose. 'Watch it, boy, if you don't want me to break your skull for you.'

Martin was about to do a little skull-breaking of his own, but Simkin restrained him. 'Easy now, lad,' he murmured into Martin's ear. 'You know you can flatten him, and we know you can flatten him; he's the only one with owt to prove, and he's only trying to show off in front of the wench. Don't give him the satisfaction. There's better ways of proving yoursen the better man.'

'Either one of you will do,' the marshal called dryly to Martin and the horse-faced man. 'You'll all get a turn soon enough.'

The horse-faced man sneered at Martin, and stepped up to the mark.

'Name?' asked the marshal, dipping a quill into an ink-horn.

'Will Caynard of Humberstone,' said the man.

The targets were set two hundred and fifty yards from the marks. Each competitor was allowed a 'sighter' – a warm-up shot – after which he had to place three shots in the yellow circle at the centre of the target to qualify for the next round. Caynard passed through, and Martin stepped up to the mark.

'What's your name, lad, and whereabouts are you from?' the marshal asked him.

'Martin . . . Martin Kemp. Of Knighton.'

The marshal made a note of his name and address. 'You can have a "sighter" first.'

Martin shook his head. 'I won't need it,' he told the marshal absently.

A group of local lads gasped mockingly. 'Looks like we got oursens a young Robin Hood here,' sneered Caynard.

Martin cast an eye over the watching crowd. In addition to the townsfolk there were a few nobles watching on horseback at the rear of the crowd, including Beaumont, Stamford and Beatrice. Martin felt a sudden pang at the sight of her, but pushed it to the back of his mind.

He had never shot in front of such a large crowd before, but he simply turned his back on it, blotting the spectators from both sight and mind. He took three target arrows from his belt. They were three feet in length, with grey goose-feather fletchings and ash shafts. Their steel tips had been designed to prevent deep penetration, so they could easily be pulled from the boss without damaging the shaft or the fletchings. Putting three arrows in the centre of the target was easy enough: he had practised archery for as long as he could remember; it was all second nature to him.

The next round was the same again, only this time without the 'sighter', and the distance was extended to two hundred and sixty yards. Consistency was as important as accuracy in this competition; one slip, and a competitor was out of the running. Sudden death, they called it.

By the end of the sixth round, the distance had been increased to three hundred yards, winnowing out all but six of the competitors, including Martin and Caynard. For the seventh and final round, a slender wooden wand was placed upright in the ground a foot in front of the butts; whoever placed his arrow closest to the wand was the winner. This time they used simple steel-tipped arrows that would not knock the wand aside if they brushed past it. The six archers drew lots to decide the order in which they would shoot. Caynard was second, and Martin fifth.

The first man to shoot barely hit the target, and knew at once he would not win, cursing his own over-confidence for betraying him when he had come so close to victory. Caynard stepped up to the mark, exuding self-confidence. After he had placed his arrow in the target, one of the marshals ran up to examine its placing.

'It's touching the wand!' he announced. The crowd cheered uproariously, the wench clapping her hands with delight. Caynard's friends hoisted him on to their shoulders and carried him through the cheering crowd.

'They're a bit premature in their celebrations, I reckon,' sniffed Sewell, although few people seemed to agree. The next two archers confirmed the general opinion, shooting well but not well enough to beat Caynard's shot.

'Go on, Martin!' shouted Sewell. 'Show them that trick I taught you.'

Martin nodded, and stepped up to the mark. He licked his index finger and held it up to check the wind's strength and direction. Then he took an arrow from the marshal and nocked it to his bowstring, taking careful aim. Keeping his mind clear and relaxed, he took in a deep breath, and let fly on the exhale. Once he had sent the arrow speeding towards it target he closed his eyes, feeling the bowstring thrumming against the bracer on his left wrist. The great gasp that arose from the crowd, and the cheer from the other Knighton villagers, were enough to confirm that he had succeeded in his aim: he had split the wand.

'You've done this before, haven't you?' the marshal remarked dryly.

Martin grinned self-consciously, and was suddenly swept off his feet as the villagers of Knighton hoisted him on to their shoulders, carrying him past the scowling

Caynard. He was eventually deposited with his family and friends, and received an embarrassingly breath-snatching hug from Alison.

'Did we win?' Martin gasped over her shoulder at Michael, who nodded.

'A shilling!' It was the equivalent of a month's wages. 'It's a pity they don't hold archery contests more often: with your skill with a bow, we could quit farming and live off the profits of your archery.'

'Now there's an idea,' said Martin, and turned to where a fairground barker was promising a ram and a ring to any man who could put Goliath on his back. 'Goliath' was a muscular young man in his late twenties. Six foot five, he towered over any man Martin had ever seen, with a shaven head and a face ferocious enough to ensure that he had few takers. Martin watched until one peasant lad decided to chance his arm – and all his other limbs, for that matter – paying the barker a penny before entering the ring with Goliath. The peasant was a big lad, even bigger than Martin, but he was no match for Goliath. They wrestled for a few moments, but sure enough it was the peasant lad who found himself flat on his back in the mud.

'What do you think?' Sewell asked Martin, as the two of them eyed Goliath speculatively. 'The trick is to go in swift, like; get him down before he knows what's hit him.'

Martin nodded. He had done enough wrestling with the other lads in the village to know what he was doing. 'The trouble is, it looks as though Master Goliath knows that, too,' he remarked wryly. 'Do we really need a ram?' he asked Michael, who was examining the beast in question.

Michael rose to his feet, satisfied that the ram was in good health. 'We can always sell it.'

Martin nodded, and paid the barker his penny. He removed his clogs and stripped to the waist, entering the ring dressed only in his breech-cloth and woollen leggings.

He started by trying to circle his opponent, but it was obvious that Goliath was growing bored with the day's succession of victories, and now wanted only to win this latest match as quickly as possible. He dashed forward, seeking to clasp Martin around the waist as a preliminary to turning him upside down and dropping him on his head, but Martin dodged out of his reach, and hooked an arm across his back. The two of them grappled for a few moments, churning the mud beneath their feet as they circled as one within the ring. Goliath tried to hook an ankle behind Martin's legs, but Martin was wise to that trick, keeping his feet out of Goliath's reach. They pushed against one another, and then Martin suddenly retreated. He broke free, and twisted Goliath's arm. The giant overbalanced, falling on his back. Martin promptly dropped on his neck, pinning him down for the count of five. Then the two of them rose, clasping hands to show that there were no hard feelings. The barker – who was Goliath's manager – handed the gold ring and the ram's lead to Michael rather more grudgingly, scowling at Goliath.

Martin was about to climb out of the ring when a man stepped up to the ropes. 'I'd like a go at that, if you don't mind.' His accent – the broad tones and short vowel-sounds of a man from the North Country – sounded strange to Martin.

'All right,' panted Goliath. 'But let me catch my breath.'

The man shook his head. 'Not wi' you. Wi' the new champion.' He indicated Martin with a nod.

Goliath turned to his barker, who shrugged truculently. 'You'll have to ask him about that,' he said, indicating Martin.

'What d'you say, lad?' the newcomer asked Martin.

'Will you give us a chance to take the ram and the ring from you?'

'What if I win?'

'Then I'll give you the equivalent in cash.'

Martin looked the man up and down. He was in his late forties, of no more than average height, a stocky man with close-cropped hair and a seamed face. 'Aye and like,' Martin agreed carelessly.

Goliath climbed out of the ring and the man climbed in. He and Martin circled each other warily, and then Martin charged forward, hoping to catch his opponent by surprise. The man dropped to one knee at the last moment. As the two of them collided, the man caught Martin in the stomach with his shoulder. He pushed himself sharply to his feet, allowing Martin's own momentum to carry him over his shoulder. Martin landed on his back in the mud, and the man placed a booted foot on his chest for the count of five.

Martin felt angry and humiliated at having been caught out so easily. 'Best out of three?' he suggested hopefully.

'Of course,' the man replied, grinning, as he helped Martin to his feet. The man's insouciance only infuriated Martin all the more.

Once again they circled warily, Martin striving to control his anger. It would only cloud his judgement, and he knew from experience that in wrestling judgement was far more important than strength or weight.

The two of them ran at each other simultaneously. The man caught Martin in a bear hug, squeezing him painfully tight. Martin reached over the man's shoulder, trying to grab him around the waist from behind. The man tried to get under Martin's centre of balance and flip him over his shoulder, but Martin kept his feet well back and firmly planted on the ground. Their feet slipped out from beneath them in the churned mud and the two of them landed in a heap, the man chest-down on the ground,

Martin on top of him. Martin caught the man in an arm-lock and rolled him over, pinning him down for the count of five.

As the two of them struggled to their feet, the man looked Martin up and down with frank appraisal. 'Not bad,' he said. 'Not bad at all. This 'un for the ram and the ring, eh?'

Martin suddenly had the feeling he was being tested in some way.

They grappled again, and this time Martin managed to hook a leg behind the man's ankle, tripping him up. The man rolled on to his back, pulling Martin with him, the soles of his feet against Martin's stomach. Martin landed heavily on his back in the mud once more, dazed. The man was on top of him immediately. Martin had to exert all his strength to push the man off, rolling on top of him. But again the man used Martin's own momentum against him, continuing the roll so that he ended up on top once more, this time bracing himself to ensure that he stayed there.

Martin knew when he had been beaten fair and square. 'That's a ram and a ring I owe you,' he told the man ruefully, as the two of them struggled to their feet and clambered out of the ring.

The man shook his head. 'Nay, lad, you keep them. What would I want with a ram and a ring? Besides, it's been a fair while since any man put me on me back. You've earned it.'

'We had a contest,' protested Martin. 'You won. It wouldn't be fair . . .'

'Listen, lad. I already get paid for fighting, and paid handsomely at that. It'd be a crime to take the prizes from you. When I entered the ring, I didn't think you stood a chance. I must confess that for a moment there, you had me worried.'

'Maybe so,' mused Martin. 'But then, when *I* entered

the ring with *you*, I never thought you stood a chance, neither.'

The man chuckled. 'What's your name, lad?'

'Martin Kemp.'

They shook hands, and the man jabbed a callused thumb at his own chest. 'Wat Preston. I saw you at the butts earlier. That were some rare archery, lad. I'll wager you're a mean customer wi' a quarter-staff, too, eh?'

Martin shrugged. 'Middling fair.'

Preston laughed again. 'Wi shoulders like that?' he asked, punching Martin on one of those self-same shoulders. 'And modest too, I'll warrant! You're an instinctive fighter if ever I saw one, lad. A bit impetuous, maybe, but then who isn't at your age? You've got brains and you use 'em, and that's a rare enough quality nowadays. You've got potential. Have you ever thought of making a living out of soldiering?'

The question caught Martin off guard, but he answered it readily enough. 'Aye and like. All the time.'

Preston regarded him in wonderment. 'Well now, I'm glad we had this little chat. Have you ever used a sword?'

This time it was Martin's turn to laugh. 'Only a wooden one. When I were a boy,' he added, by way of explanation. 'Where would I get the money for a sword?'

'It could be arranged,' Preston told him seriously. 'My master would happily lend you a sword, if you were ready to use it in the service of the king.'

'I'd like that,' Martin admitted.

'Then why not?' Preston pressed eagerly. 'My master's looking for fine young men like yourself to go to fight for the king in France. And what young man of spirit could turn down such an opportunity, eh? There's glory and booty to be won ... why, I've seen farmers' sons no better off than yourself spend a season campaigning in

Brittany, and come back laden down with enough spoils to make 'em the envy of the richest merchants in London . . .'

Martin reluctantly shook his head. 'I'm a villein, not a freeman. I'd need my lord's permission to leave the manor . . .'

'Who is your lord? I'm sure that if my master were to have a word with him, it could be sorted out easy enough . . .'

'Well, well. If it isn't my Lancelot.'

Recognising the voice, Martin immediately lost interest in what Preston was saying and turned to where Beatrice stood. He blushed, momentarily at a loss for words. 'Did you see me shoot?' he stammered.

She nodded, smiling. 'If you could use a sword as well as you ply that bow of yours, then you would indeed be a fitting champion . . .'

'You seem to be losing your touch, Wat,' observed a voice beside Preston, and he turned to see his master standing there. The two of them watched as Martin and Beatrice strolled a short distance away.

'I can't compete with the likes of her,' replied Preston, aggrieved. 'Although what a fine lass such as her can see in a villein is beyond me.'

'Beatrice Beaumont has a reputation as a tease,' Preston's master explained dismissively. 'She's probably only doing it to tease the lad, and her lover yonder.' He nodded to where Stamford stood nearby with Beaumont, glowering at the sight of Beatrice talking to the young churl. Beaumont said something to Stamford, who nodded, and walked across to where Beatrice stood.

'Come away, Beatrice,' snapped Stamford. 'People will talk!'

'Because I spoke to a churl?' she protested indignantly. 'I was merely congratulating him on his victory in the archery contest. We should be proud that it was a young

48

man from our manor who proved himself the finest archer in the county.'

'Skill at archery is nothing to be proud of,' replied Stamford, glaring at Martin. 'The bow is a weapon for churls.' He took her by the arm and all but dragged her away. She shot Martin an apologetic glance over her shoulder. He watched the two of them disappear into the crowd, and was about to turn back to Preston when someone grabbed him roughly by the arm.

'Stay away from my daughter, Kemp!' Beaumont snarled in his ear.

Martin shrugged off his grip. 'Can I help it if she prefers my company to that of your squire, Sir John?' he replied sardonically.

Beaumont hit him. The blow caught him by surprise, knocking him off his feet. More shaken than hurt, he was about to pick himself up and hurl himself at Beaumont in fury when Sewell suddenly crouched by him, holding him down. 'Easy, lad,' he murmured, and it gave Martin enough time to control his anger and realise the foolishness of trying to retaliate.

'I'll not warn you again,' growled Beaumont. 'If I see you talking to Beatrice once more, your whole family will suffer for it.' He turned his back on Martin and stalked off. Martin glared after him until he was out of sight, and then turned to where Preston had been standing. But both Preston and his master had disappeared. Disconsolate, Martin hurried off to rejoin the other villagers from Knighton.

Beatrice walked with Stamford and Edith through the crowded streets of the town, pausing to view the gowns on display on trestle tables in front of dressmakers' shops. Uninterested in such fripperies, Stamford walked ahead, trying to will the two women to hurry up. He allowed his curious eyes to linger too long on a well-dressed young woman with a painted face, and seeing his interest she quickly lifted the hem of her gown high enough to give him a brief glimpse of her crotch.

'Fancy a go?' she asked, grinning to reveal green teeth. 'Only a couple of shillings to a fine young man like yourself. I'd offer it for free, only I've a father and three little sisters to look after.'

Pop-eyed with disbelief, Stamford blushed and stammered, 'Eh? Er . . . no! No, thank you.' Crimson-faced, he hurried on, the whore's cackle of amusement ringing in his ears. Watching from the doorway of a shop, Beatrice and Edith giggled at his discomfiture, allowing him to disappear into the crowd.

'He looked as if he'd never seen a cunny before!' whispered Edith.

'Nor has he, for all I know,' replied Beatrice, more interested in a particoloured silk kirtle.

Edith regarded her sceptically. 'You mean, you haven't taken him in hand yet?' she asked archly.

'I would have thought that seducing noblemen was more your level,' said Beatrice. She was beginning to suspect there was more to Edith's relationship with her father than that of servant and master, and she could not help resenting the fact that her father loved anyone other than herself. 'Especially older noblemen,' she could not resist adding snidely.

Edith coloured. There had been a certain amount of friction between the two for as long as she could remember, as there might be between step-daughter and step-mother; but the confined world of Stone Gate Manor House forced the two of them to make an effort to get along, suppressing their mutual dislike. Edith knew what would happen if Beaumont had to choose between her and the daughter he doted on; but she promised herself she would make Beatrice pay for her last remark.

But there was nothing she could do openly to defy her master's daughter, so she forced herself to paste a smile

50

on her face and hurriedly changed the subject. 'Did you see that handsome knight who was watching young Martin Kemp wrestle? The one with only one eye?'

'Sir Thomas Holland, you mean?' asked Beatrice, forcing herself to sound indifferent. She had met Holland at the memorial service for the old Earl of Lancaster. She could not forget that day, no matter how hard she tried. She had found herself holding court to all the young squires present, as she invariably did at any event she attended. But such callow youths held little interest for her. She had spent the day trying to get Holland alone, and when she finally succeeded he had spurned her advances, saying it was neither the time nor the place, though even she could see it was just an excuse. She knew he thought himself too good for her, although he was just a member of an obscure family from Lancashire. 'How unfortunate that a Genoese crossbow bolt at the battle of Sluys should have rendered him so repulsive.'

'You think so? I thought him rather handsome. The eyepatch lends him an air of mystery.'

'Aye, for such mystery is not rightly his. All it covers is an ugly socket, I am certain. I would not choose to wake beside that each morn. Anyway, they say he is enamoured of Lady Joan Montague,' she added dismissively. Lady Joan, often referred to as the Fair Maid of Kent, was said to be the most beautiful woman in all England, and Beatrice found it very tiresome that so many young men who should have been paying court to her were instead more interested in extolling Lady Montague's virtues.

'Is she truly as fair as they say?' Edith could not resist asking. She knew full well that Beatrice did not move in the same circles as Lady Joan, who was cousin to the king and wife to the Earl of Salisbury's heir.

'I neither know nor care,' Beatrice replied coldly, nettled.

They had reached the south-west corner of the town,

51

where Leicester Castle stood on the bank of the River Soar. They passed through the arched gateway into the bailey. The castle was a relatively modest fortification. The mound of earth that had once formed the *motte* of the old Norman castle still stood, but the wooden keep had long since been allowed to rot away, while no new stone keep had been built in its place. Instead the centrepiece of the castle was its great hall, the administrative centre of the county.

There were stalls and sights to be seen inside the bailey, which was just as crowded as the streets outside. Michael and Martin Kemp were there, watching the Moorish dancers dressed in clogs and dark clothing, holly-wreaths on their heads, dancing in a circle with elaborate foot-patterns as they jingled their bells, flourished their silk scarves and clacked their staves together. The dancers were dark-skinned paynims, brought back to England by Henry of Derby following his visit to Granada on crusade.

The Kemp brothers had been inside the castle only once before, six years earlier, when Derby had held a tournament there to celebrate his daughter's wedding. Martin had only been about ten years old at the time. The knights in their shining armour, riding on their magnificent destriers, had made a great impression on him.

Seeing Martin and Michael, Beatrice nudged Edith and murmured conspiratorially in her ear. Edith was about to protest when an idea occurred to her. Here was her chance to pay Beatrice back for her earlier barbed remark. She smiled sweetly. 'As you will, my lady.'

A gypsy woman clutched at Michael's sleeve. 'Your fortunes told, if you cross my palm with silver.' She was approaching middle-age, a plump woman with a swarthy complexion who nonetheless would have appeared quite jolly had it not been for her dark, soulful eyes.

Michael was about to brush her off, but Martin, feeling flush after his victory at the butts, tossed her a penny which she caught deftly in one hand. 'Go on then, mistress,' he said with a grin. 'What does Fate have in store for my brother?'

The woman bit the coin to make sure it was not false, and then studied Michael's palm. 'You will die wealthy,' she pronounced solemnly. 'Beware a man with a scarred face.'

Michael beamed. 'You hear that, Martin? I'm going to be rich.'

'A likely story. She's just telling you what you want to hear.'

'Madame Szgany never lies,' said the woman, and reached for Martin's hand. Shrugging, he held out his palm. She began to study it, and then reacted as if she had been stung. There was real fear in her eyes, and she made a pass in the air as if warding off an evil spirit.

'What is it?' Martin asked in astonishment. 'What's wrong?'

'Death walks beside you,' the woman whispered fearfully.

Michael crossed himself, but Martin laughed. 'I'll be glad of his company, so long as he minds where he swings that scythe of his.'

'Don't jest of such things, Martin!' hissed Michael. 'Come, quickly, to yonder church that you may be shriven of the curse this paynim woman has placed on you!'

Martin grinned. 'Don't be daft. It's all a load of heathen nonsense. You know what Sewell says: a man holds his destiny in his own hands, 'tis true; but it's a destiny he must fashion for himself, not one that's writ in every line of his palm.'

'I suppose you're right,' Michael allowed dubiously, and then turned as Edith approached him.

'It's Michael Kemp, isn't it? I was so sorry to hear about what happened to your father last autumn. How are you coping now you're head of the family . . .?' She linked her arm through his, and he allowed himself to be led away, flattered by her attention, telling her of the heavy responsibilities he had to bear. There might have been more than ten years' difference in their ages, but at thirty-two she was still handsome; yet at the same time, she would be lucky to find a husband at such a late age, and not being of noble birth she could do a good deal worse than Michael Kemp.

Even so, there had been something staged about the way she approached Michael, Martin reflected as he turned his attention to the bear-baiting. He understood why a moment later when Beatrice sidled up beside him.

'I want to see you,' she said out of the corner of her mouth, without turning her head to meet his gaze.

'Sir John said I weren't to see you no more,' he stammered, confused.

'You're not scared of him, are you?' she taunted.

'Of course not,' he asserted, full of youthful bravado.

'Then meet me in Knighton Woods at noon tomorrow. Where you saved Dickon and me from those robbers.' Then, to his astonishment, she gave him a peck on the cheek before slipping away through the crowds.

Glancing at this over her shoulder as she pretended to listen to what Michael was saying, Edith permitted herself a smile of triumph. Beatrice had played right into her hands.

CHAPTER THREE

When the sun reached its zenith the following day, the peasants of Knighton broke off from harrowing the fields to sit down to a dinner of cheese, bread and ale. It was easy for Martin to slip away. He knew they would have resumed their labours by the time he got back, and he would be scolded by Croft, but it would be worth it even for a glimpse of Beatrice. He had not slept a wink the previous night, wondering why she wanted to see him. He could think of only one reason, but that was more than he dared to hope for. What could such a fine lady see in a churl like himself?

Beatrice was already waiting for him by the time he reached the clearing. He stumbled through the trees and came to a halt a few feet from where she stood as she looked up to greet him. The two of them faced one another awkwardly. Then she smiled.

'You came.'

'Aye.'

She paused. She too had lain awake most of the night thinking about what she would say, coming up with a dozen alternatives, and now she could not remember one of them. It was ridiculous, she told herself: she could hold her own in conversation with some of the wittiest young men in the Leicestershire aristocracy, yet this hulking, taciturn peasant youth always made her feel tongue-tied. There was a feeling of strength and power emanating from him that both frightened and excited her.

'My father wants me to marry Dickon Stamford,' she

blurted, and then wanted to bite off her own tongue for betraying her so clumsily.

He tried to shrug nonchalantly, though inside he suddenly felt sick at heart. He was a fool to have thought there could ever be anything between the two of them. 'Do you love him?'

'What's that got to do with anything?'

He shrugged, and they started walking side by side through the trees. 'You could run away from home,' he suggested.

She laughed mirthlessly. 'And how would I live?'

Martin had no answer to that one, so they walked on in silence while Beatrice desperately tried to think of something else to say.

'How is it that you know so much of the noble deeds of King Arthur and his Knights of the Round Table?' she asked at last.

He shrugged again. 'Uncle Simkin – Master Sewell, I mean – and my father used to tell us of them when I was a boy.'

'I'm sorry. About your father, I mean.'

'It's not you who should be sorry. It's your father.'

'My father never laid a finger on yours!' Beatrice protested hotly. 'I heard it from Treroose, our steward – he was there when it happened – it was a seizure, nothing more . . .'

'Aye, well. Your father will burn in Hell for it,' Martin said stubbornly. 'Even if I have to send him there myself.'

'Martin!' she protested angrily, and then softened. 'Must we fall out like this?'

He lapsed into a sullen silence.

'It's small wonder you and my father hate one another so,' she sighed. 'You've far too much in common.'

He stopped, and stared at her in bewildered astonishment. 'What's that supposed to mean?'

'You're both arrogant, and both as stubborn as the Devil.'

'Don't ever compare me with your father!' Martin snarled angrily.

She giggled. 'And hot-blooded, too!'

Her laughter infuriated him, and he raised a hand to strike her, barely restraining himself in time. She did not flinch, standing with her arms akimbo, her fists balled on her hips, staring at him defiantly as if daring him to hit her. Suddenly, for the first time, Kemp was aware of her not as an idealised love, but as an object of lust. Before he even realised what he was doing he had seized her in his arms and pulled her hard against him, dipping his head to kiss her clumsily.

'H . . . how dare you?' she whispered when he broke off the kiss. There was no anger in her voice, only confusion.

'There's nothing I wouldn't dare, for you,' he breathed hoarsely, and kissed her again. This time she responded, reaching up behind his head to pull his mouth down hard against her own, her lips opening into his, her tongue probing. She felt him growing hard against her, and grew fearful that she was losing control not only of the situation, but also of herself. Part of her told her to stop this before it got out of hand; to allow herself to be seduced by such a filthy peasant would be unthinkable!

She tried to push him away, but Martin had none of Stamford's courtly qualms. Carried away by his own lust, he gave no thought to the possible consequences of his actions. The two of them grappled momentarily, and then Beatrice slipped and fell amongst the bracken, pulling Martin down after her. She gasped, winded, as he fell on top of her.

'I'm sorry,' he stammered, only now realising what he had done.

'You jackass!' she squealed. 'You've got my gown all filthy, you clumsy great ox!'

'I'm sorry,' he repeated helplessly.

Then, to his astonishment, she giggled, and reached up to pull his face down against hers once more. The weight of his body on top of her filled her with an excitement she had never felt with any of her previous lovers. He could feel her breasts pressing firmly against his chest, well-rounded and disproportionately large on such a petite figure. Feeling him grow tumescent once again, she experienced a tightness in her throat, her breath coming in ragged gasps now. She reached down between them, tugging up the hem of his tunic, grasping him through the fabric of his breech-cloth. His heart pounding, he stared down at her, and she nodded solemnly. He pushed himself up, kneeling between her spread thighs as she hiked up the hem of her gown around her hips and he struggled to tug down his breech-cloth.

Then he crouched over her, clumsily trying to thrust himself inside her, and she had to reach down and expertly guide him into her. She gave a gasp of pleasure as he slid into her with a grunt, arching her body against his. He began to move against her, slowly and gently at first, uncertain of himself. Then she wrapped her bare legs around his hips, pulling him deeper inside her, moaning with pleasure. No longer in control of himself, terrified and ecstatic at one and the same time, he began to increase the violence of his thrusts, grunting with lust, and she squirmed beneath him, sobbing with delight at each stroke. Then, just when he could contain himself no longer, her body was racked with a spasm and she cried out, clutching him to her. He groaned in his moment of release, and it was over before he realised it. He slumped on top of her, gasping for breath. Beneath him Beatrice began to weep, although whether it was with joy or disappointment he could not tell and was too spent to care.

Edith was also breathing hard where she hid amongst the ferns less than fifty yards away, rubbing her crotch through the fabric of her skirt. She was disappointed that the scene had not lasted longer, although she had expected nothing more of a callow peasant youth so clearly inexperienced in such matters. But she was pleased by Beatrice's performance; she had played right into her hands. Struggling to control the rasping of her breath, she crept away through the bracken, heading back to the manor house with a triumphant smile on her face.

Riding to the manor house the following morning, Thomas Croft was about to turn off the road and up the lane when he was overtaken by a finely dressed young man in a feathered cap, riding a thoroughbred palfrey.

'Good morning!' the young man hailed him cheerfully. 'Is this the right path for Stone Gate Manor House?'

'Indeed it is,' said the reeve. 'I'm riding that way myself, if you'd care to ride a ways with me. It's not far,' he added.

'Much obliged to you,' said the young man. 'I have two letters for . . .' He paused, and reached inside one of his saddle-bags to produce an envelope, glancing at the name and address on it. '. . . Sir John Beaumont. I take it I have the right address?'

The reeve nodded. 'Aye. I'm Thomas Croft, Sir John's reeve for the village of Knighton.'

'I cannot say I am familiar with the place,' the young man said airily. 'I am John Rider, one of the king's messengers,' he added.

They heard the ringing clash of steel on steel even before they entered the courtyard of the manor house. The gate was open, and they rode through to see two men clad from head to toe in gleaming armour engaged in combat, swinging their heavy broadswords against metal-rimmed wooden shields. One knight wore a white jupon emblazoned with a red wyvern over his breastplate, the other a red jupon bearing the device of a white cinquefoil. Their faces were hidden by the visors of their egg-shaped bascinet helmets. They were only practising, but the messenger had attended enough tournaments to know that both men were clearly expert swordsmen.

The reeve and the messenger were not the only spectators to this display of swordsmanship. A young noblewoman stood on the far side of the courtyard, clapping her hands with delight at their skill, while a well-dressed servant stood by more sedately, his back three-quarters turned towards the open gate. Eventually the steward caught sight of the two visitors.

'Sir John is exercising with Master Richard,' he told the reeve. 'But I'm certain he'll see you in the dining hall as soon as he is finished, if you'd care to wait in the kitchens.'

The reeve bowed, and headed towards the kitchens. The cookhouse was set apart from the main buildilng, to reduce the risk of a fire in the kitchen leading to the destruction of the manor house. Treroose turned to the messenger. 'And what is your business, sir?'

'I have two messages from the King's Chancery for Sir John Beaumont.' The messenger showed Treroose the envelopes bearing the Chancery seal.

'If you give them to me, I'll see that he gets them,' said Treroose, reaching for his purse to tip the messenger.

'I was ordered to deliver them into Sir John's hands personally,' said the man. That was a downright lie, but he had ridden ten miles since cock-crow, and while he had other letters to deliver at Leicester town itself, he was damned if he would ride another yard without some breakfast inside him.

Treroose sighed. 'Very well. If you'd care to wait with

Master Croft in the kitchens, I'll let Sir John know that you're here. Have you eaten yet today?'

The messenger removed his cap and clutched it to his chest, suddenly all grateful humility. 'No, sir.'

'Have a word with the cook.'

As the messenger hurried after the reeve in the direction of the kitchens, Beaumont and Stamford continued to fight, oblivious to the arrival of the two visitors. Beaumont was a veteran of countless campaigns and well skilled with the broadsword, but he had trained Stamford well, and the squire had youth on his side. Eventually Stamford gained the advantage, and pressed home his attack with such vigour that Beaumont was forced down on to one knee, exhausted.

'Enough!' cried Beaumont, as Stamford landed another blow on his upheld shield. 'I yield! The field is yours, Richard, and nobly won.'

Panting from the exertion, Stamford lowered his broadsword, and the two men removed their bascinets, grinning at one another. 'At last I have beaten you, Uncle,' said Stamford, tossing the flaxen locks out of his face with a jerk of his head.

Beaumont nodded. 'You have learned well. Now there is nothing more I can teach you. All that remains for you must be learned on the field of battle.'

Stamford slotted his sword back into its scabbard with a brisk, well-practised motion. 'I only hope I have that chance.'

Beaumont shrugged. 'If there is no campaign against the French this summer, we can always travel to the east, to join the Teutonic Knights in their crusade against the paynims.' He turned to his steward, who was hovering at his elbow. 'What is it, Treroose?'

'Master Croft and a messenger have arrived to see you, Sir John.'

Beaumont nodded. 'Very well. Tell them I shall receive

them in the hall as soon as I have removed my armour.'

In the kitchens, Beaumont's cook was providing Croft and the messenger with goats' cheese, freshly baked bread and a cup of hot, spiced mead. She was a lean but cheerful woman in her late forties. 'I'm sure Sir John won't keep you long,' she assured them.

'Let him take as long as he likes, Meg,' replied Croft. Like the cook, Croft had been widowed, and he looked forward to his visits to the manor house.

'Typical of the provincial nobility,' sniffed the messenger. 'They like to keep the king's messengers waiting. It makes them feel important.'

'Like actually being one of the king's messengers, I suppose?' Croft remarked sardonically. A good man on the whole, he was instantly, unreasonably jealous of this finely-dressed messenger with his courtly airs and graces.

On this occasion he was hopelessly outclassed, however. The cook could not help but be impressed by a king's messenger from Westminster. 'What news from London?' she asked eagerly.

'Obviously I can't reveal any affairs of state,' said the messenger, and then glanced about as if searching for eavesdroppers, lowering his voice to a conspiratorial whisper. 'But it looks very much as if his Majesty intends to campaign in Gascony this summer.'

'Truly?' asked Croft.

The messenger nodded. 'A Great Council was held at Westminster last month. All the greatest noblemen of the realm were there to discuss the possibility of a campaign. Except my Lord Derby, of course: he's already in Gascony. And a great fleet of ships has been ordered to assemble at Portsmouth to carry an army beyond the seas.'

'More war,' the cook sighed in disgust. 'How many more men will be crippled? How many more women will lose their husbands and sons, I wonder?' She herself had lost her husband at the battle of Morlaix four years ago. 'And all because his Majesty, not satisfied with being King of England, wants to be King of France as well.'

'His claim to the French throne is righteous,' the messenger protested indignantly, but before he could say any more, Treroose entered the kitchen.

'Sir John will see you now.'

Having little interest in the administration of the manor, Stamford had agreed to take Beatrice out hawking, so Beaumont was seated alone in the dining hall, when the reeve and the messenger were ushered into his presence. 'What is it, Croft?' he asked the reeve.

The reeve indicated the messenger uncertainly, feeling that a letter from the King's Chancery should take precedence over his own petition on behalf of the villagers of Knighton.

Beaumont turned to the messenger. 'Well? What is it?'

'Two letters from his Majesty's Chancery, Sir John.' The messenger presented the envelopes with a flourish.

Beaumont broke open the seal on one envelope and unfolded it, casting an eye over the Latin wording:

To Sir John Beaumont of Stone Gate Manor in the County of Leicester.

Sir John has been assayed at one knight and one squire for his lands, tenements and chattels of that manor, to be found for the King's service and for his next passage into foreign parts. Sir John and his squire are requested to present themselves to Sir Thomas Holland of Broughton, Knight Banneret, at the mustering point of Bosworth village no later than the Tuesday following the feast of Saint Augustine in the twentieth year of the present reign.

Signed Michael Northburg, Clerk to the Privy Council on behalf of his Majesty King Edward the

Third after the Conquest, at Westminster on the morrow of Saint Aelred.

Beaumont's initial elation at this call to arms was dampened by the recollection that when he had first been called to serve the king, eight years ago, he had been required to provide a dozen armed men. It was a sign of his declining fortunes that he was no longer considered wealthy enough to provide such a retinue. But war brought opportunities for booty, for ransoms from captured enemy noblemen. If he could impress the king with his courage, he might even be awarded extra lands. At least he had an opportunity to reverse the wheel of fortune that until now had been turning against him.

He turned his attention to the next letter. It was a commission of *oyer* and *terminer*, addressed to him in his capacity as a justice of the peace, calling on him to catch and try whoever had been responsible for the rape and murder of a young noblewoman who had been found dead in Leicester on the morning following the May Day celebrations. A close friend of Sir James Pabenham, the under-sheriff for the County of Leicester, Beaumont knew all about the case, and he greeted his responsibility for catching the guilty party with dismay. There had been no witnesses and no evidence, and the likelihood of finding who was responsible out of the thousands of people who had visited Leicester town that day was slim.

He dismissed the messenger, ordering Treroose to tip him a shilling, and then turned his attention to Croft, listening to his report with only half an ear. Croft was requesting that the village be let off paying some of their taxes, last year's harvest having been poor. But Beaumont's mind was elsewhere. A commission of *oyer* and *terminer* was a chance to draw the attention of the court to himself; until he did that, he had little hope of gaining high office, and the revenues that came from it.

But this particular commission could only serve to make him look incompetent, for he knew he should never be able to track down the culprit of the crime.

'Am I to be blamed if the harvest is poor?' he asked Croft angrily, when the reeve had said his piece. He waved the first of the two letters he had received in Croft's face. 'See! I have been called upon to fight for the king in France! How am I to pay for my horse and armour, if my bondsmen and tenants cannot pay their taxes? Tell the villagers they will have to tighten their belts.'

Croft knew that once Beaumont's mind was made up it could not be changed, and bowed out of the hall, feeling sick at heart, knowing that people might starve as a result of Beaumont's indifference.

Once he was alone, Beaumont crossed to the narrow window and gazed down into the courtyard where Stamford and Beatrice were mounting their horses, while Wade leashed the spaniel and the falconer took Stamford's peregrine and Beatrice's merlin from the mews, placing leather hoods over the birds' heads. Edith entered the room and walked up behind Beaumont, encircling his waist with her arms and standing on tiptoes to kiss him on the side of the neck. When Lady Beaumont died in childbirth, the knight had found some degree of solace in the nursemaid's bed, and the two of them had been lovers ever since.

Edith rested her chin on Beaumont's shoulder, and the two of them gazed out of the window at the hawking party which was making its way out of the courtyard. 'I see your daughter has finally found her Lancelot, Sir John,' she remarked teasingly.

Beaumont nodded. 'I knew the girl would see sense sooner or later.'

'If you can call choosing a churl for her champion sense, aye.'

Beaumont broke free of Edith's embrace and turned to face her, seizing her roughly by the upper arms and shaking her. 'What are you saying?' he demanded angrily.

'Did you not know of the attention she has been paying to John Kemp's son?'

'I told him to stay away from her!'

'But did you tell her to stay away from him?' she asked archly.

'He has seen her again? Since Monday?'

Edith nodded. 'They met in the woods yesterday. Why else did you think she went out riding by herself?'

Beaumont blanched. 'Has she . . .?'

'Granted him the gift of mercy?' Edith laughed. 'Aye.'

Beaumont started trembling with rage. 'Damn him! Damn him to Hell!' he exploded angrily, releasing her and turning to the table. 'I'll have him hanged for rape, damn her!'

'She gave herself willingly, as far as I could see.'

'It matters not! The damned upstart! I'll . . .' He broke off, realising with despair that he could not punish Martin without humiliating Beatrice and destroying the honour of his family name. He sat down and buried his face in his hands. When he finally looked up, Edith saw he had been weeping.

He gestured at the two letters that lay on the table. 'As if I did not have enough to worry about. Richard and I have been called upon to serve our king in France.'

'Isn't that what you wanted?'

'Aye – but who will look after my Guinevere while Richard and I are absent, and protect her from that upstart villein; not to mention her own wilfulness?'

'You could try talking to her.'

Beaumont shook his head. 'I have tried. She is a headstrong girl, and will not listen to her father. And in the meantime there is this: a commission of *oyer* and *terminer*, to catch some felon who has probably already left the county.'

Casting her eyes over the commission, Edith pursed her lips thoughtfully. 'You could try killing two birds with one stone,' she suggested.

'How so?'

'You need someone to hang for this crime; and you need to dispose of young Kemp.'

'You think perhaps Kemp was the man who raped and murdered this woman?' asked Beaumont, furrowing his brow.

Edith laughed. 'Does it matter? He was in Leicester that day – it *could* have been him.'

Beaumont liked the idea, but was forced to shake his head sadly. 'I cannot convict a man without proof!'

'When you tried Sir James Pabenham's nephew for raping that peasant wench, there was plenty of evidence to suggest that he was guilty, yet you were able to procure a jury which found him innocent. It seems to me that Sir James owes you a favour.'

Beaumont nodded thoughtfully, and then folded the commission of *oyer* and *terminer*, placing it in his purse and heading for the door. 'Where are you going?' asked Edith.

'To Leicester,' explained Beaumont. 'To call on Sir James.'

Martin was working in the north field with the rest of the villagers, pulling up the weeds that had invaded the ploughed earth, when Simkin Sewell, working nearby, murmured across to him. 'You've been seeing that Lady Beatrice, haven't you?' he asked with a leer.

Martin flushed hotly. 'Who told you?'

Sewell grinned. 'A little bird told me. Take my advice, boy. Forget about her. You'd be better off spending time with Alison Forester.'

Martin grimaced. 'She's nowt like as beautiful as Lady Beatrice.'

'Aye, nor as dangerous. Young love's a fickle thing, Martin. If you've any sense you'll forget about Lady Beatrice. If you must make a fool of yourself, do it over one of your own kind. We're not people to Sir John and his family and the likes of them. We're slaves, or playthings, without feelings to be hurt.'

Martin shook his head. 'Beatrice isn't like that.'

Sewell noticed Martin had dropped the honorific from Beatrice's name, and drew his own conclusions. He shook his head sadly. 'She doesn't love you, boy. Don't try and fool yourself into thinking otherwise.'

Martin smiled to himself. He was sure Sewell was wrong. If Beatrice did not love him, why would she grant him the gift of mercy as she had done in the woods the other day?

It was past noon when Croft called a halt to their labours, and they gathered in the middle of the field to eat the usual dinner of bread, cheese and ale. Martin sat down with Michael, their backs aching from constantly bending over to root up the weeds. They had almost finished eating when they became aware of three men riding down the lane. 'Who's this, then?' asked one of the women, shading her eyes against the sun.

Croft glanced up as the horsemen turned off the lane and began to ride across the turned earth to where the peasants were gathered. The leader was a stern-faced, well-dressed man, riding a palfrey, flanked by two rough-looking men armed with cudgels and seated astride rouncies. 'It's the district constable and his bailiffs,' he mused. 'I wonder what he wants.'

Sewell chuckled. 'Someone's in trouble.'

The constable and his bailiffs reined in their horses amidst the peasants. 'Which one of you is Martin Kemp?' the constable demanded peremptorily.

Martin was not aware that he had done anything wrong, so he hesitated only a moment before stepping forward. 'I am.'

The constable made a discreet signal to the two bailiffs, who instantly swung themselves down from their saddles. Before he realised what was happening, one of them had driven the end of his cudgel into Martin's stomach. The breath driven sharply from his body, Martin doubled up in agony with a hoarse scream. The two bailiffs pinned him down in the mud while one of them quickly and expertly bound his wrists behind his back.

'What in God's name is going on?' demanded Croft.

'I have a warrant signed by the Under-Sheriff of Leicester for the arrest of Martin Kemp of Knighton,' explained the constable, drawing the said document from beneath the folds of his cloak as one of the bailiffs grabbed a fistful of Martin's hair and dragged him to his feet.

The villagers were all stunned. As a boy, Martin had always been getting into trouble, but none of them would have considered him a criminal. 'On what charge?' demanded Croft.

'Murder and rape,' explained the constable, as one of the bailiffs tied a rope around Martin's wrists, and fastened the other end to the pommel of his saddle.

'I never murdered or raped anyone!' blurted Martin.

'That's for the court to decide,' said the constable, as the bailiffs swung themselves back into their saddles. The three of them rode off without another word, forcing Martin to trot along behind them. The constable had learned from experience that it was always best to make an arrest as swiftly as possible, before the accused's friends and relatives had time to react. All too often peasant solidarity could stand in the way of justice, when an entire village would forcibly prevent the arrest of a suspected felon.

It was only two miles to Leicester, but it was one of the longest journeys Martin ever made. It was his descent into Hell. Sometimes he would stumble and fall, and be dragged painfully through the mud or across the stony track until the bailiff reined in his horse long enough for Martin to pick himself up. But Martin was hardly aware of the pain. His mind was too full of sudden and inexplicable turmoil. Why was this happening? Who was he supposed to have raped and murdered? What was going on? Part of his mind told him that this was all a mistake, that this could not be happening; but the rope around his neck was real enough, and if the trial perpetuated the mistake then the rope with which they would hang him would be real enough, too.

Eventually Martin was delivered to the dungeons of Leicester Castle, battered and bruised, his clothes ragged, his flesh torn and bleeding, his wrists raw where the rope had chafed them. Still dazed, he was handed over to the gaoler and bundled without ceremony into one of the cells. The heavy, iron-bound oak door was slammed shut, and with the turn of the key in the lock he finally found his tongue. There was a small grille set in the door, and he pressed his face against the bars.

'This is a mistake!' he protested. 'I've not done owt wrong!'

'That's what they all say,' the gaoler returned unsympathetically, moving away through the torch-lit dungeons without so much as a backward glance.

Martin threw his shoulder against the cell door. He succeeded only in hurting himself.

'You're wasting your time,' the gaoler's voice echoed back.

Infuriated, Martin flung himself at the door again, and again and again, until he had exhausted his anger. Then he sank down to the cold flagstones in despair. The dank cell was tiny, without even enough room to lie down, but

70

there was a stone ledge to sit on. Martin remained where he was, hunched on the floor, his knees against his chest, until sleep claimed him.

It was perpetual night in the darkness of the dungeons, so he had no way of knowing how much time had passed when he was woken by the door being opened. Still half-asleep, he found himself driven to the back of the cell with savage kicks. A wooden cup and a crust of barley bread were placed on the floor just inside the door, which was promptly closed again. The crust was stale, but Martin ate it ravenously, washing it down with the stagnant water in the cup.

'I can get you better food,' said the gaoler, talking through the grille. 'For a price.'

'I have no money,' replied Martin. His voice sounded hoarse and cracked even to his own ears.

The gaoler shrugged, and walked away.

After a few hours, another face appeared at the grille. 'Are you ready to plead?'

'Plead?'

'Are you innocent or guilty?' the man asked patiently. He had the plummy accent of a nobleman.

'I'm innocent!' Martin said desperately. 'I beg you, let me go! I've done nothing, I swear!'

The man waited for Martin's pleas to finish before continuing. 'Do you wish to be tried by combat or by jury?'

'But I've done nowt wrong!' protested Martin.

'Then a jury should acquit you, shouldn't it?' the nobleman said reassuringly. 'I'll put you down for trial by jury, shall I?'

'When will I be tried?'

'There's a gaol delivery at the county court in two weeks time.'

'Two weeks!'

'You can count yourself lucky. County court sessions

are held quarterly. You might have had to wait three months.'

'And after the trial? Then what?'

'If you're innocent, they'll let you go. If you're guilty, you'll be hanged the next day. In the meantime, I suggest you spend some time in prayer.' The man's face disappeared.

Martin pushed himself to his feet. 'Wait! I don't even know why I'm in here! Who am I supposed to have raped and murdered?'

But the man had already gone.

The days passed with agonising slowness. Martin could only keep track of them because he was fed twice a day, if being given a stale crust of barley bread could be described as being fed. But there were a hundred years between each such meal, and there was nothing to do but sleep and pace up and down – one step forward, one step back – while the same thoughts kept turning over and over in his mind until he thought he must go mad. This could not be happening: he had done nothing wrong, committed no crime, and he had certainly not raped anyone. All he could do was pray that when it came to the trial, the error would be cleared up and he would be set free.

He often thought of Beatrice, and such thoughts filled him with pain. He knew she must love him as much as he loved her, yet now that he had that love to live for he was going to die. He had already missed one of their regular eventide trysts in Knighton Woods. What would she think had happened to him? As a justice of the peace and lord of the manor, her father would surely know that Martin had been arrested. Would he tell his daughter? Almost certainly, if only out of spite. But would she believe him guilty of the crimes of which he had been accused? Over the past few weeks they had got to know one another quite well, and she had often jokingly referred to him as her 'gentle knight'. Surely she must realise he was not capable of such crimes? He longed to see her, to assure her of his innocence. He even dared to hope that she might learn where he was imprisoned and visit him, but as the days wore on he began even to despair of seeing her again.

He lost track of the days. Even if he had had something with which to scratch a tally on the walls, it was too dark in the cell for him to have been able to see it. But finally, after breakfast one morning, he was dragged from his cell, his limbs stiff and aching, to where the other prisoners were being marshalled under the watchful eye of the gaoler, the bailiffs and their assistants. There were a dozen prisoners in all, and they were shackled together at the ankles with heavy fetters that prevented them from taking anything but the shortest steps. Shuffling along, they were led out of the dungeons and into the courtyard. Martin blinked as the bright sunshine seared his eyes. Driven along by the buffets of the bailiffs, the prisoners were marched across the broad courtyard and into the great hall of the castle where the county court was held.

The great hall was a huge room, nearly eighty feet in length, with four pillars down either side to support the oak beams of the roof. There was a raised dais at the far end of the room where Beaumont, acting as justice of the peace, sat in his finest and most costly robes. Below him sat a handful of clerks and serjeants-at-law, while the jury sat on a couple of benches to one side. As Martin was brought in, Beaumont refused to meet his gaze, and Martin felt despair wash over him. Suddenly he knew why he was there, and he knew that there could only be one outcome to this trial.

One by one, the prisoners were released from the fetters that chained them together, although their legs were kept in irons, and they were called to enter the dock and raise their right hands. The legal proceedings were conducted in Anglo-Norman, the bastardised form of the French language spoken by the nobility. A few words were common to English and Anglo-Norman, but not enough for Martin to be able to make any sense of what was going on. Only a few minutes were devoted to each case in turn, and then each prisoner was returned to join the others. No verdicts were given as yet; the jury would listen to all twelve cases before it adjourned to consider any of them.

Finally Martin was called into the dock and told to raise his right hand. He was not asked to take an oath on the Bible; it was automatically assumed that the accused would lie to save his own skin, and the courts did not want to encourage oath-breaking. One of the serjeants-at-law rose to his feet and spoke briefly in Anglo-Norman, while a clerk busily wrote down his words. Then the justice of the peace turned to Martin, addressing him in English.

'You are Martin Kemp of Knighton?'

Martin nodded miserably.

'Are you prepared to confess your guilt, or do you wish to lodge a plea of not guilty? If you confess, you will more readily secure mercy.'

'But I haven't done owt wrong!' protested Martin.

The officials of the court discussed the case in Anglo-Norman at length, their tones moderate, as if they were discussing no more than the weather, while the members of the jury looked bored. Finally Beaumont exchanged a few words with one of the serjeants-at-law, and called for the next case.

'That's it?' Martin was incredulous. He suddenly tried to break free of the bailiffs who were chaining the fetters back to his leg-irons. 'But I didn't do it!' he screamed, lunging back towards the dais. 'Damn you, Sir John! You know I didn't do it! You've arranged this, so I'll be . . .'

Then a fist was driven into his stomach, choking off his protestations as he doubled up in agony, retching. Struggling in desperation, he tried to fight back, but there were too many against him, and he was weakened by lack of exercise and a prison diet. Another fist connected with his jaw, while someone else struck him on the back of the head with a cudgel. Nausea swept over him, and he struggled to maintain his grip on consciousness. The court was in uproar, but he was hardly aware of anything as he was dragged from the hall.

The next thing he knew, he was back in his cell. He had no recollection of either falling unconscious or waking up; but then there was little difference between unconsciousness and the dark silence of his cell anyway. Only the pain that seemed to course through every part of his body told him that he was now awake.

Torchlight flickered through the grille in the door to dance dimly on the rear wall of his cell. He heard footsteps outside, and voices.

'Walter Daubney: not guilty,' intoned a sepulchral voice. A key turned in a lock and a cell door swung open on rusty iron hinges with an eldritch groan.

'Andrew Winger: not guilty,' said the voice. Another door opened.

'Alfred Drayton: guilty of murder and sentenced to be hanged at dawn.' This time, no door was opened.

The sepulchral voice continued mercilessly. 'Stephen Brown: not guilty... Batholomew Sturdy: not guilty... Peter Samwell: guilty of murder, assault and robbery. Sentenced to be hanged at dawn.' This time, a wail of despair escaped one of the cells a few doors down.

Martin could hear his own heart thumping, and there was a painful tightness in his chest.

'Simon Emery: not guilty... David Pakeman: not guilty... Roger Rudcock: guilty of trespass of vert and venison and sentenced to be hanged at dawn... John Gaylard: not guilty... Thomas Blanchard: not guilty... Martin Kemp: guilty of rape and murder and sentenced to be hanged at dawn...'

Martin was immediately and violently sick.

CHAPTER FOUR

None of Martin's friends or family had been present at the trial – it was as if the false accusation were enough for them to disown him – but Nicholas, who had been given a few days off from his studies to deal with this family crisis, came to visit him in gaol that night. He bribed the gaoler to allow him to speak to Martin through the grille in his cell door. 'How could you do such a thing, Martin?'

'Nicholas?' Martin jumped to his feet. 'For the love of God, Nicholay, you have to get me out of here!'

'How could you do it? Your mother is half-dead with shame . . .'

'I didn't do it, Nicholay. I swear to God, I'm innocent! Speak to Lady Beatrice – she knows. She can still save me.'

Nicholas did not seem to hear him. 'I'll pray for your soul, Martin, though it's more than you deserve . . .'

'Where's our mam?' Martin demanded desperately. 'Is she well? Why hasn't she come to visit me?'

'Mother?' Nicholas spoke vaguely, as if in a daze. 'She wants no more to do with you. You have shamed her – shamed us all. Perhaps the good Lord will find it in his heart to forgive you; I know I never shall.'

'I didn't do owt, Nicholay. I'm innocent. Please, you must tell our mam . . .'

'The good Lord rest your wicked soul, Martin. I always knew as how you'd come to a bad end.' Nicholas abruptly turned his back on his brother, walking away.

Martin slumped down to the floor of his cell, repeatedly

muttering his innocence. And then he prayed to God, for earthly rather than celestial salvation. There was nothing left but prayer. He was not ready to die. Kneeling on the hard flagstones with his hands clasped before him, he recited the few prayers he knew over and over again, and then he made up a few of his own. '*Please God, do not let me die. I have done nothing to warrant death. Save me from hanging, and I swear I'll never fornicate again. I'll do anything you ask of me, I'll enter a monastery and dedicate the rest of my life to your service, if you'll only let me live . . .*'

A key turned in the lock and the cell door swung open. He blinked in the flickering torchlight as the gaoler handed him his final breakfast.

'Is it morning already?' Martin tried to sound calm, but even to his own ears his voice seemed hoarse.

The gaoler nodded wordlessly. There was little to be said. He had been unconvinced by Martin's protestations of innocence – nearly all his guests denied their guilt, but their crimes were largely a matter of indifference to him. It all came to the same thing in the end. 'There's someone come to see you.'

Martin paused in the act of biting off a mouthful of crust to look up sharply. 'Beatrice?' If only he could see her one last time, assure her that he was innocent of the crimes for which he had been condemned; if only she could confess her love for him, he might yet die a happy man. But to be hanged so unjustly, when he had such a love to live for . . .

But the gaoler shook his head, and stood to one side to reveal a black-clad priest holding a small, leather-bound Bible. With his pale, cadaverous features in the shadow of his cowl, he looked like the angel of death. Martin knew utter despair then, knew that he had been abandoned by God.

'I have come to hear your confession,' said the priest.

'Go to Hell,' Martin told him bitterly. 'I've not done owt wrong.'

'Would you go to your grave with your sins unpurged?'

'I've not committed any sins, yet I'm to die for a crime which I didn't do. I've prayed to God for salvation, but he has forsaken me. Now I'd make a pact with the Devil himself, if it would free me from this unjust fate,' spat Martin.

The priest recoiled in horror. 'Blasphemous wretch! Would you burn in the fires of Hell for eternity?'

'For a full span of life? Aye.'

The priest snapped his Bible shut and turned to the gaoler. 'There is nothing I can do for this one. He has chosen his path.'

The three other men condemned to die that morning were already being chained together in the main room of the dungeon. The first was a tall, massively built, tow-headed young man with vacuous blue eyes and a pendulous lower lip; the second was in his mid twenties, with lank, shoulder-length dark brown hair and a broken nose; and the third was a small, weasel-faced man of about forty. Martin was likewise put in irons and chained behind the man with the broken nose, and then the four of them were marched outside, surrounded by the bailiffs. The priest's voice droned in a dull monotone as he marched at the head of the procession. They marched into the courtyard and out through the main gateway of the castle, leaving the town by the south gate.

The sun was shining.

'It's a fine day to die,' remarked the man with the broken nose as they shuffled along Millstone Lane below the south wall of Leicester town. 'What's your name, then?' he asked the gigantic youth.

'Alfred Drayton,' replied the giant, speaking in the slow tones of the weak-of-brain.

'Pleased to meet you, Hal,' replied the man with the broken nose, with such *bonhomie* that if Martin had not known better, he would never have guessed that this man, like himself, was destined to be hanged by the neck until dead within a short while. 'I only wish we could have met under happier circumstances, but it's never too late to make friends, I always say. My name's Roger Rudcock, by the way, but folks call me Hodge. So, what brings you to this sorry end?'

'I killed a man,' Hal said dully. 'I didn't mean to,' he added hurriedly. 'All I did were hit him.' Looking at Hal's broad shoulders, Martin could well believe it.

'I were caught poaching, for my sins,' said Hodge Rudcock, and turned to the weasel-faced man. 'What about you?'

'Go to Hell.'

Rudcock shrugged. 'Aye and like. Chances are, that's where we'll all be before this hour is past. How about you?' he asked Martin.

'What difference does it make?' Martin demanded bitterly. 'We're all going to be hanged.'

'Never say die, lad,' replied Rudcock. 'Where there's life, there's hope.'

They rounded the Corn Wall at the south-east corner of the town and found themselves at the aptly named Gallowtree Gate, beyond the ditch below the town wall to the east. A large crowd had gathered. There were a few drawn out of ghoulish curiosity, but on the whole the sympathies of such spectators lay with the condemned, and a last-minute reprieve – not an unheard of occurrence – might provide some excitement. The crowd watched in silence as the condemned men were led to the horse-drawn cart that waited beneath the boughs of the gallows tree. Martin searched the crowd in vain for the faces of his friends and family. He was surprised to see that there was no sign of Sir John Beaumont and his entourage, either: he had expected them to be present, to gloat.

Rudcock nudged Martin, and nodded to where a nobleman dressed in red and yellow robes sat astride a mighty destrier, surrounded by a platoon of archers and a troop of men-at-arms.

'It's his lordship,' said Rudcock. 'That's got to be a good sign.'

'His lordship?' echoed Martin, in incomprehension.

'The Earl of Warwick,' explained Rudcock.

Ordinarily, a man was only appointed to the office of sheriff for twelve months, but Thomas Beauchamp, Earl of Warwick, had been appointed Sheriff of Warwick and Leicester for life as a reward for his outstanding military service for the king. While most sheriffs were expected to be present at all hangings that took place in their jurisdiction, the Earl of Warwick's appointment was largely a sinecure, whereby he took the revenues of the office while employing underlings to carry out the duties required. Hodge seemed to consider the earl's presence a good omen, although Martin could not begin to imagine why.

The condemned men had reached the cart. Martin no longer felt any fear. He had resigned himself to his fate.

'Which one of you is Kemp?' asked the bailiff.

Martin stepped forward. 'I am.'

'You're first.' The bailiff tied his hands behind his back with rope, and then began to strike off his leg-irons. In a way, Martin was glad that he was going to be hanged first. He had never seen a hanging, but Simkin had told him that it was a gruesome way to die, and he had no wish to stand and wait to witness the fate presently in store for him.

The hangman grasped him under the armpits and hauled him up on to the cart. A rope had already been slung over one of the lower boughs of the tree, and the noose hung at head-height. The hangman looped the noose around Martin's neck and drew it tight. There was very little slack: the idea was to strangle the victims slowly rather than to snap their necks with a long drop.

Then the hangman climbed down from the cart and uncoiled the whip that hung from his belt. One lash would set the horses galloping, drawing the cart away from beneath Martin's feet and leaving him swinging in the breeze, the coarse hemp rope cutting into his windpipe until he was choked to death.

Martin felt strangely calm. It was not the prospect of being hanged that filled him with trepidation so much as what might lie in the hereafter. He tried to console himself with the thought that the eternal torments of Hell could not be much worse than a peasant's life of toil.

The hangman drew back the whip, preparing to lash the horses. Martin braced himself instinctively.

'HOLD!'

For Martin, that single word was not so much a reprieve as an unwelcome prolongation.

The Earl of Warwick rode his horse forward at a slow walk, reining it in a few yards shy of the cart. He was in his early thirties, a tall, rangy man with a short, slightly pointed beard, his cheeks shaven in the current fashion, with dark, wavy, shoulder-length hair parted in the centre, framing a long, lean face with a narrow mouth and sensuous lips. His lazy eyes were dark, his nose long, with slightly flaring nostrils. Seated upright in the saddle, he gazed across to where Martin stood waiting to die.

'You are Martin Kemp of Knighton?'

Martin nodded.

'They tell me you were convicted of murder and rape, and condemned to death for it,' remarked the earl.

Martin had accepted his fate, but the false conviction still rankled. 'I never raped nor killed anyone!' he said, his eyes flashing angrily.

The earl shrugged indifferently. 'That's not what I said. A jury passed a verdict of guilty on you in an English court of law. Not that the length of hemp around your neck cares either way. They also tell me you are skilled with a bow.'

This time it was Martin's turn to shrug. 'Middling fair.'

'You are the Martin Kemp who won the archery contest on May Day, are you not? That must make you one of the finest archers in the county.'

'I had one of my good days,' sneered Martin. 'Much good it can do me now.' Condemned to death, he felt no obligation to address the earl as 'your lordship'; they could only hang him once. In a way, his imminent death gave him a tremendous sense of freedom.

'It could do you a great deal of good,' said the earl, amused by the villein's defiance. 'His Majesty the king has called for skilled archers such as yourself to serve him on his next passage into foreign parts.'

'It's a pity for the king that I'm condemned to be hanged, then, isn't it?'

'Curb your insolence, churl! The king has the power to grant pardons to condemned men, and will do so at my recommendation . . . in return for good service.'

'Good service?' echoed Martin, bewildered.

'Serve his Majesty for twelve months – serve him well, mind – and you shall be granted a full and unconditional pardon for your crime, and for any subsequent out-lawries.'

'I am to fight overseas for the king?'

The earl nodded. 'If you agree to it. The choice is yours.'

'And if I refuse?'

'Then I shall order the hangman to continue.'

Martin grimaced ruefully. 'It's not much of a choice.'

The earl shrugged. 'It's the best choice you're likely to

be offered this day.' He regarded Martin questioningly. 'Well? Which is it to be?'

'I'll fight for anyone who'll free me,' said Martin.

'Then you can start by addressing me as "my lord",' said the earl.

Martin grinned. 'Aye, my lord.'

'Untie his hands,' the earl told the hangman, before turning to the three other condemned men. 'The same offer goes for all of you – you can all use a bow, I presume?'

They nodded fervently.

'Very well, then. The same rules apply to all of you. Serve his Majesty for one year, and you'll all be granted pardons for your crimes. But pay heed: if any of you try to desert, or disobey orders, or do anything to give me cause for complaint, then by God's sweet passion I'll see to it that the judge's original sentence is carried out, even if it means hanging you from the nearest tree myself! Is that understood?'

The four men nodded. Martin had often dreamed of becoming a great warrior and fighting for his king; now it seemed he was going to get his chance.

The earl was about to wheel his horse away when he paused, and peered down at Rudcock. 'I know you, don't I?'

Rudcock nodded, grinning with pleasure at having been recognised by the earl. 'Aye, my lord. I served under your command in Flanders three summers ago.'

The earl nodded thoughtfully. 'Very well, then. You four follow me.' He wheeled his horse about, and they marched back through the town towards the old stone bridge across the Soar. The earl rode at the head of the column with a small retinue of squires, followed by the troop of men-at-arms. The four paroled convicts marched behind them, while the platoon of mounted archers brought up the rear as they headed along the dusty track towards the village of Bosworth.

Leicester Forest stretched away to the south beyond a field beside the road. Its thick foliage and leafy glades offered refuge for any outlaw, if he could cover the several hundred yards of ploughed earth. Martin was not convinced that he wanted to escape anyway. He had literally been given a new lease of life where before he had faced only despair and certain death. But he was too numbed with relief to feel any joy. As much as he looked forward to the chance to win glory and riches on the battlefield, he could not help resenting the fact that he had been forced into his current circumstances by a cruel twist of fate. He would much rather have volunteered for military service of his own free will, in his own time, though it was doubtful that Beaumont would have given his permission for one of his villeins to risk getting killed in the king's service, depriving him of a labourer; especially not when one of that villein's brothers had already left the manor to go to college and the villein in question was Martin Kemp.

Martin was more worried about Beatrice than he was about her father. He wished that there was some way he could speak to her before he left, to let her know that he was still alive. Supposing she thought him guilty of the crimes for which he had been condemned? The thought that she might never speak to him again renewed his despair.

There was some consolation, however. Perhaps this was the chance he had been waiting for. If only he could win glory in the fields of France, perhaps he too could be knighted, like Sir John Chandos, and return a worthy suitor for Beatrice's hand. He was one of the king's archers now, or as good as, and for the next twelve months he intended to make the best of it.

The weasel-faced man did not see things in the same light. 'We've been given a second chance,' he whispered to Martin as they trudged along behind the mounted men-at-arms in the hot summer sun. 'I'm damned if I'm going to throw my life away by getting slain fighting for the king; he never did owt for me. I reckon we can make it to those trees before any of these whoresons realise we've gone. Once we make it into the forest, they'll never find us.'

'Don't be a jackass!' hissed Martin. 'They'd cut us down with their arrows before we even got halfway!'

'The lad's right,' said Rudcock. 'Besides, army life isn't so bad – it's a lot better than being an outlaw with a price on your head, you can take my word for it.'

'What about you, Hal?' persisted the weasel-faced man. 'You aren't afraid of a few arrows, are you?'

Drayton was weak-brained enough to be easily influenced, but he was more influenced by the majority. 'I . . . I reckon I'll stay with these two,' he admitted uncertainly.

'Fine. It's your choice,' said the weasel-faced man. He glanced around, and suddenly broke away from the column, vaulting over the hedgerow that ran alongside the track. He landed on his feet and started sprinting across the churned soil towards the trees.

'Man away!' shouted the serjeant-at-arms in command of the archers.

The earl raised a hand, signalling for the column to come to an abrupt halt. 'Why do you tarry, then?' he called back.

The serjeant nudged one of his men, who leisurely nocked an arrow to his bow and let fly. The weasel-faced man was already over a hundred yards away, but the arrow took him cleanly in the small of his back. He flung his arms out to the side and stumbled, arching his back, before falling face-down in the shape of a crucifix.

'Well done, Leverich,' said the serjeant. 'Should we fetch the body, my lord?'

'What for?' demanded the earl. 'Leave it for the carrion crows. No, wait – you're right. We'll take it with us.

There'll be plenty of other impressed convicts at Bosworth who'll need to be reminded of the penalty for desertion.'

Martin was shocked. He had never seen anyone killed before. The very cold-bloodedness of the archers chilled him to the bone. He felt slightly sick.

As four of the archers trotted across the field to retrieve the man's body, Rudcock shaded his eyes against the noonday sun with one hand to peer after them. 'You were right, lad,' he told Martin sardonically. 'He *didn't* even get halfway.'

They reached the mustering point on Bosworth Common a couple of hours after noon. A number of large, brightly coloured tents had been erected towards the centre of the common, and all manner of banners and pennants fluttered idly in the breeze. Already, men had begun to arrive from all over the county. There were richly clad knights on horseback and their squires, indentured to serve the earl; and men-at-arms, archers and hobelars – lightly armoured mounted infantry, wearing quilted aketons, iron gauntlets, steel gorgets to protect their throats, chain-mail coifs, and bascinets – mounted on Irish 'hobby' horses and armed with swords and spears, all recruited by commissions of array. There were civilians serving the troops in an auxiliary capacity: tanners and armourers, bowyers and fletchers, farriers and cooks. And then there were the others, peasants come from the nearby town to wish their loved ones goodbye, or merely drawn by idle curiosity.

The greensward had already been churned to mud by the passage of countless feet and hooves. The camp was a hive of activity, with cooks preparing food for the troops, armourers repairing weapons, farriers reshoeing horses, and armed men everywhere, drilling, practising their archery, or simply lounging about and talking. The only other times Martin had seen this many people gathered in one place had been at the May Day festivals in Leicester. The atmosphere was not dissimilar to a festival, with men laughing and joking, practising feats of arms, and the smell of cooking; but whereas the May Day festival was a celebration of life, this was a gathering of men preparing for war.

As the earl and his retainers dismounted, handing their horses' bridles to waiting equerries, the serjeant of archers and half a dozen of his men escorted Martin, Rudcock and Drayton through the camp to where a richly embroidered banner showing a silver lion on an azure background stood before a bell-shaped, blue-and-white striped tent towards the centre of the field.

'Sir Thomas Holland's banner!' Rudcock observed joyously. 'Looks like we've landed on our feet, lads!'

'Who's Sir Thomas Holland?' asked Martin, but before Rudcock could reply, the three of them were roughly pushed into the tent. Inside were three straw-stuffed pallets at one side, and a suit of armour neatly stacked beside one of them. In the centre of the tent stood a trestle table at which sat two men. The first was a lean man of average height, in his mid-twenties, dressed in the brown habit of an Austin friar, the bright blue eyes in his youthful face full of benevolence. The light-brown hair beneath his cowl was shorn in a tonsure. The second was a handsome, sanguine lad no older than Martin, his hair bobbed, the hems of his coat and shoulder-cape fashionably scalloped, as were the cuffs of his wide sleeves.

The friar was hunched over scrolls of parchment, occasionally dipping the nib of his quill into an ink-horn as he scribbled away. The young nobleman sat beside him, lounging indolently in his chair. They both looked up as the archers escorted the three convicts into the tent.

'Three impressed convicts from the Leicester gaol delivery,' said the serjeant, handing the friar a receipt to sign. 'Alfred Drayton of Harborough, Martin Kemp of Knighton and Roger Rudcock of Blaby.'

'Hold on a moment.' The friar had a soft southern accent. He shuffled through his papers until he found the one he was looking for. 'What were those names again?' he asked, his quill poised over the parchment.

The serjeant repeated the names of the three men. The friar deftly added the names to a list he was drawing up, and then looked up again, pointing with his quill at Hodge. 'This one I already know,' he said, smiling. 'Thank you, serjeant, we'll take care of them from here.'

The serjeant nodded, and ducked back out of the tent with his men.

'You're all skilled in archery?' asked the friar. The three convicts nodded. 'Which one of you is Drayton?'

'I am,' said Drayton.

'So you must be Kemp?' said the friar, turning to Martin, who nodded. 'I'm Brother Ambrose, clerk and chaplain to Sir Thomas Holland; this is Master Adam Villiers, Sir Thomas's squire.' The young nobleman inclined his head, smiling amiably at the three convicts. 'Have either of you two ever served in the king's army before?' the friar asked Martin and Drayton. They shook their heads. 'Well, never mind. Roger's a veteran, he'll show you the ropes. Have the terms and conditions of your impressment been fully explained to you? You'll serve the king as a foot-archer for one year, at the end of which you will receive a pardon for whatever crimes you were found guilty of. You'll be paid thruppence a day, the same as any other foot-archers, commencing the first day you step foot outside this county. You'll receive the balance of your first payment tomorrow, enough to cover you until we reach the port of embarkation. In addition to your pay you'll be allowed to keep any booty you win overseas. Arms and equipment will be supplied by the agents of the Royal Armoury. You'll take your orders from Sir Thomas or his serjeants; failure to obey those orders will lead to statutory punishment under military law. Mass and communion are every Sunday morning, followed by confession if you feel you need it. Have I forgotten anything?' he asked Rudcock, who shook his head.

'Nothing that springs to mind, Brother Ambrose.'

'Right, then. If you have any questions about anything, don't hesitate to come and ask me. By the way, Roger, I've put you in Serjeant Preston's platoon. I'm sure he'll be pleased to see you back again – and you him, of course.'

'Of course,' Rudcock said wryly, an aggrieved expression on his face. 'Who else is here?'

'The usual crowd,' sighed Brother Ambrose. 'John Conyers, David Brewster, Thurstan Freeman, John Newbolt – they're all outside, behind the tent,' he added, gesturing over his shoulder with his quill. 'I suggest you go and join them.'

Hodge nodded, touching his forelock to Brother Ambrose and Villiers before ducking out of the tent, followed by Martin and Drayton.

'So, who's this Sir Thomas Holland?' asked Martin.

'Who's Sir Thomas Holland?' Rudcock echoed incredulously. 'Only one of the greatest knights in Christendom, that's all! I served under his command at the siege of Tournai a few summers back. He's the second son of Lord Holland, and a vassal of the Earl of Lancaster. I didn't reckon we'd see him here; I thought he'd be in Gascony with his lordship. It's not like Sir Thomas to miss out on an opportunity for a scrap.'

'Is he a great warrior, then?' asked Martin.

'Is he a great warrior!' echoed Rudcock. 'He's fought in more battles than you've had hot suppers.'

'That wouldn't be difficult,' Martin remarked wryly.

'I were at his side when he lost an eye at the battle of Sluys – God's soul, but it were back-and-edge there, I can tell you!' continued Rudcock. 'He fought with Robert d'Artois in Brittany, took part in the assault on Vannes, and was in command of the garrison at Bayonne in Gascony a couple of years back. Even when there's a truce between the king and Philip of Valois, Sir Thomas is off fighting wars against the heathens in distant lands. The last time I saw him, he were off to fight the paynims in Prussia, and I heard tell that he's been crusading against the Moors in Granada since then. Believe me, lads, if we're to be serving under Sir Thomas Holland, you can be sure we'll be in the thick of the fighting all the way.'

Martin smiled to himself. If he were to risk his life fighting for his king in France, he wanted a chance to win glory serving with a knight of great renown.

There were a dozen men lounging around Holland's banner, roughly dressed peasants like Martin and his new-found companions. Five of them were crouched in a circle, playing jacks. Rudcock squatted down amongst them. 'Is this a private game, or can anyone join in?'

'Well, axe my arse!' exclaimed one, a stocky man in his late thirties whose face was as coarse as his words. 'If it isn't young Hodge Rudcock. We reckoned as how we'd see you here. What took you so long?'

Rudcock grinned. 'I were detained as his Majesty's pleasure. Or rather, displeasure, as I gather he weren't too pleased about me poaching in his forests again.'

A man in his late teens who was lounging back on the grass chewing on the end of a long piece of straw chuckled. 'You must be the worst poacher in the world, Hodge,' he said. 'You're always getting caught.'

'I don't know what the king would do without me to fight his wars for him if I weren't.'

'I reckon he'd get by,' the coarse-faced man said dryly, and indicated Martin and Drayton. 'Who are these two?'

'Martin and Hal,' said Rudcock, indicating his two companions in turn. 'Martin here won the May Day archery contest in Leicester this year.'

The coarse-faced man grunted non-committally, unimpressed. Anybody could put an arrow in the centre of a target; but loosing a dozen arrows a minute at an enemy who was charging directly at you on horseback, lances crouched – now that took skill and courage.

'Martin, Hal,' said Rudcock, motioning for the two of them to crouch down beside him. 'This is Thurstan Freeman.' He indicated the coarse-faced man. Then he pointed to the young man chewing on the piece of straw. 'And this cheeky young devil is David Brewster.' Brewster was a tall, lean, handsome lad with curly, light brown hair and bright blue eyes. He acknowledged Rudcock's introduction with an affable nod in Martin's and Drayton's direction. 'David's mad, by the way,' added Rudcock.

Brewster arched a quizzical eyebrow. 'Oh aye? How d'you work that out?'

'Most soldiers I know dream of owning their own inn when they retire,' explained Rudcock. 'David's parents already own an inn, so he volunteered to be a soldier.'

Brewster shrugged indifferently. 'It's overrated. You soon get tired of lugging barrels of ale up and down the cellar steps all day and night.'

Next Rudcock indicated a short, wiry but broad-shouldered man in his mid twenties, with black, curly hair, a neat, pointed beard and a pair of dark brown eyes with a mischievous twinkle in them. 'This here's John Conyers, and the sour-faced whoreson yonder is Jankin Newbolt.' Jankin was in his late thirties, with a hooked nose, thinning hair and a dark, tangled beard. 'This one I don't know,' added Rudcock, indicating the fifth jacks player, a pink-faced youth barely sixteen years of age with a ready if nervous grin.

'That's Limkin Tate,' Freeman said dismissively. 'He's harmless.'

'That reminds me of a joke,' said Conyers. He spoke with a pronounced Yorkshire accent.

Brewster pulled a face, groaning, 'What doesn't?'

'Did I ever tell you the one about the one-armed veteran who goes into the alehouse?' asked Conyers.

'Only about a thousand times,' grumbled Newbolt.

'Is that the one where his empty sleeve trails in a man's ale-pot, and when the man complains the veteran tells him: "There's no 'arm in it"?' asked Rudcock.

Conyers' face fell. 'You've heard it before.'

'Only about a thousand times,' Brewster said with a grin.

A tall, pale, sickly looking lad of about seventeen summers wandered over to join them. He looked dazed and lost. 'Is this Sir Thomas Holland's company?' he asked uncertainly.

'Well, part of it,' said Freeman, scratching his head.

'I don't think I should be here,' the youth said pathetically.

'Then why don't you go somewhere else?' suggested Conyers, returning to his game of jacks.

'Whose company are you supposed to be in?' asked Rudcock, rather more kindly.

'Well, someone told me I was assigned to Holland's company, but I really don't think I should be here at all.'

Brewster shrugged. 'If you've come to join Holland's company, you've come to the right place,' he said.

'Sir Thomas's clerk will make out your indenture sheet, if you've come to volunteer,' teased Conyers, indicating the tent.

'You don't understand,' protested the lad. 'I'm not a soldier.'

'Who amongst us is?' Brewster mused wryly.

'My father's a franklin,' the lad explained dolefully. 'The commissioner of array decided that my father's annual income required him to provide one armed man for the king's service in foreign parts. Father said he couldn't spare any of the labourers, so he sent me instead. He said a spell of military service would help build my character.'

'Aye and like,' Conyers acknowledged jocularly. 'If it doesn't kill you first.'

The youth looked as though he were ready to burst into tears. 'Don't worry, lad,' Hodge told him kindly. 'We'll look after you. Isn't that right, lads?'

The others grunted half-heartedly. The veterans knew that they would have enough problems of their own without having to wet-nurse a milksop.

'What's your name, lad?' asked Rudcock.

'Inglewood. Peter Inglewood. Of Ashby-de-la-Zouch.'

'I once knew a man from Ashby,' mused Conyers. 'The French captured him, and cut off the first two fingers of his right hand, so he couldn't use a bow any more.'

Rudcock scowled at Conyers. 'Don't listen to him, Perkin,' he told Inglewood, automatically using the common diminutive of Peter. 'He's only teasing you.'

'It's true enough,' protested Conyers. 'My mate Rob had a cousin who was an archer, and he were captured by the French. They cut off his fingers. I saw the stumps mysen, with these very eyes.'

Brewster snorted derisively. 'He caught his fingers in a millstone, more likely.'

Newbolt shook his head. 'I heard that the French had started mutilating captured archers like that.'

'Don't talk daft,' Freeman told him. 'The French don't take the likes of us prisoner. There's nowt in it for them, see? You can't ransom an archer. Unless Conyers is going to try and tell us his mate's cousin is a nobleman.'

'Hey, kiss the Devil's arse, Freeman,' Conyers replied pettishly.

'Ah, stick it in a turd, by God and Saint Joyce!'

Martin was shocked: vulgarity was something he was used to, but he had never heard a man blaspheme so casually.

'All right, men, on your feet!' snapped a voice from behind them.

Martin rose with the others, and turned to see Wat Preston standing there. He was dressed for war, wearing a jerkin of brigandine construction – gilt-headed rivets securing small metal plates between a fabric cover and a leather foundation – a chain-mail coif, and a 'kettle' helmet. He wore a short sword at his hip, and carried a gnarled oak cudgel.

'Form a line,' snapped Preston. 'Let's see what I've got to work with here.'

'Master Wat!' exclaimed Martin, stepping forward. 'It's me, Martin Kemp. I'm here after all . . .'

'Serjeant Preston to you, lad!' snarled Preston. 'Now get back in line! Come on, shift your idle arses! Don't any of you whoresons know what a line is? You'd better learn fast, by God's guts and gizzard!'

The men began to range themselves into an uneven and straggly line.

'Nails and blood!' exclaimed Preston. 'I've seen a drunken stonemason's apprentice draw up a straighter line than that!' He began to move along the line, inspecting each man in turn. He nodded an acknowledgement to Thurstan Freeman, and paused in front of another old comrade-in-arms, a stocky, grizzled man in his early fifties. 'Hullo, Daw. Good to see you back again.' Next he halted in front of Martin. 'So, you say you know me, do you, lad?'

'It's me, Martin Kemp. We wrestled together at the May Day festival in Leicester town.'

Someone further down the line sniggered.

'You can stop your laughter, Conyers,' growled Preston, without taking his eyes from Martin's face. 'Yes, I remember you. I thought you didn't want to serve in the king's army? Change your mind, did you?'

'Sort of,' said Martin, and hung his head. 'To tell the truth, I had it changed for me.'

'I had it changed for me, *serjeant*,' corrected Preston. 'What happened? Owe someone some money, do you? Got some peasant lass into trouble?'

'No, serjeant. They were going to hang me,' he mumbled miserably.

'Convict impressment? You surprise me – I wouldn't've marked you down as that manner of man. Well, don't look so glum, lad. You may have been a convict, but now you're one of the king's archers, so head up, chest out, shoulders back. Try and look like you're proud to be given a chance to serve your king, rather than ashamed of it! Soldiering isn't such a bad life. You'll admit you were tempted to it before. In twelve months' time you'll be able to return to the bosom of your family, laden down wi' enough booty to ensure that you never have to work again.'

'If they'll still have me, serjeant,' Martin said morosely. 'They believe me to be guilty of . . .'

'Hist, lad!' snapped Preston. 'I don't know what crime you were condemned for, and I don't want to know. As far as the king's army is concerned, that can remain a matter strictly between yourself, the king, and his lordship the earl. That goes for all of you.'

A look of horror stole across Perkin Inglewood's face. 'I'm to serve with condemned criminals?' he blurted.

Preston slowly turned away from Martin and stalked across to where Perkin stood. 'And who in Christ's name are you?'

'P-P-P-Peter Inglewood, sir,' stammered Inglewood.

'P-P-P-Peter Inglewood, *serjeant*,' corrected Preston. 'I'm a serjeant-at-arms, not some God-damned knight. Tell me, P-P-P-Peter Inglewood, do you have some objection to serving with condemned criminals?'

It took Inglewood a moment to decide which reply would be wisest under the circumstances. Preston waited for Inglewood to part his lips before cutting in. 'Did you hear what I just said to Kemp?'

'Yes, sir . . .'

'*Serjeant*, damn your nose!'

'Yes, sir, serjeant, sir.'

Preston sighed. 'Well? What did I say?'

Inglewood screwed up his eyes to concentrate. 'You said that whatever crime he was condemned for was strictly between himself, the king, and his lordship the earl.'

Preston was grudgingly impressed. Most of the men who served under him had difficulty remembering their own names. At least Inglewood had been paying attention. 'Is your name Martin Kemp?'

'No, sir . . . serjeant, I mean . . .'

'Are you by any chance his lordship Thomas Beauchamp, Earl of Warwick, High Sheriff of the Counties of Warwick and Leicester?'

Inglewood grinned uneasily. 'Of course not!'

'Of course not, *serjeant*. And you're not going to tell me you're the king, are you?'

Inglewood shook his head miserably. He had never felt so humiliated in all his days.

'Speak up, P-P-P-Peter! I can't hear you!'

'No, serjeant.'

'That's more like it. So we'll have no more objections about who you're going to serve with, will we?'

'No, serjeant.'

Preston nodded in satisfaction. 'Good.' He began to move on.

'It's just that . . .'

Preston froze, and slowly turned back to face Inglewood. 'Aye?' he asked, in a tone that would have discouraged all but the most foolhardy from persisting with their protest.

'It's just that, I don't think I should be here at all,' blurted Inglewood. 'I mean, I think there's been some mistake.'

Preston looked him up and down distastefully. 'I'll wager that's what your mam told the midwife when she clapped her eyes on you for the first time.'

'I'm not a soldier,' sobbed Inglewood. 'I really don't think I should be here.'

Rudcock buried his face in his hands, but much to his astonishment Preston did not explode with wrath. Instead, the serjeant-at-arms put an arm around Inglewood's shoulders.

'To be perfectly frank with you, Inglewood, I have to agree with you. I really don't think you should be here either. But you've come this far, which means you must have been approved for service by the commissioner of array, so it looks like I'm stuck wi' you.' He squeezed Inglewood's shoulders, making the youth wince with pain. 'Now, I've oft-times boasted that I can make a soldier out of any man; whether or not you actually come into that category is a moot point, but if I can make a soldier out of you, it'll be the crowning glory of my career!'

Inglewood wiped a tear from his cheek and managed a wan smile. 'Thank you, serjeant.'

'Stop smiling, Inglewood! Don't you know when you're being insulted?'

'N . . . no, serjeant.'

Preston sighed. 'Then maybe there's hope for us both.' He moved on down the line, nodding an acknowledgement at Hodge before halting in front of Conyers. 'Back again, eh Conyers? Like a bad penny.'

Conyers grinned. 'You know me, sergeant. Never could say no to a scrap.'

'As I recall, the only reason you were with us in Flanders

was because the alternative was kicking your heels at the end of a length of hemp. Same again this time, was it?'

'Nay, serjeant. This time I volunteered.'

'What do you want? A knighthood?' sneered Preston. He walked a few paces away and turned to address the whole group. 'Now get this, all of you,' he said, raising his powerful voice. 'If it were up to me, all of the men in this kingdom between the ages of sixteen and sixty would be compelled to give their king military service, regardless of rank, income, or whether or not enough arms and armour can be provided to equip them. If you haven't got any weapons you can kill a man with your bare hands – if you know how to do it – and if you haven't got any armour, you can stop a crossbow bolt or a sword-stroke meant for a man less deserving of sudden and painful death than yourselves; and you'd still be doing no more than your duty to your king. So don't any of you start thinking that just by being here you're doing me, Sir Thomas, or his Majesty himself any great favours. Is that understood?'

'Yes, serjeant,' muttered a few of the men.

'By Him that harrowed Hell!' exploded Preston. 'D'you think the French are going to be impressed by that kind of limp enthusiasm? Because I can tell you now, they won't! They might die laughing, but I wouldn't want to stake my life on it. You're supposed to be the king's archers, not a bunch of God-damned ha'penny whores! Now what was that again?'

'Yes, serjeant!'

Preston nodded in satisfaction. 'That's more like it. Right, then. Those of you who have already served under my command are not – I hope – likely to forget me; although not for sentimental reasons, I dare say. For those of you who don't know me, my name's Wat Preston, but that's no concern of yours, as you'll all address me as "serjeant" at all times. You will do as I say at all times. If I say "jump!" you will not wait to ask "how high?" You will jump as high as you damned-well can, and pray to the Lord Christ that it's high enough to satisfy me.' He pointed to the banner. 'Now *that* is the banner of Sir Thomas Holland, God bless him. It's his command you'll be fighting under, and that is the banner you'll rally round in battle, so remember it well. Wherever it goes, you follow, even if it should lead you to the gates of Hell itself. I might also add that Sir Thomas is particularly fond of that banner. It's accompanied him as far east as Lithuania and as far south as Africa. Having brought that banner through countless campaigns, and won great glory under it on various battlefields, the last thing Sir Thomas wants is for that banner to end up hanging over some French whoreson's hearth so that the bastard can boast about how he captured Sir Thomas Holland's banner. Right? So, if that banner should be taken by the French – who are the biggest bunch of thieving scum on God's good earth, even worse than the Irish – then I shall hold each and every one of you responsible. In the event of its capture, you'd better retake it as quickly as possible or hope that you die in the attempt, because, by God's tears, if you fail and live, I'll personally make your miserable lives such a living Hell that you'll pretty soon wish you *had* died. Do I make myself clear?'

'Yes, serjeant!'

'Right! Now let's get you lot kitted up, and see if we can't disguise you as fighting men.'

They were provided with new grey tunics of coarse linen, hoods, woollen caps, black leather shoes, jerkins of hardened leather, broad leather belts with water gourds attached, leather bracers for their left forearms, and knapsacks for food and other provisions. By way of arms they were each given a short sword, a dagger, and at the bowyers' tent each man was issued with a longbow of unseasoned wych-elm that was roughly the same height as himself, with a flaxen bowstring and a woollen bow-bag to protect it from the elements. At the fletchers' tent they each received two score arrows in a leather retainer. The arrows were steel tipped with goose-feather fletchings, their long shafts made of ash, a wood that was both swift in flight yet heavy enough to deliver a powerful blow. They were one cloth-yard – three feet – in length, but later the men would cut their arrows down to suit the length of their draw.

There was no attempt at standardisation. They were given whatever arms were available, and those were not up to much. Martin's short sword – a little over two feet in length – was much pitted from hard usage, while the leather covering of the accompanying scabbard had worn away to expose the seasoned wood underneath. There was no doubting that most of the equipment had seen better days, but from glancing about the camp, Martin could see that he was no worse equipped than most of the other foot-soldiers.

Preston ordered his men to don their equipment and line up facing Holland's banner. Martin managed to attach the scabbard to the belt alongside the sheath for his rondel, a round-hafted dagger with a triangular blade; but when he tried to buckle the belt on underneath his jerkin, he found that his gourd became entangled with the strap from which his bow hung from one shoulder.

'I hope you don't mind my saying, like, but you're making a right sow's ear of that,' said Rudcock, already fully kitted and fitted out, coming to his rescue. 'Look here; you've got it all arsy-versy.'

Martin grimaced wryly. 'I've never been a soldier before.'

'You could've fooled me,' Rudcock said sardonically. 'Here, let me give you a hand with that. You fasten the belt *over* the jerkin, so you can get at your sword in a hurry if you need to. And you can wear that gourd right round here at the back, where it won't get in the way. See?' He adjusted Martin's scabbard so that the sword hung at his left hip. 'You *are* right-handed, aren't you?'

Martin nodded.

'There – how's that?'

'Awkward,' admitted Martin. The thick, heavy jerkin felt

100

bulky and cumbersome, and he was unused to having so many unfamiliar objects dangling from his belt.

'Don't worry, you'll get used to it,' Rudcock assured him.

'By the fire that burns, Rudcock, stop fussing over him!' bellowed Preston. 'He's old enough to go without a mother to wipe his nose and arse for him! Come on, the rest of you, get a God-damned move on! Nails and blood! The French could have overrun this camp before you rabble would be ready to face them!'

The men lined up in front of the banner, clutching their longbows in their woollen bags. The simple addition of jerkins and weapons had wrought an astonishing change in their appearance that even Martin could see. They no longer looked like the simple peasants they were, but like armed and dangerous men of war. Martin suddenly felt self-conscious, as if he were an impostor in their ranks.

Preston was thinking the same thing of all of them. 'Well, you might fool the French . . . at a distance . . . on a foggy night . . . but you don't fool me. Give a peasant a sword and all you've got is an idiot with a sharp piece of metal; the only person he's likely to hurt is himself. But maybe we can do something about that with a little drill. Now, I want you all to remember that the equipment with which you have just been issued remains the property of the Royal Armoury. Each and every single item must be accounted for when your term of service ends, and losses will be charged to you, so don't go losing any of it. And make sure you maintain it properly! I want those swords and daggers polished *at least* once a day, every day, regardless of whether or not you've had them out of their scabbards and sheaths since the last time you polished them. I'll be inspecting your equipment regularly, so don't think you can get away with slacking. All right, we'll worry about whether or not you can actually use those weapons at a later date. You can go and get something to eat now.'

They bought mutton from the victuallers and roasted it

over an open fire. It was charred on the outside and blood-raw in the middle, but Martin nevertheless devoured his portion with relish. Meat of any kind had been a rare luxury at home, and the march from Leicester after two weeks of prison diet had made him ravenous. As darkness fell, he was able to lie down and sleep with a full stomach and a sense of hope for the first time in weeks. In spite of the hardness of the ground, the coolness of the night air and the snoring of the others, he soon fell asleep, exhausted by the day's events.

The following morning the camp was awoken before dawn by the sound of a herald's trumpet blowing reveille. Martin was used to rising early, but not with his clothing damp with dew and his limbs all stiff and aching. They had bread and ale for breakfast, after which Preston had his men line up for inspection.

Throughout the day, men from all over the county continued to arrive at the mustering point, their ages ranging from sixteen to sixty. Like Martin, many of them were new to the business of soldiering, but also like him they had lived and worked on the land all their lives, and were strong and tough; the kind of men who would face hardship and tribulation with equanimity.

That afternoon, Rudcock showed Martin, Tate, Inglewood and the other raw recruits how to polish their weapons with bone-marrow grease until they shone. A troop of knights rode past on their coursers, caparisoned for war and accompanied by their squires. They were not dressed in armour, but with their huge broadswords hanging at their hips and their pennants flying from the tips of the lances carried upright by the squires, they still managed to look just as Martin had always imagined the Knights of the Round Table must have looked.

It was then that he recognised the arms of Sir John Beaumont.

CHAPTER FIVE

Martin stared. It was indeed Beaumont, seated astride his black courser, accompanied by Stamford, chatting amiably to his fellow knights as he rode by. Martin's first instinct was to avert his gaze before he was seen and recognised, to avoid trouble; but even as he stared, he felt anger well up within him. Here were the two men whom, Martin had no doubt, had conspired to have him executed for a crime that he had not committed. He knew he should have expected to see them at the mustering point, but their sudden appearance had caught him off guard.

As Beaumont listened absently to the light-hearted banter of the other knights, he glanced about at the warlike preparations of the camp with obvious approval. Then his gaze fell on Martin, and their eyes locked. Beaumont reined in his horse in shock and raised one hand, the index finger stretched in Martin's direction.

'By God's passion!' he roared. 'What in the name of Christ is that villainous churl doing here, for God's dignity?'

Everyone in the immediate vicinity stopped what they were doing, their eyes seeking out the object of Beaumont's wrath. The other knights, who had ridden on a few paces, wheeled their horses and rode back. 'What troubles you, Sir John?' asked one, glancing with the others towards Martin.

'That scum,' said Beaumont, slowly but clearly, 'is a murderer and a rapist, whom I personally brought to justice and sentenced to death.' It was a lie that Beaumont had been working to perpetuate for so long that he had come to believe it himself. 'It was he who was responsible for the foul murder of Sir John Seagrave's daughter.'

A shocked silence fell over the scene, not only amongst the knights and squires, but also amongst Martin's companions. Although many of them were thieves and murderers, the crime of rape – and the rape of a noblewoman at that – was one that appalled even them.

'I had thought him hanged for his villainy,' continued Beaumont, evidently struggling to keep a tight rein on his emotions. 'His continued existence makes a mockery of English justice; nay, it makes a mockery of the honour of the Seagrave family. I ask again, what ill fate allows him to be still with us, and apparently roaming free?'

'The same thing that brings us all here.' It was the voice of a nobleman, speaking in calm and measured but nonetheless firm tones. 'The service of his Majesty the king.'

Beaumont wheeled his horse about to face the new-comer. He was a dismounted knight, dressed in a white tunic and a blue cloak, the long tail of his hood wrapped about his head in a turban-like liripipe. He was in his early thirties, tall and well-built, with dark hair and a stern countenance. His bronzed, saturnine features, though regular, were somewhat angular, his face clean-shaven to reveal a firm, square jaw-line, his mouth set in hard, cruel lines. His right eye was dark, piercing and intense; the left was covered by a patch of white silk.

Beaumont was unimpressed. 'That churl,' he continued, still pointing at Martin, 'is a condemned criminal, tried and found guilty of a capital felony in a court of law. How he came to escape I cannot tell, but I intend to see to it that the sentence passed on him is duly carried out.'

Stamford smiled grimly. 'Allow me to deal with him, Uncle,' he said, drawing his broadsword with a well-practised motion.

'Put up your sword, boy!' snapped the one-eyed knight. 'Let no man confound what the king himself has decreed.'

'The king!' scoffed Beaumont. 'What is the life of this miserable villein to his Majesty?'

'The same as the life of any man bound to do the king military service,' the knight replied evenly.

'But this man is a condemned criminal!' Beaumont protested in outrage.

The knight smiled sardonically. So far he had not spared so much as a glance in Martin's direction. 'Which one? The thief? The poacher? The murderer, perhaps? Thieves and murderers they may be, sir, but it's my experience that thieves and murderers make the best fighting men. What is military service, after all, but pillage and slaughter? Dismiss your quarrel with this churl as unworthy of one of gentle birth such as yourself. He is bound to make amends for his misdeed in the king's service.'

'The king's service?' spat Beaumont. 'And what of the honour of the name of Seagrave? I'll readily cross swords with any man who tries to prevent me from defending that honour.'

The knight's face grew dark, but he refrained from reaching for the hilt of the massive broadsword that hung in an ivory scabbard from his jewelled belt. 'Then I must warn you that to do so you will have to cross swords with me, for I'll put the service of my king before the service of my God, let alone Sir John Seagrave's damned honour. I advise you to ride on, sir, safe in the knowledge that justice has found its own course.'

'How dare you address me so impertinently?' demanded Beaumont. 'Know you not who I am?'

The knight stared coolly up at Beaumont. 'Your coat of arms is as unfamiliar to me as, it would appear, mine own is to you. It seems I must perform my own introduction. I am Sir Thomas Holland of Broughton, Knight Banneret, son of Sir Robert, Lord Holland of Upholland. In the absence of my liege lord, Henry of Derby, I have been commissioned by my lord of Warwick to lead these troops to Portsmouth and beyond. I believe,' he added dryly, 'that the letter you received from his Majesty's Chancery requesting you to present yourself at this mustering point may have made mention of me?'

Abashed, Beaumont bowed stiffly in his saddle. 'My apologies, Sir Thomas.' He made a helpless gesture, while the other knights smirked and sniggered at his discomfiture. 'I did not realise . . .'

'Evidently not.' Holland's tone was full of icy menace. 'And you are, sir . . .?'

'Sir John Beaumont, Lord of Stone Gate Manor.' He gestured towards Stamford, who was hurriedly slipping his sword back into his scabbard. 'And this is my squire, Richard Stamford.'

'Indeed.' This time it was Holland who was singularly unimpressed. 'I suggest you heed well my counsel, Sir John, and ride on. And remember that whatever crimes may lurk in these men's pasts, they are the king's men now, and any man who seeks to harm them seeks to harm his Majesty's cause in France.'

Beaumont glared at Holland with a hatred almost equal to that which he reserved for Martin, but he and Stamford had no choice other than to ride on. The other knights had already contrived to distance themselves from Beaumont and his squire, riding away separately.

Martin felt sick to the stomach as he watched Beaumont and Stamford depart. He was unable to delight in their humiliation at Sir Thomas's hands. Somehow he had felt that this second chance, the offer of a pardon, would mark a complete break with a past of subjugation to Beaumont and his kin, a chance to start life anew. Now he realised that he would never escape his past, that he would always be branded a criminal; and with that realisation came the suspicion that Beaumont and his family would always dog his steps, a perpetual reminder of his humble status.

Brother Ambrose had watched the encounter from the entrance to Holland's tent. Now he stepped forward to address his master in low tones. 'I fear you may have antagonised him, Sir Thomas.'

Holland regarded his clerk with one eyebrow cocked. 'What of it?'

'If I may speak freely . . .?'

The tiniest hint of amusement flickered on Holland's stern countenance. 'You usually do, Brother Ambrose.'

'You humiliated him, if you'll pardon me for saying so. He'll not forget it.'

Holland made a dismissive gesture. 'He humiliated himself. For a man of gentle birth to harbour such feelings of hatred against a lowly churl . . . it's beyond all belief!' He shook his head sadly.

'But if you look at it from his point of view, as the injured party . . .' persisted the friar.

'A matter for the law to decide, and the law has made its decision.' Holland said firmly. Once he had made up his mind, it was rarely changed. 'I'll not tolerate the behaviour of any man who seeks to put his own interests before those of the king. Hang every condemned man in the king's service and you'll decimate our ranks!'

Holland took his leave of the friar, heading off in the direction of the earl's tent. In truth, Brother Ambrose had been pleased with the outcome of Holland's confrontation with Beaumont, if not its handling. Unlike Holland, Brother Ambrose had paid some attention to the object of Beaumont's wrath. He considered himself an excellent judge of character, and when Martin had professed his innocence the night before, the friar had been inclined to believe him. But innocent or not, Martin had been condemned by a court of law, and the young villein could considered himself lucky that he had been given this opportunity to gain a pardon. Perhaps it was the will of God. Besides which, Brother Ambrose, like Holland, was a loyal servant of the king, and agreed that his Majesty was entitled to every man he could get to serve him in France.

That night, as dusk fell over the common, Martin and his companions settled down to sleep on the ground around the camp fire once more. Martin was just beginning to drift off when he became aware of Hodge conversing in low tones with Piers Edritch, a young man who had been assigned to Preston's platoon earlier that day. Edritch was only a few months older than Martin, an aggressive young man with close-cropped hair, a pug nose and small, close-set eyes. Realising that he was the subject of their conversation, Martin pretended to be fast asleep, straining to catch their words.

'You heard what that knight said,' Edritch was saying. 'Rape! I'm damned if I'm going to fight alongside any man who has to take a woman by force – that's the lowest of the low, that is.'

'Worse than murder, Piers?' asked Rudcock.

'You shut your face!' snapped Edritch. 'The man I slew deserved to die.'

'So you appointed yoursen judge, jury and executioner, I suppose?'

'Sometimes a man must take the law into his own hands. You can't always rely on the courts for justice.'

'Aye and like,' agreed Rudcock. 'And it were the same courts that found Martin guilty of murder and rape.'

'And you reckon he might be innocent, I suppose?'

'He doesn't strike me as the kind of man who'd take advantage of a woman, that's all.'

They lapsed into a hostile silence, and after a few minutes Martin was fast asleep. His dreams, however, were by no means sweet.

*

Martin could hear the droning monotone of the priest's voice reading the last rites, and he wondered who was dying. He tried to look around, but whichever way he turned darkness surrounded him, enfolding him. He tried to reach out with his hands to feel where he was, but they were held fast behind his back. He tried to move his legs, but they were secured with irons. He felt confusion and panic well up inside him.

Then the ground beneath his feet seemed to lurch sickeningly and fall away. He felt himself spinning in the air, the rope biting into his neck, cutting into his windpipe. Choking, he struggled madly, trying to kick his legs. The rope tightened, and a new, blacker darkness began to descend over him. He tried to scream, but no sound would come out.

He awoke with a start, bathed in a cold sweat. It was a chill night, the black sky above him studded with stars. The camp fire flickered nearby, casting eerie shadows over the huddled shapes of the men who slept around it. He could hear the others snoring, and the grizzled Daw Oakley muttering something about pastry in his sleep. Throughout the camp, other fires flickered in the darkness. A torch was burning outside Sir Thomas Holland's tent, and in its light he could see Villiers conversing in low tones with Brother Ambrose.

Martin did not want to go straight back to sleep. The nightmare had been too vivid for him to want to risk dreaming it again. It was strange, but now that the threat of being hanged was past, the thought of what might have happened scared him more than it had done when it seemed inevitable, cruelly tying his innards into knots so that he felt weak and nauseous. Perhaps in some way he had never faced up to the fact that he might truly be executed for a crime he had not committed.

Feeling cold, he pushed himself to his feet, stepping carefully over the sleeping bodies of his companions to get nearer to the fire. Villiers bade Father Ambrose good night, and slipped inside Holland's tent. Brother Ambrose walked across to join Martin by the fire, warming his hands over it.

'Why abroad so late, my son?' murmured the friar. 'Is sleep elusive this night?'

Martin nodded. 'I was just thinking how lucky I am to be alive.'

Brother Ambrose nodded. 'Life is precious, is it not?' he said, smiling. 'Often we do not realise that fact until it is too late. Enjoy it while you can, that would be my counsel to a man of your age.'

Martin grimaced. 'Most folk of my class don't get the chance to enjoy life, whether or not they realise how precious it is,' he pointed out.

'Aye, true enough. But we must all be thankful for what little we have.'

'Aye, I reckon so.' Martin hesitated before plunging into a new topic of conversation. The friar seemed like a kindly man, but Martin did not know how far he could trust him. 'I were wondering about my family, like ... they probably think I'm dead by now.'

'I dare say word will get back to your village that you've gone to serve in the king's army overseas. If the good Lord smiles on you, you could be returning to your village a hero in twelve months' time.'

'I suppose so. It's just that ... I'd feel a lot happier if I could see them before I go.'

Brother Ambrose smiled. 'Are you certain you would not prefer to redeem yourself first?'

'I've not done owt wrong to redeem,' Martin insisted stoically. 'I were wrongly condemned.'

The friar shrugged. 'Man was born to suffer as the sparks fly upwards.'

'I were wondering how long it'll be before we set out for France?' Martin continued obliquely.

Brother Ambrose chuckled. 'We have to get to Portsmouth first.'

'Portsmouth?'

'That's where we'll be sailing from for France.'

'How long till we leave for Portsmouth, then?'

'A few days yet. The muster rolls are still some way from being completed.'

Martin decided to take the plunge. 'Only, I were thinking, I could return to Knighton – that's my village – and be back here in a few hours . . . it's not that far . . .'

'Do not even think of it,' the friar told him harshly. 'You know what the penalty is for desertion. Because that's what they'll assume you've done if you're found missing, even if only for a few hours.'

'Maybe if I had permission, like?' Martin persisted desperately. He was terrified that Beatrice, thinking him to be a rapist, would not wait for him to return from France. 'Could you not have a word with Sir Thomas?'

'I should dismiss such hopes if I were you. Sir Thomas is hardly a sentimentalist,' Brother Ambrose remarked dryly. 'Now you'd best get some sleep. And forget about trying to slip away when you think no one is looking; that path leads only to the end of a rope.'

Three days later was the Eve of Saint Justin, the last day of May. It was also the final day of the muster. After the general inspection of troops that was to be held at noon, they would set off marching for Portsmouth. Preston sent Martin and Brewster to the well near the town common to fetch water so that they could boil some mutton for breakfast. It was nice to be able to get away from the hurly-burly of the camp into the relative quiet of the town, if only for a few moments. Martin was winching the bucket of water to the surface when he heard someone call out his name, and he turned in time to see Beatrice running towards him. His heart leapt, and then she was in

111

his arms, kissing him. Brewster had to jump forward and catch the handle of the winch before the bucket was allowed to drop down again, rolling his eyes in mock despair.

She broke off the embrace, aware that Brewster was watching them with an amused smile, and suddenly felt embarrassed. 'Is there somewhere we can talk in private?' she asked breathlessly.

Martin glanced uncertainly at Brewster, who grinned. 'Oh, go on!' he said, emptying the water into the pail they had brought. 'I'll cover for you.'

Grinning, Martin thanked him, and led Beatrice behind one of the inns in the town. 'Is your father around?' he asked her.

She shook her head. 'He's sleeping in a tent with Dickon on the common,' she observed with a smile, but then she bit her lip. 'He told me that you were dead – hanged for rape and murder. Is . . . is it true?'

He smiled. 'That I'm dead?'

She punched him playfully. 'No, silly! What Father said, about you having raped and murdered Sir John Seagrave's daughter.'

'Of course it isn't true.'

She hugged him again. 'I knew it must be a mistake, that you could never do anything like that.'

'It was no mistake,' growled Martin. 'Your father deliberately arranged it, to stop us from seeing one another.'

She bridled. 'Martin! How dare you suggest such a thing! I know my father disapproves of my talking to you, but to suggest that he would deliberately have you put to death . . .'

To his dismay, Martin could see at once that he would not be able to convince her of the truth of the matter, and decided until he could come up with some proof the topic was one that was best avoided. 'What are you doing here, anyway?' he asked her, to change the subject.

'I've come to see Dickon and my father off. But what about you?' She took in his new clothes and arms. 'You're not . . .?'

He nodded. 'It's the only way I can get a pardon, even though I didn't do it. I have to serve the king overseas for a year.' Her face fell. 'What's the matter?'

'So, you're going to die after all,' she said sadly.

He grimaced. 'I don't intend to let any God-damned French whoreson kill me . . .'

'Martin!' she exclaimed, shocked.

'What?'

'You never used to take the Lord's name in vain like that.'

He blushed. 'I'm sorry. It's living with all these soldiers; they're an ungodly lot.' He smiled. 'Cheer up, my duck. I'll be back in a year's time, laden down with booty and glory. Why, I might even be given a knighthood for valour, and then . . . well, who knows?' He looked at her expectantly, but her expression was sceptical. 'Why not?' he demanded defensively. 'It happened to Sir John Chandos.'

'You believe yourself as good a man as Chandos?'

'Better,' Martin asserted proudly. 'You wait and see. I'll be back in a year's time, as noble a man as your father, and just as rich. No, richer! I'll catch some French nobleman, and hold him to ransom! They won't be able to refuse me a knighthood then!'

'And I'll thatch Groby Pool with pancakes!' she replied, smiling. 'How are you? Are they treating you well?'

He nodded. 'Aye and like. For the first time in my life, I can finish a meal without feeling hungry at the end of it. They're fattening me up for the kill, I reckon.'

'Please, Martin, don't speak of such things! Not even in jest!' She hung her head.

'I'm sorry.' He raised his hand – unsure of himself at first, fearful that she might recoil from his touch – to gently caress her cheek. When she did not protest, he touched her under the chin and raised her head so that she looked into his eyes. 'I'll be back, my duck. I promise you.'

She smiled wanly. 'I'll miss you.' Then a thought occurred to her. 'At least take this,' she said, and unwrapped the white silk coverchief she wore, tying it about his neck with a tearful smile. 'Your lady's favour, as befits my champion,' she explained. 'Wear it into battle, as Sir Lancelot wore Guinevere's favour. Perhaps it will bring you luck.'

'I'll always wear it, to remind me of you,' he promised, and they kissed. Her fingers clawed at his hood, pulling it back so that she could run her fingers through his crisp hair. Then she broke off the embrace and stood staring up at him, their eyes locked, hers solemn, his pleading, and she nodded, taking him by the hand and leading him into the inn's stables. She found a pitchfork and propped it against the door, wedging it shut from the inside, while he found an empty stall and piled up some clean hay to make a bed. When he turned, she was standing right behind him. He kissed her again, and began to fumble with the laces of her bodice. When her breasts were exposed, he dropped to his knees and began to nuzzle her. She moaned softly, clutching his head to her chest. Then, when he lifted his head to gaze up at her, she suddenly pushed him back so that he sprawled in the hay. He stared up at her in bewilderment, frightened that this might yet be a joke of which he was the butt, but she smiled tenderly, standing astride him and lifting her skirts. Feeling as taut as a drawn bow, Martin hastily pushed down his breech-cloth. She threw back her head and gasped with delight as she lowered herself slowly on top of him. Then, as she began to move against him, he reached up and caressed her breasts.

Their lovemaking was more tender this time, as if they both knew they might never see one another again and were trying to draw it out, to make it last for ever. This time when the throes of ecstasy finally caught up with Beatrice the spasms were even more uncontrolled, and Martin cried out as his own body responded, until she subsided on top of him with a final shudder, sobbing against his chest.

They lay there in silence, for how long Martin neither knew nor cared. Finally he gently lifted her off him, as easily as if she were no more than a rag doll, and straightened his clothes. The silence between them felt uncomfortable, thick with forboding. 'Will you wait for me?' he asked hesitantly.

She paused before responding. 'I'll wait.'

The ambiguity was not wasted on Martin. 'For me? Or for Stamford?' he asked bitterly.

'I could never marry a commoner, Martin,' she pleaded. 'You must see that.'

'And if I won a knighthood?'

She smiled sadly. 'If you were a knight, Martin, I'd marry you today, and the Devil take my father.'

Martin was grinning by the time he rejoined his new-found companions-in-arms on the common. 'You took your time, didn't you?' Brewster observed sardonically.

Martin blushed. 'We had much to discuss.'

'Oh yes?' said Brewster, grinning archly, and Martin scowled. 'Looks like you've got a rival in the womanising stakes,' Brewster added to Conyers, who grinned good-naturedly.

'What's she like then, this lass of his?' asked the Yorkshireman.

'She's a noblewoman,' said Rudcock. 'Isn't that so, Martin?' Martin declined to reply, and then Rudcock noticed the coverchief he now wore about his neck.

'What's the muffler for? Frightened of catching cold?'

Martin blushed again. 'A parting gift.'

'I see. Going to wear it into battle, like, are you? Your lady's favour?'

Martin grinned shyly. 'Summat o' that. How about you, Hodge? Have you got a girl?'

'Aye and like. I'm married, me. Three times, and all.'

'Three times!' exclaimed Inglewood, shocked.

Rudcock nodded. 'I've got one wife in Blaby, one in Sandwich, and another in Ghent.'

'But that's polygamy!' protested Inglewood, who had been to school.

'Polygamy?' echoed Rudcock. 'What's that when it's at home?'

'Having more than one wife.'

Rudcock rubbed his jaw while the implications of Inglewood's definition sank in. 'I reckon you're right. If that's polygamy, then I'm a polygamer,' he admitted vaguely.

Before Inglewood could explain that the word Hodge was looking for was 'polygamist', and that polygamy was contrary to the law of God, a voice that Martin found familiar cut in.

'Well, well, well! If it isn't young Robin Hood!'

Martin looked up, and recognised the horse-faced man from the archery contest in Leicester less than a month ago; though it seemed more like a lifetime ago. The horse-faced man was accompanied by two of his friends, each of them carrying a longbow in a woollen bow-bag.

Rudcock recognised the horse-faced man, too. 'Will Caynard,' he observed, his tone making it clear that he was less than overjoyed to see him.

Caynard ignored Rudcock. 'Come to be a soldier, then, boy?' he asked Martin.

'Aye,' said Martin, without looking up from the sword-blade he was polishing.

'"Aye"?' Caynard echoed mockingly. '"Aye"? Is that all you got to say for yoursen?'

Martin decided it would be best to stick to Simkin's advice, and ignore him.

'Hey! I'm talking to you, boy!'

'I noticed,' muttered Martin. 'I wish you'd give it a rest.'

'What were that?' Caynard demanded incredulously.

'Leave him alone, Will,' suggested Brewster, stretched out on his back on the greensward, hands clasped behind his head as he squinted up at the sun, a piece of straw jutting from the corner of his mouth. 'Can't you see he's new to all this?'

'I weren't talking to you, Brewster,' snapped Caynard, and turned back to Martin, grabbing a fistful of his coverchief. 'What's this then?' he jeered. 'A muffler? What are you, a gelding? Got to wear a girl's muffler to keep the cold off your chest, have you?'

'It's a gift from a friend,' muttered Martin, dropping the sword he had been polishing and trying to brush Caynard's hand away.

'Are you sure it's not a present from your mam?' scoffed Caynard. 'Who in the name of Christ do you think you are? Sir Lancelot, wearing your lady's favour? I'll bet she's a God-damned whore, your "friend"!' He suddenly pulled the coverchief upwards, jerking Martin to his feet.

Whether it was anger or instinct that made Martin lash out he could never afterwards be sure, but the blow he landed on Caynard's jaw took Will completely by surprise, knocking him on to his backside. John Conyers and some of the other veterans laughed. Enraged, Caynard jumped up and took a swing at Martin, hitting him on the cheek. Even as Martin went down he lashed out with one foot, catching Caynard under the kneecap. Caynard followed him to the ground with a scream of pain.

Suddenly Martin felt himself seized by the arms by

Caynard's two friends. They hauled him to his feet and held him there so that Caynard could pummel him in the stomach.

Rudcock leapt to his feet. 'Hey, that's enough,' he protested, trying to pull Caynard away.

Caynard punched him on the jaw, sending him sprawling in the mud. 'Keep out of it, Rudcock,' he snarled, kicking him sharply in the ribs. Rudcock doubled up in agony, and Caynard turned back to where his friends held a dazed and winded Martin between them. Will spat on his knuckles, and punched Martin on the nose. Martin could taste the blood on his lips as it coursed from his nostrils.

'He said: "That's enough",' said a deeper voice, and Caynard felt a heavy hand on his shoulder spin him around, before a massive fist smashed into his face. Drayton then turned and punched one of the men holding Martin. With one arm free, Martin was able to punch his remaining captor repeatedly in the stomach.

The brawl was about to turn into a free-for-all when Preston steamed up like an enraged bull and started to pull them apart, using his cudgel to get the attention of those too intent on their own private battles to notice that there was a new knight in the lists. He pulled Drayton off one of Caynard's friends. 'Nails and blood! What the Devil in Hell do you think you're doing?' the serjeant demanded furiously.

'They were beating him up,' Drayton explained ponderously, indicating Martin.

'I didn't ask what *they* were doing, I asked what *you* were doing,' snarled Preston.

Caynard was helped to his feet by his two friends. Preston turned on them. 'Will Caynard, Gilbert Murray and Bartholomew Lefthand,' he observed grimly. 'I might have known you three would be involved in it somewhere. You should have been here yesterday.'

'We got held up,' Bart Lefthand said insouciantly.

'Hold your tongue, damn your nose! Who struck the first blow?' the serjeant demanded of the platoon in general.

No one spoke.

'Very well, then. Five lashes for each of you, and don't think I don't mean it. I've flayed the hides off an entire company in my time . . .'

'It were me,' said Martin, wiping his bloody nose with his sleeve. 'I struck the first blow.'

'How very noble of you,' sneered Preston. He stepped up to Martin and drove the end of his cudgel into his stomach. It was an expert blow, driving all the wind from Martin's body so that he doubled up in agony, retching.

'That isn't fair!' protested Drayton, and indicated Caynard. 'He started it.'

'Did I ask you?' growled Preston, turning on Drayton. He had a way of looking at the men under his command as if they were something he might scrape off the sole of his boot. He looked the gigantic Drayton up and down contemptuously. 'I suppose you think you're pretty tough, eh? Since you're so worried about what's fair and what ain't, maybe you'd like to take a poke at me, eh?'

'But they started it!' protested Drayton.

'And I finished it. So what are you going to do about it, Samson? You want to take a poke at me now, eh? Come on, Drayton, you big, lumbering ox! No comebacks, just you and me.' Preston tossed his cudgel aside. 'Now's your chance. I'm unarmed. Why don't you try it? Surely a big, strong lad like yourself ain't afraid of a little fellow like me?' As he spoke, Preston punctuated his words by shoving Drayton in the chest, until the big youth lost his temper and took a swing at the serjeant's head. Preston ducked beneath the blow and drove his gauntleted fist into Drayton's stomach with an impressive economy of movement. As Drayton bent double, Preston clasped his

119

hands together and brought them down on the back of Drayton's neck, knocking him to the ground.

Unsmiling, Preston turned to face the others. 'Anyone else feel like fighting?' he demanded angrily. Apparently, no one did. 'In future, save your strength for the French. The inspection takes place in less than an hour; you're supposed to look like you're ready to go into battle, not as if you've just come out of one!' He snatched up his cudgel. 'God-damned rabble!'

As Preston stalked away, Rudcock crouched by Martin, who was trying to staunch the flow of blood from his nostrils. 'Are you all right, lad?'

Martin nodded. 'Bastard,' he muttered thickly, indicating Preston's receding back.

'He gets paid to be a bastard,' Rudcock pointed out evenly. 'What did you expect him to do? Reward you for your honesty?'

'What were he trying to prove?' demanded Martin, gazing across to where Drayton crouched in the mud on all fours, shaking his head muzzily.

'That no matter how tough we may reckon we are, he's tougher.' Hodge glanced across to where Caynard, Left-hand and Murray were sulking, nursing their own bruises. 'Don't feel too bad about it, mind. You and Hal gave a pretty good account of yourselves.' He grinned. 'I reckon you can safely say you've won your spurs as far as defending your lady's honour is concerned, Sir Lancelot. I don't expect Will Caynard and his mates will try picking on you again for a while. But if you've any sense you'll take my advice and try to make up with Will. I know he's not the nicest bloke to have around, but if the two of you are going to be serving together in this platoon, you're going to have to learn to get on with each other. We've got enemies enough awaiting us on the other side of the sea, without making enemies in our own ranks. We've got to stick together.'

Martin nodded, but as he glanced across to where Caynard sat, and their eyes locked, Caynard glared at him malevolently.

'How serious is it?' asked Rudcock.

'It's just a nosebleed.'

'No, I mean this thing between you and this noble-woman.'

Martin scowled. 'I don't reckon it's any of your business.'

Rudcock shrugged. 'It's just it seems strange to me, a fine lady like her paying attention to a churl like yourself. No disrespect, Martin, but I'd be just as suspicious if such a woman paid any attention to me.'

'I'm just as good a man as any nobleman,' asserted Martin. 'Better than some.'

'Aye and like,' acknowledged Rudcock. 'But you try telling a noblewoman that.'

'Beatrice loves me.'

'As long as you're sure. I wouldn't like to think you'd got your heart set on her, only to find that she was leading you on just to tease you.'

'Beatrice isn't like that,' insisted Martin.

Rudcock shrugged again.

Martin took his hand away from his nostrils. 'How is it?'

'It's stopped bleeding,' Rudcock assured him.

'Is it broken?'

Rudcock grinned. 'You mean, are you as handsome as me yet? You should be so lucky!'

Martin tried to cuff him playfully across the back of the head, but Rudcock scrambled out of his reach, laughing. Martin picked himself up and crossed to where Drayton sat, clutching at his midriff with one hand while rubbing the back of his neck with the other. 'Are you all right?'

Drayton nodded, and immediately regretted it, wincing as fresh shoots of pain lanced through his neck and into his skull. 'I made a muck-up of things, didn't I?' he said dolefully. 'I'm sorry. I always seem to get things wrong.'

'Sorry!' Martin exclaimed incredulously. 'If you hadn't joined in, God alone knows what sort of state Will and his mates would have left me in by the time Preston came along. It should be me who's apologising. If I hadn't lost my temper in the first place, Preston would never have hit you like that.'

Drayton shook his head. 'He'd've found some excuse sooner or later. They always do. I reckon it's because of my size. Folks always reckon they can prove something by hitting me. Sometimes they're right. I'm not very good at fighting.'

'I've seen worse,' said Martin, laughing. 'Much worse.'

They finished polishing their equipment. The whole encampment was in a froth of activity. Heralds ran to and fro, marshalling the troops, while squires struggled to saddle their masters' horses. The massive coursers pranced friskily and champed at the bit, the scent of war in their nostrils.

As the hour of the inspection drew near, the serjeants-at-arms drew their men up into their units on the open field adjoining the encampment. There were over a hundred men in Holland's company alone: in addition to Preston's platoon of twenty foot-archers, there were eight knights bachelor, including Beaumont; fifteen squires, including Richard Stamford and Adam Villiers; twenty mounted archers; and a troop of thirty-five men-at-arms, mounted on rouncies, armed with shields, swords and lances, dressed in chain-mail hauberks and 'kettle' helmets.

Holland sat astride his war-horse, a powerfully built dappled-grey courser, and watched dispassionately as his serjeants arrayed his men in their loose formations, each command accompanied by a punch or a kick when it was carried out too slowly for a serjeant's liking.

The foot-soldiers stood fully armed in their platoons, clutching spears or bows, while the knights sat in full armour astride their coursers, accompanied by their squires on rouncies, holding pennanted lances upright on the felt butts on their saddle bows. The knights' colourful jupons and brightly burnished plate armour made a proud display that put the foot-soldiers to shame.

The Chief Baron of the Exchequer had come to the inspection to see what kind of men the king would be getting for his money. He rode along with the Earl of Warwick before the assembled formations, exchanging a few words with each of the knights commanding a company. To Martin, the whole process seemed little more than a formality, but the sight of the armed men around him made him proud.

The earl greeted Holland amicably. It was obvious that the two of them were old comrades-in-arms with a great deal of respect for one another. Both the earl and the baron regarded Holland's men with evident approval, before moving on. After the inspection was completed, the men were ordered to remain in their formations to watch as three captured deserters were hanged from the boughs of a large oak tree that stood at the edge of the field. There was no law against desertion as such, but since the men had waited until they had received their first payment before leaving they were considered guilty of theft.

Martin watched uneasily as the three men died, kicking and struggling, their faces grotesquely distorted as the life was choked out of them. There but for the grace of God go I, he thought to himself; then he corrected himself with a grimace: if God had any grace, he would not have been unjustly accused and condemned.

For Inglewood, the gruesome sight of the hanged men, on top of being made to stand in the blazing sun in full kit for well over an hour, was too much, and he stumbled against the man next to him before collapsing to the ground in a dead faint. Some of the veterans laughed. Preston directed Rudcock to fetch a pail of water from a nearby well and tip it over Inglewood's head to revive him.

The bodies of the three deserters were left swinging from the bows of the oak tree to feed the carrion crows, and the order was given to strike camp. The tents were dismantled and loaded aboard the carts and wagons of the baggage train along with the pots, pans and cauldrons of the field kitchens. Sheaves of arrows were packed in wicker baskets and loaded on horse-drawn carts, covered over with horse-hair tarpaulins. The knights and men-at-arms removed their hot and heavy armour and equipment and fastened it on to their packhorses.

The marshals began to form the men up into a column on the road leading south. It was a time-consuming process, taking even longer than it had done to get them into formation for the inspection; for now draught animals had to be harnessed to the carts and wagons, and there were the packhorses to be taken into account. No one seemed to know where they were supposed to be, while the serjeants argued with the marshals, the marshals argued with one another, and the knights squabbled for the place of honour at the head of the column. The horses would not stand still, and neither would some of the men. Tempers quickly frayed in the hot May sunshine.

Nevertheless, through persistence and industry, the marshals managed to hammer some kind of order out of the chaos and confusion. Holland rose above the squabbling of the knights, and as a consequence the earl awarded his company the place of honour at the head of the column; or perhaps Holland had known all along that the earl had reserved the place of honour for him and his men, so he had not needed to get involved in the squabbles in the first place.

The earl gave the signal to move off with his marshal's baton, the heralds sounded the march on their trumpets, and the column moved hesitantly forward.

Martin Kemp was marching to war.

CHAPTER SIX

The Earl of Warwick rode at the very head of the column, one of his squires riding alongside him carrying aloft his banner, three red crosslets above and below a band of red on a yellow background. With him rode his retinue, and behind them marched Holland's company, Sir Thomas himself astride his massive courser at their head. Beside him Adam Villiers rode a bay rouncy, holding Holland's banner aloft, and Brother Ambrose rode a skewbald pony. Next came the knights and squires under Holland's command, including Beaumont and Stamford, followed by a hundred archers slogging it on foot. It was John Conyers who pointed out that a dismounted man who marched in the place of honour had the advantage of having to walk through less horse-muck than the dismounted men at the rear of the column.

Preston marched at the head of his platoon, puffing away at a set of bagpipes. He was not the only musician in the column; there were other men, armed with trumpets, horns, clarions and pipes, and drummers beating out the rhythm of the march on tabors and nakers. As they marched, their music combined with the jingle of harness and the clatter of mail to give their progress a martial air. At the centre of the column was the baggage train, a dozen carts and wagons piled high with victuals, equipment and spare arms. There were over six hundred armed men of one kind or another in the column, which stretched back along the dusty track for nearly half a mile. The horsemen moved off at a trot, forcing the foot-soldiers to jog along in their wake, and it was not long before the tail of the column began to straggle, merging with the host of camp followers who came in their wake. Most of these were pedlars who knew that they could exhaust their wares sooner or later if they stuck with the column long enough, but there was also a troupe of tumblers heading south seeking protection against any bands of brigands who might be lying in wait on England's lawless roads, and a handful of enterprising prostitutes who cruelly mocked the peasant girls running after the column to wish their loved ones goodbye.

Marching so close to the head of the column, Martin was unaware of the carnival it degenerated into towards the rear. He was looking at the well-armed and disciplined troops around him. He had heard that Philip of Valois ruled over the richest and greatest country in the world; yet he found it hard to believe that Valois could ever hope to muster an army as magnificent as this one. And this was only what was left in the county after Henry of Derby had taken the pick of the men to Gascony the previous year. Rudcock and some of the other veterans speculated as to what their ultimate destination might be. Would the king join Derby in Gascony, unite with his allies in Flanders, or would he land in Brittany, where the English had established a foothold following the Earl of Northampton's defeat of the French at Morlaix a few years ago?

It was a warm day, and before long the hot sun began to squeeze sweat from every pore in Martin's body. He still felt awkward and ungainly in his heavy leather jerkin, and the sword that hung at his hip knocked irritatingly against his thigh with every step. The earl forced a punishing pace, and Martin soon developed a stitch in his side. But there could be no stopping to rest. Martin was consoled by the fact that none of the other new recruits seemed to be faring any better, and he was glad that after his sojourn in gaol he had had a few days to rest and recoup his strength. Inglewood was obviously suffering, being more used to riding when travelling over a distance.

'Come on, Perkin, keep it up,' Rudcock told him, panting through gritted teeth. 'It won't be a very good start to your military career if you collapse on your first day of marching, will it now?'

They had set out from Bosworth later than the earl had intended, and he was determined to make up for lost time, forcing the pace. They crossed the border into the County of Warwick shortly before dusk. For many of the new recruits, including Martin, it was the first time they had set foot outside their native county. Darkness fell, and the earl ordered torches to be lit so that they could march on through the twilight, not stopping until they reached the village of Brinklow at the hour of vespers. The men made camp below an old Norman motte and bailey castle, while the noblemen found lodgings in the village inn or slept inside their tents. The men were able to forage enough dead wood to make camp fires, and they dined on roast beef beneath the stars, chatting merrily and boasting about the feats of prowess they hoped to perform in the fields of France. They slept soundly that night, exhausted by the day's march.

They were roused early the following morning by reveille. After their usual breakfast of bread and ale, the veterans of Preston's platoon initiated the new recruits by seizing them bodily and throwing them into a brook that ran alongside the camp. Most of the new recruits knew it was all in fun and put up only a token resistance, but Inglewood did not see it in the same light, struggling furiously as he was dragged to the edge of the stream. When he landed in the water, the old hands laughing as they looked down at him from the bank, it seemed for a moment as if the red-faced Inglewood might burst into tears, but he managed to choke back his sobs and settled for glowering sulkily at the pranksters.

It was a very different story with Hal Drayton. Rudcock and Conyers managed to drag the muscular youth to the brook, but there Hal broke free, pushing Conyers into the water. As he did so he lost his balance, slipping in the churned mud on the bank and toppling in himself, but he nevertheless managed to pull Rudcock in after him.

Preston appeared on the bank. 'All right lads, play time's over,' he said sternly, but not unkindly. 'Time to strike camp. We've a long way to go yet before we reach Portsmouth.'

The men formed up into a column once more; they were rapidly learning to obey the orders of the marshals and the serjeants promptly. It was the first day of June, and the warm sunshine soon dried out the clothes and equipment of those who had had a soaking.

They reached the village of Coventry shortly after noon. Coventry Common was the mustering point for the men of the County of Warwick, and it was there that the rest of the earl's command waited. The Leicester men pitched camp alongside the Warwick men's encampment while the earl inspected the men who had been raised in his county in his name. Inevitably, there were a few fights that night between the men of Leicester and the men of Warwick; but the two counties were so closely bound together administratively that there was more amity than enmity. The serjeants kept a tight rein on the troops under their command to ensure that the few brawls that did break out were not allowed to escalate into all-out rioting.

More than doubled in size by the addition of the men of Warwick, the column set out immediately the following day at dawn. Whenever it passed through a village, the peasants gathered to line the roadside, waving and cheering; the king's propaganda had spread word of

Valois' usurpation throughout the realm, and there were few Englishmen who would have even contemplated questioning the righteousness of the king's cause. From his customary place at the head of the column, the earl led them on at the usual punishing pace, but the weather was fine and morale was high, the men chatting amongst themselves and laughing gaily, or singing along raucously to the martial airs played by the pipers.

They continued south in this manner for several days, through the Forest of Arden and across the Cotswolds into the County of Oxford. They marched along the bank of the River Cherwell to its confluence with the Isis just outside the town of Oxford itself, where they camped one night. Martin toyed briefly with the idea of slipping from the camp to visit his brother Nicholas, but he was not sure that he would be able to find Merton College in the large town in the dark; besides which, the sight of the three men being hanged for desertion was still grimly fresh in his memory, and he did not want to risk being hanged just so that he could see his sanctimonious brother.

South of Oxford, the column passed between the White Horse Hills and the Chilterns into the Vale of Kennet, crossing into Hampshire and marching over the South Downs. Towards late afternoon on the ninth day of the march, they emerged from the Forest of Bere and began a steep climb up the north face of a ridge, the draught animals straining to haul the wagons up behind them. Martin could detect an unfamiliar tang in the air, and he caught sight of white birds circling overhead, their harsh cries clearly audible above the clatter of the marching men. They were birds with which even Martin was familiar, being occasional visitors to the fields of Knighton during the winter months: seagulls. The crest of the ridge formed the horizon, drawing ever closer until finally the men had breasted it, and the harbour of Portsmouth suddenly came into view below them.

Martin had never seen anything like it. The harbour itself was huge – far bigger than Groby Pool, the broadest expanse of water he had seen up to that day – and teeming with literally hundreds of wooden ships, of all shapes and sizes. There were cogs, carracks and crayers, barges and ballingers, hakeboats, loadships, pickers, doggers and galleys. Their striped red and white sails were furled, and many of the larger ships had wooden turrets built fore and aft.

A castle stood on a promontory jutting out into the harbour, the king's flag flying from atop the massive stone keep to show that his Majesty was in residence. The town of Portsmouth itself stood on the east side of the harbour's narrow opening, a close-packed huddle of slate-roofed houses, the tower of a church rising up from their midst. A little to the north-east of the town, an even larger settlement stood on the flat expanse of Southsea Common, stretching out along the roads to London and Winchester: a mass of tents and pavilions that formed the camp of the king's army.

And beyond all this was the sea, stretching away for as far as the eye could see, the deep blue waves rolling in to break in a welter of foam against the shore. Martin had often tried to picture the sea in his mind's eye, but even the mental image of a lake so broad that the far side could not be seen simply had not prepared him for the mind-numbing reality: he had not thought there could be so much water in the whole world. He wondered how far across one would have to sail before one reached the coast of France.

'All right, lads, let's show these whoresons how the men of Leicester go to war,' Preston growled, as they began to descend the south-facing slope of the ridge towards the encampment. He blew a tune on his bagpipes, a martial air with which they had all become familiar during the march from Bosworth, and the men joined in, singing raucously and lustily with their banners and pennants raised once more. At the foot of the ridge they crossed the old stone bridge on to Portsea Island, which formed the eastern side of the harbour. It was dusk by the time they drew near the encampment, but even the fast-fading light could not hide the fact that it was even larger than Martin had first thought. Even the experienced veterans seemed astonished by the size of the army being assembled by the king, averring that it must be the greatest force of men that the kingdom had ever seen. Surely Valois could not hope to muster an army strong enough to face this threat?

The Earl of Warwick had already been appointed Marshal of the King's Army for the forthcoming campaign, and as such it was nominally his responsibility to see that the arriving troops were quartered on the common; in his absence, he had delegated the task to the Under-Marshal, Robert Howell, who met the earl at the outskirts of the camp. Howell was accompanied by Sir Thomas Norwich, both of them mounted on fine palfreys. The earl signalled the men behind him to silence.

'My lord of Warwick,' said Norwich. He was a tall, lean man in his mid forties, with dark hair fading to iron-grey, a lean-jawed, wedge-shaped face, and a long, straight nose. His cold grey eyes were piercing, and his countenance could match the earl's for sternness. At that moment he exuded *bonhomie*, a frequent trick of his, but the earl was no longer taken in; behind his amiability was hidden a mind that was as ruthless as it was razor-sharp. 'You are most welcome. These are the men from the counties of Warwick and Leicester?'

The earl nodded.

'I'll have to check their names off against my copies of the muster rolls, my lord, but that can wait until the morrow, when I have the indenture sheets made out.'

The earl made a dismissive gesture. 'I'll have one of my

clerks attend to it.' Unlike Norwich, he had always found the administrative side of soldiering tedious in the extreme.

Norwich smiled thinly. 'As you will, my lord.'

Howell gestured to a stretch of greensward a short distance from where they sat astride their horses. 'With your permission, my lord? If you and your men would be willing to pitch your tents yonder?'

The earl inclined his head. He had every confidence in his subordinate's ability to marshal such a vast army of men – he would not have agreed to his appointment, otherwise – and since Howell already seemed to have the organisation of the camp well in hand, the earl saw no reason to interfere in his underling's work at this late stage. He barked out a few curt orders to his marshals, and immediately his men began to pitch their tents adjoining the main camp, where Howell had indicated. Since leaving Bosworth, the raw recruits had become as adept at pitching camp as the veterans.

The routine at the great encampment on Southsea Common proved to be more or less the same as it had been at the camps which the Earl of Warwick's column had set up on the march from Bosworth. Reveille was sounded throughout the encampment before dawn the following morning. Preston's men rose to their feet and stretched stiff and aching limbs. The serjeant ordered Daw Oakley and Thurstan Freeman to buy some breakfast from the victuallers while Brother Ambrose performed a morning mass for Holland's men, but apart from a handful of knights and squires attendance was low, being non-compulsory. Perkin Inglewood insisted on attending, but most of Martin's new companions could not be bothered. Martin had attended mass every Sunday morning for as long as he could remember, but that had been at his parents' insistence. He had never been one for singing, even less for sermons, and now he took guilty pleasure in not attending.

'All right, you God-damned miserable bunch of idle whoresons,' Preston snarled at his men when they had finished eating breakfast. 'It's time to start turning you into soldiers.'

'What, all of us?' moaned Newbolt.

'Aye, that includes you, Newbolt. Just because you've survived one campaign, you may fall into the trap of thinking you know all there is to know about fighting, but the chances are there's at least one Frenchman in Gascony who can prove otherwise. Come on, get a move on! Nails and blood! The fleet will have sailed without us before you God-damned sluggards wake up.'

Grumbling, Preston's men gathered up their arms and followed him to an open patch of greensward adjoining the encampment. A platoon of men-at-arms were already drilling on foot nearby. They handled their spears with impressive proficiency, levelling them as they might to receive a mounted charge.

Preston's men stood in a loose gaggle while the serjeant stood before them. 'Right!' yelled Preston, to make sure he had their undivided attention. 'When you lot of old washerwomen have finished gossiping, perhaps you might like to bend your ears in my direction. You might learn something that could one day save your wretched and worthless hides. I'm sure you've all noticed by now that I'm no tonsured scholar from Oxford and Cambridge like Brother Ambrose, but for those of you who haven't already had the honour of serving with me before, I'll have you know that I graduated *summa cum laude* from the School of Hard Knocks.' He grinned. 'You didn't know I spoke Greek, did you, Conyers? For those of you not fluent in Greek, *summa cum laude* means I'm a nasty bastard who can snap any one of you in two just by batting my left eyelid . . . yes, what is it, Inglewood?'

'Pardon me for interrupting, serjeant, but *summa cum*

laude isn't Greek, it's Latin,' said Inglewood. 'It means . . .'

'Were you born a pain in the arse, Inglewood, or do you have to work at it?' asked Preston. 'One word of advice: no one likes a God-damned smart-arse, all right? Now, where was I? Oh, yes. In addition to your so-called skill with the bow, eventually you're all going to have to learn to use your swords; for those of you who don't know, that's the sharp, pointy bit of metal hanging down from your belts. But right now I wouldn't trust most of you to shave your own pig-like faces wi'out giving yourselves a mortal wound. So we're going to start with the basics: unarmed combat.'

The veterans groaned. Many of them suspected that this was just an excuse for Preston to beat the living daylights out of them.

'Oh, yes!' said Preston, grinning sadistically. He drew his short sword from its scabbard and tossed it to the ground a few feet from where he stood. 'Right! Here's the situation: you've used all your arrows and your bow-string's snapped; your sword is broken and is about as much use to you as a gelding is to a mare on heat; some whoreson Irishman has pinched your dagger; and there's some French devil charging towards you with every intention of thrusting his poxed spearhead clean through your gizzard. So what are you going to do?'

'Run away?' suggested Conyers, raising a laugh from the others.

Preston smiled tolerantly – he did not mind the occasional joke, if it kept spirits up – and waited for the laughter to die down, rubbing his bristly jaw as he thought for a moment. 'Wrong, as usual, Conyers; but I'm glad you brought the subject up. Since we're talking about running away, I'll tell you all something now and not repeat it, but that doesn't mean I want any of you to forget it,' he said, his face growing dark. 'If I see any of you running away in the face of the enemy, I'll kill you myself,' he told them grimly. 'And if any of you are stupid enough to think I'm jesting or bluffing, then just ask Daw Oakley there. He's seen me do it enough times before now, so he *knows* I'm not kidding. Understood?'

The men nodded dumbly, the new recruits chilled by the gravity of Preston's tone.

'Right!' continued Preston. He had a way of saying 'right!' that made people listen. 'No arrows, no sword, and no dagger. There's some French whoreson charging at you, and you can't run away because I'm standing right behind you. Luckily you've still got four deadly weapons on you. So who's going to tell me what they are? Not you, Murray, I know you know already. How about one of the new lads? Tate? Kemp? Wighton? No?'

When no response was forthcoming, he tugged off his chain-mail gauntlets and tossed them to the ground, displaying a pair of calloused and grimy hands. 'Two arms . . . and two legs. Not much use against a knight in full armour, I'll grant you, but a lot of the time you'll be up against peasant levies no better equipped than yourselves. So, who's going to be our first volunteer? Who wants to be the evil, murdering French whoreson? Inglewood?'

Inglewood shrank back.

'Perhaps not,' Preston agreed, grimacing with distaste. 'Come on, one of you bunch of field mice must be dying to stick your sword in my guts.'

'How about if you have both hands tied behind your back?' suggested Conyers, who had seen this all before and knew what was coming next.

'Are you volunteering, Conyers?'

'No, serjeant,' the Yorkshireman replied hurriedly.

'Then God-damned shut up,' said Preston, and smiled. 'I'll tell you all what. I'll turn my back on you so's I can't see you coming. Can't say fairer'n that, can I?'

136

There were still no volunteers, the raw recruits suspecting that it might be harder than Preston made out, and the old hands knowing it was.

'Drayton!' exclaimed Preston, as if noticing an old friend in their ranks for the first time. 'How about you? You like fighting, don't you? I'll wager you're still smarting from that punch in the guts I gave you at Bosworth, eh? Want a chance to even the score?'

Drayton stepped forward reluctantly, toying uncertainly with a short sword that looked little more than a dagger in his massive paw. 'What if I kill you?' he asked unhappily.

Preston chuckled. 'You won't.'

'But what if I do?'

Preston sighed. 'Drayton, you have my full permission to try and kill me. In the event of my death, I absolve you of all responsibility, and these lads here can be witnesses to that, all right? Now come on, thrust that God-damned sword right through my back and out the front of my belly! It shouldn't be too difficult for a big, strong lad like yourself. Run me through! Hang my gizzard out to dry!' He turned his back on his men.

After a moment's uncertain hesitation, Drayton raised his sword and charged. Without even so much as a glance over his shoulder, Preston side-stepped at the last possible moment, tripping Drayton up and wresting the sword from his grip as the big lad went down. Drayton rolled on to his back, and Preston put a booted foot on his chest, tickling his Adam's apple with the tip of the sword. He made it all look embarrassingly easy.

'All right, lad, on your feet,' said Preston, helping Drayton up. 'Not too bad, considering you've never used a sword before.' He turned to the others. 'Does anyone want to tell me what Drayton's mistake was?'

'He attacked you with the sun at his back,' Brewster drawled laconically. 'You saw his shadow.'

Preston nodded. 'That's it, Brewster. Spot on.'

'But that wasn't fair!' protested Inglewood. 'He didn't have any choice in the matter!'

'That's because I deliberately positioned myself to my own advantage, boy,' Preston told him, not unkindly. 'That's the first rule of combat: wherever possible, position yourself to your own advantage. When it comes to a pitched battle, it'll be up to their lordships to select the battlefield, but there'll be plenty of times when you can make a few decisions of your own. Height is another good advantage to look for. Can you gain the advantage of height over your opponent? A rock, a fallen tree-trunk, a slight slope in the ground; a few inches that could make all the difference between life and death: your life, his death. Do you want the sun in your enemy's eyes? Will your shadow give you away if you try to sneak up on someone? Small details, but maybe vital. These are questions I want you to ask yourselves every time you reach for the hilt of your sword. And don't any of you give me any God-damned nonsense about creeping up behind people being unfair. Leave the chivalry to your betters. Your job is to kill as many Frenchmen as possible, and I don't care how you do it. Because believe you me, the French won't treat you any more chivalrously if your positions are reversed.'

'Is it true that when the French capture archers, they cut off the first two fingers of their right hands so that they can't use a bow any more?' asked Limkin Tate.

'I've heard a rumour to that effect,' admitted Preston. 'Whether or not it's true I can't say. Churls like us aren't usually taken captive. We aren't worth ransoming, see? So if any of you are captured and only have two fingers cut off, you can count yourselves lucky.' He smiled grimly. 'And then you can start learning to use a bow left-handed, because I'm damned if I'll accept the loss of two fingers as an excuse to wriggle out of doing your duty to your king.

'But back to today's first lesson: the best soldier isn't necessarily the strongest soldier or the bravest soldier, it's the one who shows some nous, right? So . . . who's our next volunteer?'

No one stepped forward.

'I'll stand facing the sun, so that I can't see your shadow this time,' Preston offered cajolingly.

Still no one offered.

'I don't know what's up with you lot, you're the most lily-livered bunch of recruits I've ever had the misfortune to have to lead,' Preston protested in disgust.

'You said we should use our heads, serjeant,' Conyers said sardonically, getting his second laugh of the day.

'All right,' said Preston, with a tolerant smile. 'But we'd best be getting on, otherwise you won't learn anything more, and believe you me, we haven't even begun to scratch the surface of all there is to learn. Come on, if someone doesn't step forward, I'll pick a volunteer; only this time, I'll have the sword, and you can go unarmed.'

Martin stepped forward. 'I'd like to give it a go, sergeant.'

'Good lad, Kemp,' said Preston. 'Ready when you are.'

Martin drew his sword and charged, swinging the blade at Preston's head. Preston ducked beneath the blow, catching Martin's stomach against his shoulder. Then he straightened, tossing Martin over his shoulder. Martin landed flat on his back, winded. Preston helped him to his feet and handed him back his sword.

'You all saw how I used his own momentum against him?' Preston asked the others. 'Stay low – think of it as a see-saw, and you're the pivot. Got it? Watch again . . . another volunteer?'

'Can I have another try?' Martin asked ruefully. 'I think I'm getting the hang of it.'

Preston stared at him in astonishment. 'You are a glutton for punishment, aren't you? All right, one more demonstration courtesy of young Kemp here, and then you can pair off and start practising amongst yourselves.' He braced himself for Martin's next attack. 'Ready when you are, Kemp.'

Martin levelled the sword and charged, holding it low this time, ready to thrust it into Preston's stomach. Preston side-stepped, but the sword-thrust was a feint, and Martin smashed the knuckles of his left hand into the serjeant's face. Dazed, Preston staggered back.

'How's that?' asked Martin, adding, 'You did say we wasn't to fight fair.'

'Not bad,' Preston mumbled thickly. 'You're learning fast. Class dismissed,' he concluded, before collapsing.

Warwick and Holland made their way to Porchester Castle to pay their respects to the king first thing that morning. When Holland returned to his tent towards noon, he found Preston seated there, taking a break. Preston immediately rose to his feet and snapped more or less to attention. 'Sir Thomas.'

'Hullo, Wat,' Holland replied absently, removing his cloak and folding it once before placing it over the back of a chair. 'How goes the training?'

'Not too bad, Sir Thomas.' The doubtful tone in Preston's voice did not worry Holland; he was accustomed to the serjeant playing down the ability of his men, so that he would not be disappointed when they came to fight. In the event, Holland usually found himself anything but disappointed with the results of Preston's training. 'One or two of the new lads are showing a fair bit of promise,' Preston allowed on a higher note.

'Good.' Holland spoke vaguely, his mind on other things. He had every confidence in Preston's ability to transform the rawest recruits into tough fighting men. 'Tell me, Wat . . .'

'Sir Thomas?'

'Why are you clasping a dead fish to your left eye?'

'The victuallers wouldn't give me a steak, Sir Thomas.'

'I see,' said Holland, peeling away the fish to reveal Preston's black eye. 'That's an impressive shiner you've got there, Wat.'

Preston grimaced. 'I'm not as young as I used to be,' he admitted ruefully.

'Who amongst us is?' acknowledged Holland, with a wry smile. 'Who gave you that, then?'

'One of the new lads, sir. Martin Kemp, of Knighton. The one Sir John Beaumont accused of rape and murder.'

'Hmm. Tell me, Wat, what do you make of him?'

'Sir John Beaumont, sir?'

Holland shook his head. 'Nay, I suspect I have that one's measure already,' he said, with a grimace. 'I meant the lad that hit you.'

'Kemp, you mean? He's a difficult one to make out. Some of the lads call him Sir Lancelot, on account of how he wears some lass's coverchief – his lady's favour, so to speak. He doesn't have much to say for himself. He's a fine archer, and not a bad wrestler – for a young 'un.'

'Not bad with his fists either, by the look of it,' added Holland, with a smile. 'Keep me informed of his progress.'

CHAPTER SEVEN

Later that day Martin strolled through the encampment with Rudcock, Conyers, Brewster, Inglewood, Drayton and Tate. The whole camp was alive with activity, noisy with the sounds of men at work and pervaded by a wide variety of smells both familiar and unfamiliar: horse-muck, tanned leather, wood smoke, roasting meat, and vegetables fresh and rotten.

This whirl of the senses reminded Martin of the annual trade fair at Leicester. There were armourers sharpening weapons on grindstones or repairing coats of mail; fletchers cording sheaves of arrows and packing them in large wicker baskets; farriers reshoeing horses; cooks baking bread and roasting meat; heralds riding to and fro with messages; and squires, young and old, scurrying about on their masters' errands. And everywhere there were soldiers: professionals, veterans, raw recruits; Welsh spearmen and Cheshire archers; wild Irish kerns with long hair and flowing moustaches, dressed in yellow tunics with baggy sleeves, armed with javelins and axes; sappers from the Forest of Dean; men from all over the country. Hodge pointed out the banners of the earls of Arundel, Huntingdon, Northampton, Oxford and Suffolk, as well as those of Lord Bartholomew Burghersh and Thomas Hatfield, the bellicose Bishop of Durham. And then there were the Welsh archers; the Earl of Arundel's men, from Chirkland, in their red-and-white parti-coloured livery; and the Prince of Wales's archers in white and green. Limkin noticed that many of the Welsh

142

troops wore only one shoe, and pointed this out to the others.

'That's because the Welsh are too poor to be able to afford a whole pair of shoes each, so they have to share,' explained Conyers, grinning.

They left the encampment behind them and entered the narrow streets of Portsmouth. The port seemed just as busy as the camp – little more than an extension of it, really, under the present circumstances – with armed men and mariners hurrying to and fro. It seemed as if the military preparations had more than doubled the town's population. Martin and his friends strolled along the quayside, watching the mariners prepare their vessels for war by fitting them out with double tackle.

Dusk was falling fast. They were about to turn back when they came to a waterfront tavern. Torchlight blazed through the open front door, splashing across the cobbles of the quayside, and the raucous noise of merriment came from within. 'Come on,' said Rudcock, heading towards the door.

'Are you sure we should be going in there?' Tate asked nervously. 'The serjeant didn't say we could.'

'He didn't say we couldn't, neither,' Conyers pointed out reasonably.

'I'm not going in there,' Inglewood said firmly. 'My mother told me to stay away from alehouses.'

'Well, she's not here now, is she?' said Conyers. 'I won't tell her if you don't. Besides, this isn't an alehouse, it's a tavern.'

'What's the difference?' asked Drayton.

'Alehouses don't serve wine,' explained Rudcock, licking his lips.

'Or girls,' added Conyers.

But Inglewood was adamant. 'I'm not going in there.'

'Suit yourself,' retorted Conyers, leading the others

towards the entrance. 'If you change your mind, you know where to find us.'

Inglewood watched his five friends enter the tavern, torn between his desire to stick with them and his fear of the eternal damnation he would suffer if he went into the house of Satan, filled as it was – according to Old Mother Inglewood – with the Devil's snares. Fear won out over friendship, and he slunk back to the encampment.

Inside, the tavern was as crowded as it was noisy, with soldiers and mariners occupying every table. Martin and his friends stood in one corner by the counter, and eventually the innkeeper approached them.

'Five flagons of Gascon wine,' Conyers told him, and indicated Tate. 'The skinny one's paying.'

'You boys just arrived in Portsmouth?' asked the innkeeper, as he handed them their flagons. His soft Hampshire accent sounded strange to the Leicester men's ears.

Rudcock nodded. 'We got here yesterday evening.'

'Whereabouts are you all from?'

'Leicester County.'

'That's quite a step away.'

'Nine days' march,' asserted Rudcock.

'I'll wager you're all missing your wives already?' the innkeeper probed.

Rudcock snorted derisively into his flagon. 'Glad to get away from them, more like.'

Conyers had caught the innkeeper's drift, however, and he waved Rudcock to silence. 'Not that we'd say no to a bit of female company, aye and like.'

The innkeeper grinned, showing yellow and crooked teeth. 'There's my daughter, Agnes,' he said, nodding towards a serving wench who was collecting empty cups. She was in her early teens, a scrawny creature with dirty blonde hair, but her pale face was pretty enough beneath the grime that coated it.

Conyers glanced at Tate, who, along with Drayton and Brewster, was engaged in a conversation with local fishermen standing further along the counter, oblivious to the conversation with the innkeeper.

'Ha'penny a go,' the innkeeper stated firmly, in a voice that would brook no haggling. 'She's completely clean; no risk of catching the perilous disease – I swear it, by Saint Quenet's belly.'

Martin furrowed his brow, vaguely aware that some kind of transaction was taking place, but unable to fathom its nature. He took a sip of his wine, another new experience for him. It was less sweet than ale, more sour, and had a strong, sharp, fruity flavour, but it lacked the crisp, clear edge of ale, and was thick with scummy dregs so that he had to grit his teeth to drink it.

Conyers opened his purse and slipped the innkeeper a couple of farthings. 'It's not for me, though; it's for the skinny lad over there.'

The innkeeper glanced across to where Tate was still engrossed in his conversation with Drayton and the fishermen, and regarded Conyers askance.

'He's a bit shy,' Conyers explained with a wink. 'Make sure she's gentle with him.'

Understanding, the innkeeper grinned, and closed his hand over the two coins. 'Gentle as a lamb, our Agnes,' he said with a chuckle, and pushed his way across the room to Agnes's side, whispering in her ear. She glanced up from what she was doing and looked directly at Tate, nodding wordlessly in response to her father's instructions.

'What were all that about?' asked Martin.

'Shh!' Conyers nudged him sharply in the ribs, and winked conspiratorially.

Tate, Brewster and Drayton turned back from their conversation with the fishermen. 'Did you hear that?' Tate asked Rudcock, Conyers and Martin. 'Apparently, this town was attacked by the French a few years back . . .'

'Whoresons!' put in Drayton, whose empathy often outweighed his eloquence.

'They burned all the houses and all the ships in the harbour, stole everything of value they could carry away, did . . . unspeakable things to the women, and killed hundreds of people,' continued Tate.

'*Hundreds* of people?' Conyers echoed sceptically. 'I don't believe there's ever been hundreds of people in this town *to* kill before now.'

Before Tate could reply, Agnes slipped between them and pressed herself up against him, kissing him on the lips with more force than genuine passion; not that Tate knew the difference. He was too stunned to defend himself. She put her arms around his neck and whispered something in his ear. His face flushed bright crimson. 'I . . . I think you must've mistook me for someone else,' he blurted.

Rudcock and Conyers exchanged wicked glances.

Agnes took Tate firmly by the hand, half-dragging him towards the stairs. He turned back appealingly to his friends. 'Hodge!' he called, his face a mask of panic. 'Explain to her . . . there's been some kind of mistake . . .!'

Rudcock shook his head, grinning. 'You're on your own now, lad.'

'Where are they going?' asked Martin, as Tate disappeared up the stairs with Agnes.

'Somewhere where they can get some privacy, like, I should imagine,' said Rudcock.

Martin suspected that he already knew the answer to his next question, but his mind simply refused to accept it, so he went ahead and asked anyway. 'Why?'

Rudcock stared at him in astonishment. 'Why do you think a young lad and a young lass might want to be alone together?'

'But ... what if the innkeeper ...?' stuttered Martin.

'What did you think I was paying him for just now?' asked Conyers.

'You mean ... you paid him ... so that Limkin could ...?' asked Martin, the light slowly beginning to dawn. Prostitution did not exist in Knighton, and while Martin had seen painted women on his occasional visits to Leicester, his mother had explained them by saying that they suffered from a highly contagious disfiguring disease that forced them to cover their faces with paint. As the years went by, Martin had eventually gained a vague understanding of why so many men seemed willing to spend so much time in such close proximity to supposedly diseased women.

'The lad's got to dip his wick some time,' Conyers said sententiously.

'But ... how can the innkeeper ...?' stammered Martin. 'I mean, his own daughter ...?'

Rudcock shrugged. 'It's money in his purse, isn't it? He's got to feed her somehow.' He reached for Tate's flagon, abandoned on the counter, and shared its contents between the four of them. 'Waste not, want not, that's what I always say.'

They stood drinking and talking for a short while, until a table was abandoned, and then they hurriedly claimed it for themselves.

Martin turned to Conyers. 'You're not from the County of Leicester, are you?' he asked, curious about Conyers's accent.

'Oh, so you noticed, did you?' Conyers said sarcastically. 'I'm from Doncaster, in the West Riding of the County of York.'

'County of York indeed!' scoffed Rudcock. 'John's grandfather came from France, didn't he? John here's the enemy!'

'The Devil carry you to Hell!' Conyers responded irritably to Rudcock's teasing. 'At least my grandfather had sense enough to leave that God-forsaken country. Both me mam and me dad were born in the County of York, and I reckon that makes me a Yorkshireman born and bred.'

'Why did you leave Doncaster?' asked Martin.

'Had to, didn't I? The Law was after me.'

Rudcock laughed again. 'Don't believe a word of it. The only reason the Law was after him was because he seduced the wife of some justice of the peace!"

Before long they had exhausted the contents of their flagons, and Conyers waved the innkeeper across to order some more wine.

'Is everything to your satisfaction?' asked the innkeeper. 'And to your young friend's?' he added, with a lecherous smirk.

'It must be,' said Rudcock. 'He's not come down yet.'

'He probably hasn't even got it *up* yet,' guffawed Conyers, and slipped the innkeeper another couple of farthings. 'I'll have a go when he's through. She'll probably need a good seeing to after fumbling around with our Limkin for half an hour.'

'New boys first, John,' Rudcock reminded him. 'Let the young 'uns have a bite at the cherry. How about it, Hal?'

Drayton nodded with idiotic enthusiasm, fumbling for his purse.

'What about you, Martin?' asked Rudcock.

Martin pulled a face. 'I'll not sully myself by lying with whores – Beatrice would never even speak to me again!'

'So don't tell her,' said Rudcock. 'I'm thrice married, but you don't think I'm going to let that stop me when Hal and John are through, do you?'

'When you lot are finished, the poor lass will probably be glad of a rest,' Martin said distastefully.

Rudcock shrugged. 'If you're sure . . .'

'If he's not interested, don't push the boy,' said Conyers, leaning back in his chair and falling against a man sitting behind him so that the man's pot of ale was upset. The two of them promptly got into a heated argument.

Martin drained his flagon for the second time. 'I think I'll turn in early,' he said, struggling to conceal the disgust he felt about his friends' indulgence in prostitution. He pushed himself to his feet, and suddenly the whole tavern seemed to whirl around him in an unnerving manner.

'Are you all right?' Rudcock's voice seemed to come from a long way away.

'I'm fine,' Martin mumbled thickly.

'Are you sure? You look a bit green about the gills, if you ask me.'

'I said, I'm fine,' snapped Martin, his voice slurred, his temper flaring.

Rudcock shrugged. 'If you say so.'

Martin walked towards the door, struggling to keep his body upright. Outside, he drew the cool night air into his lungs, only vaguely aware of the brawl that was breaking out behind him. The wine had been much more potent than he had realised, much stronger than the ale he was used to. At first the fresh air seemed to clear his head a little, and then he suddenly felt a chill. A wave of nausea swept through him, and he stumbled against the wall of the tavern, retching. He'd brought up all the wine he had drunk and his supper as well, and felt much better for it. It just went to show that a peasant should stick to ale, and leave the wine to the nobility. No, that couldn't be right, he told himself, shaking his head muzzily; nobility was just a matter of ancestry, and everyone was descended from Adam and Eve, weren't they? Whether noble or churl, a man was still a man, of that much he was certain. What was good for the goose . . .

He was sick again.

In future he would steer clear of the filthy French muck and stick with good, honest, English ale.

When Martin was cruelly awoken by the reveille the following morning, his head ached as if it had been repeatedly battered with cudgels, while his mouth tasted as if he had been dining on cow-muck. Buckling on his sword-belt, he silently vowed never to let another drop of Gascon wine pass his lips.

The mood was distinctly subdued during breakfast, and Martin was reassured to see that his friends looked as ill as he felt. After they had eaten, Preston had the platoon parade for inspection as usual. Recognising the hung-over condition of his men, he took obvious relish in putting them through their paces, taking them for a route march in full kit, their backpacks filled with rocks so that the straps bit cruelly into the men's shoulders. Unencumbered by a pack, Preston ran circles around his men, belabouring their lacklustre performance.

'Come on, you sluggards, shift your arses!' he bellowed, as the men wheezed their way up the side of a steep hill in the hot June sun, the sweat pouring from their bodies in torrents. He stood to one side to let them pass, taking a quick head count to make sure no one had slipped away for a breather. 'Nails and blood! You'll move a lot faster than that when the whole of Valois' army is breathing down your necks! I don't know what you're smiling at, Tate, we've another five miles to go,' he added. Tate had been grinning like the cat that drank the cream all morning. 'What are you supposed to be doing, Inglewood? Did I tell you to bring up the rear?' He speeded the franklin's son on his way with a kick up the backside.

Preston continued to drill his men rigorously in the weeks that followed. If any of the raw recruits had thought that they knew all there was to know about archery – and most of them had, Martin not least – they were soon proved to be hopelessly wrong. Nearly all of them could put an arrow in the bull's-eye at two hundred and fifty yards; what they had to learn now was how to do so at least eight times a minute; how to shoot on volleys at a given command; and how to stop a charging, fully armoured knight in his tracks with a single shot.

'Half a dozen volleys will usually break a charge,' Preston told them. 'A good shot with a bodkin-tipped arrow will pierce the best chain-mail at fifty yards. But when in doubt, aim for the horse. An armoured knight on foot is about as much use in a charge as a straw castle. He'll only get in the way of his friends riding up behind him; chances are they'll do the job of killing him for you.'

They had to learn to fight with sword and dagger. They started out using thick wooden stakes driven upright into the ground as targets, until they had got the hang of using their swords. Then they worked in pairs, fencing together to practise parrying and riposting, the sharp tips of their short swords covered with leather sheaths to prevent them from wounding one another accidentally. Martin had grown up with premanently scabby knuckles from fighting with wooden swords as a child, but that had just been playing. Now he had to learn how to fight for his life: how to parry a potentially fatal thrust; how to hack off an opponent's sword-arm; how to deal with a mounted knight at close-quarters; and how to thrust at the weak spots in a knight's armour. Preston taught his men to work in pairs or even threes when dealing with armoured knights, so at least one man could pinion the knight's arms while another thrust his blade through a gap in the armour.

'A man can clad himself from head to toe in steel,' said Preston, 'but unless he wants to blind himself, he'll always leave two of his most vulnerable points open to attack: his eyes. A good thrust through an eyeball and into the brain will kill your opponent before he knows what's hit him. And always remember what I told you about not fighting fair. If you lot were noblemen, your opponents might let you yield so they can hold you for ransom; but your miserable hides aren't worth an oyster to anyone but yourselves, so the French will kill you with as much thought as they'd give to crushing an insect, if you give them half a chance. Leave chivalry to them as was born to it; your job is to kill or be killed, so make sure it's the former rather than the latter.'

In the afternoons, if Preston had not already exhausted them with a fifteen-mile route march, they usually lost themselves in the rough-and-tumble exhilaration of football. Sometimes they would be put to work helping to load the ships that vied for moorings alongside the quays in the harbour. Martin had not realised how much work was involved in transporting an army overseas. In addition to arms and armour, there were food, water and ale, cooking utensils, fodder for the horses, harnesses of red leather, dismantled carts and wagons, complicated siege engines such as mangons and trebuchets, and cannon, the latest innovation in warfare. These cannon were ribauds, clusters of slender tubes fashioned from toughened copper and mounted on hand-carts. Each tube fired a small iron bolt or pellet, and the tubes could be fired individually, in quick succession, or simultaneously. Martin had never seen any kind of cannon in action, but it was said that the pellets fired from a ribaud could pierce the best armour when an arrow might be deflected.

When everything had been loaded on to the ships except the men, horses and the more perishable food-stuffs, Preston began to step up his training, drilling his men during the afternoons as well as the mornings. Any day now, the prevailing winds might swing around to a more favourable direction, allowing the fleet to set sail for France. Preston wanted to teach his men as much of what he knew about fighting as he possibly could before they left. While other serjeants-at-arms were content to teach their men the most basic rudiments of drill and swordplay and leave it at that, Preston felt compelled to pass on all the tricks and techniques that he had had to learn for himself on the field of battle. Each little trick might be enough to save the life of one of his men. A dead man was no good to anyone. The serjeant had sense enough to realise that he could not hope to impart thirty-two years of military experience in the space of a few short weeks, but he hoped that at least some of it would sink into their thick skulls, to be remembered when it was needed. He liked to think that every little thing he could teach them gave them an edge over other fighting men, and he had always taken a carefully concealed pride in being able to train and command the finest platoons of archers that ever served the king.

Although Preston's men were often drilling when most of the other men were free to do as they pleased, it did not especially bother them, except perhaps Jankin Newbolt, who would always find something to complain about. There was precious little to do in Portsmouth except visit the inns and taverns, and there was always enough time for that after supper. The rest of the time, while other men grew bored through idleness, Preston's men were maintaining a high standard of morale, and with that came what Brother Ambrose liked to refer to as an *esprit de corps*: a vague awareness that however inexperienced half of them might be, they were receiving the best training that any of the serjeants-at-arms in the king's service could offer.

As for young Martin Kemp, he settled down to an archer's life with an ease that surprised himself not least of all. He had yearned to escape from the soil-bound drudgery of a peasant's life for as long as he could remember. Having achieved a complete break with the monotony of his previous existence, he had found himself in an entirely unfamiliar world, and at first the whole experience had been rather unnerving. Now he was beginning to realise that life in camp was no worse than life in Knighton, and in many ways it was a good deal better. The routine of constant drilling that Preston imposed on his men might have been tedious at times, but it was as nothing compared with the mind-numbing monotony of tilling the soil. Now at least he was learning the skills of war, the very skills that had set his childhood heroes – the Knights of the Round Table – up above all other men. Unlike some of the other raw recruits, who had been better off in civilian life, Martin did not long for the comforts of home. Inglewood might complain about the quality of the food, but he was used to the rich fare of a franklin's table. While Martin's mother had been an able cook, she had been hampered by never having enough money to buy food, and meat in particular. Although the men had to buy the food they ate from the victuallers out of their wages, the prices were reasonable and their wages generous enough not to make this too much of an imposition. In the army, Martin discovered a whole new sensation, and in time he came to realise that it was called 'not being hungry'. Nor did he miss the comfort of a straw-filled pallet barely softer than the ground on which he now slept; and the weather that summer was warm enough for him not to regret the absence of a roof over his head. The only thing Martin felt he lacked was female company, yet he could not bring himself to betray Beatrice by dallying with the whores in town as his companions often did.

Just under a fortnight after Martin and his companions arrived at Portsmouth, Sir Thomas Norwich rode up to Holland's tent to find Villiers sharpening his master's broadsword with a whetstone. Villiers immediately replaced the sword in its scabbard and rose to his feet.

'Good morning, young Master Adam,' said Norwich, with his crocodile smile. 'Is your master about?'

'He's still asleep, I think, Sir Thomas,' replied Villiers.

'Then would you be so kind as to rouse him? I have a message for him from his Majesty.'

Villiers nodded, and ducked inside the tent, where he found Holland, woken from his sleep by the sound of voices, rising from his pallet. 'What is it, Adam?' he asked, blinking blearily at his squire.

'Sir Thomas Norwich says he has a message for you from the king.'

'Then don't just stand there, boy; show him in,' Holland replied irritably. 'Then fetch me some clean water to bathe my face in.'

Villier had already anticipated his master's second command. 'There's fresh water in the jug,' he said, grinning, as he held the tent flap to one side to usher Norwich inside. Once Norwich was in the tent, Villiers discreetly slipped outside.

'Good morning, Sir Thomas.' Never one to stand on ceremony, Holland poured some water from the jug into a shallow basin, and splashed some on his face.

'Good morning,' Norwich returned evenly. 'His Majesty sends his compliments, and requests that you attend him at Porchester Castle at noon.'

Holland began to shave himself with his razor-sharp dagger. 'What hour is it now?'

'Just before prime.'

'Return my compliments to his Majesty and inform him I shall be there,' said Holland, as if there had ever been any doubt that he would answer his liege's summons.

Norwich nodded, and took his leave of Holland. The king was holding a council of his closest military advisers that day, and Holland was not the only nobleman to be summoned.

When Holland had finished shaving, he towelled his face dry and began to dress in his finest robes. A soldier rather than a courtier, Holland's finest robes would have provoked dismay in the Court at Windsor, but the king himself was generally unimpressed by mere finery. He dispatched Villiers to fetch his palfrey, before breakfasting on cold meat left over from supper, and a little fresh bread which Villiers fetched from the bakers.

Holland emerged from his tent to find Preston's men practising their drill, as usual. Some of the less experienced knights often mocked the way Holland's serjeant perpetually drilled his men, but Holland would merely exchange a quiet smile with the more seasoned campaigners who had seen men trained by Preston in action, and knew how well the constant drilling paid off.

The serjeant had split his men into pairs for sword drill; he was fortunate in that there were nine old hands to the ten raw recruits in his platoon, so that each new recruit was able to drill with a more experienced veteran, Preston himself pairing with the left-over recruit. The sound of steel clashing against steel rang out, combined with the grunts of the men, while their sword blades flashed in the early morning sun. Martin had teamed up with Rudcock, and now Holland watched with satisfaction as the two of them fenced up and down in front of his tent: cut, thrust, parry, slash. Martin's enthusiasm drove the somewhat more lackadaisical Hodge slowly but surely backwards, until Rudcock's sword flew out of his hand, landing point-first in the mud at Holland's feet.

'Easy now, Martin!' protested Rudcock, nursing a jarred wrist. 'You almost had my hand off there! Save it for the French, can't you?' He turned to retrieve his sword, and it was not until then that he saw Holland watching them both with a stern expression. He swallowed hard. 'Good morning, Sir Thomas,' he said tremulously.

Holland stooped to pick up the sword, handing it back to him. 'You will find you get a better grip if you twine a leather thong about the hilt,' he remarked dryly.

'Aye, Sir Thomas,' mumbled Rudcock, abashed.

Holland turned to Martin. 'Good,' he said curtly. 'Very good. You have fenced before, have you not?'

'Aye, Sir Thomas,' admitted Martin, as Preston hurried up to ensure that his men did not embarrass him in front of Holland. 'The serjeant's been teaching us since Friday,' Martin added ingenuously.

Preston cuffed him roughly around the back of the head. 'Jackass! Before you joined the army, Sir Thomas means.'

Martin hung his head to hide his blushes. 'My apologies, Sir Thomas,' he muttered awkwardly. 'I mean, no; not unless you count playing with wooden swords.'

Holland chuckled. 'The kitten that plays at stalking becomes the best hunter as a cat. Even I had to start somewhere. You don't suppose I was given a broadsword of steel when I was first learning to fight, do you?'

'Nay, sir.'

'You show signs of promise, boy.'

'He's not too bad, Sir Thomas,' Preston admitted grudgingly.

'Not too bad!' exclaimed Holland. 'I fear you do the lad an injustice, Wat. If what I just witnessed is the result of but a few days' training, then you have surely surpassed yourself.'

'If you say so, Sir Thomas.' Preston had been training men for over a quarter of a century, and one thing he had never ceased to maintain was that there was no such thing as a natural warrior. A good soldier was made, not born, he had always claimed; but when watching Martin drill, he had to confess to himself that he was beginning to have his doubts.

157

As Villiers returned with Holland's palfrey, the knight turned back to Martin. 'What is your name, boy?'

'Kemp, sir. Martin Kemp, of Knighton.'

'Martin Kemp, eh? It seems to me I have heard that name somewhere before.' Smiling, Holland stole a glance at Preston, who unconsciously raised a hand to his recently bruised eye. 'Keep up the good work, Kemp,' said Holland, swinging himself up into his palfrey's saddle. 'You have a promising career in the king's service ahead of you, should you desire it. Who knows? Perchance some day you too may be a serjeant-at-arms, like old Wat here.'

'Nothing would please me more, sir,' responded Martin, with poorly disguised irony.

Preston scowled, but Holland threw back his head and laughed loudly, before digging his spurred heels into the palfrey's flanks and riding north out of the vast camp, towards Porchester Castle.

'All right, Kemp, you can stop grinning just because Sir Thomas noticed you,' growled Preston. 'I've seen him marvel at queer-shaped cow-pats before now, let alone a villein who knew one end of a sword from t'other, so don't let it go to your head. You may show signs of becoming a near-competent swordsman compared to this rag-taggle bunch of no-hopers who like to call themselves soldiers, but it'll be a long time before you're a match for the puniest Parisian levy. Now back to work, all of you!'

The subject for discussion at the king's military council that day was the forthcoming campaign. Whatever decision was reached regarding the fleet's destination, it was not made public beyond the king's closest advisers – who were sworn to secrecy – for fear of French spies.

Rumours abounded, nevertheless. Word soon got around that the king had asked the Church authorities in London to say prayers for the success of his expedition to

Gascony earlier in May, and since the fleet's mariners confirmed that the ships were being provisioned with enough victuals for a two-week voyage, Gascony did seem to be the most likely destination.

A few days after the Feast of Saint John, in a solemn ceremony before the high altar in the nearby church at Fareham, the King's Seals were transferred to the Archbishop of Canterbury, who would lead the Government in his Majesty's absence. The wind had finally changed, and there was a new sense of urgency throughout the encampment as the men prepared to embark for France. The king and the young Prince of Wales boarded their ship, the *Philip of Dartmouth*, at the end of June. The ship set sail, and anchored off the Isle of Wight, waiting for the rest of the fleet to assemble behind it.

It was a long and arduous process. There were only a few quays in the harbour, and over fifteen thousand men to be crammed on board seven hundred ships of various shapes and sizes. Each troop or platoon of men eagerly awaited the command to pack up its equipment and make its way down to the docks, while the marshals struggled to maintain some semblance of order in the collapsing encampment. After several days of intense frustration for Holland and his company, Sir Thomas Norwich finally arrived with instructions for them to make their way down to the harbour.

Martin's nerves were tightly coiled with excitement as he struggled to gather up his equipment. After endless weeks of training, the moment he had been so eagerly awaiting had finally come. Only a few days earlier, after the platoon had completed a fifteen-mile march in a record two and a half hours, Preston had grudgingly admitted that he had taught them as much as he could about fighting, adding that how much of his training they remembered in the heat of battle was up to them.

'Are we soldiers now?' Tate had asked, almost plaintively. The older, more experienced members of the platoon had laughed cynically.

'Soldiers, is it now?' Preston had roared in reply, but not without a certain amount of humour in his tone. 'Nails and blood! God-damned miserable excuses for fighting men you lot are, the whole God-damned bunch of you! But you'll have to do for now,' he added soberly.

And now those God-damned miserable excuses for fighting men were trooping through the streets of Portsmouth, encumbered with their arms and equipment, dreaming of the glory and the booty they would soon win overseas in the service of their king.

The quayside was a scene of chaos and confusion as the mariners struggled to load the last of the cargo aboard each ship, hampered by hundreds of troops milling about on the waterfront, waiting their turn to be directed on board a vessel. Holland led his company on to a stone pier where a hundred-tonne cog named the *Trinity* was moored, its red and white flag furled. A gangplank wide enough for horses led up to the cog's deck, and Holland dismounted, exchanging a few words with the ship's master before leading his palfrey up on to the deck. Specially made hurdles had been arranged on the deck to provide stalls for the horses, and plenty of fodder was stored nearby. Villiers came next, leading his own rouncy, Holland's courser, and the packhorse. He handed the halter of the rouncy and the courser to a mariner who stood on the dock steadying the gangplank, before leading the packhorse up on deck.

Villiers had been handling horses all his life, and it had so much become second nature to him that it never occurred to him that another man lacking his experience with the beasts might be nervous about having to hold the halter of such a massive warhorse. Peledargent, usually a placid and patient animal, was already made nervous by the noise and bustle around it, and could sense the mariner's fear. Martin could see the courser's nervousness in its tensed body, flared nostrils, wide eyes and pricked-up ears. The mariner held Peledargent's halter at arm's length until Villiers returned to collect it. He was so glad to be rid of the responsibility that when Villiers returned for the courser, the mariner released the halter before the squire had grasped it, allowing it to fall to the surface of the pier.

'Clumsy jackass!' Villiers snapped irritably. Muttering apologies, the mariner ducked down to pick up the halter for the young nobleman. The courser flinched at the sudden movement beneath its head, rearing up with its teeth bared and its nostrils wrinkled back. Forgetting all about the halter, the mariner fled in terror, bumping into Villiers and bowling him over. This sudden commotion immediately caused a panic, the men on the pier pushing and shoving in their desperation to get away from the wildly rearing courser. The shouts of alarm only served to frighten the horse even more, and it wheeled to flee, only to find the way blocked by a stack of casks. It wheeled again, lashing out with both hind legs, staving in one of the casks and knocking another to the cobbles. Villiers barely managed to roll clear before the cask crashed down on the spot where he had lain, spreading billowing clouds of flour across the pier.

As the other archers were struggling to get away, Martin instinctively stepped forward. Peledargent was a lot bigger than his father's horse, but Martin swallowed his fear by telling himself that the principles that applied to dealing with hackney nags must also apply to the biggest warhorse. He moved into the courser's field of vision, taking care not to make any sudden movements that might alarm it even further and giving it a chance to get used to his presence. While the panic of the other men had only served to excite the horse, Martin's apparent calm had a calming effect on the beast, which stopped rearing long enough for him to grasp the bridle. The courser tried to rear up again, but Martin's grip was firm.

'Easy, boy, easy,' he muttered soothingly. He blew into its nostrils – the horses' way of making friends – and the courser allowed him to reach up and stroke its mane, whinnying softly. As the marshal in charge of the dock managed to restore some semblance of order to the scene with the help of the serjeants, Martin took the courser's halter and led it up the gangplank. Once on deck, he backed it into one of the specially made stalls, and a mariner tied its halter to an iron ring set in the ship's bulwark. Then he turned about to see Holland standing by the mast, watching him thoughtfully.

'Come here, boy.'

'Sir?'

'It's Kemp, isn't it?'

'Aye, sir.'

'How is it that when everyone else was running away from Peledargent, you walked towards him and calmly seized his bridle? Were you not scared?'

'Not as scared as he was, sir, I reckon,' replied Martin, jerking a thumb in the direction of the courser.

'You've worked with horses before?'

'Sort of, sir. We used to have a hackney mare . . .'

'How is it you did not volunteer to be a mounted archer?'

Martin hung his head. 'I didn't volunteer at all, sir,' he reminded Holland.

'Ah, yes. Very well, then. That will be all.'

'Aye, sir.' Martin had to wait at the top of the gangplank until Villiers had brought up his rouncy. Once the rouncy had been tethered, Villiers turned to his master.

'I'm sorry, Sir Thomas.' The squire was uncharacter-istically abashed. Happy-go-lucky by temperament, he had not been serving with Holland for long, and he was desperate to impress his new master. 'If that damn' fool mariner hadn't dropped the halter . . .'

'If you had not given the mariner the halter to drop in the first place,' Holland cut in coldly, before turning his back on his squire and greeting the knights of his company as they led their own horses up the gangplank.

Eventually all the knights and squires of Holland's company were quartered on the *Trinity* with their horses, and the ship slipped away from its moorings to make way for the next, which took on board Holland's men-at-arms and half of his troop of mounted archers. Finally Preston's platoon had its turn. They were embarked on another cog, the *Saint Thomas of Kent*, along with Brother Ambrose and the rest of Holland's mounted archers. The gangplank was raised behind them, the mariners scuttling back and forth across the decks, casting off the mooring ropes and unfurling the sail, foully cursing the lubberly archers who got in their way. The vast canvas of the square red and white striped sail billowed with the freshening breeze behind it, and the cog glided smoothly away from the dock, St George's pennant fluttering from the top of the single mast. The *Saint Thomas of Kent* slipped through the narrow channel at the harbour mouth and sailed into the Solent, following the ship ahead and presently followed in turn by the ship behind, until within a few hours they had joined the vast fleet that was assembling off the north-west coast of the Isle of Wight.

Then the wind, capricious to the last, changed direction once more.

Five days later there was not a single man in Preston's platoon who did not wish himself dead.

Ever since setting sail from Portsmouth, they had been huddled on the rolling deck of the *Saint Thomas of Kent* while the cog was tossed about on the white-capped swell of the sea, along with all the other ships in the fleet, their sails tightly furled. Gale-force winds howled through the rigging, and the ice-cold sea spray stung the men's faces each time a wave crashed over the cog's sides.

Like his companions, Martin had spent most of the first night at sea bent over the side. The crew's subsequent attempts to feed the archers had been met with limited enthusiasm. Their innards caught fast in the grip of a bone-chilling nausea, the archers found it impossible to keep any food down. Martin's companions had turned a pallid green, and he did not doubt that he looked at least as bad. They were no longer aware of anything beyond their own enclosed world of sea-sickness, wishing only that the purgatory in which they now found themselves might soon be brought to an end one way or another. Only Brewster, unflappable as ever, leant unconcernedly against the bulwark, the inevitable straw jutting from the corner of his mouth, enjoying the salt-water sting of the spume on his face.

'Are we nearly there yet?' Inglewood asked one of the mariners, who laughed and helped him to his feet, pointing through the gloom towards a dark mass of land just visible beyond the starboard quarter.

'See that?' asked the mariner, grinning.

'Is that France?' Inglewood asked weakly, hardly daring to hope.

The mariner laughed again. 'That there's Portsmouth, that is! We been riding at anchor ever since the fleet turned back from the Needles, waiting to ride out this storm until the wind changes.'

'Oh, God . . .!' Inglewood sank back to the deck, his arms wrapped tightly about his midriff.

The ship's master emerged from the round-house below the after-castle and hailed Preston, who appeared to be infuriatingly immune to the sickening effect of the pitching deck. 'Good morning!' he bellowed above the howl of the wind, as more sea-spray lashed the men on deck who were already too wet and cold to care. 'Another fine day, eh, Master Preston?' he asked, grinning evilly through his luxuriant black beard.

'Aye,' Preston agreed dryly. 'Middling fair.' Although blessedly unaffected by sea-sickness, the serjeant did not share the mariners' apparent relish for the storm.

The master paused, tilting his head back slightly as if sniffing the wind, and after a few moments the wind suddenly began to veer round. He smiled with satisfaction. This was promising, he told himself; the sooner he unloaded this wretched and unprofitable cargo of lubberly archers, not even fit for ballast, and returned to his normal business of trading – with just a little piracy on the side – the happier he would be.

'Master Garston!' shouted the lookout on duty at the mast-head. 'The *Philip of Dartmouth* is unfurling her sails.'

The master waved in acknowledgement, and turned to the ship's constable. 'Well, lad, you know what to do.'

'Aye, sir.' The constable bellowed orders at the mariners to weigh anchor and hoist the sail, before turning back to the master. 'What course should I tell the steersman to lay in?'

'I know no more'n you,' replied the master. 'We're to follow the rest of the fleet.' He glanced at Preston, who merely nodded. The serjeant was carrying sealed orders, wrapped in an oilskin package, that revealed the fleet's destination; but in accordance with the king's passion for secrecy, the package was not to be opened unless they became separated from the rest of the fleet.

'Aye, we'll follow them straight to Hell,' grumbled the constable, making his way aft where the steersman grasped the tiller.

The *Saint Thomas of Kent* weighed anchor and set forth once more, this time sailing past the Needles and out into the open sea with the rest of the fleet, heading south across the Channel. The voyage was brief, and entirely without incident. There were no sightings of any French ships, and even if there had been, it would have been a foolhardy master indeed who would have sailed his vessel against so mighty a fleet.

When dawn rose the following day, the weather had calmed enough for the archers to recover from their sea-sickness a little, and Martin and some of the other, hardier members of the platoon pushed themselves to their feet to see that the cog was coasting in towards a great, open, windswept beach.

'Is that France?' asked Martin. He was not sure what he had been expecting, but it certainly had not been this ordinary-looking landscape of dunes and grasses that lay beyond the stretch of pale sand.

'Aye,' grunted Preston, and turned to the others. 'Come on lads, on your feet. We're here.'

'It can't be Gascony,' mused Rudcock. 'We've not been at sea long enough. Is it Brittany?'

'Normandy, I reckon,' said Preston, the oilskin package tucked inside his tunic still dutifully unopened.

'Normandy!' exclaimed Conyers. He and Rudcock had organised a sweepstake on the fleet's destination: Gascony had been odds-on favourite, with Brittany and Flanders close behind it in popularity. Normandy had been a clear outsider, never having been invaded by the king's men before. 'This is the last place I expected us to make landfall.'

'Aye,' said Preston, grinning. 'I reckon that's what the French were thinking, too. He's a cunning devil, is his Majesty.'

There was certainly no sign of any enemy activity on the shore, just a dozen French ships beached nearby, most of them rigged for war. A score of English ships had already landed, including the *Trinity*. The *Saint Thomas of Kent* ran in beside it, coasting in through the breakers until her keel touched bottom.

'All right, lads, this is it,' growled Preston. 'Shift your arses!' He was the first over the side, lowering himself down a knotted rope into the cold, waist-deep water that surged between the ships' hulls.

His men needed no further bidding. They jumped down, stumbling in the heavy waves that washed over them. The mariners lowered the end of the broad gangplank into the water, and two of the mounted archers held it steady while their companions led their horses down into the surf. Finally they were followed by Brother Ambrose, hauling on the halter of his obstinate skewbald pony.

Holding his longbow in its bag above his head to keep the bowstrings dry, Martin waded unsteadily up through the surf with the others, stumbling awkwardly through the undertow that dragged at his ankles. It felt strange to be back on solid ground once more, but it was a welcome return nonetheless.

Adam Villiers had erected his master's banner a short way up the beach, and Holland himself sat astride his palfrey, marshalling his knights and men-at-arms. Martin could see Beaumont and Stamford amongst them, but they did not notice him amongst the anonymous archers rallying around Holland's banner. More and more men were pouring on to the beach from other vessels, rallying around other banners, while the *Trinity* and the *Saint Thomas of Kent* were already slipping back out to sea to make way for the other ships that waited in the bay to unload their cargoes of men and horses.

Preston formed his men into two ranks and took a quick head-count to make sure that no one had been left on board ship. 'All present and correct, Wat?' asked Holland.

'All present, Sir Thomas,' responded Preston, glaring

at his wan and bedraggled men. 'I don't know about correct . . .'

Holland was too busy to acknowledge the jest. 'Throw up a cordon of pickets along that line of dunes,' he ordered, gesturing a short distance inland.

'Aye, sir.' Preston turned to his men, dividing them into groups of four and directing them to set up pickets on the dunes overlooking the beach. 'Keep your eyes skinned for enemy troops,' he told them. 'We don't want to be caught with our breeches down by a counter-attack before we've even begun the campaign.'

Martin went with Conyers, Rudcock and Inglewood, scrambling up the side of a dune to the right of the beachhead, the soft sand shifting beneath his feet. The weather promised a sunny day, but there was a cool breeze blowing in from the sea, even more pronounced at the crest of the dune. From there they could see inland, a rich countryside of green fields, trees, hedges and narrow lanes. It all looked so ordinary and peaceful. A flock of seagulls, disturbed by the disembarking troops, wheeled and screeched in the clear blue sky overhead.

Martin gazed inland with the others, searching the rural landscape for any signs of French troops, but there was no one, not even a single peasant at work in the fields. In the distance they could see a herd of cattle, but there was no sign of a cowherd watching over them.

'Where are the French?' demanded Inglewood, almost plaintively.

'In Gascony, with any luck,' replied Rudcock. 'That's about a hundred leagues from here, I reckon. Hopefully we'll be long gone from this place by the time they've learned of our landing.'

'But I thought we'd come to fight them!' protested Inglewood, the pacific franklin's son keyed up for battle by weeks of intensive training.

'Maybe. Maybe not,' Rudcock replied non-committally.

'If the nearest French troops are a hundred leagues away, what are we supposed to be looking for?' demanded Martin.

'The local warden may try to cobble together a militia,' explained Rudcock, his eyes constantly scanning the horizon. 'We're at our weakest while we're still disembarking, and he'll know it.'

Martin stole a glance back down to the beach. A tide of men was streaming off the ships. The troops rallied around their masters' banners and formed up into their platoons and companies, but for every man on the beach there were another thirty still waiting to disembark from ships anchored out in the bay. Someone had put the French ships to the torch, and the dry wooden vessels were burning fiercely in the morning sun. He watched as Sir Godefroi d'Harcourt, a Norman knight who had sworn fealty to the King of England after being exiled from France by Valois, sank to his knees in the surf and kissed the sand of his homeland.

Martin turned his attention back inland. There was still no sign of the enemy, but somehow that did not surprise him in the least. He was beginning to suspect that this picket duty was a mere formality, a complete waste of time. He felt another sharp pang of hunger, and wished he could go and get something to eat. He could see an orchard about two miles away, and could picture the ripening apples that were almost certainly hanging from the trees. 'How long do we have to keep this up for?' he asked.

'For as long as it takes,' said Rudcock. Martin had noticed a subtle change come over his friend now that they were effectively on enemy territory. Back in Portsmouth Rudcock had always seemed somewhat indolent, approaching the training with the blasé attitude of a man who has already done it before for real, as indeed he had. But now his attitude had suddenly gained a workman-like edge as he rapidly settled back into the mentality of a soldier on campaign.

Martin's stomach rumbled audibly, voicing the thoughts of all four of them.

'I'm hungry,' grumbled Inglewood.

Rudcock sighed, and as if by magic he produced some cheese and biscuits that he had scrounged off the mariners on board the *Saint Thomas of Kent*. 'I were saving this for a special occasion, like, but your plight has touched my heart.' He portioned the cheese and biscuits up between himself and his three very grateful companions. There was not much for each of them once it had been divided four ways, but it was better than nothing at all, and they devoured the morsels rapidly.

'Keep your eyes open, mind,' Rudcock cautioned them as they crammed the food into their mouths. 'Remember that story in the Bible about the man who needed to pick only the best soldiers, so he told them all to drink from a stream, and sent away the ones who didn't keep an eye out while they were drinking. We want to be like the best soldiers, and all.'

'Are we soldiers yet?' Conyers imitated Tate's plaintive tones, echoing the question the youth had asked Preston at the end of their training. The others laughed.

'Which man was that?' Martin asked, after a pause.

'Come again?' said Rudcock.

'The man in the Bible.'

Rudcock pushed his hood back from his head to scratch his scalp. 'Solomon, I reckon.'

Conyers shook his head. 'Nay, it were David, weren't it?'

'I reckon it were Solomon,' said Rudcock, 'because he were the clever one, weren't he?'

'I'm sure it were David,' insisted Conyers.

'You're getting it all arsy-versy,' Rudcock told him. 'David were the one as killed the giant with the sling shot.'

'Aye, and the one who had to pick the best men.'

'It was Gideon,' put in Inglewood, wearying of the theological discussion.

'What?'

'It was Gideon who picked the best men by sending away the ones who didn't keep their eyes open when they drank from the stream,' said Inglewood. 'Judges, Chapter Seven.'

'Oh. Well, there you have it,' said Rudcock. 'It were Gideon.'

'Isn't education a wonderful thing,' Conyers sighed wryly.

They lapsed into silence, four pairs of eyes scanning the countryside, four minds lost in their own thoughts. Behind them, the English, Welsh and Irish troops continued to disembark from the ships.

'Christ's blood, but this is dull!' sighed Martin after a while.

'You'd best get used to it,' Rudcock told him. 'This is soldiering for you. You don't want to believe what they say in the ballads. In real life, it's a thousand parts boredom mixed with one part sheer terror. If you've any sense, you'll enjoy the boredom while it lasts.'

'What were you expecting?' Conyers asked Martin. 'To find the French waiting for us on the beach, so that we could charge off the boats and fight them there and then?'

'Summat o' that, I suppose,' Martin admitted vaguely. He gestured listlessly. 'I don't know.'

'Hey, Conyers,' Rudcock said suddenly.

'What?'

'Know any good stories?'

'None you've not heard already,' Conyers replied sourly.

'How about the one about the bull?'

'Which one's that?'

'You know, the one about the bull and the reeve's son.'

'Oh, that 'un. I must've told you that 'un a hundred times. A *thousand* times.'

'It's a good story,' asserted Rudcock. 'Martin and Perkin haven't heard it.'

Conyers sighed. 'Do you *want* to hear this story?' he asked Martin and Inglewood.

Inglewood shrugged.

'We won't know until we've heard it, will we?' Martin pointed out reasonably, his eyes still searching the hedgerows – more because it gave him something to do than because he thought he might actually see something important.

'By then it could be too late,' Rudcock said jocularly.

'Do you want to hear this story, or not?' demanded Conyers.

Rudcock nodded. 'Aye and like. I said so, didn't I?'

Conyers sighed. 'There's this reeve, see? And he's all awkward about summat, so he goes round to the franklin's house and hammers on the door with his fist.' Conyers mimed the action to suit the words. 'The franklin's out, but his daughter opens the door and . . .'

'Little girl,' put in Rudcock. 'She's just a little girl, remember?'

Conyers broke off the story to glare at him. 'Who's telling the story, you or me?'

'It's not as funny if you don't tell them she's a little girl, all wide-eyed and solemn-faced and all . . .'

'I know that,' Conyers said irritably. 'I were just coming to that part, weren't I?'

'Sorry. Go on.'

'So the franklin's little girl opens the door,' continued Conyers. 'But before the reeve can say owt, she tells him: "If you've come here to hire the pedigree bull, my da' charges a shilling for it to swyve a cow." So the reeve shakes his head sternly and says: "I'm not interested in any pedigree bull, little girl. Is your father in?" The little girl shakes her head, and says: "If you wants summat cheaper, we've got another bull, only it's not a pedigree," see? So the reeve says . . .'

'What's that?' cut in Martin.

'What's what?' Conyers demanded, irritated at another interruption.

'That.' Martin pointed to something he could see moving beyond a coppice about a mile away.

'I don't see owt,' said Rudcock, peering in the direction where Martin was pointing.

'Are you sure it's not just an animal of some kind?' asked Inglewood.

'Do you want to hear this joke, or not?' demanded Conyers.

Ignoring him, Martin lowered his outstretched arm hesitantly. 'I could've sworn I saw summat . . .'

Rudcock shrugged. 'It were probably just some beast, like Perkin said . . .'

Something glittered in the landscape, sunlight reflecting off polished metal. 'There!' Martin said urgently, pointing once more. 'Don't tell me you didn't see that!'

'I saw it,' Rudcock agreed soberly.

'Look!' Inglewood said unnecessarily, as a yellow and green banner emerged from the trees a little to the left of where they had seen the flash of sunlight. It was carried by a man on horseback who rode along behind a hedge that came up to the horse's withers.

'That's not one of ours,' said Rudcock, as a line of helmets emerged behind the banner. 'Looks like they're coming this way.'

CHAPTER EIGHT

'What should we do?' Inglewood asked nervously.

'Martin, go and find Preston,' Rudcock ordered briskly.

Martin nodded, glancing around in search of the serjeant. Preston was making his way along the lines of pickets and was talking to Oakley, Drayton, Newbolt and Tate on the next dune along. They seemed to be oblivious to the approaching troops. Without another word, Martin slithered down the side of the dune and scrambled up the next to where Preston stood. By the time he got there, Preston was already peering towards the advancing column.

'It's all right, lad,' he told Martin calmly. 'I've seen 'em.'

The French column was more clearly visible from the second dune, marching in close formation along a narrow lane between two hedgerows. Their path would lead them to a point a little to the left of where Martin and Preston stood.

'Run and find Sir Thomas,' Preston told Martin, without taking his eyes off the column. 'Tell him there's about . . . three hundred foot-soldiers about half a mile away, approaching from the north-west. Have you got that?'

Martin nodded.

'Then repeat it back to me.'

'Three hundred foot-soldiers about half a mile away, approaching from the north-west.'

'Good lad. Off you go.'

Martin scrambled back down the side of the dune to the beach, pushing through the gathering throng of men, to where Holland sat astride his palfrey, talking to Sir Thomas Norwich, Sir Godefroi d'Harcourt and a young nobleman. D'Harcourt was a tall, lean man in his early thirties, with a bronzed complexion, flaming red hair and bright blue eyes set in an angular face. The young nobleman was in his late teens with long, dark hair, a thin face, dark, narrow eyes and a weak chin covered with a stubbly excuse for a beard. As Holland spoke, his tone seemed to be calm but cold, a sure sign that he was displeased, and the object of his displeasure was the young nobleman, red-faced and not a little frightened by Holland's anger. Norwich and d'Harcourt watched the confrontation with evident discomfort.

'Sir Thomas?' Martin said nervously.

Holland did not seem to hear him, continuing his harangue against the young nobleman.

'Sir Thomas!' Martin persisted, a little more boldly.

Both Holland and Norwich, sharing the same christian name, glanced down at him. 'What is it, boy?' Holland demanded irritably.

Martin swallowed hard. 'Serjeant Preston told me to tell you there's about three hundred foot-soldiers about half a mile away, approaching from the north-west.'

Holland exchanged glances with Norwich and d'Harcourt.

'French troops?' the young nobleman asked, wide-eyed.

'Hell's teeth, Montague!' snapped Holland. 'My serjeant would hardly bother to warn me if they were English!'

'They *are* French, are they not?' Norwich asked Martin, in a diplomatic attempt to make Montague's question seem less naïve.

175

'They aren't ours,' replied Martin, aware that he did not know for certain that they were French. He suddenly realised that his reply had sounded sarcastic when no sarcasm was intended; but while Norwich scowled, Holland smiled, as if Martin had backed him up in his argument with Montague.

'Where's Preston now?' Holland asked him.

Martin pointed. Holland dug his spurs into his palfrey's flanks, goading it up the side of the dune, and d'Harcourt, Montague and Norwich followed, Martin sprinting in their wake. The four noblemen reined in their horses on the crest of the dune, and Preston wordlessly pointed out the advancing troops.

'God's love!' exclaimed Montague. 'They've not squandered their time, have they?'

'What did you expect, my lord?' Holland responded snidely. Although Montague's father, the Earl of Salisbury, had been killed in a tournament at Windsor two years earlier, Montague himself was still not old enough to inherit the earldom; nevertheless, he theoretically outranked Holland, a fact Holland clearly resented, and he took no pains to conceal his resentment. 'Three hours have passed since sun-up, and they most likely saw our lanterns when we anchored in the bay last night.' Holland turned to d'Harcourt. 'Do you recognise that banner, Sir Godefroi?'

D'Harcourt nodded slowly. 'Those are the arms of Robert Bertrand, the Marshal of Normandy.' He spoke English with a thick Norman accent. 'He is the warden of these parts. He will remain loyal to Valois, regardless of the odds stacked against him.'

'Hmm,' mused Holland, and turned to Preston. 'What do you make of those troops, Wat?'

'An ill-assorted lot, Sir Thomas.'

D'Harcourt nodded in agreement. 'A hastily gathered citizen's militia, I would say.'

'Order the heralds to sound the call to arms,' Holland told Norwich, taking charge of the situation. Norwich nodded, wheeling his horse about and riding back down to the beach.

'We should get as many men as possible off the beach, and meet them beyond the dunes,' said Montague, trying to reassert his command of the beachhead.

'There's not enough time,' replied Holland, although he was clearly unconcerned by the threat of approaching enemy troops. 'At best we could get a couple of companies beyond the dunes to fight a holding action – trying to meet them on equal terms would be a useless waste of men.' He threw a casual glance back to the beach. There were already several thousand men on shore, and more arriving with every passing moment. He smiled, wondering if Bertrand and his militia had any idea of what they were up against. 'We should throw up a defensive cordon of archers and men-at-arms here on the beach, and wait for the French to come to us. If they *are* just a militia, they'll be ill-disciplined and have little morale – they'll soon enough think twice when they see how heavily we outnumber them.'

D'Harcourt nodded in agreement. 'Sir Thomas is right, my lord.'

Montague nodded ruefully. 'Then let it be so,' he told Holland and d'Harcourt, still clinging to the theory that as the first to land on the beach, he was still nominally in command of the beachhead until a more senior nobleman arrived on the scene.

Holland smiled at Montague's discomfiture, and wheeled his courser about, signalling for Preston to jog alongside him as he rode back to the beach where the rest of his company had rallied around his banner. 'Since your men were the first to espy the enemy, would they like the opportunity to draw first blood, Wat?'

'I'd consider it a great honour, Sir Thomas,' replied Preston.

'Are your men up to it, do you think? At least half of them are raw recruits, are they not?'

Preston grimaced. 'There's a first time for everyone, sir. At least now, when we have such a weight of numbers on our side, there is no risk of their losing us the battle.'

The heralds were sounding the call to arms, and Preston's men fell back from the dunes, rallying around Holland's banner. Holland and d'Harcourt directed the marshals to draw a line in the sand, and three companies were formed up along it, facing in the direction from which the French would approach. Archers were alternated with dismounted men-at-arms who stood with their spears ready to hold off the attack.

'They are brave men, for so few to attack so many,' Villiers observed to his master. 'I see little honour for us in this battle.'

'Aye,' agreed Holland. 'But what would you have us do? Yield to them? If they wish to die, it is only right that we should afford them the opportunity to do so with honour,' he added sardonically.

D'Harcourt studied the scene with the practised eye of an experienced tactician. Holland had drawn up the battle line with the clear intention of relying on numerical superiority and better discipline, with minimal regard for the terrain. These were probably the same tactics d'Harcourt himself would have used if he had been in command, but they were not without their disadvantages. 'We shall not see the enemy until they emerge from the dunes,' he remarked dubiously to Holland.

Villiers nodded in agreement. 'We need a look-out,' he said, and turned to Holland. 'With your permission, Sir Thomas?'

Holland hesitated momentarily, and then gave a curt nod.

Villiers slid out of his saddle. 'I shall signal thus, when they are halfway through the dunes,' he told Norwich, with a downward slice of his open hand. Norwich nodded, and Villiers ran out in front of the battle-line, crossing the beach and scrambling up the nearest dune. He crawled on his belly as he drew near to the crest, so that he would not be seen by the enemy. Lying flat, he peered over the top of a clump of grasses, watching the approaching troops.

Holland's company stood at the right of the line of troops, furthest from the dunes and closest to where the waves lapped against the shore. Preston's men strung their bows and took some arrows from their belts, planting them upright in the sand at their feet, heads-down, the way Preston had taught them, the quicker to nock a fresh arrow after each shot. Holland's mounted archers had dismounted, leaving their hackney cobs tethered to stakes that they had driven deep into the sand. Behind them, more men-at-arms and hobelars were being drawn up as reserves, but most of the men on the beach were left to continue unloading the ships. Many of them paused in their work to watch the impending battle with the bored indifference of spectators at a fairground sideshow; most of them had seen it all before, but it was more interesting than hefting barrels and sacks.

'Wait for my order,' Preston told his men coolly, as if this were just another drill. Martin knew that the odds were very much on the side of the English, but he nevertheless felt a cold tightness gripping his innards, and his mouth was dry. At the same time, he suddenly felt unaccountably hot, despite the cool breeze that blew in from the sea. He was standing in the front rank; if any of the English were to die that day, he was likely to be one of the first. He had awaited this moment for so long, and now that it was almost upon him he was not sure that he was ready for it.

'I don't think I can do it, serjeant,' Inglewood moaned tremulously.

'You can do it, Inglewood,' growled Preston. 'You did it at Portsmouth enough times.'

'I mean, I don't think I can actually kill a man. Isn't it written in the Bible that it's a sin to kill?'

'Nails and blood, Inglewood, but you've picked a fine time to air such theological concerns!' expostulated Preston, and some of the veterans around them laughed. 'These are Frenchmen – you'll kill them, or they'll kill you. I suggest you stop being so selfish and take their souls into consideration – you wouldn't want your death on their conscience, would you?'

Villiers scrambled a short way back down the dune, signalling frantically to Norwich, who raised a baton in his right arm.

'Ready!' ordered Preston. 'And remember, I'll thrash seven shades of shit out of any man who shoots before I give the word!'

Martin plucked another arrow from his leather retainer and nocked it to his bow. Perkin's protests had set him thinking, making him feel uneasy. Until this moment, he had never really considered the full implications of killing a fellow man, French or otherwise. His concerns were more instinctive than theological. What *right* had he to deprive another man of his life?

An armoured knight on horseback suddenly rode out from between the dunes, carrying a long lance upright. The foot-soldiers charged out behind him, roaring furiously when they caught sight of the enemy, the foreign invaders who had landed in their territory. The sound sent a chill down Martin's spine, and he felt a droplet of cold sweat trickle down from his temple.

'Wait for it!' growled Preston.

The charging men were an ill-assorted bunch, lightly armoured, some of them wielding swords or spears, but most of them armed with farming implements such as sickles, scythes and flails. They charged in a closely bunched mass, forced together by their passage through the dunes.

The knight had covered nearly half the distance between the dunes and the middle of the English front rank, his men charging close behind, still more of them continuing to emerge from the dunes. Three hundred? It seemed more like three thousand to Martin. His qualms about killing vanished like a field of corn before the onslaught of a gale.

The knight couched his lance, resting it in a specially made indentation in his shield.

Martin braced himself, pushing out the bowstave. He tried to will Preston to give the order to shoot.

The knight seemed almost upon them, the point of his lance reaching forward to spit its first victim. Martin took careful aim at the knight's head.

Norwich brought the baton down sharply.

'Loose!' barked Preston.

Martin loosed his first shot. He tried to follow its progress, but it was lost in the volley of arrows that flew over the sand towards the charging men. An arrow that might have been Martin's glanced harmlessly off the knight's helmet. Several more arrows struck the knight's horse. The beast stumbled, pitching its rider on to the sand. Other arrows claimed the charging foot-soldiers, bringing down their front rank as if they were stalks of wheat mown down with a scythe, but there were more men behind.

The English archers were shooting as fast as they could now. Martin plucked an arrow from the sand at his feet. He fumbled the shot in his panic, the shaft harmlessly burying itself in the sand. He cursed the trembling fingers that had suddenly decided to betray him at this critical moment.

The impetus of the French attack had been shattered by the volleys of arrows, but still the men behind pressed on, stumbling over the bodies of their dead and wounded comrades. Now they were almost upon the English front rank.

'Draw your swords!' ordered Preston, his short sword scraping from its scabbard. Martin, caught in the act of nocking a third arrow to his bow, dithered momentarily before dropping both bow and arrow and reaching for his sword. The English men-at-arms dropped their spears and stepped forward, drawing their swords. The clash of steel against steel rang out, and war-cries turned into screams of agony.

A Frenchman brandishing a sickle was almost upon Martin, his face contorted as he roared with aggression. Martin's fingers, damp with sweat, scrabbled uselessly at the hilt of his sword. Then the Frenchman was upon him. Martin raised his arms to defend himself, desperately clawing at the man's right wrist. The man's body slammed into him, bowling him over and driving the breath from his lungs. Martin sprawled on his back in the sand, the Frenchman astride him, forcing the point of his sickle-blade down towards Martin's eye, putting his whole weight on top of it. Martin braced his arms, grunting with the effort of holding the blade at bay. His whole attention was transfixed by the sharp point that trembled inches from his face, straining to pierce the soft jelly of his eye.

The physical effort of keeping that point away combined with the paralysing terror that froze his bowels threatened to overcome Martin. The Frenchman was too strong for him, he had gained the advantage, Martin was going to die. Part of his mind asked him why he sought to prolong the terror and the agony. Why not accept the inevitable and relax, and allow the Frenchman to finish it? Then it would all be over, he would be free from this hellish nightmare, he could rest. But another part of his mind, deeper, stronger, said *no*. No French whoreson was going to kill him now. He was not going to give up. He refused to let himself be killed.

The Frenchman punched Martin in the ribs with his free hand, catching him off guard. Martin's arms buckled, and the sickle-blade came down. Martin jerked his head aside and felt a cold flame sear his cheek. The pain broke through the terror to release him from his overwhelming sense of panic.

The sickle-blade plunged into the sand beside Martin's head. The Frenchman's callused hand gripped the sickle's handle less than an inch from Martin's face. Martin sank his teeth into the heel of the man's thumb, biting through to the bone. The man roared in pain, but refused to relinquish his grip on the sickle. Martin brought his knee up sharply between the man's thighs with all his might, the full strength of his rage and defiance behind the blow. The man screamed in agony. Martin pushed him off. He was winning now, a calmness settling over his mind in the midst of his fury like the eye of a storm. He rolled on top of the Frenchman, his fingers effortlessly finding the hilt of his rondel. He plucked it from its sheath and plunged its blade into the man's stomach, burying it up to the hilt. The man jerked spasmodically, puking blood. Martin tugged the blade clear and then brought it down again, and again, and again. He did not stop when the man fell still, but went on repeatedly plunging the blade into the man's stomach until his abdomen was a mass of bloody stab wounds.

'I think he's dead, Kemp,' remarked Preston.

Martin did not hear him, stabbing again and again at his victim's body in a frenzy of blood-lust. Preston had to seize him by the shoulder and pull him clear.

'It's over, lad. We've won.'

Martin looked up as if in a daze. The French were falling back into the dunes, their attack completely

183

broken. They were fleeing for their lives, a troop of English mounted knights galloping after them. Martin saw Beaumont ride down one of the laggards, spitting him on the point of his lance. The man screamed briefly. Beaumont threw back his head and laughed. It was the first time Martin had ever seen him happy.

Stamford was also there, whirling his broadsword above his head as he rode after the fleeing Frenchmen. Like Beaumont, he was not wearing mail: there had not been time for the English knights and men-at-arms to don their armour. As he overtook one man, he leaned down from the saddle to slash at his back. The man stumbled and fell, his back bloody, but Stamford's rouncy was charging forward, so he could not tell if the man was dead. The squire's eyes lit upon another man. This time he aimed a back-handed slash at the man's face as he rode past, just the way Beaumont had taught him, and was rewarded with the sight of a piece of the man's head being sliced off. Born a nobleman, for as long as he could remember he had been trained to fight, to kill. Now that moment had come, and it felt like fulfilment. The excitement of the moment gave him a thrill that was almost sexual. He giggled nervously. He could not believe how easy it was! His eyes fell on another man, and he spurred his horse after him. It was just like stag hunting, only easier! Stags were faster, nimbler than these pathetic Frenchmen!

As he aimed a blow at the third man, his prey dodged out of the way at the last moment, and Stamford's sword clove through nothing but air. Stamford cursed, and wheeled his horse about after his quarry, determined not to let him get away. The man plunged through a hedgerow. Stamford gripped his reins tightly in his left hand, his rouncy easily clearing the top of the hedge. As the horse's hooves thundered down on the opposite side, two more French peasants who had been hiding behind the hedge rose up. Stamford suddenly realised that in his determination to catch up with his quarry, he had allowed himself to become separated from the other English horsemen. Panic welled up within him as he tasted fear for the first time.

But the panic was soon replaced by the rage of desperation. One of the peasants tried to thrust a spear at him. Stamford brought his sword down, slicing through the spear's wooden haft, before urging his horse through a half-turn the better to aim a stroke at the spearman's head. The blade of his broadsword bit deep into the man's skull. Stamford tugged the blade free. Another of the peasants was trying to seize the rouncy's reins. The horse reared up, striking at the peasant with its hooves. Stamford lost his balance and fell from the saddle, rolling on the grass. The peasant was staggering back, his forehead stove in by the rouncy's hooves. Another ran at Stamford, whirling a flail above his head. Stamford remembered the sword he still gripped in his hand, and swung it at the man's midriff. The blade bit deep into his side, cutting into the spine, where it was wedged so deeply that he was unable to withdraw it. He felt hands grab him from behind, pinioning his arms. Another peasant appeared, a short sword in his hand drawn back to be thrust into the squire's stomach. Stamford lashed out with one leg, his booted foot catching the man with the short sword in the crotch so that he doubled up with a scream of agony. Then Stamford was able to get one arm free, and he smashed his elbow into his captor's ribs, breaking free. He whirled around, snatching his dagger from the jewelled sheath at his belt, and driving the blade deep into the man's chest. The man went down, coughing blood. Stamford turned to where his sword was still embedded in the dead man's torso. He placed one foot on the corpse's chest, and managed to pull his sword free with a grunt.

The man with the short sword had recovered sufficiently to come at Stamford again. The squire parried the thrust easily, before swinging his broadsword at the man's neck. The blade sliced cleanly through flesh, bone and sinew.

Stamford looked around. Suddenly, there were no more Frenchmen left to kill. He wiped the blades of his sword and dagger clean on the tunic of a dead peasant and returned them to their sheaths before vaulting nimbly back into the saddle of his horse. He wheeled the animal about, his eyes searching eagerly for fresh victims, but there were none. He suddenly realised that he had killed at least six men. He turned his blood-speckled face to the sky and let out a whoop of sheer exhilaration, before spurring his horse back in the direction of the beach. Let Beatrice try to mock his vow to win glory in the fields of France now!

Back on the beach, it was clear that the fight had been a total rout. The bodies of dozens of Frenchmen littered the sand. Miraculously, not one Englishman had been killed. Inglewood was kneeling in the sand, his shoulders heaving as he gasped great gulps of air into his lungs. A broad, damp patch streaked one of his leggings where he had wet himself, but the bloody sword that lay by his side proved that he had not been found wanting in the moment of truth. Piers Edritch was dancing a jig, waving his bloodied sword above his head and whooping with joy. Tate was crouched on all fours in the sand, dry-retching, while Bart Lefthand was slicing off one of his victim's ears as a souvenir. Brewster was wiping blood from the blade of his short sword with a calm professionalism that belied his years, absent-mindedly chewing the same piece of reed that had been in his mouth before the skirmish. Martin suddenly realised that his own cheeks were wet with tears.

'Are we soldiers now?' asked Conyers, once again imitating Tate's naïvely eager tones. Some of the other raw recruits laughed hysterically in a massive release of tension.

Martin felt completely drained, both physically and emotionally. He stared numbly at the rondel in his blood-drenched hands, and then at the corpse of the Frenchman he had killed. He had half-expected the bogeyman of his childhood to have horns, a forked tail, and cloven goat's hooves for feet; but this was just a man, a man not unlike himself, except that the Frenchman was dead while Martin lived. He wondered what manner of man he had been before he had been called upon to die defending his native soil at such short notice. A peasant farmer like himself, no doubt, by the look of him. Martin wondered if the Frenchman had a woman like Beatrice waiting for him somewhere. A wife, maybe, perhaps even children. Well, that was their tough luck, he told himself, hardening his heart. This was one Frenchman who would not be returning home.

'Martin? Are you all right?' asked Rudcock.

Martin looked up sharply. 'Hmm?'

'I said, are you all right?'

Martin wiped blood from his cheek with the back of his sleeve. 'I'm fine,' he said, and meant it.

Villiers swaggered back from the dunes, wiping the bloodied blade of his broadsword on a rag. He was his usual, grinning self. 'Did you see, Sir Thomas?' he asked Holland. 'I slew three of the scum, falling upon them as they sought to flee through the dunes.'

'Aye, and near got yourself killed, you damned young fool!' replied Holland, scowling. He gestured at the corpses strewn across the beach. 'Where is their honour now? They've earned their glory, but at what price? The only glory in war is won by the victors, the men who live to bask in it.'

Villiers' face fell as the truth of Holland's cynical words struck home. He suddenly felt strangely ashamed.

'All right, lads, just because you can fight off a peasant rabble you outnumber fifty to one, don't let it go to your heads,' Preston told his men. 'This is no time to start resting on your laurels; this is just the beginning. Retrieve as many arrows as you can and form up around the banner.'

Martin replenished the contents of his leather retainer and washed his hands and face in the surf. The salt water stung the scratch on his cheek, but he had received worse wounds playing with wooden swords as a child. He rinsed the blood off his rondel and wiped it on the hem of his tunic before returning it to its sheath.

By the time the platoon was gathered around Holland's banner, the troop of knights was riding back on to the beach, the knights' lances blooded and their faces aglow with victory. The Earl of Warwick rode up, the sopping hem of his cloak and the wet sand clinging to his boots attesting to the fact that he had only just led his horse ashore. He exchanged a few words with Holland, Norwich and Montague before ordering several troops of hobelars and mounted archers to be dispatched to search the countryside for further units of French soldiers. While more troops continued to come ashore, Holland's serjeants formed his company into marching order, and they headed north along the beach with the company under Montague's command.

There was a moderate-sized port about a mile to the north of the beach, a town slightly smaller than Portsmouth. Martin gazed about at the buildings, taking in his first look at a French settlement. It looked little different from any of the handful of English towns he had seen. Doubtless the written signs over some of the shop fronts were in French rather than English, but that made little difference to Martin, who could not read in any language. The sight of a well-kept church surprised him: he had not expected men repeatedly described as devils to attend

God's services. Like the French countryside, it all seemed so disappointingly ordinary.

There was something not quite right about the town, though, and it took him several seconds to realise what it was. 'Where are all the people?' he asked. The place seemed completely deserted. It was unnatural, unnerving. He had always associated towns with bustling crowds. He half expected the townsfolk to be waiting for them in ambush somewhere, and found himself nervously eyeing windows, doors and side streets.

'They probably fled the moment they saw our fleet out in the bay,' sneered Preston. 'Can you blame them? I'll wager the mightiest army in England's history was the last thing they expected to find on their doorstep when they awoke this morning.'

They made a cursory search of the streets, alleyways, and some of the larger buildings, but all they found were a few women, children and old men. D'Harcourt questioned a few of them, but it was obvious that most of the townsfolk had indeed fled. Martin had heard how badly the French treated non-combatants when raiding foreign territory, and guessed that they must have assumed they could expect no better treatment in return.

The two companies assembled on the waterfront, and Norwich signalled to the three English ships anchored in the middle of the harbour. Many more of the fleet's vessels rode at anchor beyond the harbour mouth.

Villiers rode his horse at a walk down to where Preston stood with his men. 'My lord of Warwick would like you and your men to form the guard of honour, Wat.'

'This wet-nosed rabble?' Preston scowled at his men. 'Just because they happened to be present when a handful of French peasants decided to commit suicide on our sword-points?'

Villiers smiled. 'Your men *were* the first to sight the enemy and engage them,' he pointed out.

'They just happened to be at the right place at the right time,' sneered Preston. 'A blind simpleton could have *smelt* that rabble approaching long before any of my lads chanced to spot them. However, far be it from me to deny the wishes of his lordship the earl,' he added, with an extravagant sigh.

Preston's men trooped on to the stone pier, preceded by Warwick, Montague, Holland and Norwich. The four noblemen dismounted. As the *Philip of Dartmouth* glided in alongside the pier, Preston had his men line up opposite. 'Come on, you worthless scum, at least try and *look* like God-damned soldiers,' he groaned.

Four mariners jumped down from the ship on to the pier and made the mooring ropes fast to the iron rings set into the stonework. The gangplank was lowered, and a man in his early thirties began to descend. He was a tall and well-made man, dressed in a jupon embroidered with three golden lions on a crimson background quartered with a pattern of fleurs-de-lys on an azure field, over which he wore a scarlet mantle trimmed with ermine. His shoulder-length hair was golden-brown, and he wore a short, neatly trimmed, slightly pointed beard, his cheeks shaven. His eyes were a piercing blue, set in a handsome face made up of regular and even features. It was a face that was proud without being haughty, with sternness written in the firm jaw-line, eyes that sparkled with intelligence, and lips that would be equally swift to curse or smile. He seemed to dominate the whole cavalcade by the very power of his presence, and it was obvious even to the watching archers that this could be none other than their king. They cheered, and he accepted their cheers with a smile and a gracious wave. The noblemen on the pier went down on one knee, as did Preston, signalling for his men to do likewise.

Striding regally down the gangplank, his Majesty tripped over as he stepped on to the pier and landed flat on his face. Martin could not be sure, but he thought he heard the king swear under his breath.

There was a stunned, horrified silence. After a few heartbeats that seemed to stretch out like aeons, the king placed his palms flat against the stones and began to lever himself upright. The movement stung Warwick and Montague into action, the two noblemen hurriedly stepping forward and helping the king to his feet.

'Is your Majesty all right?' Montague asked solicitously.

'I'm fine,' the king snapped irritably. 'Unhand me, you idiots. Contrary to appearances, I am perfectly capable of standing on my own two feet unsupported; let me assure you that I am not in the habit of tripping over twice in one day.' He spoke with difficulty, clasping one hand to his nostrils in an attempt to stanch the flow of blood that gushed on to his white chemise.

Warwick smiled, pleased to see that the king was quite himself, but the expression on Montague's face remained one of acute concern. He gestured helplessly. 'An ill omen, sire. Please, I beg you – land not this day, but return on board your ship. Start out afresh on the morrow, and we shall all pray that the lord God may smile more kindly on this venture then.'

'Spend another day cooped up on that God-damned . . .' spluttered the king, and then broke off, smiling. 'An ill omen?' He laughed heartily. 'No, by my faith! To me it is a good omen – it proves that this land is longing to embrace me!'

The other nobles present laughed with relief. The king glanced at his bloody hand. The flow of blood from his nostrils had not abated. 'For God's sweet love! Will no one give me a rag with which to stifle this gore?'

The nobles were at a loss; except, that is, for Holland, who snapped his fingers at Martin.

'S . . . Sir Thomas?' whispered Martin, bewildered.

'Your coverchief, boy!' hissed the knight.

Realisation dawned. Martin stepped forward, struggling to unwind the coverchief from about his neck and bowing clumsily before presenting it to his Majesty. He felt awkward and uncomfortable at suddenly finding himself the focus of such high-ranking attention. A young nobleman the same age as Martin was coming down the gangplank, and he stared penetratingly at the young archer. He bore an uncanny resemblance to the king, and Martin realised that this must be the king's eldest son, Edward of Woodstock, Prince of Wales, Duke of Cornwall and Earl of Chester.

The coverchief was grimy from constant wear, and now it was spotted with a dead Frenchman's blood. Martin felt ashamed to present such a dirty piece of cloth to the king. His Majesty took the coverchief from him, regarding it dubiously before turning his gaze on Martin, who quailed before him. 'Much obliged to you, boy,' he said rather gruffly, folding the coverchief into a wad which he pressed to his nose. Then he turned back to the ship. 'Well? Don't just stand there, you God-damned idle lay-abouts! Bring my horses!'

Martin bowed again, as clumsily as the first time, but the king no longer paid him any heed. He stepped back into line, glad of the opportunity to sink back into the obscurity of the ranks. He suddenly felt naked without his coverchief. He wondered if he would ever see it again, and consoled himself with the thought that at least he had lost it for a noble purpose. He smiled inwardly, thinking that if Beatrice asked him how he had come to lose it, she would never believe what he told her.

The rest of the king's nobles had disembarked from their various ships within the hour, and they made their way with his Majesty to a tall dune just outside the town, overlooking the north end of the beach, where the king knighted his son, along with Montague, Sir Thomas's younger brother Otho, who was serving in another company, and several other young noblemen. The supply ships were sailing into the harbour now, beginning the mammoth task of unloading all the arms, armour, equipment and victuals, a task that would take the best part of a week.

Large bodies of troops were beginning to move off the beach and into the surrounding countryside. Preston and his men rested at the foot of a dune, watching from a distance as the king performed the dubbing ritual. Once knighted, the Prince of Wales began to dub some of his own retainers.

'How come that lot get to bask in all the glory when we were the ones who did all the fighting?' grumbled Newbolt. 'Most of them weren't even there.'

'I'm sure his Majesty will give you a knighthood too, if you ask him nicely,' Preston sneered sarcastically. 'How can he refuse, after that outstanding display of swordsmanship you gave us down on the beach?' Newbolt had dropped his sword at a critical moment, and would have been killed had not Caynard stepped in to help him.

'At least ways I didn't piss myself, not like some others I could mention not a thousand leagues from here,' said Newbolt, glaring at Inglewood, who flushed hotly.

'I see that coverchief of yours finally came into its own, then,' Rudcock remarked to Martin, who grinned inanely.

'Aye,' agreed Conyers. 'The laugh'll be on him if he catches a fever now, and it kills him.'

'I'm starving,' Newbolt announced to no one in particular.

'We're *all* hungry,' Gilbert Murray snapped pettishly. 'Why don't you shut your face?'

'Actually, for once I'm inclined to agree with Newbolt,' admitted Preston, licking his lips. 'I'm quite hungry myself. Rudcock, take Conyers, Lancelot and Perkin Pisspants here into town and see what you can forage.'

'Aye, serjeant,' Rudcock said eagerly, as he and Conyers picked themselves up and led the way into town.

Martin and Inglewood followed rather more reluctantly.

'So what happened?' Inglewood asked Conyers.

'What?'

'In the story,' said Inglewood. 'The one about the reeve and the franklin's daughter.'

'Let's try this 'un,' suggested Rudcock, indicating a large, two-storey house at the edge of the town.

'Where did I get up to?' asked Conyers.

'The franklin's daughter was telling the reeve about the other bull, the one that wasn't a pedigree,' said Inglewood.

Rudcock tried the latch on the front door. It opened to his touch.

'Should we be doing this?' Inglewood asked nervously.

Rudcock shrugged. 'There's no one here to stop us,' he said, leading the way inside.

'Do you want to hear this story, or not?' demanded Conyers.

'I'm listening,' Inglewood protested petulantly.

'We'll probably find the larder at the back,' said Rudcock.

'Lead the way,' Martin told him.

'Right, so the little girls says: "If you want summat cheaper, we've got another bull, only it's not a pedigree",' continued Conyers, following Rudcock and Martin through the gloomy front room. 'So the reeve says: "I'm not interested in any bulls, little girl. I want to see your father. Your brother Jankin has dishonoured my daughter . . ."'

'Big house,' observed Martin.

'Big enough,' Rudcock agreed absently, trying a door at the other end of the room. It opened into a flagstone-floored kitchen. 'Here we are. What did I tell you?'

'So the little girl says: "In that case you'll *have* to talk to my father,"' Conyers chuckled. '"I don't know what he charges for our Jankin."'

Rudcock found the larder and peered inside. 'The promised land,' he observed with satisfaction.

'And?' said Inglewood.

'And what?' asked Conyers.

'What happened next?'

'Nowt happened next. That's it. That's the story.'

Rudcock took a side of bacon down from a butcher's hook and handed it to Martin, before reaching for a couple of plucked capons. 'John, see if you can find a blanket or summat we can carry this lot in.'

'I don't get it,' said Inglewood.

'The little girl thinks... her brother Jankin...' Conyers threw up his hands in exasperation. 'You get it, don't you, Lancelot?'

'Aye and like,' replied Martin, clutching the cheeses that Rudcock piled in his arms.

'You didn't laugh,' Inglewood said accusingly.

'It weren't very funny,' Martin said reasonably, carrying the cheeses across to the wooden kitchen table and pilling them up next to the capons and the side of bacon.

Conyers took the stopper from a small wooden cask and sniffed the contents. 'Ah-ha!' he said reverently. 'Liquid gold.'

'What is it?' Suddenly Rudcock and Martin were crowding round him.

'Calvados.' Conyers hefted the cask in his arms and managed to tip some of it down his throat.

'Hey!' protested Rudcock. 'Leave summat for the rest of us.'

'Are you sure we should be helping ourselves to all this?' asked Inglewood.

'If the owners wanted it, they shouldn't have left it here,' Rudcock pointed out evenly. 'They knew we were coming.'

'That's why they left,' chuckled Conyers.

'Besides, half of this lot will probably go rotten before the owners get back,' continued Rudcock. 'We're doing them a favour, if you think about it. Would you want to come back to a home that stank of rotting meat?'

'Shh!' Martin hissed suddenly. The others froze instinctively.

'What is it?' whispered Rudcock.

'There's someone upstairs. I can hear them moving about.'

The four of them remained motionless for a few heartbeats, listening to the silence. If there was anyone upstairs, they were keeping very quiet about it. Conyers relaxed visibly, and was about to say something disparaging about Martin's ears when a floorboard directly overhead creaked ponderously.

They exchanged worried glances. Stealing food from an abandoned house was fair game, but stealing it from a house still in occupation was another matter entirely. Rudcock raised a finger to his lips and slowly eased his short sword out of its scabbard, motioning for the others to follow him. Martin, Conyers and Inglewood likewise drew their swords as they followed Rudcock back into the the front room and up the wooden stairs that creaked alarmingly under their weight.

There were three doors at the top of the stairs, but only one of them could lead to a room above the kitchen. Rudcock turned to Inglewood, and indicated the other two doors. 'Watch our backs,' he whispered.

White-faced, Inglewood nodded, gripping his sword tightly.

Rudcock tip-toed across to the first door and laid his left hand on the latch, glancing over his shoulder to make sure that Conyers and Martin were ready. Martin felt that he was as ready as he would ever be; but it was Conyers who nodded, his features uncharacteristically taut. Rudcock threw the door open, jumping aside in case there were a couple of archers waiting on the other side with arrows nocked to their bows.

There *were* a couple of archers waiting on the other side, arrows nocked against taut bowstrings, but they did not shoot. They were dressed in tunics and coarse woollen cloaks, their faces clean-shaven and their dark hair cut in pudding-bowl fringes. Rudcock froze, his arms spread in what he hoped was an unaggressive stance.

'Who are you?' he asked, after a couple of moments that seemed to last for ever.

'We might well be asking you the same question,' replied one of the archers. He spoke English, but with a strange, rather sing-song accent that sounded alien to Martin's ears.

Rudcock noticed that both the archers wore only one shoe each, and relaxed. He had already recognised the accent. 'Archers,' he told them, lowering his sword. 'Sir Thomas Holland's company. You're Welsh, right?'

The two archers nodded, lowering their bows and tucking their arrows back under their belts. 'You want to be careful who you go creeping up on, boys. You might have got yourselves killed.'

'So might you,' countered Rudcock. It was sheer bravado: it did not fool Martin, who doubted that it fooled the Welshmen, either. 'What are you doing here?' he continued.

One of the Welshmen glanced down guiltily at the open jewel casket that lay on the bed between them. The scene told its own tale. 'Looking for Frenchmen,' he said.

'You won't find any in there,' said Martin, indicating the jewel casket with the point of his sword.

'Get back to your unit,' ordered Rudcock, with more conviction than he felt.

The Welshmen hesitated, but the long knives they wore tucked into the back of their belts would be no match for the four short swords the Englishmen held. Scowling, they shouldered their way brusquely past Rudcock and Martin, and clumped down the stairs. Conyers watched them until they had passed out of the front door.

'Have they gone?' asked Rudcock, sheathing his sword.

'Aye,' reported Conyers.

'Thieving Welsh whoresons.' Rudcock stepped into the bedroom and tipped the contents of the casket out on to the bed. The contents consisted mostly of cheap trinkets – low-grade metals and poor craftsmanship – but still worth more than a peasant could hope to earn in a year. Rudcock started to pick out items more or less at random, looping a medallion around his neck before tossing a bracelet to Martin.

'What am I supposed to do with this?' demanded Martin.

Rudcock shrugged. 'Keep it. Sell it. Give it to your lass,' he suggested irritably. '*I* don't know.'

Inglewood clutched instinctively at the brooch that Rudcock threw him. 'But this is stealing!'

'Spoils of war,' Rudcock told him. 'If the owners wanted to keep it, they shouldn't have left it behind. Same as with the food.'

'But the serjeant didn't tell us we could take all this stuff!'

'Aye and like,' agreed Conyers. 'On the other hand, he'd reckon we were crazy if he found out we'd left it behind. Besides, if we don't take it, others will come along and help themselves.'

Rudcock finished dividing up the booty, and tugged the coverlet from the bed. 'Come on. We've wasted enough time as it is.'

They went back downstairs, where he wrapped up the food in the coverlet, carrying it slung over one shoulder, and they returned to where the others waited. Rudcock lowered the coverlet to the ground and opened it up to reveal the bounties within.

'You took your time, didn't you?' grumbled Preston.

'Are you joking?' retorted Conyers, and indicated the two plucked capons. 'Those were running around someone's back yard when we found them.'

Some of the others had already got a fire going, and they roasted the meat over it. Presently, Sir Thomas Holland returned with Villiers and Brother Ambrose.

'Something smells good, Wat,' said Holland.

'Me and the lads got a little peckish, Sir Thomas,' explained Preston, breaking off a leg of capon and passing it up to Holland. 'I hope you don't mind.'

'Not in the least.' Holland bit into the meat, tearing off the roasted flesh with his teeth. 'Good,' he said, talking around his mouthful of food. 'Very good.' He turned to his squire. 'My lord of Warwick wants us to seek out some suitable lodgings for the next few days. I want you to take Preston and his men and seek out some likely manor house. There should be a small village about two miles in that direction,' he added, gesturing with the remains of the leg of capon. 'See what you can find. I have to speak further with his Majesty and my lord of Warwick, but when they no longer require me I'll round up the rest of the company and come and join you. Send back one of the men to guide us. Where's Kemp?'

Martin pushed himself to his feet. 'Here, Sir Thomas.'

'You can handle horses. Can you ride them?'

'After a fashion, sir.'

Holland chuckled. 'Good. There's your man then, Adam.'

Brother Ambrose remained with Holland, while Villiers led Preston and his men inland, marching down a narrow, dusty lane with tangled thicket hedges growing on either side. They passed across a meadow between two areas of woodland, finally spotting a small manor house not unlike Beaumont's house at Stone Gate.

The master of the house was gone, but the menial staff remained, wisely making no attempt to prevent the entry of Preston's men into the courtyard.

Villiers questioned the steward in Anglo-Norman as he selected quarters for Warwick and the other knights in his retinue. Who was the lord of the manor? The Seigneur de Quettehou. Where was he? Out. When would he be back? The steward did not know. What about the rest of the seigneur's family? The seigneur only had one younger brother, fighting the English in Gascony. Villiers asked politely if there would be any problems if the Earl of Warwick and his retinue were to spend the next few nights at the manor house. The steward despondently asked if there was any alternative. Villiers smiled: the two of them understood one another well enough.

'He's a shifty-looking whoreson,' observed Daw Oakley, as the steward emerged from the house with Villiers. 'Can't say as how I like the looks of him.'

'He's a Frenchman,' said Freeman. 'What do you expect?'

'Can we trust him?' asked Inglewood. 'Supposing he tries to . . . you know, kill us . . . during the night?'

'If he does try anything, we'll slit his gizzard for him,' said Preston, and grinned. 'And he knows it. If he's a good little boy, maybe we'll leave this place without razing his master's house to the ground.'

Villiers approached. 'Kemp?'

Martin stepped forward. 'Master Adam?'

'This place will do for a few nights,' Villiers told him. 'Take a horse from the stables and ride back to Saint-Vaast-la-Hougue, where we left Sir Thomas. Give him my compliments, and when his business with his Majesty is complete, lead him back here. Think you can manage that?'

'Aye, Master Adam.'

Martin found a fleabitten grey cob in the stables and saddled it before leading it out into the courtyard, swinging himself up into the saddle.

'Well, axe my arse!' sneered Caynard. 'Looks like Lancelot's finally found himself a destrier. Where's your lance, Lancelot?'

Martin ignored him, digging his heels into the horse's flanks. 'Come on, gee-up!' But the animal refused to budge.

It was Rudcock who realised what was wrong. 'It's a French horse,' he explained to Martin. 'It doesn't understand English commands.'

'Great,' Martin said wryly. 'What's the French for "gee-up"?'

'Try "*allez*",' suggested Rudcock.

'*Allez*!' commanded Martin, and immediately the horse set off at a trot. Guiding it with his knees, Martin rode out through the gateway.

Conyers watched him depart, before turning to Rudcock. 'Very impressive,' he said. 'But don't you think you should have taught him the French for "whoa!" while you were about it?'

Rudcock grinned. 'He's a bright lad – let him work it out for himself.'

Martin left the manor house behind him and rode across the open country towards the road leading back to the harbour. It was a sunny day, and he was able to relax and enjoy the ride. It was a long time since he had sat astride a horse, but it soon came back to him. He rode at a Canterbury-trot, the swift but comfortable pace at which pilgrims on their way to the shrine there liked to ride. He thought about the fight on the beach and his encounter with the king, and wondered which had been the most frightening.

The road came into sight. He could see two men riding along it, their brightly coloured robes and fine horses marking them out as noblemen. If Martin continued on his present course – and he had no intention of doing otherwise – he would meet them where he rejoined the road. Holding the cob's reins in his left hand, he reached instinctively for the hilt of his sword, but as he drew nearer he recognised the banner that one of them carried as that of the Earl of Warwick, the man who had saved him from the gallows in Leicester. He relaxed, and it was at that moment that a dozen riders burst out of the woods on the far side of the road. They galloped towards the two noblemen, brandishing their weapons, their warlike cries carried to Martin on the wind.

Intent on the two English noblemen they now surrounded, the twelve riders had not seen Martin, and his first instinct was to wheel his horse about and ride for safety. But he had not come to France just to flee at the sight of the enemy. After only a moment's hesitation he dug his heels into the cob's flanks, urging it forward at a gallop. The cob leapt the hedge at the side of the road with ease, Martin gripping on to the reins for dear life. As the horse came down on the dusty track, he drew his short sword, goading the cob into the fight.

The scene was a confused mêlée of clashing swords, men shouting, and horses rearing wildly. The two Englishmen were putting up a spirited defence, giving a good account of themselves as they hacked at the Frenchmen who surrounded them. The Frenchmen were more timid, seeking to capture rather than kill this richly dressed English nobleman and his squire, and it counted against them: the Englishmen were not taking prisoners.

No one noticed Martin until he had attacked the French from behind, breaking the loose circle of horsemen as he rode through their ranks, slashing clumsily and ineffectually at one man-at-arms with his sword as he rode past. Another man-at-arms closed with him. Martin struggled to defend himself, barely managing to parry the forceful blows of his opponent. He tried to recall all that Preston had taught him about swordplay, but that had been as a foot-soldier. He had not been trained to fight on horseback, and his attention was fully occupied with trying to stay in the saddle without getting his head cut off.

The cob had not been trained for war, and it reared up on its hind legs, throwing Martin to the ground. He landed painfully on the stony track, his sword flying from his hand. Before he could move, another horseman tried to ride him down, wielding his broadsword above his head to bring it cleaving down against Martin's skull.

CHAPTER NINE

Martin threw himself flat, below the reach of the arcing tip of the horseman's broadsword. The horse reared up, instinctively avoiding stepping on the prone youth, its rider cursing foully. The horseman backed away, giving Martin a chance to scramble to where his sword had fallen. As he snatched it up and rose to his feet, a man-at-arms threatened to ride him down, but the first horseman shouted something in French that made him back away.

The horseman charged. It all happened too quickly for Martin to have time to think, to be afraid. The horseman swung his broadsword at Martin's neck as he rode past, but Martin ducked beneath the stroke, jabbing the point of his sword at the horseman's hip. The horseman was wearing armour, and the thrust glanced harmlessly off his chain-mail hauberk. He swiftly wheeled his mount, riding at Martin yet again, aiming a down-stroke at him. Martin raised his sword to parry the blow. The impact was terrific, agonisingly jarring Martin's arm. It shattered the cheap and light-weight blade of his sword so it broke off near the hilt. Martin could feel the wind of the broadsword as it passed within an inch of his head. He staggered back, his bowels turning to water as the horseman pressed home his attack.

'*When in doubt, aim for the horse.*' Preston's words came unbidden to Martin's mind. He stabbed desperately at the horseman's mount, the ragged end of the broken sword gouging a bloody wound in the horse's neck. The horse reared up, and Martin stumbled out of the way of its flailing hooves, tripping over and sprawling on his back. At the same time, the horseman lost his balance, sliding from the saddle and falling to the stony ground with a crash. Unencumbered by armour, Martin was the first to pick himself up. Seeing the youth approach, the horseman reached for his fallen sword. His gauntleted hand closed around the hilt. Martin brought his foot down heavily on the horseman's wrist and had the satisfaction of feeling the bone snap. He drew his rondel and dropped on to the man's chest, pinning him to the ground.

'Yield!' Martin held the tip of his rondel poised above the man's face.

'Yield to a churl?' The man spoke thickly accented English, his voice sour with contempt. 'I would rather die!'

'Then die!' Martin plunged the rondel's blade down through the jelly of the man's eye and into his brain. Blood fountained briefly, but the man was dead almost instantaneously.

Gasping for breath like a drowning man, Martin glanced up to see the remaining Frenchmen falter at the sight of their lord lying dead, slain by a peasant's hand. They had been disheartened by the refusal of the two English noblemen to yield without a fight; the death of their master was the final straw. It had been their lord's idea to try to capture the English noblemen, anyway. Almost as one, they broke off their attack and wheeled their horses about, riding back towards the cover of the trees.

'Shall we pursue them, my lord?' asked one of the noblemen, a young squire, elated by their victory.

The other shook his head. 'They are not worth the effort. The only prize here lies yonder, and our young friend seems to have claimed that.' He rode his horse over to where Martin still straddled the dead knight's body. 'What is your name, boy?'

Martin rose hurriedly to his feet, recognising the Earl of Warwick. 'Martin Kemp, my lord.'

Warwick frowned. 'I know you, do I not?'

'Aye, my lord. You saved me from the gallows at Leicester the month before last.'

'It seems you have returned the favour, then.'

Another troop of horsemen rode up, this time from the direction of the port. Martin gripped his rondel tightly, but Warwick and the squire remained relaxed, wiping the blades of their broadswords clean before returning them to their scabbards.

'My lord!' exclaimed the leader of the newcomers, a knight of about fifty wearing a red jupon emblazoned with three black stars on a yellow chevron. Martin recognised him as Sir Reginald Cobham, another knight in Warwick's retinue. 'Are you hurt in any way?'

'Not at all, Sir Reginald.' Warwick was dismissive, speaking with good humour. He gestured to his squire. 'Young Alan and I have merely been exercising ourselves with these French dogs, that is all.' The corpses that littered the road told their own tale.

No longer the subject of Warwick's attention, Martin wiped the blade of his rondel clean on the dead knight's jupon and slipped it back into its sheath. He gazed despondently at the broken pieces of his short sword, wondering what Preston would say. He picked them up and slotted them into his scabbard. He did not know if a blacksmith could repair the sword, but at least he could prove he had not simply lost it. Then he turned to the cob which stood, quite unharmed, calmly cropping the grass at the side of the road as if nothing had happened. Martin took the bridle, and was about to remount when Warwick's stern tones arrested him.

'Kemp!'

Martin started guiltily, and turned back.

'Are you not forgetting something?'

At a loss, wondering what he had done wrong, Martin flushed with confusion. 'My lord?'

Warwick indicated the broadsword that lay in the dead knight's grasp. 'The sword. You've earned it, by right of conquest.' A hint of a smile flickered at the corners of the earl's mouth.

Martin picked up the weapon uncertainly. It was wrought from one piece of finely tempered steel, the hilt twined with a leather thong, with a wheel-shaped pommel and a curved crossguard drooping towards the blade. The blade itself was almost three feet long, three inches across at the hilt and tapering to a finely honed point. It was not a gilt-handled, jewel-encrusted sword for ceremonial occasions; it was a sword for killing people. It was considerably heavier than his short sword had been, but it was well-balanced and felt comfortable in his hand.

'And the scabbard too,' added Warwick.

The wooden scabbard was covered in pattern-stamped black leather bound with brass. Like the sword it had been crafted to contain, it was workmanlike rather than showy, but of good quality nonetheless.

'A fine weapon for an archer to carry,' Warwick continued, as Martin buckled the sword-belt around his hips, so that the broadsword hung at his left side. 'But wield it as nobly as you have fought this day, and you'll not disgrace it.'

'Th . . . thank you, my lord.' Overwhelmed with gratitude, Martin bowed away.

Two more horsemen rode up from the rear of the column, Holland on his palfrey and Brother Ambrose on his pony. 'I hope this boy hasn't been giving you any trouble, my lord?' Holland asked Warwick with a smile.

The earl shook his head. 'To the contrary, I'm much obliged to the lad.'

'Did you find us some lodgings?' asked Holland, as Martin scrambled back into the cob's saddle.

'Aye, Sir Thomas.'

'Then lead the way, young man,' said the earl.

As they rode across the fields to the manor house, the earl explained to Holland and Cobham how Martin had come to his rescue, admitting that while Martin's help had been minimal, it had swung the balance in his favour.

'You *have* had a busy day, haven't you?' Holland remarked to Martin, when the earl had concluded his account. 'On your first day in France, you are one of the first to sight the enemy, and one of the first to engage them,' recounted Holland. 'Not content with that, you are bold enough to offer your coverchief to his Majesty, and then ride to the rescue of my lord of Warwick, slaying a French knight into the bargain.' He smiled. 'Tell me, Kemp, have you any more adventures planned before nightfall?'

Martin knew when he was being teased, even when it was by a knight as stern and gruff as Sir Thomas Holland. He managed a smile, although he still felt shaken from his encounter with the French knight. 'Not that I know of, sir.'

When they reached the manor house, Holland noted with satisfaction that someone had thought to post two men – Piers Edritch and Ned Skeffington – on sentry duty. Holland suspected that had been Preston's idea rather than Villiers'. The squire was courageous enough, and both a skilled horseman and swordsman; but he would never be a great warlord without the practical, hard-headed campaigning experience that Holland had learned from Preston.

They rode into the courtyard, where Preston and the rest of his men hurriedly rose to their feet. The riders dismounted, the noblemen leading their horses into the stable while the mounted archers and men-at-arms tethered their steeds to whatever makeshift tethering posts they could find in the courtyard. Martin rejoined his platoon.

'New sword, Kemp?' asked Preston. It was impossible not to notice the huge broadsword that hung at Martin's hip.

'My lord of Warwick gave it to me,' said Martin. 'I mean to say, I won it in battle.'

Preston raised his eyebrows sceptically. 'Well, which was it? Did the earl give it to you, or did you win it in battle? Both explanations seem highly unlikely to me.'

'Both, serjeant. I won it in battle, and the earl told me to keep it.'

'That's a noblemen's sword, Kemp. Are you trying to tell me you killed a French noblemen on your first day in France?'

'I were lucky,' admitted Martin. 'And I took your advice, serjeant,' he added. 'You know – about aiming for the horse, and stabbing at the eyes?'

'Don't try and butter me up, Kemp. It won't work.'

'I weren't trying to . . .'

'And don't interrupt me when I'm talking to you; I haven't finished yet. I suppose you can confirm all this?'

Martin nodded eagerly. 'You can ask Sir Thomas if you like.'

'I may just do that.'

'My own sword got broken,' said Martin, showing Preston the truncated hilt. 'Will I have to pay for a new one?'

Preston stared at Martin in wry disbelief. He could not work out whether Martin was dishonest and very clever indeed, or honest and extremely dim-witted. 'Not if what you've told me is true, lad,' he decided at last. 'And it had better be, because I'll check, and if I find out you've been lying to me, I'll . . .'

Martin never found out what Preston would do to him if he had been lying, because at that moment Villiers emerged from the house and approached the serjeant. 'Sir Thomas wants you in the hall,' said the squire. 'He says to bring Caynard and Kemp.'

Preston glanced speculatively at Caynard. 'Well, I know what Lancelot's been up to,' he said. 'He's been thieving swords. What have you been up to this time, Caynard?'

Caynard scowled, and followed Villiers, Preston and Martin into the manor house. It was the largest private building Martin had ever entered. Relatively humble though it was, Martin was awed by its grandiosity. He was about to follow Preston through the door into the hall when Will seized him by the arm and pulled him back so that he could precede Martin, apparently for no reason other than sheer spite. Martin was unimpressed by such pettiness, and did not rise to the provocation.

The walls of the hall were hung with intricately woven tapestries depicting different scenes from the Song of Roland, while three stags' heads were mounted on the far wall. A large fire was blazing in the hearth at the centre of the room, the flickering flames adding to the illumination provided by the sickly sunlight that filtered through the high, narrow windows. Holland was standing by the fire, lost in contemplation as he gazed into the flames. He glanced up as the four men entered the room. 'Fetch the steward, would you, Adam?' he asked his squire, and as Villiers nodded and disappeared back through the door, Holland turned to the serjeant. 'We're going to question him,' he explained.

Preston nodded in full understanding. 'Aye, Sir Thomas.' He turned to Martin and Will. 'You two stand here, on either side of the door. Make sure he doesn't try to make a run for it.'

Caynard grinned. He had been through this before. 'You want me to toy with my dagger, serjeant?'

Preston nodded. 'That might help.'

Villiers entered, chattering amiably with the steward, who was clearly having a hard time keeping up with the squire's Anglo-Norman. The steward looked disconsolate at the occupation of his master's home, but by no means unduly concerned. Then he saw Holland and Preston waiting for him, their faces grim. A trace of fear entered his eyes. He tried to back out of the hall, but Caynard moved to block the exit. 'Oh no you don't, monsewer.'

The steward whimpered softly.

Holland gestured to a wooden stool he had positioned in the middle of the floor, facing the roaring fire. He addressed the steward in French, his tone mild and unthreatening. He had spent enough time in France to have a better idea than his squire of how French was spoken by the natives.

The steward walked forward slowly, the trepidation evident on his face, and sat down on the stool. Holland had carefully positioned it close enough to the fire to ensure that the steward broke out in a sweat the moment he sat down. Holland stood in front of him and a little to the right, just inside the glow of light cast across the floor by the fire, while Preston had positioned himself behind the stool, out of the steward's line of vision. Caynard took his dagger from its sheath and began to pare his grubby fingernails with it.

Villiers said something in soothing tones to the steward. The Frenchman nodded, but if Villiers had sought to reassure him, then the expression on the steward's face made it clear that he had failed.

Holland asked the steward a question in French. He spoke in mild tones, quite unlike his characteristic gruff and sardonic mode of expression. The steward replied briefly, thrusting out his lower lip and shrugging, lowering his head as much as he raised his shoulders. Holland made a dismissive gesture, and tried another question. It elicited the same response as before. Preston took a step forward and raised a hand as if to strike the Frenchman, but Holland signalled for him to stop.

'Hold, Wat. I have a better idea.' He glanced across to Martin – or, more specifically, to the broadsword that now hung at Martin's hip – with a speculative expression. 'Come here, Kemp.'

Martin crossed the room to stand before Holland, who gestured at the seated Frenchman.

'Show him your new sword.'

Martin was completely bewildered by all this, but he saw no reason not to comply. He drew the broadsword from its scabbard and held it out for the steward to see. The Frenchman's eyes widened as if in recognition.

Holland permitted himself the faintest of smiles. 'Tell him how you came by that sword, Kemp.'

Martin guessed that a succinct reply was called for. 'I killed the knight who bore it.'

The steward flinched as if Martin had struck him, and Preston chuckled. 'It seems our friend here understands some English after all.'

'You understand, do you not?' Holland asked the steward. 'The Seigneur de Quettehou lies slain, his men dispersed in the woods. They won't be returning here tonight or any other night, so you'd best reconcile yourself to the fact that we're here to stay. Now I'll ask you again: what forces does Valois have garrisoned in the Cotentin Peninsula?'

The steward seemed to crumple. 'The marshal was in the process of levying troops for a militia . . . ' His accent was thick, but nonetheless intelligible.

'The marshal,' echoed Holland. 'You mean Robert Bertrand?'

The steward nodded.

'How many men?'

'I don't know,' admitted the steward. 'There was to be

an inspection of the men at Saint-Vaast-la-Hougue this day. The arrival of your fleet prevented it,' he added bitterly.

Which explains why the French were able to attack us on the beach so soon after we'd landed, thought Holland. 'What about professional troops?' he asked the steward.

'There were some Italian mercenaries . . . '

'Genoese crossbowmen?'

The steward nodded.

'Where are they now?'

'They deserted three days ago,' spat the steward, angry at the recollection. 'I don't know where they went.'

'Any other forces?'

'Not that I know of.'

Holland nodded, satisfied that the steward had spoken the truth. 'Very well, you may go.'

The steward rose to his feet and bowed low, the relief evident on his face.

'But don't go far,' put in Preston, gesturing with his rondel. 'I've got my eye on you.'

Ashen-faced, the steward nodded again, and scurried out of the room.

Holland dismissed Preston, Martin and Caynard, before making his way to Warwick's quarters to brief the earl on what he had learned.

The cellars of the manor house proved to be well-stocked with food, and the men of Holland's company dined heartily that night. As darkness fell, Preston organised a rota for sentry duty, and those men who were not on the first watch bedded down in the courtyard for the night.

At first, Martin slept soundly. He dreamed of Beatrice, and in his dream she was able to marry him because he had won great glory and been knighted by the king for valour. At some point during the small hours of the morning his dreams turned to nightmares when his conscience caught up with him. He dreamed not of the skirmish on the beach, but of the mêlée on the road from Saint-Vaast-la-Hougue. The mounted knight was trying to ride him down again, hacking at him with that great broadsword. Then his assailant removed his helm, and it was not a knight at all, but Beatrice, and she laughed at him as she lifted the sword to deliver the death-stroke. He stood there, staring up at her in disbelief, unable to move as the blade came arcing down towards his head . . .

He awoke with a start, and found himself staring into the dying embers of the fire that had been lit in the courtyard. He sat upright with a gasp, shaken by the vivid dream. The others still slumbered, some of them moaning fitfully in their sleep. The sky overhead was a dark and dingy blue, but beyond the walls of the courtyard to the east the undersides of the clouds were illuminated in a brilliant orange gash. Sunrise, Martin told himself, and pushed himself to his feet. It would be reveille soon; there seemed little point in trying to get back to sleep. He picked his way between his sleeping companions to the gateway, where Brewster and Robin Wighton were on sentry duty. Preston stood with them, leaning with both hands on his cudgel. None of them saw Martin arrive. They were too busy gazing across the countryside to where the sunrise set the horizon ablaze, as if the town of Saint-Vaast-la-Hougue were being consumed by a huge conflagration.

It was then that Martin realised that sunrise was still the best part of an hour away. He stared at the blaze in horrified fascination. Only the very rich could afford houses made entirely of stone; for the poor, like Martin, fire was the ultimate nightmare, destroying homes and crops alike, ruining livelihoods.

'What is it?' he asked, unable to grasp the significance of the huge blaze.

'That?' Preston shrugged. 'That's Saint-Vaast-la-Hougue going up in smoke,' he said absently. 'Beautiful sight, isn't it?'

Martin still did not understand. 'Is it a French attack?'

'The French?' Preston stared at him in bewilderment. 'Why should they burn one of their own towns? No, it's more likely to be some of our own lads, getting a bit careless accidentally on purpose. Such things happen,' he added, with a chuckle. 'That's why we're here. Someone's got to show these French whoresons who their rightful king is.'

'By burning their homes?' Martin could not keep the disgust out of his voice.

'Aye, if needs be.' Preston was unperturbed by Martin's angry tone. He was used to having the occasional idealist like Kemp under his command; he consoled himself with the knowledge that the harsh realities of war would cure the lad soon enough. 'Peasants work for their lords in return for protection,' he explained patiently. 'If we show them that their lords are incapable of protecting them, they'll switch their allegiance soon enough.'

'To the king whose army burnt their homes?'

Preston shrugged. 'Who else can they turn to? We're demonstrating the power of our king, his ability to ravage the towns and countryside of France with impunity. The folks hereabouts may not like it, but there's little they can do about it. They have to think about the future.'

Martin tried to see it from the peasants' point of view, but it still made no sense. The County of Leicester had not known the scourge of war in his lifetime, or even in his father's, and he had never seen Beaumont as his protector; perhaps that was one of the reasons why he resented Beaumont's lordship so much. He wondered how he would feel if it was the other way around, with Valois claiming the throne of England and his armies ravaging the English countryside. He might be tempted to applaud

214

them if they slew Beaumont and Stamford, but not if they burnt the village of Knighton.

Sir Thomas Norwich rode up to the manor house shortly after dawn with orders from the king for Warwick and his retinue to prepare for a march. They did not have far to go. Following the burning of Saint-Vaast-la-Hougue, the king had decided to move his headquarters three and a half miles inland, to an inn in the town of Morselines, and Warwick was requested to join him there.

The king's army was spreading throughout the Cotentin Peninsula. Escorted by troops of hobelars and mounted archers, the wagons of the king's victuallers ranged far and wide in search of forage to supplement the supplies the army had brought with it. Much of the local populace had fled in the face of the invasion, so that the English seemed to outnumber the French resident in the area. The roads were crammed with English troops, marching in companies like Holland's men or working in smaller groups, searching for booty and burning villages and crops. The French knights and men-at-arms of the region had withdrawn behind the walls of their castles and fortified towns, while the peasantry who remained, abandoned by their lords and masters, had no choice but to accept the depredations of the English.

Holland's company encamped just outside Morselines. Norwich and Holland returned from a meeting with the king and his closest advisers at the inn where his Majesty was lodged around mid-afternoon. Holland had his serjeants form up their platoons so that Norwich could address them with an edict that the king had decided to issue to his troops.

'We know not who was responsible for putting the port of Saint-Vaast-la-Hougue to the torch; nor do we desire to know.' Norwich sat astride his palfrey as he addressed the men. He did not shout; his voice was strong enough to carry to the four-score men who were gathered before him. 'However, his Majesty has decreed that henceforth, out of compassion for his French subjects, no town or manor house is to be burnt, no church or holy place is to be put to the sack, nor are any old men, women or children to be threatened, harmed or molested, on pain of life and limb. Furthermore, any man catching anyone in the act of these or any other criminal deeds and bringing them to the attention of his Majesty's marshals, will receive a reward of forty shillings. By order of his Royal Majesty King Edward Plantagenet the Third after the Conquest, at Morselines, on the Feast of Saint Mildred, Thursday the thirteenth day of July in the twentieth year of his reign.'

Recalling his earlier conversation with Preston, Martin felt vindicated by the proclamation, and was pleased that his king remained true to the tenets of chivalry. Some of the veterans were stunned with disbelief, however, grumbling loudly as they were dismissed by the serjeants. Caynard, Lefthand and Murray approached Preston later that afternoon.

'It don't make any sense, serjeant,' protested Caynard. 'I've been fighting the king's wars for upwards of half a dozen years now, and this is the first time I've ever heard of owt like this.'

'What sort of campaign is this going to be, if we aren't allowed to demonstrate our power to the French?' agreed Murray. 'I wouldn't've volunteered if I'd known it were going to be like this.'

'Next they'll be telling us we aren't supposed to hurt any of the French at all,' grumbled Lefthand.

'That's as maybe,' said Preston. 'But let me remind you all that you enlisted to serve the king, and if he chooses to issue such an edict, then by God's bones you'll obey it, or you'll answer to me!'

Caynard and his friends left Preston truculently, clearly

216

unsatisfied with his response but knowing better than to defy him openly. Nevertheless, Preston could understand their bewilderment, and that evening he broached the subject with Holland while the two of them were alone in Holland's tent.

'Begging your pardon, Sir Thomas, but some of the lads aren't happy with his Majesty's latest proclamation.'

Holland was staring at a chess puzzle he had laid out on the chess set he had brought with him. 'What of it?' he asked coldly, without looking up from the board.

'It's just that . . . well, I've got a certain amount of sympathy with them on this matter. It's like telling them the opposite of what they expected to hear. They're all confused, and to tell the truth so am I.'

Holland picked up a pawn and toyed with it for a moment. 'Are you questioning his Majesty's edict?'

'Nay, sir!' Preston said hurriedly. 'It's just that . . . I think we'd all be a lot happier if we could see some point in marching through Valois' lands without doing any damage.'

Holland replaced the pawn with a sigh. He had anticipated the men's confusion, and had already broached the subject with Warwick before the edict had been read to them. Now he gave Preston more or less the same reply that he had received from Warwick.

'As you well know, Wat, his Majesty hopes to win his rightful place on the throne of France. To do so he needs the acceptance of the French people. He needs to be seen not only as a powerful warlord but also as a just and kindly ruler.' He paused, choosing his next words with care. 'I think he recognises the difficulty in expecting veterans more used to burning and pillaging suddenly to change their ways. What is important is that henceforth any such behaviour by the men in his service is *seen* to be condemned rather than condoned. Do you follow me?'

Preston nodded.

'As regards the next few weeks, I think we can rely on the men to behave as troops on campaign are expected to behave,' continued Holland. 'Can his Majesty be held accountable if, somewhere between the ravages of his men and the curbs of his marshals, a certain number of transgressions of the king's edict go unpunished?'

'Aye, sir.' Preston understood now. The men were to behave as they had done on previous campaigns – burning, raping and pillaging – while the serjeants must be ready to turn a blind eye, so long as the damage done were not so wanton, and the culprits so obvious, that the king's marshals could not ignore them.

Preston was bowing out of the tent when Holland called out to him.

'Wat?'

'Aye, Sir Thomas?'

'I think you may find it useful to acquaint some of your men – at your own discretion – with the Eleventh Commandment.'

Preston creased his brow. 'The Eleventh Commandment, sir?'

Holland nodded. '"Thou shalt not get caught."'

Grinning, Preston nodded, and ducked out of the tent.

Early the following morning Norwich rode out to where Holland's men had pitched camp. Holland greeted Norwich outside his tent. 'Orders?'

Norwich nodded, dismounting. 'My lord of Warwick requests that you and your men accompany him on a reconnaissance to the north today, to a port called Barfleur.'

'I know of it,' said Holland.

Norwich started to rummage around in one of his saddle bags. 'By the way, before I forget,' he said, producing Martin's coverchief, neatly folded. 'His

Majesty asked me to see to it that this was returned to its rightful owner, with his gratitude.'

Holland chuckled, and waved Preston across. 'Return this to Kemp, would you?'

'Aye, sir.' Preston took the coverchief across to where his men were breakfasting. Martin had already finished eating, and was polishing his broadsword with all the pride of new ownership. Preston tossed him the coverchief. 'With his Majesty's compliments.'

Martin dropped the rag he had been using to polish his sword and caught the coverchief one-handed before he had a chance to recognise it. He had not expected to see it again, and was astonished that the king had remembered to arrange its return. He held it delicately, as if it might dissolve in the morning breeze. The coverchief that had stanched the king's blood – *his* coverchief.

'Now there's a souvenir for you,' remarked Rudcock, as Preston stalked away.

Martin slowly unfolded the coverchief. It had even been laundered and pressed, and smelled strongly of lavender.

'The blood's been washed off it!' Conyers exclaimed in disbelief. 'What kind of a souvenir is that?'

Martin grimaced. 'I don't want my coverchief stiff with blood!'

'Ah, but it weren't any old blood,' Conyers pointed out. 'That were the king's blood, that were! You could've kept it for ever, to show to your grandchildren.'

'I haven't got any grandchildren,' said Martin, winding the coverchief about his neck once more. 'I haven't even got any children. Not yet, at least ways.'

'Well then,' said Conyers, with a leer. 'You'd best not waste any time when you get back to that girl of yours.'

Rudcock grinned. 'What's the point, since he's not got owt to show them anyway?'

Sitting down to join them, Newbolt caught the tail-end

of the conversation. 'What's the point in our being here at all, that's what I'd like to know,' he grumbled. 'No towns or manor houses to be burnt, no churches or holy places to be sacked, no old men, women or children to be threatened, harmed or molested? The king don't want archers, he wants a bunch of God-damned friars!'

Conyers laughed. 'I wouldn't trust a friar to leave the women alone.'

'Jankin's right, though,' said Lefthand. 'What's the point in us being here, if not to pillage and burn French territory?'

'To fight the French, perhaps?' Martin suggested sardonically.

Lefthand scowled. 'Don't talk daft. If we come up against Valois' army, we might as well dig our own graves. We'll be outnumbered a hundred to one. Isn't that right, Daw?'

Oakley scratched his grizzled jaw. 'Maybe. Maybe not. The odds were against us when we faced the French at Morlaix, but we still beat them.'

'They won't make the same mistakes again, you mark my words,' asserted Lefthand.

Before Oakley could reply, Holland emerged from his tent and gave his serjeants the command to form their men up into marching order. They were soon joined by Warwick, riding with Cobham and his company. The two companies formed a single column, with Warwick riding at its head. They headed north, the foot-soldiers struggling to keep up as they marched in the dusty wake of the mounted troops. Jankin complained about the dust kicked up by the horses' hooves getting in his eyes and throat; Martin simply pulled up his coverchief so that it covered his nose and mouth, his eyes smiling smugly at Newbolt, and the others who had mocked him for wearing it.

The column reached Barfleur without incident. The

town was another port, slightly larger than Saint-Vaast-la-Hougue had been. The streets were deserted, and the English troops entered without opposition. Some of the ships from the English fleet had already entered the harbour, and when the troops signalled that the town was in English hands they tied up at the stone piers, while other ships waited beyond the harbour entrance. It had taken weeks to load the fleet at Portsmouth, and to save time they would start unloading some of the supplies at this second port.

Cobham's men were detailed to help unload the ships, while Holland ordered his men to set fire to nine French warships they found tied up in the harbour, along with a couple of fishing boats for good measure, to make way for the English transport ships. Despite his natural horror of fire, it gave Martin a strange thrill to touch a blazing torch to a ship's rigging until it was burning nicely, the flaming ropes tracing out a fiery web. He stood back to watch as the furled sails caught fire, pieces of burning canvas floating in the breeze over the water, and then the flames were fiercely devouring the boat's timbers, sending great billows of smoke up into the air, until finally the hull had burnt down to the water-line and the boat sank below the waves with a loud, prolonged hiss. It had taken men weeks, if not months, to build these ships, and Martin and his companions had destroyed them in less than an hour. He was horrified, not only at what he had done, but at the guilty pleasure he had taken in the spectacle. Fire was something he feared, but it was also something that could be used as a weapon. It gave Martin a sense of power, but at the same time left him feeling cold and empty inside. There was no fun in doing something that, in the normal run of things, would be considered wicked, if it was sanctioned – nay, ordered – by his betters. As a villein he had been bound by the commands of his lord and master, Sir John Beaumont. Simkin had always told him that he could find freedom as a soldier. But this was no kind of freedom at all: he was still bound by the commands of a master; the fact that he had a new master in Sir Thomas Holland did not alter the underlying reality of his servitude.

And then he thought of the fishermen who had depended on those boats for their livelihood, and he felt even more guilty than he had after killing the foot-soldier on the beach or the knight on the road. Those men had taken up arms against his king, in defence of the usurper Valois. What crime had the fishermen committed? He had come to France in the hope of winning glory on the battlefield. But there was no glory here. Had not the king himself ordered that no wrong should be done to the people of Normandy? And now he had been commanded to destroy the livelihoods of some of those people. Aye, and he had obeyed unquestioningly, too. Once again he had to harden his heart: the fishermen could build new boats. They could count themselves lucky they still had their lives, assuming they had not been amongst the levies killed on the beach. This was war, he told himself, and in war people got hurt. Had not the French themselves – the people of Normandy, no less – ravaged Portsmouth and the Isle of Wight a few years ago?

As Preston and his men watched the last of the charred hulks slip below the waves, Holland rode up and ordered them to undertake a house-to-house search of the town. Martin assumed he meant that they should look for people – French troops in hiding – but once the search got underway it soon became apparent that he was alone in this assumption. Most of the others seemed to think that they were looking for plunder, Preston not excepted. In one house the serjeant found a large, iron-bound oak chest. He smashed the clasp with the heavy pommel of his broadsword and prised open the lid to reveal the contents, gold and silver coins neatly stacked on one side, jewellery piled on the other.

'Well, look what we got here!' he exclaimed in delight, wide-eyed in wonderment. 'We're rich men, lads!' He started to divide the coins among them equally. The others in the room paused in the act of going through the fine clothing they found to gather up their shares, but one pile remained on the bed. 'Did I miscount?' asked Preston. 'Who hasn't taken his share?'

The others looked at one another with suspicion. Rudcock noticed that Martin stood back with his arms folded, an expression of distaste on his face. 'Lancelot?'

'This is wrong,' said Martin.

'What?' Preston stared at him incredulously.

'This is wrong,' repeated Martin. 'The king ordered that we do no wrong to the people of France. This is stealing.'

'It's only stealing if you get caught,' said Preston. 'Now I'm sure none of these lads are going to tell, and I *know* I'm not going to tell.' He made a dismissive gesture. 'Besides, the king's edict was for the benefit of the French, not for us. His Majesty wants them to think he's kind, noble and chivalrous – which he is, of course. That's why he's leaving the sack and pillage to us. Come on, Lancelot, this is war. No one expects us to wipe our God-damned feet each time we enter a God-damned house!'

'It's *wrong*,' Martin repeated stubbornly.

'You didn't say owt when I gave you that bracelet the day before yesterday,' Rudcock pointed out.

'That were before the king issued his edict. I wish I hadn't taken it, now.'

'For Christ's sake, Martin!' Rudcock exclaimed impatiently. 'If you don't take that lot, someone else will, so don't think you're doing the rightful owners any favours.'

'The Devil take him,' spat Edritch. 'If he don't want it, the rest of us can divide up his share. All the more for us, aye?'

'Oh aye?' sneered Caynard. 'And how do we know Lancelot here won't go running to the king's marshals to claim his forty shillings, eh? Or should that be thirty pieces of silver?'

'Shut your face, Caynard,' snapped Preston. 'Kemp won't say owt to the marshals, because it's only his word against ours, and he knows what I'll do to him if he tries it. Besides, he'll be as guilty as the rest of us, because he's going to take that share. Aren't you, Kemp?'

Martin unfolded his arms, but did not move from where he stood.

'Kemp?' persisted Preston.

'Think of your family,' urged Rudcock, gesturing at the small pile of coins and jewellery. 'With what's there, you can buy yoursen a small tavern somewheres and earn a decent living, instead of spending the rest of your life slaving in the fields for someone else's benefit.'

Martin bit his lip. Rudcock's tack had touched a nerve, and he was sorely tempted. 'I *can't*. If our mam thought we were living off . . . '

'So don't tell her,' Conyers suggested simply.

Martin shook his head. 'I can't leave my lord's manor . . . '

Preston put an arm around Martin's shoulders. 'Listen, lad. With that much money you can do what the hell you like. Or do you want to be a lowly villein all your life?'

Martin hesitated momentarily, and then snatched up the coins, red-faced, pouring them into his purse until it bulged. Some of the others cheered, and began to drift out of the room in search of other booty: fine clothes, food, wine. Finally Martin and Rudcock were left alone in the room. Martin sat on the edge of the bed, staring despondently at the floor.

Rudcock clasped him by the shoulder. 'You made the right choice, Martin. Everyone does it. It's expected, king's edict or no king's edict. Why should you miss out?'

Martin nodded, wiping his nose on his sleeve. Then he looked up at Rudcock with a wan smile. 'I'm not sure I feel safe carrying this much money on me. They say the man who travels with an empty purse sleeps soundest.'

'Don't be daft,' Rudcock told him with a grin. 'Who's going to risk getting into a fight with you for the contents of your purse when they can walk into any house hereabouts and help theirselves?'

Martin and Rudcock were the last to leave the house. As they emerged on to the street, they immediately had to press themselves flat against the wall as a handful of young squires rode by. 'Watch out, you God-damned churls!' shouted one.

Another, recognising Martin, immediately reined in his horse and stared at him. 'You!' he exclaimed in disgust.

'Aye.' Martin lifted his chin to regard Richard Stamford contemptuously. Rudcock's words earlier had struck a chord within him: he was sick of bowing and scraping to the likes of Stamford. 'What of it?'

Stamford noticed the broadsword that hung at Martin's side. 'Where did you get that sword?' he demanded.

'I won it,' Martin told him proudly. 'In battle.'

'Liar!' spat Stamford. 'That is the sword of a noblemen.'

'More likely the churl stole it,' said another squire.

'I didn't steal it!' protested Martin. 'I won it fairly, in battle. I killed the knight who bore it.'

'Aye, like as not you stabbed him in the back to steal it,' sneered Stamford, flicking back his head.

'Know you not there is a penalty for stealing, by the king's decree?' said the second squire.

'Aye,' said a third. 'And a reward of forty shillings for

225

any man who brings such a miscreant to the attention of the king's marshals.'

'Give me the sword, churl, and we'll say no more about it,' suggested Stamford, with a toss of his head. The broadsword was clearly a better weapon than his own ancient and ill-kept blade, and probably worth more than forty shillings.

Martin hesitated. There were five squires, all on horseback, against himself and Rudcock, who was looking extremely nervous. 'Give him the sword,' Rudcock hissed. 'It's not worth getting killed over.'

'Your friend speaks wisely,' said the second squire. 'Hand it over to Master Richard.'

Martin pulled the sword from his scabbard, holding it with both hands, in a defensive posture. 'Come and take it.'

The other squires laughed. 'It seems he wants a fight, Richard,' said one.

'A fight?' Stamford drew his own sword. 'God's love, I'll give him a fight!' He rode his horse a few steps towards Martin and tried to bring his sword down on Martin's head. Wielding the broadsword with both hands, Martin managed to parry the blow. Then he reached up with one hand to seize Stamford by the wrist, and with one powerful tug he heaved the squire out of his saddle. Stamford hit the ground painfully, losing his grip on his sword.

Rudcock kept his hand away from the hilt of his own short sword; for the moment, the other squires seemed content to spectate, laughing at Stamford's discomfiture; if Rudcock interfered, they might feel obliged likewise to lend a hand, tipping the balance against the two archers. Besides which, Martin seemed to be holding his own.

Stamford snatched up his sword and rolled away from Kemp, nimbly rising to his feet. The two of them circled one another, swords poised to strike, while the other squires cheered and shouted encouragement at Stamford. A crowd was beginning to gather, Caynard and his friends watching the scene with amusement.

'For all loves!' a voice suddenly boomed. 'What in the name of God is going on here?'

All eyes turned to the four horsemen who had arrived on the scene unnoticed. The speaker was the Earl of Warwick, his face as black as thunder. With him were Cobham, Holland and Villiers.

'Put up your swords!' commanded Warwick. Both Martin and Stamford truculently replaced their swords in their scabbards. 'Squires fighting churls?' Warwick continued angrily. 'By my truth, I have never seen such a thing! What is the cause of this quarrel?'

Stamford pointed to Martin. 'This churl carries a sword that he has obviously stolen. The man is a criminal, and should be hanged.'

'I'll decide who's to be hanged, if anyone is,' growled Warwick. '*I* gave him that sword. He earned it.' He wheeled his horse without another word, and rode on.

Stamford was red-faced with anger and humiliation. Not knowing what to say, he took refuge in silence. This was the third time Kemp had made him look foolish.

'Next time you level an accusation at one of my men, I suggest you be certain of your facts,' Holland told Stamford coldly. 'Now get back on your horse and ride on.' He wheeled his horse after Warwick, and Cobham and Villiers went with him, the latter grinning with amusement.

'I'll see you in Hell for this, Kemp,' snarled Stamford.

'Aye and like' Martin agreed with a savage grin. 'But you'll have to wait for me there.'

CHAPTER TEN

The mammoth task of unloading the fleet's supplies and equipment was completed three days later, and Warwick, Holland and Sir Reginald Cobham were called to attend a war council at the inn where the king was lodged. A plan of campaign was drawn up, and the following morning the army prepared to set out on its march across northern France.

The process of getting the vast army into marching order took up most of the morning. The army was divided into three battalions: the vanguard, under the nominal command of the young Prince of Wales, with the Earls of Warwick and Northampton to advise him; the main body, including the baggage train, commanded by the king himself; and the rearguard, under the joint command of the Earls of Arundel, Huntingdon and Suffolk, and the Bishop of Durham. Holland's company was to march in the vanguard, and was thus one of the first units to be formed up on the road. He and his men had to wait impatiently while the harassed-looking marshals rode back and forth along the column, struggling to organise the units that were to follow.

The rearguard was still forming up when Norwich brought the order for the vanguard to set off. The prince rode at the forefront with his retinue, and behind them came fifty hand-picked archers from Chester, said to be the finest archers in the whole of England and Wales. Like the Welsh archers who followed them on foot, they were dressed in the prince's green and white parti-coloured livery.

Holland's company came next, with Sir Thomas, Villiers and Brother Ambrose riding at the head of the troop of knights and squires, followed by the men-at-arms and then the two platoons of archers. The archers sang as they set off marching. After the debilitating voyage and the five days spent around Morselines where they had recouped their strength while the ships were unloaded, it was good to be on the move at last. The sun was shining, and spirits were as high as they had been on the day they ⸱⸱† out from Bosworth. There was little doubt in t⸍   that this was the mightiest army ever fielded   an English king, and with Valois' fo⸍   ⸍o far away, it seemed that little ⸍   nce. The men boasted that they ⸍   ⸍ring in Paris within a month; ⸍   n, Valois would be forced to ⸍   ⸍o the French throne.

                ⸍oon, marching south-west
do⸍   ⸍ thickly wooded countryside.
They⸍   part of ten miles that afternoon,
reachi⸍   ⸍vn with a castle shortly after nightfall.
Unlike ⸍   ⸍ aast-la-Hougue and Barfleur, the inhabitants ᴏ⸍ this town had not had a chance to flee before the English advance. A deputation of the townsfolk was escorted to the king, with whom they pleaded only that their lives and those of their fellow citizens be spared. As Preston explained to his new recruits, the inhabitants of a town or fortress that surrendered immediately were to be treated with honour and respect, while any place that put up any kind of resistance condemned itself to massacre, sack and pillage should it eventually fall to the besieging army, in accordance with the accepted rules of war. That was the theory, at least. In practice, troops would sack and pillage any settlement they came to, regardless of whether or not the inhabitants tried to resist. The difference was that in a town that resisted, the

ensuing blood bath would have official sanction and sometimes even – at the end of a long and bitter siege – approval.

Word soon came back from the king that he had received the deputation of burghers kindly and had admitted the townsfolk to his peace. Theoretically this meant that they were as much entitled to English justice as any freeman back in England. These new-found privileges did not, however, stop them from having their larders raided by the king's victuallers searching for supplies for the army; but then those victuallers took the same high-handed approach when they operated on English soil. Apart from this, the inhabitants were left largely unharmed, which was perhaps more than they could have dared to hope for.

Valois' eldest son, the Duke of Normandy, had a manor house just outside the town, although he was absent, presumably still campaigning in Gascony. The king lodged in the manor house for the night, while the Earl of Warwick and his retinue found rather more humble lodgings at an inn to the south of the town, not far from the Bishop of Coutance's palace, where the prince and the Earl of Northampton spent the night.

That evening, many of the men from Holland's company made their way into town, including a group of squires still full of themselves following their first taste of victory at Saint-Vaast-la-Hougue. They were in high spirits, singing songs of love and glory, cursing the townsfolk who got in their way. They found a tavern which was not too full, where English knights and men-at-arms rubbed shoulders with humbler archers. The young squires were the rowdiest of the lot, lustfully pawing at the serving girls who struggled to serve wine without asking for payment, hoping only to make it through the next few days without being molested by the English troops; the arrival of the squires soon put paid to that vain hope. As some of them dragged serving girls upstairs, leaving the other men present to help themselves to wine, one of them turned to where Stamford sat in a corner. Unlike his friends, Stamford had been silent all night, showing little enthusiasm for their boisterous japes.

'Come on, Dickon!' said the squire, waving a flagon about and sloshing dark red wine on to the sawdust-covered floor with one hand as he sought to maintain his grasp around the waist of a struggling girl. 'Don't you want to join in the fun?'

Stamford shook his head and waved dismissively at the squire, scowling. The other squire was curious to know what was troubling his friend, but not to the extent that he would let it interfere with his enjoyment. He shrugged, and hoisted the girl on to his shoulder like a sack of grain, carrying her kicking and struggling upstairs.

Stamford was still brooding over his latest humiliation at Kemp's hands. It was insufferable that a mere villein should be allowed to get away with all that Kemp had done, without any punishment whatsoever. Sometimes it seemed as if the whole world was laughing at him.

'It's that squire, isn't it? The one who Lancelot got into an argument with at Barfleur,' said a voice nearby.

'They got into an argument long before that. I saw him and his master demanding that Lancelot be hanged for rape at Bosworth,' responded another.

'Rape? Lancelot!' snorted the first. 'That gelding couldn't rape a woman if she were stripped naked and tied spread-eagled to a bed!'

'What did Sir Thomas say?' asked a third voice.

'Told him to go to Hell,' asserted the second.

Stamford gave the new arrivals a sidelong glance. Their faces were vaguely familiar: four archers from Holland's company, in the same platoon as Kemp.

'Why that squire lets a villein like Lancelot push him around is beyond me,' said the first.

'Maybe he's a gelding, too,' chuckled a fourth.

'"This churl carries a sword that he has obviously stolen",' mimicked one of them, exaggerating Stamford's noble accent. '"He's a criminal, and should be hanged."' All four of them laughed raucously.

His ears burning with rage, Stamford could stand it no longer. It might be dishonourable to quarrel with churls; but it would be an even greater dishonour if he were to sit by and allow such mockery to go unchallenged. He pushed himself sharply to his feet, upsetting his stool with a crash. The sudden sound commanded silence in the tavern. Everyone stopped what they were doing to stare as Stamford made his way around the table to confront the four archers.

'Does something amuse you?' Stamford asked them coldly, toying with the rings on the fingers of his right hand, as if it required a conscious effort for him to keep his hand from the hilt of his sword. 'Perhaps you would care to share your jest with me? I am much in need of amusement.'

All four archers had blanched and fallen silent. They moved into a huddle, shrinking away from the squire.

'I'm addressing you, if you would have the courtesy to respond . . . ?'

'Please, we didn't . . .' began one.

Stamford drove his fist into the speaker's jaw, the powerful blow sending him sprawling on the floor. 'Doff your cap when you address your betters, you unmannerly dog!' he snarled.

The other three hurriedly removed their caps as one.

'Well?' persisted Stamford.

'We didn't mean no offence, your lordship,' stammered one of the others.

'That's right,' said the leader of the four archers, a rough, horse-faced individual. 'I were just saying how disgraceful it is for a villein like Kemp to be allowed to treat a man like yourself so disrespectfully. He shouldn't be allowed to get away with it. Isn't that right, lads?'

The other three archers nodded in fervent agreement, murmuring their assent.

'It's a crying shame, it is, the way thieves and rapists like Kemp are allowed to get away with murder,' continued the horse-faced man. 'But that's the way of the world, isn't it? The innocent are punished while the guilty go free.'

'What would you know about it?' scoffed Stamford.

'Oh, I like to think I know a fair bit about justice, having been through the legal system myself a couple of times. Now me, I'm a great believer in natural justice. God takes care of what the courts leave unpunished. Take Kemp, for example. If he were suddenly to suffer a fatal accident in the next couple of days, that might seem like a judgement of God, mightn't it?'

'A dagger-thrust to the heart,' suggested one of the other archers, catching the horse-faced man's drift. 'Men are killed all the time on campaign without anyone asking too closely about the whys and wherefores. Who's to say if it was a French hand that held the dagger, or an English one?'

'And what would the hand that held the dagger seek in return?' demanded Stamford.

'I've always found that gold oils the wheels of justice to make them turn more smoothly,' said the horse-faced man.

Stamford sighed. 'How much?'

'Fifty shillings,' said Caynard, expecting to have to haggle. When Stamford reached for the purse that hung at his belt, it was obvious he had misunderstood. 'Each,' added Caynard.

'That's ten pounds of gold!' protested Stamford.

Caynard glanced about to make sure that no one was eavesdropping; but the other men in the tavern had long

233

since returned to their drinking. 'We're talking murder here, your lordship. If anyone finds out, it'll be our necks they stretch.'

Stamford sighed again. He would have preferred to have reserved the pleasure of killing Kemp for himself, but too many people had admonished him too many times for brawling with the churl. Certainly it would be better not to soil his hands from further contact with the villein, but to leave the dirty work to these archers. The important thing was that Kemp's existence ceased to make a mockery of Stamford's honour. And with a purse now bulging with looted gold, he considered ten pounds a bargain when his honour was at stake. 'Very well,' he agreed, discreetly passing them a few coins. 'Five pounds now, and the other five when it's done. But if you make a botch of the job, don't come crawling back to me. I'll forget I ever met you.'

'Of course,' agreed Caynard, grinning evilly. 'But don't worry, we won't.'

Stamford eyed him appraisingly. 'You've done this kind of thing before, haven't you?'

Caynard's grin was broader than ever. 'When your roof needs mending you go to a thatcher. What you pay for is craftsmanship.' He winked grotesquely at the squire, and then led his three friends out of the tavern, back to where the rest of the company was encamped to the south of the town.

As soon as they had turned into the next street, Edritch whooped with joy. 'Twenty-five shillings for nothing! What a jackass that squire must be!'

Caynard shook his head. 'Fifty shillings. For killing Kemp.'

'But why risk being hanged for murder?' demanded Edritch. 'That squire's not going to turn around and accuse us of taking his money without doing the job for him is he?'

'That squire is perfectly capable of exacting his own justice, if he feels we've given him cause for grievance,' warned Caynard. 'And I for one don't intend to give him cause. Oh, no. We're going to kill Kemp, all right. And I intend to enjoy it.'

The army was roused before dawn by reveille the following morning, and after breakfast the heralds reiterated the king's edict that no harm should be done to women, children or the elderly, no churches or holy places robbed, nor any towns or manor houses put to the torch; and the promise of forty shillings to any man who apprehended someone performing such crimes was repeated. Nevertheless, when the rearguard departed from the town they left it in flames. If anyone was punished for starting the fire, Martin did not hear of it. The huge column of smoke that rose from the town behind them made a mockery of the king's promise to admit the townsfolk to his peace.

By now everyone had a better idea of the marching order, and this time it did not take more than a couple of hours to form the army up into its three columns. They set out much earlier than they had done the previous day. Now their route veered to the south-east. The men sang, chatted, and exchanged jests to relieve the monotony of the march. Martin found himself wishing that they could encounter the enemy, if only to relieve the tedium.

They covered over fifteen miles on the second day of the march, reaching another town about an hour before dusk. There the townsfolk told them that the bridge across the River Douve had been broken down to slow the advance of the English. The Earl of Northampton, who had been appointed constable of the army, dispatched two troops of hobelars to search for an alternative crossing, but the reconnaissance parties returned within a couple of hours to report that there was no sign of a crossing for several miles in either direction.

Holland's men were seated around their camp-fires just outside the town, finishing their supper, when Norwich rode up and ordered them to escort the team of pioneers to the site of the broken-down bridge. At Preston's command, his men gathered up their arms once more, and under cover of darkness they escorted the pioneers with their ox-drawn lumber wagons to the river-bank. There they found Cobham and two other knights in command of the crossing point.

The bridge's stone foundations remained intact, but the main wooden span had been hacked and burnt out of existence. The water was too deep to ford, and looked dark and sluggish. There was no moon, and the far bank was barely visible through the gloom. One of the pioneers crossed first, swimming at an angle as he fought the deceptively powerful current. A rope was tied around his waist which his fellow pioneers on the river-bank played out behind him. Finally he reached the far side, scrambling up the bank and disappearing into the darkness. Presently he reappeared, waving to signify that the rope had been secured, and the pioneers hauled it in until it was taut, making it fast to a sturdy tree-stump.

The master carpenter in charge of the pioneers turned to Preston. 'Your turn, now. One at a time.'

Preston ordered his men to take the bowstrings from their bow-bags, coiling them up and placing them under their hoods and caps: if a bowstring became wet, it would slacken and be rendered useless.

'Serjeant . . . ' piped up Inglewood, eyeing the dark water unhappily.

'What?' Preston demanded impatiently.

'I can't swim.'

'No one's asking you to swim,' Preston told him

irritably. 'Just hang on to the rope and haul yourself across.'

'I can't do it!'

'You're a king's archer now,' Preston reminded him. 'You don't know the meaning of the word "can't".'

The serjeant went across first. The rope sagged underneath his weight, so that he found himself hanging waist-deep in the water. Oakley went next, slinging his longbow in its cover across his back by its strap. Martin climbed down to the river's edge next, one hand on the rope, keen to get the crossing over with. He waited until Oakley had clambered out at the other side. Preston signalled for the next man to cross, and Martin gripped the wet rope tightly, lowering his legs into the water.

He gasped as he sank up to his waist in the cold water. It swirled about his hips, the current trying to drag him away from the rope. He found himself more concerned that the current would pull his shoes off his feet than he was about losing his grip. He inched his way along the rope, the water buffeting his buttocks, and soon fell into a steady rhythm as his powerful arms and shoulders hauled him across to the far side. He managed to get one foot on the muddy bank, and then Oakley clasped his hand, heaving him up to safety. He stood shivering in the cold as Preston waved the next man across.

'Come on, you lot, keep moving!'

Once the whole platoon was across, Preston divided them into groups of three or four and ordered them to form a line of pickets along the perimeter of the bridge-head. Martin found himself with Newbolt, Pip Herrick and Ned Skeffington, standing in the darkness by a clump of marsh reeds about forty yards from the wrecked bridge. He took his bowstave from its cover and restrung it, his eyes searching the darkness ahead for any signs of movement. All was quiet apart from the steady croaking of frogs. Suddenly, an eerie sound boomed across the marshes. Martin instinctively reached for one of his arrows.

'Marsh bittern,' Newbolt told him, sitting down to take off his shoes to tip the water out of them. 'Christ's pain, I'm cold!' he grumbled. It was characteristic of him that he started nearly every conversation with a gripe of some kind. 'Let's see if we can get a fire going.'

'Are you sure we ought to?' Martin asked dubiously. 'If there are any Frenchmen nearby . . . '

'We're in the God-damned middle of nowhere, for the love of Christ! Who's going to see a fire out here? Besides, if we don't get ourselves dried out, we'll like as not freeze to death.'

Of the four of them, Newbolt was the only one who had served in the king's army before, so Martin reluctantly acceded to his greater experience, although he half-expected Preston to come thundering out of the darkness the moment they had got it going, ordering them to douse it. Behind them, however, several more of the pioneers had crossed the river, and one of the first things they did was to set up flaming torches on either side of the banks so that they could see what they were doing.

Herrick and Skeffington managed to find enough dead wood scattered about to make a fire, while Jankin stomped up and down, alternatively beating his arms against his sides and blowing into his cupped hands. Martin stood by placidly, gazing across the marshes into the darkness. Behind them, the pioneers quickly set up a pulley system across the river and began to rebuild the bridge. When Martin had first realised that the army could not move on until the bridge was repaired, he had thought it would require a halt of several days, but each time he stole a backwards glance he was astonished by how much progress the pioneers had made in such a short space of time. The noise of hammering and sawing was constant, accompanied by the occasional shout, a call for more nails or a request for help in driving a new strut into the river-bank. The skeleton of the new bridge was completed in a matter of hours, the pioneers scrambling nimbly across the wooden framework with the agility of squirrels. They were obviously used to labouring as a close-knit team in such conditions, and it was almost a pleasure to watch them work.

The night wore on. Preston came by at irregular intervals to make sure that they had not fallen asleep. Martin felt dog-tired, but in spite of the meagre fire that Jankin had managed to get going, the cold kept him awake. Halfway through the night some archers from Sir Hugh Despenser's company came to relieve them. By then the pioneers had laid enough of the bridge's planks to enable men to cross on foot in single file. They encamped for the rest of the night on the north bank of the river, and Martin immediately fell asleep.

It seemed as if he had no sooner closed his eyes than Preston was kicking him awake. Dawn was rising to find the bridge completed, and the rest of the vanguard marching up from the town. Daylight revealed the landscape ahead of them, a vast expanse of marshland with a narrow causeway barely wide enough for six men to march abreast snaking away from the bridge, towards the east.

They marched across the causeway for about three miles until they came to a large, walled town surrounded by an extensive network of dykes and moats. A strong fortress dominated it, and even to Martin's inexperienced eyes the place looked impregnable. As they drew near to the town, however, Sir Godefroi d'Harcourt rode to the front of the column with Norwich and met two Norman knights at its entrance. D'Harcourt and the two Normans greeted one another amicably as if they were old friends, and before long the army was marching into the town unopposed.

At first the streets seemed deserted, but wherever Martin looked he saw nervous eyes peering from windows, or shutters being hurriedly slammed shut. He drew Preston's attention to the fact, instinctively taking his longbow from its bag.

Preston had already seen them. 'Townsfolk,' he said dismissively.

'How can we be certain it's not an ambush?' Martin asked uncertainly.

Preston chuckled. 'If it was an ambush, they would've been sure not to let us see them. Not until it was too late, anyway.'

It was the first French settlement they had reached that had not been largely abandoned by its populace, and somehow that seemed to keep looting and pillaging to a minimum. It transpired that the two Norman knights in command of the town's garrison were protégés of d'Harcourt, in the pay of the English, so the orders to do no harm to the townsfolk were to be strictly enforced. Nevertheless, the army needed to replenish its stock of food, and after a late breakfast Holland's men were put to work foraging for victuals from a whole street of houses.

Martin and Rudcock approached one of the houses. Rudcock tried the door, but it was locked. He hammered on it with his fist. 'Come on, open up! *Ouvrez, ouvrez!*'

Martin stared at him. 'What?'

'It's French,' explained Rudcock. 'It means "open up".'

'Oh.' Martin tried to make a mental note of it. He did not know how long he was going to be in France, but it could do no harm to learn a little of the language.

No one opened up. Rudcock threw his shoulder against the door. It splintered open. Inside, a terrified-looking man stood in front of his family – a wife, two children and their grandmother – who cowered in one corner. The man was wielding an iron poker, but Rudcock snatched it from his hand and tossed it out into the street. He kept his sword in his scabbard to show that he meant no harm, and Martin followed his lead. The family was clearly unconvinced; when Martin raised a hand to push back his hood and run his fingers through his tangled mop of hair, they all flinched as if he had threatened them. It bemused him to find that people could be so terrified of him. These people were all well-dressed compared to peasants, not unlike the townsfolk of Leicester; but Martin had always associated fine clothes with the nobility, whom he held in reluctant awe. Yet here were these well-dressed, important-looking people all trembling with fear at the sight of him. He tried to view the situation from their point of view. How would he have felt if two armed men had broken into the Kemps' cottage at Knighton? Angry, perhaps, but he would certainly not have cowered in fear like these contemptuous creatures, he decided.

Once disarmed, the master of the house tried to be helpful and compliant, but Rudcock was not interested. He knew what he was looking for and where he would find it. With a vaguely apologetic shrug to the family, Martin followed him through to the larder. They gathered up as much food as they could carry between them.

The army spent the rest of that day in and around the town. Exhaustion suddenly caught up with Martin around late afternoon, and after an early supper he fell into a deep sleep, waking up shortly before reveille the following morning.

Its supplies replenished, the army set out shortly after dawn, leaving another town burning in its wake contrary to orders. They marched across a dozen miles of low, marshy ground until they came to a small village on the west bank of another river. There the army halted, and after the best part of an hour spent waiting around, the order was given to make camp. Another bridge in their path had been broken down, and once again the pioneers had to be brought forward to effect repairs.

Preston and his men lit a fire and began to roast some beef. As they were eating, Holland came by. 'You'd best make sure you and your men get a good night's rest,' he told Preston in a low voice. Preston nodded.

'What's going on, Sir Thomas?' Inglewood, belonging to a slightly higher stratum of society than his fellow archers, had no qualms about speaking to Sir Thomas without waiting to be spoken to.

Holland rubbed his jaw, glancing across the river. He took a deep breath. 'There's a town on the other side of the river, about four miles from here,' he explained curtly. 'We were hoping to reach it by nightfall, but since the bridge has been destroyed that's out of the question. Our spies tell us that the Marshal of Normandy has levied a sizeable body of troops, and intends to make a stand at the town.'

'There's going to be a battle?' asked Inglewood, wide-eyed.

Holland nodded absently. 'Aye, it looks that way.'

The following day was the Feast of Saint Mary Magdalen. Once again the pioneers had finished repairing the bridge by dawn, and after a hurried breakfast the vanguard crossed the river and climbed to the top of a nearby ridge overlooking the town that Holland had told them about. The English knights and men-at-arms dismounted, leaving their horses tied behind the ridge, while the marshals hurried to get the troops into battle array. The archers were formed into a long line facing the town, interspersed with dismounted men-at-arms and hobelars, while the Welsh archers were positioned at the flanks. Much activity was visible in and around the walled town less than two miles away, but there was no sign of any French troops approaching.

Martin's mouth felt dry as he took his bow from its cover and planted a dozen arrows in the ground at his feet. The veterans seemed unconcerned at the prospect of imminent battle, chatting and joking amongst themselves as they waited. He tried to feign a similar lack of concern. Inglewood, Tate and Wighton were white-faced and trembling. Martin held a hand in front of his own face and detected a slight tremor. He flexed his fingers. His legs felt weak, and his bowels churned like a mill-race.

Holland had dismounted to stand with his men. Somehow Martin found that reassuring. He had always thought of the nobility as too proud to get down off their horses and face the enemy on foot with the men. Holland had put on armour that morning, the first time Martin had seen him wearing it. He wore a steel breastplate over a coat of mail, cuisses on his thighs made of steel plates riveted to hardened leather, steel greaves on his calves, articulated steel sabatons on his feet, and steel rerebraces, vambraces and couters to protect his arms. A pair of articulated steel gauntlets protected his hands, and on his head he wore a vizored bascinet over a chain-mail coif. His coat of arms was proudly displayed on both his shield and his jupon. He looked dangerous and threatening as he marched up and down the ranks of his company, exchanging a few words here and there with his serjeants and one or two of his men. He was in good humour; it seemed that the prospect of battle pleased him.

Martin wished he could share the knight's feelings. This had been what he had wanted, after all: a chance to fight for his king. Why, then, did he feel so frightened? But he already knew the answer to that one. The battles of his imagination, where he rode gloriously against the foe, cutting a swathe of death and destruction before him, were very different from the grim reality he had encountered on the beach south of Saint-Vaast-la-Hougue, and after that on the road to Quettehou. He was not a knight in armour, able to fight with the advantage of sitting astride a massive war-horse; he was an archer, a foot-soldier, condemned to stand and fight – and perhaps die – on the very patch of ground he now occupied. There could be neither advance nor retreat; he had just to stand and await the French attack. The waiting was the worst part of all: it gave him time to think of all the ways a man might be killed in battle through no fault of his own. In a one-on-one situation he feared no man, but anything could happen in the confusion of a mêlée. He might be spitted on a lance, decapitated by the wildest stroke of a sword, or even killed by an arrow that he never saw coming . . .

'It looks like they're moving, Sir Thomas,' rumbled Preston.

Martin snapped out of his reverie and glanced up. Sure enough, a column of armed men was emerging from one of the town gates, led by the banner that Martin had seen on that first day on the beach – a green lion rampant on a yellow background.

'Hold your positions,' growled Preston. 'It won't be long now.'

The column continued to emerge from the town. There were several hundred men as far as Martin could tell, perhaps even one or two thousand. And how many on the English side? It was hard to tell from the middle of the ranks, but Martin guessed at least two and a half thousand, maybe even as many as three. The bulk of the army remained on the west bank of the river. The men in the English vanguard seemed to outnumber the French, but the French column was still emerging from the town. How many more men were there yet to appear?

At least the English had gained the advantage of height, Martin noted with approval. The Frenchmen charging on foot up the hill towards them would be sorely tired even before they got to grips with the waiting English . . .

244

'Where are they going?' asked Villiers, standing beside his master.

Martin looked towards the French column again. It had not turned to advance on the English position as might have been expected, but was continuing along the road leading east, away from the ridge.

One of the men-at-arms behind Martin laughed nervously. 'They're running away!'

'Retreating, perhaps, but not running away,' Preston observed, almost to himself.

The rear of the French column had emerged from the town now. Two thousand men at the most, Martin guessed; barely two-thirds the number of men in the English formation. The column continued along the road leading to the east.

Norwich rode up on his palfrey and reined in alongside Holland, who now stood with the Prince of Wales, Warwick, Cobham and Despenser, a short distance from where Martin was positioned; close enough for him to be able to hear their conference.

'What's happening?' demanded Norwich.

'The French are withdrawing,' Holland said coolly.

'That much I can see for myself,' Norwich snapped irritably.

No one in the English ranks cheered. It was some time before the realisation that there was to be no battle sank in. In spite of his earlier fear, Martin felt disappointed, deflated. He felt like an iron poker that had been heated up until it was white hot, and then put aside, unused and left to cool. The burning in his blood needed to be quenched in battle, not left to cool in the breeze.

The men were forced to stay in their positions for another interminable hour while two troops of mounted archers were sent to follow the retreating French at a distance, to make sure that the manoeuvre was not a feint. By now it was boredom rather than fear that troubled

Martin. There was little doubt in the English ranks that the French retreat was genuine, and not a ruse of any kind. Just to make sure, d'Harcourt rode down to the town with Norwich and a troop of hobelars. Norwich presently returned to report that there were no enemy troops left in the town. As far as d'Harcourt could tell from questioning a few of the townsfolk, Marshal Bertrand had been planning to make a stand, but had not expected the English to cross the river so swiftly, and had found himself outflanked.

The battle lines were broken up, the men complaining about the cowardice of the French and boasting about the great deeds of valour they would have performed if there had been a battle. The vanguard advanced down the side of the ridge in a series of loose formations. Earthworks were visible around the town walls, hastily begun and abandoned incomplete. As Preston's platoon approached the north gate. Martin saw d'Harcourt seated astride his courser, giving terse commands in French to one of his squires. The Norman knight's voice was terse with barely controlled emotion as he indicated two round objects stuck on poles atop the battlements directly over the gateway. Martin had never seen such objects before, but there could be no mistaking them: human skulls, picked clean of flesh by carrion birds and bleached by the elements, their grinning jaws hanging slackly. White-faced, the squire nodded and dismounted, hurriedly climbing up to the battlements to remove the offending objects.

'I wonder who they were?' mused Villiers, riding alongside his master at the head of the company. There was neither shock nor outrage in his voice: dismembered body parts displayed in public places as an example to others were a common enough sight in many parts of Christendom.

'Doubtless friends of Sir Godefroi's, executed for

treason,' Holland replied absently. 'There were many Norman knights who fought with us in Brittany.' He did not seem to care that at least two of his former allies had been decapitated for having fought alongside the English.

Many of the town's narrow streets had been blocked by barricades of furniture, but with no one to defend them they were easily pushed over by the English troops, each splintering crash of wood accompanied by cheers. Cheated of an opportunity to face the French on the field of battle, they had to slake their thirst for destruction on the property of the townsfolk.

Like the last town they had passed through, this one had not been deserted by its inhabitants, but for an altogether different reason. The last town had been friendly to the English; or at least, the commanders of its garrison had been, and that was what had counted. But it was clear that the folk of this town had been expecting Bertrand and his men to protect them, and had even been helping the French troops to prepare the town for a siege. Bertrand's sudden withdrawal had left them unexpectedly undefended, and now they found themselves at the mercy of the English. The English troops knew that the townsfolk had been planning to resist, and they treated them more roughly than they had done at the last town when searching for food. This time, money and jewellery were seized right from under the noses of the owners. The townsfolk were helpless to prevent it. They could see that the Englishmen, cheated of their battle, were spoiling for a fight, and the townsfolk had to tread warily to avoid provoking them, stoically suffering indignities and humiliations.

Martin watched with Preston as a group of archers robbed a handful of terrified burghers at sword-point, first ordering them to hand over their valuables and then likewise demanding their fine clothes. They were not satisfied even when the burghers stood naked and shivering in the thin sunshine.

'Now kneel,' ordered the leader of the archers. 'Go on, get down on your knees!'

The burghers did not seem to understand, so the archer punched one of them in the stomach with a gauntleted fist. As the burgher bent double, the archer grabbed a fistful of his hair and forced him down on to his knees. The other burghers got the message, and knelt hurriedly.

'Lie down – flat, on your stomachs! Crawl like the worms you are!' The archer kicked another burgher between the shoulder-blades so that he sprawled in the ordure-filled gutter, whimpering. 'Come on, down on your bellies, you French scum!' When they were all lying down, the archer raised the hem of his tunic and urinated on them. His comrades joined in the game, laughing.

'We should do summat,' Martin whispered to Preston.

The serjeant turned to regard him with amusement. 'Like what? Join in, perhaps?'

Martin pulled an expression of disgust. 'The king's edict . . . '

'The rules of war take precedence, lad,' Preston reminded him. 'If a town surrenders immediately, the citizens are to be treated honourably. If they resist, on the other hand . . . '

'These people hardly resisted . . . '

'They were planning to. They would've done, too, if Bertrand and his men hadn't turned tail and fled, like the cowardly scum these French dogs are.'

Martin slipped away from Preston and the others shortly after that. He needed some time by himself, to think. But wherever he went he saw more scenes of brutality. Soldiers trooped in and out of the larger houses, emptying them of food and valuables. Pieces of furniture were thrown from upper-storey windows for the sheer fun of watching them smash against the ground. Martin saw women of all ages pinned to the ground, struggling and screaming while English troops took turns at raping them, laughing, goading one another on. Women who tried to resist were savagely beaten. Sometimes they were beaten even if they did not resist, just for the hell of it. Martin wanted to intervene, but he knew he would only earn himself a beating if he tried to interfere. He was an idealist, but pragmatic enough not to want to get beaten up on principle. There was nothing he could do to defend these people; it made him feel impotent, sick with rage and despair at the senseless brutality of it all.

He thought about what Preston had said about the rules of war. It made no sense to him. He had always considered it chivalrous to admire courage and despise cowardice; yet those who tried to defend their homes were punished, while those who surrendered immediately were to be treated honourably. That was the theory, anyway, but then Martin recalled how the last town had readily surrendered, and the English had nonetheless left it in flames. It might have been argued that that had been the handiwork of common soldiers like himself rather than chivalrous noblemen bound by the rules of war, but the king's edict to protect the people of Normandy did not seem to be too strictly enforced. Martin was learning that pillage, brutality and destruction were an integral part of warfare, and that the nobility evaded the constraints of the chivalric code by leaving the dirty work to the common soldiery, most of whom seemed more than happy to oblige.

He suddenly noticed that dusk was falling. He had not realised how late in the day it was, and hurried through the gloomy streets in search of the rest of his unit, or at least a familiar face. He was making his way down a back alley when two armed men stepped out of the shadows ahead of him, blocking the way. At first he thought they must be French, and he panicked, reaching for the hilt of his broadsword. Then he recognised them as Edritch and Lefthand. His first reaction was one of relief at seeing someone he recognised, and he raised one hand in an uncertain greeting. He was not particularly friendly with Edritch or Lefthand, but that was not enough to explain why they made no attempt to return his greeting. His instincts were screaming that something was wrong long before he heard Caynard's voice behind him.

'Get him!'

Martin glanced over his shoulder to see Caynard and Murray standing at the other end of the alley, blocking his retreat. The two pairs of men advanced, closing in on him. He turned to a back door in one wall of the alley. It was locked. He threw his shoulder against it, but it held firm. He turned his back on the door to face the four men. They stood around him in a half-circle, their faces grim but uncertain.

'What the devil do you want?' Martin demanded angrily, unnerved by their strange and threatening behaviour.

Caynard grinned, showing dirty and jagged teeth in the gloom. 'Scared, Lancelot? You should be.'

'Go to Hell.'

'Go on, Piers!' urged Murray.

Edritch drew a dagger from his belt, taking a step forward as he thrust the blade towards Martin's stomach. It was so sudden, so unexpected, Martin did not have a chance to draw his rondel. He stepped aside to avoid the dagger thrust, at the same time throwing a punch at Edritch, catching him on the jaw. As Edritch staggered back, the other three closed in. Martin tried to break away, but Lefthand grabbed him by the shoulder and threw him back against the wall. Murray drove his fist into Martin's stomach, kneeing him in the face as he doubled up. Pain exploded through Martin's skull. He struggled to keep his grip on consciousness. It was obvious that they intended to kill him, although he could not understand why. He knew that if he fainted now, they must surely finish him.

He felt hands grab him roughly by the arms and haul him upright, so that he was face to face with Caynard. There was a dagger in Caynard's hand, and as Lefthand and Murray struggled to hold Martin steady, Caynard tried to plunge the blade into his chest. Martin tried to squirm aside. The razor-sharp blade sliced through his leather jerkin. He felt an icy, burning sensation in his left side. The blade came away with blood on it, and Martin could see a dark stain spreading rapidly across his tunic.

'Hold still, you God-damned whoreson!' snarled Caynard. 'You'll only make it worse for yourself.'

Martin struggled with renewed frenzy. He might be badly cut, but he was not dead yet, and he was damned if he was going to let these whoresons kill him. He lashed out with his right foot, catching Caynard just below the kneecap. Caynard cried out in agony, dropping the dagger. Then Lefthand's elbow smashed into Martin's cheek. Bright lights exploded in his head. He felt his consciousness slipping away from him. The cloth of his tunic was warm and sticky where it was soaked with his own blood.

'What the bloody hell's going on here?' demanded an unfamiliar voice with a strange accent. It distracted Lefthand long enough for Martin to get his right arm free. He lashed out with his fist, but it failed to connect with anything.

'Scarper!' Caynard's voice, hoarse, panicky. Murray threw Martin against the wall again. His head struck the stonework with an audible crack, and suddenly his legs refused to support him any longer. As he slid to the ground, he felt someone kick him viciously in the stomach. He no longer cared. He heard running footsteps, a scream of agony, but it all sounded very distant, and he was not convinced that it had anything to do with him any more. Not any of it.

CHAPTER ELEVEN

Martin awoke to find himself adrift on a sea of pain. His head throbbed dully, his right cheek felt sore and swollen, his stomach was churning, and the whole of his left side seemed to be aflame with agony. He welcomed the pain: it told him he was still alive.

He came to slowly and reluctantly. He seemed to be lying face-down on a straw-stuffed pallet of some kind. He could hear distant voices, talking in a foreign tongue. The accent was melodic yet the tone was terse, as if the two speakers were arguing about something.

He opened his eyes cautiously. A burning brazier stood in the centre of the room, an iron thrust amongst the glowing coals to heat it. By the brazier's light he could see the two men who were arguing. One was tall, thin and elderly, with a long white beard that came down to his belt, dressed in a coarse, knee-length woollen tunic and a long cloak; the other was stocky and broad-shouldered, with a shaggy mane of hair, bushy eyebrows, and a luxuriant beard. His torso was naked except for a leather jerkin, exposing a shaggy mat of hair on his chest, and equally hairy, muscular arms. Martin could not recognise the language, but he guessed it must be French. Beyond the two men he could just make out Piers Edritch, sitting hunched in one corner, bound hand and foot and tightly gagged. So, they had both been captured by the French.

Nearer the pallet – less than an arm's length away – Martin could see his broadsword in its scabbard, propped against the wall. The two foreigners did not seem to be paying any attention to him. He dared not move for fear of attracting their notice, but as far as he could tell the men had neglected to tie him up. He wondered what they were arguing about. It must have been obvious to them that he was only a churl, not worth trying to ransom, so why they had not simply killed him was a mystery. They might yet change their minds on that score, so this was probably the last chance he would get. Slowly, with barely perceptible movements, he began to reach out for his sword.

'I wouldn't bother if I were you, boy,' said a voice close by, speaking with the same sing-song accent that Martin had heard in the alley. He had heard it somewhere else before, too, but he could not place it. He twisted his head around, ignoring the pain that lanced through his neck and up into his skull, and searched for the speaker. He had not previously noticed the fifth man in the room, seated in a chair by the foot of the pallet. He was in his late twenties, short and stocky, with dark brown hair cut in a pudding-basin fringe emerging from beneath a greasy woollen Monmouth cap, and a bushy, drooping moustache. His dark eyes twinkled with amusement in the candle light. 'We're all on the same side, or supposed to be,' he continued. 'You *are* English, aren't you, boy?'

Martin nodded, in spite of the pain. 'Aye,' he managed to gasp. Now he was able to make out the green and white livery of the three foreigners, despite the gloom. He breathed a sigh of relief, the tension melting from his body.

The other two men broke off their argument and turned to face him. 'Oh, so he's awake, is he?' said the broad-shouldered one. 'Who's your master, boy?' he asked Martin.

'Sir Thomas Holland.'

The three Welshman exchanged glances. They were obviously familiar with the name.

'I should be getting back to my platoon,' added Martin, making as if to rise from the pallet.

The man with the bushy moustache rose to his feet and gently forced Martin back down. 'You rest easy, boy. You've got yourself a nasty wound there. It needs to be cauterised.'

The word meant nothing to Martin. 'What do you mean?'

The broad-shouldered one chuckled. 'You'll find out soon enough.' He turned to address the elderly man with the long white beard. 'How's that cautery iron coming along, Dafydd?'

'Nearly ready.'

'Have you got a name, boy?' asked the man with the moustache.

Martin nodded. 'It's Kemp. Martin Kemp.'

'I'm Ieuan ap Morgan. This here is Madog Fychan, and old greybeard over there is Dafydd ap Trahaiarn, our physician.'

'Why were this fellow and his friends trying to kill you?' Dafydd demanded sternly, indicating Edritch.

Martin shook his head. 'I don't know.'

'And you expect us to believe that?' Madog demanded angrily.

'If you want my opinion, it's the wrong person we're questioning,' said Ieuan, and indicated Edritch. 'If we want to know what was going through his mind, it's him we should be asking.'

'We'll come to him presently,' grunted Madog. 'Is that iron ready yet, Dafydd?'

The physician nodded, wrapping a cloth round the fingers of his right hand and binding it in place with a leather thong. He knotted the thong tightly with his left hand and his teeth. 'Hold him down.'

Before Martin realised what was happening, Madog was seated on his ankles, pinning his legs to the pallet.

'You'd best sink your teeth into this,' said Ieuan, holding a folded leather strap for Martin to bite on. 'We don't want you biting your own tongue off, do we?' He grabbed Martin's wrists and pinned down his arms. In spite of his wiry frame, Ieuan was deceptively muscular.

'Tell me, boy, do you know what extreme pain is like?' Dafydd asked conversationally, drawing the iron from the brazier and inspecting the white-hot tip with a critical eye.

Martin nodded, gripping the leather thong between his teeth.

'Good,' said Dafydd. 'Then this shouldn't come as too much of a shock to you.' He applied the white-hot tip of the cautery iron to Martin's side.

The agony was excruciating. Martin tried to buck on the pallet, but Ieuan and Madog held him down firmly. He could hear the sizzle of burning flesh, and a stench not unlike charred pork filled the room. He squeezed shut his eyes, sobbing through the leather strap on which he had clamped his teeth as if his very life depended on it. The agony was far worse than the pain of the original wound had been. It seemed to last for ever. Just when he thought he must mercifully faint, Dafydd took the glowing blade away. The agony receded, leaving a dull but insistent pain that was mild only by comparison.

Dafydd replaced the iron in the brazier and picked up a candle, bending over Martin's torso to inspect his handiwork. 'That seems to have done the trick,' he remarked, stroking his beard thoughtfully. 'Fortunately for you, it wasn't a deep cut. I'll put an ointment of groundsel beaten with salt-free grease on it – that should take away some of the pain, and help it heal up nicely. You'll have a nice big scar, of course.'

Madog moved off the pallet, and Ieuan released Martin's wrists, clapping him on the other shoulder. 'Something to talk about on your wedding night, eh, boy?'

Martin barely managed to spit out the leather strap. The ordeal had left him too drained to talk.

'You're lucky it was us that rescued you,' added Ieuan. 'Dafydd's a real master at this kind of thing.'

'So I should be,' retorted Dafydd. 'I've been healing wounds like that one ever since I was at Cambuskenneth – long before any of you lot were born.' He produced a mortar and pestle and began to grind up a mixture of mustard seeds and herbs, occasionally adding oils and ointments to the mixture.

'Now, let's find out what all this was about, shall we?' suggested Madog, bending over Edritch and seizing him by the throat. He lifted him easily with one brawny arm and placed him in a chair, before ripping the gag off roughly. Edritch was evidently terrified, his eyes bulging from his head. 'Now then, why don't you start by telling us who you are?'

'Piers Edritch. I'm in the same platoon as Kemp.'

'Why were you trying to kill him?'

'I weren't trying to kill him!' bleated Edritch.

'Ballocks!' scoffed Madog. 'We saw you with our own eyes.' He wrapped a cloth around his hand and grasped the handle of the iron being heated in the brazier. 'The truth now, before I start giving you the same treatment Dafydd just gave your companion. We'll see how much you like it, eh, boy?'

Ashen-faced, Edritch broke out in a sweat. 'You wouldn't dare! I'm one of Sir Thomas Holland's men. If he found out . . . '

'If he found out, I'm sure he'd be just as interested as we are to know why his men are trying to kill one another,' said Madog. 'But he's not going to find out. In Gwent we like to sort out our own problems, without recourse to your English lords and your English justice. We dispense our own.'

'Look, boy, you're a dead man already,' Ieuan told

Edritch mildly. 'How much you suffer before you die is entirely up to you.'

A spasm shook Edritch's body, and he vomited into his own lap. Dafydd grimaced with distaste, while Madog patiently waited for the spasms to die down before drawing the iron's glowing tip from the brazier.

'What about the screams?' asked Dafydd.

Madog laughed. 'The English have been murdering the townsfolk since dusk. Who can tell an English scream from a French one?' He held the tip of the iron an inch from Edritch's nose. 'The truth now, boy.'

'In God's name! Please! I beg you! Don't kill me!' wailed Edritch. 'For the love of Jesus! I'll tell you everything, I swear!'

'Why were you trying to kill him?' demanded Madog.

'We were to be paid fifty shillings each to do it.'

'Fifty shillings!' Madog exclaimed incredulously.

'Someone with a fat purse must hate you a lot, boy,' Ieuan remarked to Martin.

'Who was going to pay you?' Dafydd asked Edritch.

'I don't know.'

Madog flicked the iron against Edritch's cheek. The red-hot metal was in contact with his skin for only a moment, but it was long enough for the flesh to blister and burst. Edritch screamed in agony. Martin felt sick, but only because he knew his own skin must have done likewise when Dafydd had cauterised his wound.

'Who was going to pay you?' repeated Dafydd.

Edritch was sobbing with pain. 'I don't know,' he mumbled, his cracked voice muffled by the awful wound on his cheek. 'I swear it, by the soul of my dead father!'

'Oh aye?' said Ieuan. 'And which one of the thousands you doubtless have to choose from would that be?'

'You must have some idea who was going to pay you,' persisted Dafydd.

Edritch shook his head. 'It were Will who came up with the job. He arranged it all.'

'Who's Will?' demanded Ieuan.

'He means Will Caynard,' Martin managed to gasp. 'One of the other three men who attacked me.'

'And does he have a hundred and fifty shillings to spare?' Ieuan asked him.

Martin shook his head. 'I wouldn't have thought so,' he croaked. It was a princely sum, as much as a ploughman could hope to earn in eleven years.

'There was a squire,' sobbed Edritch. 'I don't know his name . . . '

'His master's arms?' demanded Dafydd.

'A red dragon with two legs on a white background.' With tears streaming down his blistered face, Edritch nodded in Martin's direction. 'He knows who it is.'

Dafydd turned to Martin, his eyebrows arched questioningly.

Martin managed a faint nod. It was beginning to make some kind of sense at last.

'What about the others who helped you?' demanded Madog, returning the iron to the brazier. 'What were their names?'

'Bartholomew Lefthand and Gilbert Murray.'

'I know them,' said Martin. 'I recognised them when they attacked me. They're in my platoon.'

Madog nodded in satisfaction, and turned away, casually reaching for the haft of a great battleaxe that was propped against the wall nearby. He swung back suddenly, almost casually lopping Edritch's head clean off his shoulders. Blood fountained briefly from his truncated neck. His head rolled into a corner, a look of terror and defeat frozen on its features. Martin buried his face in the pallet. He had not liked Edritch, but even under the circumstances he was not convinced that he had deserved to be so callously murdered, defenceless and bound hand and foot.

Ieuan put a hand on Martin's shoulder. 'It had to be done, boy,' he said grimly. 'If we'd let him live, he would have had no choice but to try to kill you again – not just for the money, but to stop you from talking.'

'But . . . surely we should've taken him to the king's marshals . . . ?' protested Martin.

'Then it would've been your word against theirs as to who started the quarrel,' said Dafydd. 'And even if the marshals had believed your word above the four of them, they would have just stretched Edritch's neck for him. Believe me, Madog's way is quicker.' The way Dafydd used the present tense suggested to Martin that he was not ruling out Madog's way for future use. Martin shuddered, the sight of Piers' head flying across the room imprinted on his memory.

'You know this squire he spoke of?' asked Madog, as Dafydd began to daub his poultice on Martin's wound. It looked and smelled repulsive, but felt cool and soothing.

Martin nodded. 'I think so. The arms that Edritch described are the arms of Sir John Beaumont – my master from England. He has a squire named Richard Stamford who believes . . . that he has cause to hate me.'

'For ten pounds, he must hate you a great deal,' Ieuan remarked sardonically. 'What did you do to earn such a hatred?'

'He can afford it,' Martin said dismissively.

'That's not what I asked.'

Martin shrugged. 'It's a long story.'

Ieuan chuckled. 'Then save it for a long winter's evening.'

'I have to get back to my platoon.' Martin did not want to be accused of deserting. As he tried to raise himself from the pallet, however, he found himself too weak, and Ieuan had little difficulty in gently forcing him back down.

'You're not going anywhere,' the Welshman told him firmly. 'What you need now is rest, boy.'

Martin slept feverishly that night. He dreamed that he was back on the road to Quettehou, only this time he watched from a distance as the mounted knight charged at Edritch, who stood stock-still as if frozen in time. The knight bore the arms of Sir John Beaumont, but when he took off his helmet once again it was Beatrice's face that was revealed. Laughing, she swung at Edritch's neck with the broadsword that Warwick had given to Martin. Edritch's head was lopped from his shoulders, and rolled down the road until it came to rest at Martin's feet. He glanced down at the disembodied head, but instead of seeing Edritch's face he saw his own, laughing up at him.

He woke with a scream. He was still lying on the pallet in the room where the Welshman had tortured and killed Edritch in the hellish glow of the brazier, but now, with the coming of dawn, sunlight streamed through the cracks in the shutters on the windows. He sat upright for a moment, gasping for breath.

The door opened, and Ieuan entered. 'What was that?'

'I . . . I must have had a nightmare,' admitted Martin, feeling foolish.

Ieuan smiled, and began to remove the shutters so that sunlight and fresh air flooded into the room. 'You don't surprise me. You were tossing and turning feverishly all night. We didn't think you'd make it at one point, but you look well enough this morning, considering all you've been through. You stay there,' he added, heading back towards the door. 'I'll get you something to eat. You lost a fair amount of blood last night. You need to build your strength up.' He left the room, and Martin heard his feet descending a creaking flight of wooden steps. Martin swung his legs off the mattress and sat on the edge of the pallet. Even that much movement left him feeling completely drained. There was a dull throbbing in his head, and the wound in his side still smarted painfully.

There was no sign of Edritch's body or the brazier, nothing to remind him of the nightmarish events of the previous night. He wondered if they too had been nightmares. He glanced out of the window, across the rooftops of the town they had entered after Bertrand's men had abandoned it. The sky was blue, the sun already over the horizon. Martin knew that Preston and the others must be wondering where he had got to.

There were more footsteps on the stairs, lighter this time, and Dafydd entered the room. 'I don't remember saying you could sit up,' he told Martin sternly.

'I don't remember you saying I couldn't,' Martin grunted irritably.

Dafydd chuckled, and held the back of one hand to Martin's forehead. 'The fever's gone, anyway,' he said, sitting down on the pallet beside Martin so that he could unbind the dressing he had wrapped around his torso. 'Let's see how that wound of yours is.'

The wound had neither burst again nor gone septic. Dafydd applied some more of his poultice and put on a fresh dressing.

'Will I be able to move about?' asked Martin.

Dafydd pursed his lips. 'You need time to rest and recuperate, to give this wound a chance to heal properly. In the normal run of things I'd insist that you spent at least another week in this bed.'

'To Hell with that,' said Martin, to Dafydd's amusement. 'This isn't the normal run of things.'

'Most of the army's already moved on, and our company is moving out today,' admitted Dafydd. 'While I'm not happy about letting you set out on the march, it has to be healthier for you than leaving you here to the tender mercies of the townsfolk. Those few of them who weren't slain in last night's excesses, that is.'

261

'Do you know if my company – Sir Thomas Holland's – is still in the town?'

Dafydd shook his head. 'Madog's gone to see if he can find someone from your company to let them know you haven't deserted.'

'Will he tell them how I were wounded?'

Dafydd chuckled again. 'Ieuan thought it might be best if we made out you were ambushed by a couple of Frenchmen. Your Master Caynard and his friends won't be inclined to contradict you, and Ieuan thought you might like a chance to take care of them personally.'

Martin nodded dubiously. 'Surely you can't approve?' he asked tentatively.

Dafydd regarded him in incomprehension. 'Why not?'

'Doesn't the Bible say "Thou shalt not kill"?'

'That doesn't stop the Bishop of Durham. What's good enough for his grace is good enough for me. Are you trying to tell me you've never killed before?'

Martin hung his head. 'Twice,' he whispered. 'But they were both Frenchmen,' he added hurriedly. 'It was my duty to my king . . . '

'If you can kill a Frenchman, you can kill an Englishman,' Dafydd said with another chuckle. 'The Bible also teaches us "An eye for an eye and a tooth for a tooth." Because if you don't kill them, then believe me, boy, they'll kill you now. Maybe you'd best stop worrying about your duty to your king and start worrying about your duty to yourself.'

Martin still did not understand, but before he could ask Dafydd to explain further, Ieuan returned with a bowl of broth. 'Get this inside you, boy. Soup just like my old mother used to make. It should help you get your strength back.'

Dafydd finished tying the dressing. 'There. Put a fresh dressing on each day, and make sure you keep the wound clean.'

Martin tried Ieuan's broth. It tasted foul, but he felt it would be churlish to say so, considering all that Ieuan and his friends had done to help him. Besides which he was ravenous, and foul or not he devoured it hungrily.

'He's got a healthy appetite on him this morning,' Dafydd remarked to Ieuan. 'That's always a good sign. Here,' he added to Martin, reaching inside a pouch at his belt and pulling out what appeared to be a small twig. 'Chew on this for a while,' he recommended.

Martin eyed the twig dubiously. 'What is it?'

'Liquorice root.'

'Will it help to heal my wound?'

'No,' admitted Dafydd. 'But it tastes nice, and it'll keep your breath fresh.'

Martin shook his head, chuckling, and washed his hands and face in a basin of cold water Dafydd had placed by his pallet. Ieuan searched through the chests and wardrobes in the house until he found a white linen chemise, holding it up for Martin to see. 'I'm afraid your own tunic is beyond repair, but this looks to be about your size.'

'Thank you.'

Ieuan helped him to pull the chemise over his head, and he finished dressing. He was buckling on his sword-belt when Madog returned. 'Holland's company has already moved on,' he announced. 'But the king has sent word for the army to gather at a place called Torigny, a few miles from here. We should catch up with the rest of the vanguard there.'

'Do you feel well enough to walk?' Ieuan asked Martin.

Martin pushed himself to his feet. He felt a little dizzy for a moment, but the feeling soon passed. He nodded. 'Aye.'

'Good lad.'

The Welshmen gathered up their equipment and left the house with Martin, joining the rest of their band outside the east gate of the town. There were about two hundred of them in all, foot-archers under the command of Sir Gruffydd ap Llywelyn. Martin was introduced to all of them, or so it seemed to him. Few of them spoke English as well as Ieuan, Dafydd or Madog, but they welcomed him into their ranks amicably enough.

Martin noticed once again that many of the Welshmen wore only one shoe, and asked Ieuan why this was so.

'So's we can get a better grip on the ground when we're fighting,' Ieuan explained with a grin. 'We Welsh like to stay in tune with nature, not like you English, who prefer to cut yourselves off from it.'

As they set out marching to Torigny, Dafydd rode amongst them on a small white palfrey, playing soft and subtle harmonies on a small harp while the others sang along. In spite of looking like the wildest and most villainous bunch of brigands Martin had ever encountered – and since he had been recruited into the army, he had encountered many – they sang beautifully. They all started on the same note, and then each seemed to break away into different modes and modulations, each one complementing the whole in perfect harmony. As the song drew to a close, they all returned to the same note on which they had started out, to round off the melody. It was so beautiful that even Martin – who had little appreciation for the finer things in life – was entranced, and he quite forgot about the pain of his wound.

'You can count yourself lucky to have heard the finest singers in all the world, English,' Madog told Martin. 'It's the bardic tradition, see? It never dies.'

One of the others said something in Welsh, and the men around him nodded in agreement. 'They say it's your turn to give us a tune,' explained Ieuan, grinning.

Martin shook his head, blushing. 'I can't sing.'

'Of course not,' said Madog. 'You're English. But since

we've just entertained you, it's only fair that you repay the debt in kind.'

Martin grimaced; it was clear that he was not going to get out of this one. 'Very well. But don't say I didn't warn you.' And having said that, he launched into the only song he could think of, a half-understood old song called 'The Knight Stained from Battle':

Who is he, this lordling, that cometh from the fight?
With blood-red clothing arrayed to cause fright
Yet apparelled so finely, so seemly a sight
So fearless of tread, so peerless a knight.

'It is I, it is I, who speaks naught but right
A champion to heal all mankind in fight.'

Why, then, is thy raiment all stained crimson with blood
As men from the wine-press with the grapes they have trod?

'I have trampled the wine-press all on my own
And for all of mankind I did stand alone.
I have trampled the people in anger and wrath
And my cloak is besmirched with their bloody froth
And it is to their great shame they have fouled its cloth.
The day of vengeance liveth in my thought;
The season of reck'ning I forget not.
I looked all about for some helping hand;
Help was there none though I searched all my band.
Mine own strength it was that this cure wrought,
Mine own doughtiness help to me brought.
I have trampled the folk in wrath and ire,
And cast them down into their shameful mire.'

The Welshmen laughed and cheered. 'You're right, English,' Madog chuckled. 'You can't sing to save your life.'

'From the Book of Isaiah, unless I'm much mistaken, though it seems to me you must have left out a couple of lines,' Dafydd observed with amusement.

At that moment, an English herald galloped up from behind them until he was riding level with Llywelyn at the head of the band. 'New orders, Sir Gruffydd,' he panted. 'All troops are to make for Cormolain.'

'Cormolain, is it?' Llywelyn bellowed good-humouredly. 'And where the Devil is Cormolain?'

'From here?' The herald removed his cap to scratch his head while he glanced about to get his bearings. 'About four miles yonder,' he said, pointing to the north-east. 'The army is to regroup. Word is that Valois has gathered a fresh army and is marching to meet us.'

A murmur of excitement rippled through the Welsh band, but the herald had already taken his leave of Llywelyn and spurred his horse on, galloping on towards Torigny to pass the word on to the other units of the vanguard that had gone ahead. Llywelyn turned his horse about and led his men off the track, across the fields towards Cormolain.

'Did you hear that?' asked Madog, his eyes shining with the promise of battle. 'The French are coming to give us a warm welcome at last.'

'Aye,' said Ieuan, rather more sceptically. 'How many times have I heard that one before?'

'I have to rejoin my company!' Martin said desperately. 'If there's to be a battle . . .'

'You can fight with us,' offered Madog. 'That way you'll get to see some *real* archers in action.'

'I shouldn't go worrying if I were you,' Ieuan assured Martin. 'We're all in the prince's battalion. If the order's gone out for the army to regroup in Cormolain, then I expect that applies equally to Sir Thomas Holland's company. You'll be reunited with your countrymen soon enough.'

Llywelyn's band reached Cormolain around mid-afternoon, where they found the nucleus of the vanguard setting up camp just outside the village. Martin recognised the banners of the Prince of Wales and the Earl of Warwick, and knew that Holland could not be far away. He took his leave of Ieuan, Dafydd and Madog.

'I expect we'll see each other soon enough,' remarked Ieuan. 'We are marching in the same battalion, after all. Why don't you bring some of your English friends to meet us?'

'Aye,' said Madog. 'Like this Will Caynard and his friends.' Grinning, he drew his finger across his throat in a highly expressive gesture.

Martin shook his head with a wan smile. 'That's summat I'll have to deal with in my own way.'

'Fair enough,' said Ieuan. 'But remember what I told you last night: it's you or them.'

'What about this squire who wants you dead so badly?' asked Dafydd, dismounting from his palfrey. 'Even if you succeed in killing Caynard and his friends, this Richard Stamford may just hire other men to kill you.'

Martin shrugged. He had spent the past two hours considering the situation. He had thought about Stamford's vendetta, Caynard's callous greed and murderous brutality, and the lack of justice in a world where a man could be condemned for a crime he had not committed. It seemed to him that there were two kinds of people in the world, the victors and the victims. He was determined to stop being a victim, and start dishing out some justice of his own. 'If I can kill Will Caynard, I can do the same for Richard Stamford,' he said simply.

Ieuan chuckled. 'That's the spirit. You'll be all right, boy. But make sure that Stamford's death looks like an accident. No one's going to pay much mind if men like Caynard are killed, but if a young nobleman like Stamford dies in suspicious circumstances, there'll be questions asked.'

Martin nodded.

'Better still, make it look like French handiwork. No point in bringing more trouble on yourself than you've already got. No one will question his death if he's found with a Genoese crossbow bolt in his back.'

'Genoese?'

'The French employ Genoese mercenaries as archers,' explained Ieuan. 'Can you use a crossbow?'

Martin shook his head.

'Then learn. If you find a crossbow, bring it to me and I'll teach you. It's a lousy weapon compared to an honest length of yew, but it has its uses – as your present circumstances demonstrate,' he added.

'You sound as if you've had some experience at this kind of thing,' Martin said drily.

Ieuan flashed his teeth in a savage grin. 'Ask no questions, hear no lies, boy.'

'I don't know how to thank you all for all you've done,' Martin told the three of them awkwardly.

Ieuan shrugged, embarrassed. 'Perhaps one day you'll have a chance to return the favour; but if you don't, don't go out of your way to find one. God be with you, Martin Kemp.'

Martin took his leave of the Welshmen and made his way into the village, where he found Villiers and Brother Ambrose erecting Holland's banner in front of one of the larger houses. 'Hullo, young Kemp,' the friar greeted him cheerfully. 'Where've you been? We thought perhaps you'd been killed.'

'Or that you had deserted,' Villiers added with a grin.

'I were wounded, but some Welsh archers treated my wound and brought me here.' Martin avoided telling a lie to the friar and the squire, hoping that they would naturally assume he had been wounded by the French. He had decided that the closer he stuck to the truth, the more likely he was to be believed; at least he had the wound to corroborate most of his story, and his battered face spoke for itself.

'Well, you're here now,' said Brother Ambrose. 'And of your own free will, it seems, rather than dragged back by the marshals. That proves you weren't trying to desert.'

'Here ahead of the rest of your company,' added Villiers. 'We'd almost reached Torigny when word came that his Majesty had changed his mind, and that we were to head here. Sir Thomas sent the two of us ahead to find some lodgings.' He gestured to the house.

'What about the rest of the army?' asked Martin. The tents erected outside the village had seemed pitifully few to him.

Villiers grimaced. 'It's all over the place. The main body was at a place called Sept-Vents, the last I heard. If the French attack us now, they'll be able to wipe us all out piecemeal.'

'Is it true, then? That Valois has gathered a fresh army, and is marching to do battle with us?'

'That's what they're saying,' said Villiers.

'Here come Sir Thomas and Norwich now,' observed Brother Ambrose. 'Perhaps they have some news.'

Villiers and Martin turned to see Holland and Norwich riding up the street at the head of the company, arguing. 'Rumours!' spat Holland. 'Has anyone seen this French army for themselves? No! It's always a friend of a friend, a serjeant-at-arms in some mythical troop of hobelars who interrogated a Norman peasant whose great-aunt in Caen spoke to a Parisian man-at-arms who was told by a lady-in-waiting to Valois' chambermaid that Valois was talking of going to Saint-Denys to fetch the Oriflamme! I'll wait until I've seen this army for myself before I don my armour.' Holland dismounted, handing his bridle to Villiers.

Brother Ambrose indicated Martin. 'The prodigal son has returned, Sir Thomas.'

Holland cast the briefest of glances in Martin's direction.

'So I see. You'd best get back to your platoon, boy.'

Martin nodded, and made his way back to where Preston stood with his men.

'Where the devil have you been?' Preston demanded angrily. 'Nails and blood! You can count yourself lucky you weren't hanged as a deserter.'

'I were ambushed,' explained Martin, once again avoiding a direct lie. 'I were wounded in the side, but some Welshmen took care of me.'

'Oh aye? Did you check your purse after?' Preston asked cynically.

Martin instinctively put a hand to the purse that hung from his belt. It still bulged with coins. He instantly felt guilty for having thought that Ieuan and his friends might do such a thing.

'I hope you killed the whoresons that attacked you,' grunted Preston.

Martin hesitated before replying. 'One of them lies dead,' he said carefully. 'But the other three escaped when the Welshmen came to my aid,' he added, glancing across to where Caynard stood. Caynard avoided meeting his gaze, and Martin suddenly had the satisfaction of realising that Caynard and his friends had had no sleep that night following their botched attempt to kill him. He was determined that they should never sleep easy again. 'But if I ever catch up with them again . . .' He let the threat hang in the air.

'I see,' Preston remarked dubiously. He was more inclined to believe that Lancelot Kemp had tried to stop some English troops from maltreating the townsfolk, and had received a savage beating for his pains, but he was prepared to let it pass. Whatever Martin had been up to, his bruised face indicated that he might have learned his lesson. 'In future, make sure you don't get separated from your mates,' he said gruffly. 'There's safety in numbers, and you can't trust these Norman dogs. By the way, you haven't seen

Piers Edritch since yesterday, have you? It seems he's disappeared as well.'

Martin shook his head. 'Not since yesterday,' he said truthfully.

'All right,' said Preston. 'Get back with your companions.' He jerked a thumb towards the platoon behind him, and then turned to address them all. 'Make camp, lads – we'll be spending the night here.'

The rest of the vanguard reached Cormolain by nightfall. Martin slept little that night, keeping an eye on Caynard, Lefthand and Murray, and one hand on the hilt of his rondel. Occasionally he would catch one of them sneaking a furtive glance in his direction, but none of them tried anything, perhaps thinking that there were too many witnesses around. He realised with a cold certainty that Dafydd had been right: he would never be able to sleep soundly while one of them still lived; and by not reporting their actions to Preston, he had committed himself to dealing with them personally.

He got his first chance much sooner than he expected. The following morning they ate breakfast before dawn, after which Martin changed the dressing on his wound in accordance with the instructions that Dafydd had given him.

'By the Cross that Saint Helen found!' exclaimed Rudcock, seeing the cauterised wound. 'When you said as how you'd been wounded, I didn't think . . .'

'It looks worse than it is,' Martin cut in curtly.

'Doesn't it hurt?' asked Tate.

'Like the Devil,' admitted Martin.

'You should show that to Preston,' said Rudcock. 'If he saw how serious it is, I'm certain he'd be able to arrange for you to ride with the baggage train for a few days . . .'

'I'm fine,' insisted Martin. Wounded or not, if there was going to be a battle, he did not want to be left twiddling his thumbs in the rearguard.

After the morning inspection, they started to ransack

the village for plunder. Martin was wandering down an alleyway when he glimpsed Lefthand and Murray walking down the street up ahead. He immediately realised that he had been careless enough to become separated from his friends again. But Lefthand and Murray had not seen him, their minds occupied with the task of finding what meagre booty the village could provide. Perhaps here was his chance to even the score. He watched them enter a small wooden house with a thatched roof, closing the door behind them. Martin glanced up and down the street to see if anyone else was in the vicinity. There was no sign of Caynard. The only people in sight were some men-at-arms setting alight some houses a short distance away. That gave him an idea. He hurried down the street to beg a burning brand from one of the men-at-arms. As he made his way back, he noticed a pitchfork thrust into the midden by the door of the house that Lefthand and Murray had entered, and used it to prop the door shut.

He sprinted around the back of the house to make sure there was no other exit, and then hesitated. Killing men in battle was one thing, but murdering them in cold blood . . . ? Just because these men had tried to kill him, did that give him the right to exact retribution? But no one had ever given any thought to *his* rights. He had none, he was a villein. He could expect no justice in this world. He began to ask himself what Sir Lancelot would have done in this situation, and then caught himself. He was not Sir Lancelot, he was Martin Kemp. No one would ever treat him with chivalry, and in return he was not expected to show chivalry to anyone else. If it was justice he wanted, he would have to forge it himself.

He tossed the flaming brand on to the thatched roof and stepped back.

The flames spread across the dry straw with a rapidity that astounded him, crackling noisily. Lefthand and Murray must have realised what was happening, for he heard their shouts of alarm and their heavy, hurried footfalls on the wooden steps within. He saw the latch on the door rattle, and then the whole door shuddered as one of them threw his weight against it. But the door was sturdy, and wedged firmly shut.

Martin suddenly realised that he had made a careless mistake: they could easily open one of the shuttered windows and climb out. But the two men were panicking, concentrating their efforts on a door they would never open. By the time they thought of looking for the windows, dark grey smoke was oozing out from behind the shutters. Martin could hear them choking as the acrid smoke clawed at their lungs. Now they would be blinded, their eyes stinging, unable to find a window. He could hear them blundering about helplessly inside, disorientated by the smoke. A pity Caynard had not been with them, thought Martin; but at least he had evened the odds in his favour.

The whole building was ablaze now. Martin could hear the screams of the two men as they were roasted alive. He watched as part of the roof collapsed with a roar, sending up a shower of sparks, and then the screams were suddenly silenced.

Martin's lips curled upwards in a grim smile of satisfaction.

The vanguard reached the village of Cheux the next day, while the main body of the army, marching east on a parallel course, reached the Cistercian priory at Fontenay-le-Pesnel, less than ten miles from Caen.

The disappearance of Lefthand and Murray had been noticed as soon as Preston's men had gathered to leave Cormolain the previous evening. Piers Edritch had been the first man lost by Holland's company since they landed in France, but the serjeant had let it pass. When two more men went missing from Preston's platoon, the other serjeants in the company began to snigger that old Wat was losing his touch when it came to keeping a tight rein on his men. Irritated by their sniggers, Preston had ordered a thorough search of the village. Lefthand's and Murray's charred corpses had been found in the ruins of one of the burnt houses, the pitchfork propping shut what was left of the door bearing mute testimony to the fact that their deaths had not been accidental. Naturally everyone assumed the murderers to have been French men-at-arms lying in wait, or perhaps even the villagers themselves. By way of retribution, the whole village was burnt to the ground, along with the crops in the surrounding fields. Martin's conscience was not troubled in the least; by now he had learned that such wanton destruction would have occurred regardless of whether or not the locals had done anything to warrant it. Indeed, he had found his conscience surprisingly untroubled by any aspect of the incident. He no longer gave a damn about anything, and it was as if a great burden had been lifted from his shoulders.

Only one man guessed that it might not have been the French who had been responsible for the deaths of Lefthand and Murray. It seemed too much of a coincidence to Caynard that of the four men who had attacked Martin, he was now the only survivor. He could hardly believe that the same callow peasant youth who insisted on wearing a girl's muffler and had been so reluctant to claim his share of the booty at Barfleur could also be responsible for the cold-blooded murder of his friends. But he had noticed that a change had come over Martin in the past three days. Perhaps it was only his perception of the man, coloured by the knowledge that if he did not kill Martin, Martin would kill him; but looking at him he no longer saw a precocious lad skilled with a bow, inexperienced in war, his head filled with misplaced ideals of chivalry. Now he saw a young man both willing and able to kill, ready to murder in cold blood if need be. Perhaps what Edritch had once told him about Martin having raped a woman was true after all.

In turn, Martin caught Caynard giving him a glance that told him he had guessed the truth of the matter, and had the satisfaction of knowing that in future it would be Caynard who would spend sleepless nights with his fingers curled around the haft of his dagger.

Norwich rode into Cheux shortly after dawn the following day, and found Warwick breakfasting in one of the town's inns with Sir Reginald Cobham, Holland and Villiers. 'What news?' Warwick asked him, after the briefest exchange of pleasantries.

'Last night his Majesty sent a messenger to the burghers of Caen, with letters calling upon them to surrender with the honours of war,' explained Norwich. The honours of war meant that the persons and property of the people of Caen would not be harmed – theoretically, at least. 'The messenger should have returned hours ago, yet still there is no sign of him.'

'Any news of Valois' army?' asked Holland.

'Scouting parties have been sent out, but those that have returned report there is no sign of it. However, reliable reports indicate that the Constable and Chamberlain of France are in Caen with a sizeable body of men-at-arms and Genoese crossbowmen. His Majesty sends his compliments, and suggests that the army regroups on the road to Caen two miles south-east of here.'

'He intends that we should attack Caen?' asked Cobham.

'Aye, Sir Reginald,' said Norwich.

Warwick nodded thoughtfully. 'We may have by-passed Bayeux, but we cannot afford to leave a city as large as Caen still in hostile hands to the rear.

'On the other hand, his Majesty is reluctant to allow the campaign to become bogged down in a prolonged siege that might give Valois more time to raise an army, in the north of this realm,' said Norwich. 'Either we take Caen by storm, or not at all.'

Warwick nodded in agreement. 'Return his Majesty my

compliments, and assure him I will see him at the appointed place.'

Preston's men were ordered to strike camp and before long they were marching south-east to where the army was forming up on the road to Caen. When the advance scouts reported that they were drawing near to the city, Warwick had the vanguard spread out on either side of the road, each company marching across the fields in its own column so that they would approach the city on a broad front from several directions, to make their numbers seem greater. 'His Majesty wishes to avoid a siege,' Warwick explained to Holland. 'If the citizens can be scared into submission, we may yet win the day without bloodshed.'

Riding at the head of his company, Holland reined in his steed on the crest of a ridge towards mid-morning. He paused momentarily to gaze into the middle distance.

'Caen,' breathed Villiers, riding up beside him.

Holland nodded, and signalled the column forward once more, spurring his horse into a trot. As they surmounted the crest of the ridge, Martin and his companions saw their target laid out in the vale before them.

The second largest city in Normandy after Rouen, Caen was far bigger than any other town Martin had seen before. It stood at the confluence of two rivers, where the Odon ran into the Orne, dividing the city into two distinct halves. To the north-west was the old town, dominated by a strong castle that stood on a slight eminence to the north and was joined to the town walls. Where the castle's curtain wall jutted out from the town wall, it was surrounded by a broad moat. In stark contrast to the fortress, the ancient stone walls of the old town were poorly maintained, although it was obvious that for the past few days the citizens had been strengthening the defences to the north and west with trenches and palisades. To the south, the old town was protected by a branch of the Odon, separating it from the new town which lay to the south-east. The new town was a rich and prosperous suburb, containing the largest and grandest houses in the city. It had no wall, for it stood on an island, surrounded on three sides by the two arms of the Odon, and on the fourth by the Orne. A bridge across the Odon connected the old town to the new, while a third bridge spanned the Orne to the south.

Led by the Prince of Wales and the earls of Warwick and Northampton, the vanguard marched around the north side of the old town, giving the forbidding castle a wide berth: the fortress was clearly well-manned. A walled convent stood nearly four hundred yards to the east of the city; finding it deserted, the prince's troops quickly occupied it. Look-outs were posted in the convent's bell-tower to watch any activity in the city. While Holland and Cobham met with the prince and the two earls inside the convent, his men rested in the shadow of its walls.

'What happens, now?' asked Tate.

'Now we wait,' Preston told his men. 'You might like to use your time to check your tackle,' he added. 'I don't want you trying to storm the walls only to find you've left your swords at Cheux.

Martin inspected his bowstring and counted his arrows, but he knew he was only going through the motions, trying to keep his mind from dwelling on the forthcoming battle. He repolished the blade of his broadsword for the sake of having something to do, watching as the main body of the army marched into sight in three columns, forming up into battle array facing the north and west walls.

A field kitchen was brought up to the convent and began to serve out food. The army had already marched over ten miles that morning, and many of the men were hungry. Martin was not one of them. There was a tightness in his chest and his stomach felt knotted with excitement. Even though the sun surmounted the convent wall at noon to beat directly down upon him, he still felt cold and numb.

He glanced to the south. Beyond the rooftops of the new

town, he could see dozens of Caen's citizens streaming across the bridge over the Orne, scattering into the countryside beyond.

Preston had seen them, too. 'There go the wise ones,' he remarked cynically.

'And here wait the fools,' muttered Newbolt. If Preston heard him this time, he gave no indication of it. Newbolt's words were only symptomatic of the tension that lay heavy over the whole company, like a shroud of apprehension.

'Are we soldiers yet?' asked Conyers, in a conscious effort to relieve some of the tension. By now those words had become something between a running in-joke and a platoon motto. This time they solicited only the weakest laughter.

Villiers emerged from the convent on his rouncy, and Preston hailed him. 'Any news?'

'The look-outs report that the people of the old town seem to be withdrawing across the bridges into the Île Saint-Jean,' replied Villiers, spurring his horse towards the king's banner, which could be seen above the main body of the army.

Martin sighed, and slotted his gleaming sword back into its scabbard. He guessed that the Île Saint-Jean must be the name for the new town. He had a feeling that either the French would withdraw from the city, or the king would postpone the attack. Either way, he was reminded of the events of four days previously, when they had failed to get to grips with Bertrand's men. He was plagued by the same feeling of disappointment after all the fear and tension of waiting.

A troop of men-at-arms saddled up their rouncies and began to form up into a loose column, their pennants hanging limply in the still air, their armour and harness jingling lackadaisically. Martin watched them with an air of bored curiosity as they trotted away from the convent.

Towards the city.

Martin sat up sharply and rubbed his eyes, as if not believing what he saw. What did they think they were doing? Did they not realise that the old town was still in enemy hands? No, not the old town – had not the squire said that the townsfolk had withdrawn across the bridge into the new town on the Île Saint-Jean? But the Valois banner of a pattern of yellow fleurs-de-lys on a blue background still hung over the castle, which loomed over the eastern gate that the men-at-arms were now approaching.

Then realisation slowly dawned on him: this was it, this was the attack. No trumpet's blare, no armoured knights charging to the fore with their lances couched. Just three-score men-at-arms riding along a dusty track as calmly as if they were returning from a day's hunting.

The men stationed in the castle seemed to be taken equally by surprise. Martin could see them moving about on the battlements of the curtain wall, but no one shot at the advancing English troops.

The Earl of Warwick emerged from the convent, foll-owed by Holland and Cobham. All three of them were on foot and in armour. The earl started to march slowly but purposefully after the men-at-arms, his armour clanking noisily. Holland paused only long enough to order his men to follow him, before marching after Warwick.

'All right, lads, on your feet!' ordered Preston. He might have been ordering them to rise for an inspection. 'Let's go.'

'Well, it looks like this is it,' remarked Rudcock, pushing himself upright. Brewster hurriedly followed, tossing down the straw he had been chewing as he rose to his feet. Martin followed. There was no time to form up into an orderly column, the archers marching along behind Warwick, Holland and Cobham in a loose gaggle. Ahead of them, the men-at-arms had dismounted, seizing control of the eastern gate unopposed. The men in the castle had not started shooting at anyone yet, but then Martin reckoned that he and his companions had another hundred yards of open ground to cross before they would be within effective range of bows. Before them loomed the walls of the old town. Clustered in their shadows were the hovels of peasants too poor to be able to afford land within the walls, many of them built actually leaning against the wall.

Martin did not notice that they had come within a bowshot of the castle that loomed to their right until a crossbow bolt plunged into the earth a few yards short of where he marched. After a few moments a couple more bolts sailed over the archers' heads, but it was hardly a withering hail of missiles.

Now they had entered the suburbs, and were hidden from the castle's battlements by the tightly packed hovels. The men-at-arms on guard at the gate ahead of them grinned jovially, the gateway itself gaping like a huge maw waiting to devour the advancing men. Martin felt a sudden chill as he followed Preston through the shadows of the gateway. Then they emerged into the sunlight once more, marching along a dusty, deserted street in the old town. Surely this must be a trap of some kind? Martin could see no one waiting in ambush, but had not Preston told him that if anyone had been lying in ambush, he would not see them until it was too late?

They came to a T-junction, still marching at a steady walking pace. The old town was unnaturally quiet. Martin could see the entrance of the castle to their right. By withdrawing into the new town, the defenders of the old town had left the castle's garrison cut off from the rest of the city's defenders. Warwick led Holland and his men to the left, away from the castle and towards the Île Saint-Jean.

A church rose up ahead of them. As they passed it, the bridge across the Odon into the new town came into view. A towering stone gateway had been built at the far end of the bridge, just over a hundred yards away. A barricade of furniture and lumber, about the height of a man, had been built across the entrance to the gateway, and behind it

Martin could make out the faint sheen of dozens of steel helmets in the shadows below the tower.

Warwick signalled for Holland and his men to halt. At Holland's direction, Preston formed his men up into two ranks at the north end of the bridge, facing the well-defended tower. 'All right, lads, let's give 'em a few volleys of ash.' Preston's men took their arrows from their leather retainers. 'Nock! Mark!'

Martin nocked his arrow to the bowstring, picking his mark – the head of a man he could just make out behind the barricade.

'Draw!'

Kemp raised the bow, drawing back the arrow until the fletching touched his ear, pushing out the bowstave with his left arm.

'Loose!'

Nineteen arrows sped through the air towards the men crowded behind the barricade. Martin saw his own target fall back in a welter of blood. It was the first time he had ever shot a man. He was pleased that in spite of the situation he was still calm enough to shoot well.

'Draw!'

Martin selected another arrow and nocked it, taking careful aim.

'Loose!'

The platoon let fly. A dozen more men fell dead.

Some crossbowmen stationed on the roof of the tower started to return the archers' fire, but because of the awkwardness of the angle, none of the Englishmen were killed. The crossbowmen ducked back down behind the parapet to reload.

'Heads up!' ordered Preston. 'Mark! Aim for the embrasures! Draw! Wait for it!'

After an interminably long wait, the crossbowmen bobbed back up over the parapet for their next volley.

'Loose!'

Five of the crossbowmen fell back from the embrasures with arrows protruding from their faces. A crossbow fell from the parapet and splashed into the water below the bridge.

Within two minutes Preston's men had used up their arrows. There was still no sign of the men-at-arms that the Earl of Northampton was supposed to be bringing up to reinforce them. More crossbowmen were appearing on the roof of the tower to replace their fallen comrades.

'We should fall back!' said Cobham. 'We'll be cut to pieces if we stay here.'

'We're not staying here,' Holland told him, drawing his broadsword. 'My lord?'

Warwick drew his own broadsword, and nodded. 'Charge!' he ordered, and began to run across the bridge towards the barricade.

Holland followed suit. 'Saint George for Edward!'

Preston had his sword in his hands and was lumbering after his master. 'Come on, lads, up and at 'em!' he roared.

Running along close behind Preston, Martin drew his own broadsword and waved it experimentally above his head. He felt vaguely foolish. This was ridiculous: he was not supposed to be here; he was a peasant, a mere villein, not a warrior.

Then he heard the sound of crossbow bolts whistling through the air, raining down on the bridge, and he remembered that this was not a game, this was war; which meant that one side would win, the other side would lose, and those on the losing side would die.

CHAPTER TWELVE

Martin heard a scream of agony as one of the crossbow bolts struck home, but there was no time to glance over his shoulder to see who had been hit. Warwick and Holland had already reached the barricade, hurling themselves at the heaped furniture and slashing at the men behind it with their broadswords as they struggled to clamber over. Martin broke into a sprint for the last few yards. He heard a warlike shout of desperation and defiance, and realised it had come from his own lips.

He threw himself at the barricade, as if the weight of his own body would be enough to dash it asunder. He landed awkwardly on the piled furniture. His wounded left side exploded in pain. Winded, he felt himself slipping back down to the surface of the bridge. He reached out with his left hand to grab a table leg while scrabbling for support with his feet. Gaining purchase with one foot, he hauled himself up the side of the barricade. A man at the other side was trying to stab at his face with a spear. Martin hacked at it with his sword, chopping it clean in two. His spear rendered useless, the man began to clamber up the other side of the barricade to meet him, reaching for the hilt of his sword. Martin stabbed him in the throat without hesitation. The man fell back, dead; but there were plenty more men behind to replace him.

It looked as if there were hundreds of Frenchmen waiting for them behind the barricade: men-at-arms wielding swords and spears, ordinary citizens armed with tools or farming implements. Two more men clambered up, swinging their swords at Martin. He parried one blow, barely managing to duck beneath the other. He felt a momentary panic at the precariousness of his situation, and then his companions were climbing up on either side of him. There was no time to look to see who they were, but it did not matter; it was reassuring enough to know that he was not alone. A sword-thrust killed the Frenchman to his left. The one to his right shouted something incomprehensible, and drew back his sword to strike a blow at Martin's head. Martin aimed a back-handed blow at his neck, seeking to lop off his head. He misjudged the distance and succeeded only in slashing the man's throat open, but it was enough. Blood gouted everywhere, blinding him. Something heavy struck him a glancing blow on the head. His blood-drenched hand was unable to maintain its grip on the table leg. He felt himself slipping, falling back to the surface of the bridge. He lay there panting for a moment, trying to wipe the blood from his eyes while another man leapt up to take his place at the barricade.

'. . . But I'm wounded, serjeant!' To Martin's left, Newbolt was clutching at his upper left arm. The sleeve of his tunic was soaked with blood, while more blood seeped between his fingers.

'You're not wounded!' Preston was snarling. '*He's* wounded!' The serjeant gestured with his sword to young Ned Skeffington, lying on his back at the foot of the barricade, the broken-off haft of a spear jutting from the gory mess that had once been his throat. 'Go on, get back in there!' Preston shoved Newbolt roughly back towards the fray, before turning to where Martin lay. 'Come on, Lancelot, this is no time to be taking a nap!'

Feeling foolish, and not wanting to be thought a coward, Martin reached for his fallen sword and picked himself up, once again clambering up the side of the barricade. As he reached the top, a man tried to strike at him with an axe. Martin parried the blow with a roar of aggression, and hacked at the man's shoulder. His blade bit down to the bone, and Martin grunted with the effort of withdrawing his sword from where it had become embedded in cartilage. Then he thrust the point of his sword into another man's chest and saw his victim fall back, coughing up blood.

Standing beside Martin, Drayton picked up a chair and lifted it above his head, hurling it down on the men behind the barricade. That gave the two of them enough of a breathing space to seize a heavy wooden table between them, and send it after the chair. The centre of the barricade suddenly began to shift under the weight of the men pressed against it. It was as if the table had somehow been holding the structure together. Realising that the barricade was about to collapse, Martin struggled to regain his balance. Then he toppled over as a mass of tables and benches crashed down on to the Frenchmen seething behind it. Men screamed in agony as wood and bone splintered. Martin felt himself tumble over and over. He found himself sprawled on the ground, dazed, surrounded by Frenchmen baying for blood.

He reached for his fallen sword, but someone deliberately put their foot on it, pinning it to the cobbles. Martin swivelled on his back, driving the sole of his foot into the man's crotch with all his might. Another man tried to plunge the blade of a scythe in his chest. Martin barely rolled clear in time, the blade striking sparks from the cobbles. He pushed himself to his feet and smashed his fist into the man's jaw, feeling the bone snap. Another man ran at Martin with a sword. Drayton rose up behind him, holding a sturdy chair aloft. The chair came down, and the man crumpled and fell, his neck broken, his skull smashed in. Martin scrabbled for his sword, and rolled on to his back to parry another blow.

He smashed a foot into his assailant's kneecap. The man screamed in agony, and Martin stabbed him in the groin.

The breach in the barricade was widened as a troop of dismounted men-at-arms pushed through from the English-held side. The French tried to rally, surging forward to meet them. Drenched in blood and gasping for breath, Martin crawled out of the way, into the lee of the barricade where it met the balustrade at the side of the bridge. Hunched in the corner, he watched as the two sides strove to push through. The din was terrific as steel clashed against steel, battle-cries were roared in English and French, and horribly wounded men cried out in agony. But the French had the weight of numbers on their side in the enclosed space beneath the tower. In the small square beyond, Martin could see what looked like hundreds more Frenchmen tightly packed between the houses, struggling to support their comrades on the bridge. Slowly but surely, the English men-at-arms felt themselves pushed back towards the barricade.

He felt a hand grab him beneath one armpit and hoist him to his feet. It was Preston. 'Come on, Lancelot, we've done our bit. Northampton's brought up fresh troops – let's leave it to them, eh?' Martin followed the serjeant back across the barricade with reluctance. He did not want to abandon the fight now; he was just getting his second wind.

The order to fall back was given by an English trumpeter, and while some of the men-at-arms fought a desperate holding action beneath the tower, the rest followed Preston and Martin back across the bridge. On the other side, Welsh archers were forming up in ranks to shoot at the enemy. Martin recognised Ieuan and Madog amongst them, but they were too busy to acknowledge him as he retreated behind their lines with the shattered remnants of his platoon.

Smoke drifted across the scene, blotting out the sun.

The tall, slate-roofed houses across the street from the church had been put to the torch, and were burning fiercely. The few survivors of the troop of men-at-arms scrambled back across the barricade, closely followed by the French. As the French tried to pursue them across the bridge, they were cut down by repeated volleys of arrows from the Welsh, their concentrated hail wreaking havoc in the confined space. The cobbles were piled with blood-soaked corpses. Martin glimpsed the Earl of Warwick through the drifting smoke. He was on horseback now, seemingly unhurt, giving orders and directing troops. The English troops were rallying on the north side of the bridge. The French started trying to rebuild the barricade.

Martin stood to one side as another troop of dismounted men-at-arms was brought up to support the Welsh archers on the bridge. He saw a man climbing up on to the road from the river-bank. His sword drawn, the man suddenly charged at him. Martin's broadsword was still in his hand. Almost instinctively, he slashed at the man with a back-handed up-stroke, neatly severing his arm just below the elbow. The man staggered back screaming, blood jetting from the stump.

More men were pouring up on to the road from below the bridge. Martin hacked at one and parried a blow from another, before driving the point of his sword into the first man's throat.

'Ambush!' roared Preston. The Frenchmen must have been hiding beneath the bridge, lying in wait until the English were entrenched on the bridge before falling on their flanks. But the bloodied men of Preston's platoon met them with an unexpected ferocity, holding them off until more men-at-arms could be brought up to support them. The ambushers were pitifully few, and soon found themselves pushed back to the river's edge. With the river at their back, they fought desperately to defend themselves against the English counter-attack.

Up on the bridge, the Welsh archers stood aside at a given signal to let a fresh troop of men-at-arms rush the barricade. It came to bloody hand-to-hand fighting once again. Having exhausted their supply of bolts, the Genoese crossbowmen on top of the tower hurled rocks down at the English troops below. Mortally wounded, a man fell screaming from the bridge to land in the river with a splash, his heavy armour pulling him straight under. The houses on the north bank of the river were roaring noisily as the flames consumed them, sending a vast pillar of smoke up into the blue sky over the city.

Below the bridge, Martin found himself facing three men. He lunged at one with his sword, stabbing him in the stomach. He punched the second in the throat with his left hand, before parrying a blow from the third. Then Rudcock came to his aid, stabbing the third in the back, allowing Martin to concentrate on the second. He parried another blow before booting the man in the crotch. As the man doubled up with a howl, Martin brought his sword down on the back of the man's head, splitting his skull open.

The fighting below the bridge ended suddenly. Realising that they had lost the element of surprise and were hopelessly outnumbered, the few remaining Frenchmen dropped their weapons and dived into the river. They swam upstream, where a line of boats had been tied up to block the channel, protecting the north-west side of the new town. Martin and his companions rejoiced at having repelled the ambush, and clambered back up the bank to street-level. There they found Ieuan and his friends pulling back, while more men-at-arms were thrown forward into the fray.

Holland was there, directing troops, trying to bring order to the confusion. His armour appeared to be dented in one or two places, but he seemed otherwise unhurt.

'Everything all right?' he demanded of Preston, shouting above the din of battle.

The serjeant nodded. 'It was back-and-edge back there for a while, but we beat 'em.'

Holland glanced to where the mêlée continued on the bridge. 'It won't make much difference if we cannot force a passage into the new town,' he observed grimly. 'All right, Preston, take your men out of here. You've done more than your fair share for today.'

Preston nodded, and signalled for his men to follow him. 'Come on, lads.'

Martin did not seem to hear him. He was gazing up-river to where the retreating ambushers were wading against the current towards the line of boats. Rudcock tugged at his sleeve. 'Come on, Martin, we're just getting in the way here.'

Realisation dawned slowly on Martin. 'There's a ford,' he breathed incredulously. Rudcock did not hear him over the din. 'Christ's blood, there's a God-damned ford!' he shouted.

'A what?' asked Rudcock, distracted.

'A God-damned ford, by my hood!' exclaimed Martin. 'Where's the serjeant?'

'He's gone – and so should we be.' A crossbow bolt struck a man standing nearby in the neck. 'For the love of Saint Peter, Martin, let's get out of this!'

Martin was no longer listening. He was trying to attract Holland's attention. 'Sir Thomas!' he shouted, waving.

'Hell's teeth, boy! Can't you see I'm busy?' snapped the knight.

'There's a ford across the river, sir!' shouted Martin, gesturing frantically.

But Holland had already turned his attention back to the mêlée on the bridge. Martin felt someone grab him by the arm and pull him to one side, a moment before he would have been knocked down by an armoured knight riding past.

He glanced at his saviour. It was Ieuan. 'Trying to get yourself killed, boy?'

'There's a ford!' Martin insisted excitedly. 'We can cross the river there!'

'It's not exactly undefended,' Rudcock remarked wryly, indicating the crossbowmen who manned the line of boats.

'He's right though,' said Ieuan. 'It's a chance. If we can get to the other side, we can outflank the Frenchmen on the bridge.' The stocky little Welshman quickly took charge of the situation, issuing orders for some of his comrades to lay down a covering hail of arrows from the river-bank, before telling the rest to follow him.

Martin and a reluctant Rudcock scrambled back down to the river's edge with Ieuan, Madog, and a dozen other Welshmen. Seeing what they intended, and preferring it to the carnage on the bridge, a few hobelars followed them, wading into the sluggish river. So far it had been a dry, hot summer, and the level of the water was low, only coming up to their chests. Half-wading and half-swimming, they made their way diagonally against the current towards the line of boats.

Seeing them approach, the men on the boats started shooting with their crossbows. Almost immediately, the Welsh archers on the river-bank opened up with a steady hail of arrows, picking off crossbowmen with lethal accuracy and forcing the rest to keep their heads down. Crouching down behind the wooden sides of the boats, they popped up occasionally to shoot at the men who swam towards them.

The crossbowmen wore steel helmets and leather brigandines over chain-mail hauberks. 'Genoese mercenaries,' gasped Ieuan, swimming alongside Martin. Crossbow bolts sliced into the water all around them. A bolt struck a hobelar in the left shoulder, and he jerked spasmodically for a moment before floating still, face-down in the water.

Ieuan ducked under the surface, coming up for air a few yards further on. As a child, Martin had often gone swimming in the mill-pond at Knighton on hot summer afternoons. Now the skill readily came back to him, but he was no match for the Welshmen, who seemed to be as much at home in the water as ducks.

Madog was the first to reach the boats. The nearest Genoese dropped his crossbow and reached for the short sword he wore at his hip. Madog hooked his left hand on the edge of the boat and flung a dagger with his right. It hit the Genoese in the throat, killing him instantly. One of the Welshmen swimming alongside Martin died as a bolt pierced his skull. Madog swung himself up into the boat, taking a huge battleaxe from his belt in time to face another Genoese who sought to close with him. More Welshmen were struggling up into the boats. The Genoese tried to repel them, stamping on their fingers and stabbing at their faces. Other Welshmen, like Ieuan, ducked below the surface to swim under the keels of the boats, coming up behind the Genoese to slaughter them mercilessly. Martin had reached one of the boats now. A Genoese loomed over him, sword in hand. Before he could thrust the sword at Martin's face, Martin had stabbed him in the chest. Martin pressed himself close to the side of the boat as the Genoese keeled over, landing in the water with a splash. Then Madog seized Martin's left hand, hauling him out of the water and on to the deck beside Ieuan.

There was no time for self-congratulation. The Genoese in the next boat were struggling to reload their crossbows, lining up for a volley. Madog hurled his axe at one. The razor-sharp head buried itself deep in the man's chest. Then Madog snatched a short sword from a corpse's hand and jumped on to the deck of the next boat. He fought like a wild man, maniacally hacking and slashing. Ieuan, Martin and Rudcock followed, closing with the rest of the Genoese.

Unable to do any more good from the river-bank, the rest of the Welsh archers were wading into the water. The battle still raged fiercely on the bridge and below the tower. More and more English troops were being brought up from the rear. There was not enough room for all of them to engage the French on the bridge. Many of them followed the Welshmen into the water, wading towards the boats.

After a savage fight, Martin and his friends killed or maimed about a dozen of the Genoese and put the rest to flight, leaping from boat to boat towards the French-held bank of the river. Nearly three dozen Genoese manning the boats nearest the English-held bank found themselves cut off from the new town by the Welshmen's seizure of three boats at the centre of the line. The Genoese began to advance along the line of boats towards them, intending to fight their way to the far bank before the archers in the water could reinforce those already on the boats. Spotting a smouldering brazier on the deck, Martin snatched up an unlit reed-torch and thrust it into the glowing coals until it began to burn fiercely, sending dark wisps of smoke up into the bright summer sky. He waited until the torch was fully ablaze before tossing it on to the next boat between him and the Genoese. The flames licked at some trailing rigging. Suddenly the furled canvas sail was alight, the flames spreading rapidly throughout the small ship. By the time the Genoese had reached the next boat, their way was blocked by the roaring inferno.

The gentle breeze was enough to fan some of the flames towards the barge on which Martin and the others now stood. Madog retrieved his battleaxe, and they jumped into the next boat. They hacked through the painters that held the line of boats together, setting the burning ships adrift.

Some of the archers in the water had already reached the boats still moored to the south bank and were helped up on deck by Martin and his friends. Others swam directly to the far bank of the river. Madog led the way along the line of boats, leaping from deck to deck, Martin, Ieuan and Rudcock close behind him, until they came to the last boat. There they jumped into the waist-deep water and waded to the bank, scrambling out of the river. A handful of French soldiers came to meet them on the bank, determined to stop the English from gaining a foothold on the Île Saint-Jean. One of them tried to run Martin through with a spear. Martin knocked the spear-head aside with his left hand before smashing the man's skull with his broadsword. His arms were beginning to ache with fatigue. He ignored his exhaustion, thrusting his sword at another man's chest. He was still trying to withdraw the blade from the dead man's ribcage when a third ran at him wielding a sword. Madog stepped in and split the man's skull apart with his axe. Behind them, more and more English and Welsh troops were swarming up the bank. The English had finally got their foothold on the Île Saint-Jean. Realising that they were massively outnumbered, the French rapidly turned tail and fled into the streets of the new town.

Many of the archers collapsed on to the ground, gasping for breath. Martin found himself urging them on. He too desperately wanted to lie down and rest, but he was frightened that if he did so he might not find the strength to get up again, and he had not forgotten that they had made the crossing for a specific purpose. If they stopped where they were, then the fight on the boats would have been for nothing.

'Come on, keep moving!' he roared, kicking at the men who lay down. Some of them swore at him and refused to budge, but the rest rose wearily to their feet and followed him. They charged through the broad streets, Martin brandishing his sword as he led the way. Now Madog and Ieuan were struggling to keep up with him. A few French troops in the streets ahead of them were taken completely by surprise, thinking that the men charging up behind them must be on their side. Martin reached the nearest, hacking at his face before the man had a chance to realise his mistake. The next man was too numb with shock to react in time. Martin thrust his sword through the man's stomach, hardly slowing as he ran past, twisting the dying man around as he tugged his blade free. Realising now that they were facing the enemy, the rest of the Frenchmen fled for cover before this wild mob of English and Welsh troops.

Martin led the way into the next street, turning left and left again until suddenly the tower at the French-held side of the bridge was directly ahead of him. The two sides still strove against one another furiously in the enclosed space below. By now the English were beginning to make some headway, forcing the French back inch by inch.

Seeing his goal in sight, Martin redoubled his efforts, his feet pounding the cobbles as he sprinted towards the enemies' backs. He heard himself roar with bestial fury. Hearing him, some of the Frenchmen turned, but he was already upon them, hacking and slashing left and right. The others still with him likewise fell upon the French ranks. The French at the rear tried to face this new threat, but they were so closely packed in the confined space below the tower that there was hardly room to turn. A wave of panic spread through the French ranks as they realised that they were hemmed in, attacked from behind as well as before. A few of them dashed through a heavy oak door into the tower, slamming it behind them. Others tried to follow them, clawing at the iron-bound door and finding it barred from within. The French ranks broke and fled, retreating into the new town, barging past the English and Welsh troops who tried to block their path. Martin stood in their way, slashing with his sword at the men who ran past him, but none of them were in a mood to stop and challenge him. Someone cannoned into him, sending him sprawling on the cobbles. Feet stampeded all around him. Someone kicked him in the side. Too numb to feel any pain, Martin picked himself up. He was about to pursue the fleeing Frenchmen when someone grabbed him by the arm and dragged him down a side alley behind the tower moments before an English troop of men-at-arms charged past, riding down the French with their lances.

'God's soul, Martin, have you lost your wits?' panted Rudcock. 'Do you want to get yourself killed?'

Martin broke free of his grip with a snarl and stepped back into the street, joining the English foot-soldiers who were now charging past, whooping victoriously, bellowing 'Havoc!' – no quarter.

'For the love of Saint Michael!' Rudcock shouted after him. 'Martin, it's over! We've won!'

Martin gave no indication that he had heard. Rudcock sighed wearily and went after him.

Many of the French were throwing down their arms and trying to surrender, but they were slaughtered without mercy. The streets were filled with carnage as soldiers and civilians alike were dragged from houses and put to the sword. Everything the English had done so far during the fortnight since they landed in France paled into insignificance compared to the butchery of that afternoon. The people of Caen had tried to resist the advancing English army and, in accordance with the rules of war, now they had to pay the penalty. The English and Welsh troops rampaged through the new town, killing everyone and everything that moved in an orgy of bloodshed and destruction. Whether or not the people they encountered were armed did not enter into it: children and old men were slaughtered as a matter of course, women subjected to mass-rape before being horribly mutilated. In their desperation, many of the citizens barricaded themselves in their houses and hurled slates and wooden beams down from the rooftops on to the English troops in the streets below.

It was in the midst of one such scene of carnage that Rudcock caught up with Martin, grabbing his arm. 'Christ's passion, Martin! Will you stop a moment? It's over! We've won!'

'It isn't over until every last one of these whoresons . . .'

Before he could finish, Rudcock suddenly seized him, throwing him to the ground, and a moment later a heavy wooden bench crashed to the cobbles where the two of them had been standing.

'God's blood!' Martin flinched as a roof-slate shattered near his head, showering him with fragments. As more missiles were showered down around them, they picked themselves up and ran to the house from which the attack was being launched. Pressing themselves up against the outside front wall, they were out of sight from above, protected from the hail of slates by the eaves, but otherwise pinned down.

Rudcock threw his shoulder against the door, but it held fast. 'Let's see if there's a back way,' he suggested.

Martin shook his head and took a few steps back, hurling himself bodily against one of the shuttered windows. It splintered under his weight and he fell through, rolling on the floor of the front room. He rose up on one knee, pulling his sword from its scabbard. The room was empty. He climbed to his feet and hurried to the front door, removing the bar and lifting the latch to allow Rudcock to slip inside.

They ran up the stairs, Martin leading the way, sword in hand. A dark figure loomed up in front of him at the top of the first flight, and he thrust his sword forward. Blood spattered on the floorboards, and the figure fell back into a pool of sunlight cast through a window. It was a red-haired woman in her early thirties. In life she must have been handsome. Martin found himself wondering what it might have been like to make love to her. A waste of a fair face and a good body, he concluded cynically. He felt no remorse. It served her right for being in the wrong place at the wrong time. Her family should have considered the possible consequences when they started trying to drop furniture on the king's archers.

They stepped over her body and continued up the next flight of stairs until they reached the top, where they found a hatch in the ceiling. They exchanged glances.

'They'll be waiting for us,' whispered Rudcock.

Martin nodded, and sheathed his sword, climbing up the short ladder leading to the hatch. He placed one palm on the underside of the hatch, took a deep breath, and threw it open.

A spear was thrust down at him. He squirmed out of the way, catching the haft of the spear in one hand and tugging on it with all his might. The man holding the spear lost his balance and fell through the hatch, cracking his head as he hit the floor below. Rudcock plunged the tip of his sword into the man's heart to make sure he was dead.

Martin was already hauling himself out on to the sloping roof. A man was scrambling along the side of the roof to attack him, but he was unarmed. Martin drew his sword once more. The man stopped short. Martin grinned savagely, advancing slowly across the slope of the roof towards him. The man prised up a roof-slate and hurled it at Martin's head. Martin ducked, struggling to maintain his footing. The slate sailed over his head and smashed against the cobbles three storeys below. Martin straight-ened, resuming his implacable advance. Terrified, the man panicked, and tried to run to the top of the roof. He had almost made it when his feet slipped out from under him and he landed heavily on his front. He managed to hook his hands over the apex of the roof, and scrabbled for a foothold on the tiles. Martin hacked at his legs with a grunt of frustration, chopping one of the man's feet clean off. Blood gushed from the stump, coursing down the tiles towards the guttering. After a few shocked seconds, the man realised what had happened and gave a strangled gasp of agony. He released his grip to clutch at his stump, and rolled down the roof, shooting over the edge and plummeting to the street far below with a wail. Martin plucked his dismembered foot from the guttering and carelessly tossed it down after him.

By now, Rudcock had joined him on the roof. 'I saw at least three men up here when we were down below,' he said nervously. It was not the height that made him nervous so much as the strange look on Martin's face.

Martin nodded, and gestured with one hand to encompass a circuit of the roof. 'You go that way, I'll go this.'

Turning the corner of the roof, Martin found a tow-headed, freckle-faced youth pressing himself flat against the tiles. Seeing Martin, the youth began to inch away from him. He was the same age as Martin, but lacked his size and strength. Martin sheathed his sword with a contemptuous sneer.

'So, you like throwing things off rooftops, do you?'

The youth did not understand him, but shook his head anyway, trembling.

Martin reached out and seized him by the collar of his tunic, pulling him upright. 'Do you?' he repeated.

A damp stain began to spread down the youth's leggings. Martin grimaced in disgust.

'Well, I'll let you into a little secret,' he hissed. 'So do I.' He swung the youth around so that his back was to the edge of the roof, and shoved him in the face. The youth teetered, his arms flailing, and then he was gone, plummeting with a scream of terror that was soon cut short by the cobbles below.

Martin noticed Rudcock, pale-faced, standing at the next corner, and gestured to the broken body far below. 'Found him.'

'Aye,' Rudcock said softly.

They climbed back in from the roof, and Rudcock hurried back down the stairs without so much as a backward glance. Martin was about to follow when he heard a floorboard creak in one of the rooms leading off the top landing. Facing the door, he eased his sword out of its scabbard and kicked the door open.

The room was dominated by a large four-poster bed, its heavy velvet drapes tied back to the posts. Martin guessed that the people who had lived there must have been nobles, or at least wealthy burghers. Seeing no one in the bedroom, he entered cautiously, his eyes searching the room, sword poised to strike.

Two large blue eyes peered back at him over the edge of the bed.

'Come out from behind there,' he ordered. 'Show yourself.'

She understood the gist of his words, and rose trembling to her feet. She was a young woman, younger than himself, with a pale face and red hair. There was something vulnerable about her as she stood there before him, shaking with fear. Martin's throat was dry, his stomach knotted inside. He suddenly realised he wanted her – more than he had ever wanted anything in his whole life – and there was nothing to stop him from taking her. The other men did as they pleased with the women of Normandy. Why should he be any different? No one expected him to be any different; he was a churl, not bound by the strictures of chivalry.

He fumbled his sword back into its scabbard and closed the door behind him, propping it shut with a chair so that he would not be disturbed. His hands were shaking uncontrollably. He forgot about Rudcock and the rest of his companions, he forgot about Beatrice, and he forgot about the king's edict: after all, everyone else seemed to. Nothing existed for him any more except this woman, and the urgent need he felt to slake this sudden lust that threatened to consume him from within. Part of his mind screamed at him that what he was about to do was wrong, but that part was no longer in control. The same bestial instincts that controlled his actions in battle now took over.

He walked around to the other side of the bed to face her. She shrank away from him, but he caught her around the waist, pulling her against him. She tried to cry out, but he pressed his lips against hers, trying to force his tongue between her clenched teeth. She attempted to push him away, pounding with her tiny fists on his chest, but the ineffectual blows only made him laugh. They emphasised her powerlessness, only serving to increase his lust. She babbled away in French, her eyes pleading with him, but he would no longer meet her eyes. He grabbed the front of her dress and ripped it open. She gasped in horror and tried to break away from him, but he seized her by the arm and hauled her back, throwing her against the wall. She cried out in pain. He slapped her back-handed across the face, drawing blood from the corner of her mouth. He tore the rest of her clothes from her body, using the blade of his rondel when the complex fastenings proved too frustrating for his trembling fingers. She no longer tried to escape, standing there stock-still, her eyes closed, moaning with terror. He pushed her back against the wall with one hand on her throat, the other fumbling with the hem of his tunic. He pushed his breech-cloth down over his hips, and forced himself into her. She screamed in pain as he violated her, but he was oblivious to her suffering. There was no satisfaction in his release, only a sense of anti-climax. Breathing hard, he pressed his forehead against the cold bricks behind her head.

Then the full magnitude of what he had done hit him, and he pulled away from her. He was filled with self-loathing as he realised he had betrayed everything he had believed in, acting the part of the vilest churl in an Arthurian legend by taking advantage of the weak and helpless. He hunched himself up on the floor in one corner of the room, his knees drawn up against his chest and his face buried in his hands as his shoulders shook with sobs of shame.

How long he crouched there he could not be sure, but after a while he felt something touch him lightly on the forehead, and looked up sharply. The girl quickly withdrew her hand. She was kneeling on the floor before him, still trembling, a bedsheet wrapped around herself. Her face was streaked with tears. He noticed now that she was actually quite plain. There was no hatred in her eyes, only fear and . . . pity? It was the first time in his life he had ever felt completely inadequate. 'I'm so sorry,' he whispered. 'Oh, Christ forgive me! What have I done? I'm so sorry!'

After a while he mopped the tears from his cheeks with his hands, wiped his nose on his sleeve and pushed himself to his feet, readjusting his clothing. Then, after a moment's hesitation, he took the purse from his belt and tossed it on to the bed between them. 'It's not much, I know, but if it will help make amends . . . '

She stared first at the bulging purse, and then at him. There was no longer pity in her eyes, only contempt. She snatched up the purse and flung it in his face with all her might.

'*Bâtard! Je ne suis pas une putain!*'

The purse was heavy, and the blow hurt his cheek, but

not as much as it wounded his conscience. He left the purse where it fell and stumbled out of the room, racked with guilt and shame.

Except for the castle, which still held out with a garrison of a few hundred men, the entire city of Caen had fallen to the English. The houses opposite the church were still burning fiercely, sending smoke wafting over the scene of the battle. Corpses lay everywhere, in the streets, on the river-bank, floating in the river itself. The corpses on the bridge lay so thick that the cobbles below were only visible in one or two places. A couple of figures moved amongst the heaps of the dead, helping themselves to the contents of their purses. The looters might have been camp followers or soldiers, but Holland did not much care either way. It was accepted that even the professional soldiers would loot to supplement their pay. One thing was certain: the rightful owners no longer needed the money.

Holland's palfrey picked its way fastidiously across the bridge. Beside him rode Villiers and Sir Thomas Daniels, a knight in the prince's retinue. 'A hard battle,' observed Daniels, as the three of them rode past the shattered barricade.

'Aye,' agreed Holland, ducking his head as they passed under the archway beneath the tower. 'We lost a great many good men.' By which he meant good fighters, rather than men who would be missed by their friends and families.

Some men-at-arms were trying to break down the door of the tower, and making heavy weather of it. Holland, Daniels and Villiers rode past, emerging into the small square behind the tower where some hobelars were trying to torture a merchant into revealing the whereabouts of his cache of gold. The merchant was trying to explain that all his money was invested in overseas trading ventures, but the hobelars did not understand, so they went on with the torture.

A young nun emerged from a side alley at a run. Her features contorted with terror, she glanced over her shoulder at her pursuers, and did not see Holland until she had bumped into his palfrey. The horse shied away skittishly.

'By charity!' Holland exclaimed irritably, patting the beast's neck to soothe it.

The nun backed away, staring up at the bloodied warrior in fear. Her pursuers, three archers, emerged from the alleyway, cackling lecherously. Seeing Holland, they stopped short.

'You!' snapped Holland, indicating one of the archers at random. 'Come here.'

The man doffed his cap and approached Holland, bowing and scraping obsequiously. 'My lord?'

Holland leant forward on the pommel of his saddle to address the archer. 'Have you forgotten the king's edict forbidding the violation of holy places?'

The archer furrowed his brow, not understanding the *double-entendre* at first.

Holland smiled at him benevolently.

The archer's brow cleared, and he was unable to stifle a chuckle. Holland laughed. The other two archers thought it would be diplomatic to join in the laughter, until all four of them were guffawing merrily. It was at that point that Holland's face suddenly fell stern again, and in the same instant he viciously kicked the first archer in the face. He was still wearing his armour, and the steel toecap of his sabaton knocked the archer unconscious before he had even hit the ground.

Holland waved the other two archers across. 'Your friend seems to have fallen ill. Doubtless a judgement from God for his impure thoughts. I suggest you take him away before I have all three of you hanged, so that you can explain yourselves to the Almighty in person.'

The two archers approached Holland fearfully, lest he

should mete out similar treatment to them, but he merely watched while they gathered up their friend between them and dragged him away. 'Scum,' Holland muttered under his breath.

'I suppose you expect me to be grateful,' the nun told him coldly. Her English was passable, though thickly accented.

Holland removed his bascinet. 'I expect nothing from you, madam.'

'I cannot say that I approve of the violent means by which my salvation was effected,' she continued. 'You act as though you were the instrument of God's justice.'

'Yet you think me an agent of the Devil,' Holland observed perceptively, with a faint smile.

'Had it not been for you and your countrymen, I should not have needed rescuing at all.'

'And had not the people of Caen resisted, I might not have seen so many of the king's men die in today's attack,' Holland said with a shrug.

The nun was unimpressed. 'They were God's children, not your king's men.'

'God gave them life,' admitted Holland. 'But my king – your king too, by right – gave them something to live for.'

'Something to die for, you mean,' she sneered.

'Better to die for a noble cause than to die uselessly.'

'You call this a noble cause?' She gestured at the blood-soaked streets.

'Aye. Do not tell me you would not also die for a cause. Your faith, perhaps?'

'Naturally. But if I die, at least I can be certain of receiving my just reward in Heaven.'

'That is as maybe,' acknowledged Holland, growing bored with the debate. 'But unless you wish to do so today, I suggest you stay close by me.'

'The Devil's protection!' she spat.

'Perhaps. But will you accept it, I wonder?'

The nun did not reply, but she lingered in Holland's company nonetheless.

One of Holland's archers appeared, walking back towards the tower from the heart of the new town. Recognising him, Holland struggled to put a name to his face. 'Rudcock!' he exclaimed at last. 'What the Devil are you doing here? The rest of the company is seeking quarters in the old town. Why aren't you with them?'

'Sorry, Sir Thomas. Me and Martin got separated from the others during the battle.'

'Separated? How? I thought I gave orders for your platoon to fall back?' Holland said angrily.

'That you did, sir. But Martin saw a ford across the river, and we thought if we could cross to the other side and attack the French on the bridge from behind . . . '

'You mean, that was you and Kemp I saw leading those Welsh archers across the river to attack the boats?'

'Well, we weren't exactly *leading* them, sir,' squirmed Rudcock.

'And neither of you sought to consult myself or Serjeant Preston before you initiated this flanking attack?' Holland continued sternly.

'Begging your pardon, sir, but you were a bit preoccupied, like, and we didn't think there'd be time to find the serjeant before the French reinforced the boats . . . '

'So the pair of you decided to take matters into your own hands and acted entirely on your own initiative?' Holland's tone was incredulous.

'You could put it like that, sir.'

'That is exactly how I am putting it, Rudcock. Whose idea was this?'

Rudcock hung his head. 'Mine, sir. It seemed like the right thing to do . . . ' he pleaded nervously.

'It was the right thing to do,' said Holland, reaching for his purse and tossing a shilling to the astounded Rudcock. 'That rear attack turned the enemy flank not a moment too soon.' He permitted himself one of his rare smiles. 'Well done, Rudcock.'

'In that case, sir, you'd best give this to Martin,' said Rudcock, offering back the coin. 'It were his idea, not mine.'

'And you were covering for him, thinking I might be wrathful?'

'Aye, sir.'

'Then keep it. Honesty deserves its own reward as much as initiative. Where is Kemp now?'

'I lost him somewhere in the new town,' admitted Rudcock, gesturing back the way he had come. 'He's not himsen today, sir. To tell the truth, he's been acting queer for a few days now. I'm worried about him . . .'

But Holland was no longer listening, his attention caught by the sound of a man's voice, calling out his name. *'Sieur Thomas! Est-il vraiment vous? Sauvez-nous, pour la grâce de Dieu!'*

Holland and Daniels both glanced around, but saw no one.

'Ici! Up here!'

They glanced up, and saw a pale face at an upper-storey window of the tower. Holland walked his horse backwards a few paces, shading his eye with one hand as he gazed up at the window. 'Should I know you?' he demanded coldly.

'Oui! C'est moi! It is I, Raoul de Brienne, Comte d'Eu! We campaigned together in Prussia and Granada, *n'est-ce-pas?'*

Holland remembered d'Eu. Three years ago, immediately following the Truce of Malestroit, Holland had travelled to Spain with Henry of Derby and the Earl of Salisbury to crusade against the Moors in Granada. The Comtes d'Eu and de Tancarville had travelled with them, and the five had been present at the siege of Algeçiras. D'Eu was an honourable man, but a little naïve: he had never suspected that the three Englishmen had been on a secret mission to draw the King of Castile away from his alliance with Valois.

D'Eu was also the Constable of France, and as such would earn his captor a handsome ransom. Holland smiled, and bowed in his saddle. 'Good day to you, my lord. Do you wish to surrender?'

'Yes, if you can offer us safe conduct.'

'How many of you are there?'

'Myself; Jean de Melun, Comte de Tancarville, with whom you are also acquainted; and a dozen men-at-arms.'

Holland and Daniels exchanged glances. De Tancarville was the Chamberlain of France and, like d'Eu, he would fetch an impressive ransom. 'Throw your weapons out of the window, and then let us in,' ordered Holland. D'Eu nodded, and disappeared from the window. 'Fetch Preston and his platoon,' Holland told Villiers, who nodded, digging his heels into his palfrey's flanks and galloping back across the bridge.

As a collection of swords, spears and daggers dropped out of one of the windows, Holland and Daniels rode back under the archway to where the men-at-arms were still trying to prise open the tower door. 'Who's in charge here?' demanded Holland.

One of the men-at-arms, a grim-faced young serjeant, stepped forward. 'I suppose I am, sir,' he said.

'Do you know who I am, serjeant?'

'Aye, sir. You're Sir Thomas Holland.'

Holland nodded in satisfaction. 'The gentlemen in this building have surrendered to myself and Sir Thomas Daniels here. They are not to be harmed. Do you understand?'

The serjeant nodded. 'Aye, sir, right you are.' He turned to his companions. 'Right, lads, you heard Sir Thomas. Come away from there.'

Holland and Daniels dismounted, handing their bridles to Rudcock, and presently the door to the tower was opened from within. When Villiers returned with Preston and his men, Holland took some of them inside with Daniels. D'Eu formally surrendered to Holland, while de Tancarville did likewise to Daniels, and since Daniels was a knight in the prince's retinue, de Tancarville became a prisoner of the prince himself, no small honour in a way. Holland ordered some of his men to take the French men-at-arms to where the captives were being assembled. The two French noblemen gave their word of honour that they would make no attempt to escape, and were allowed to keep their swords as a symbol of their honourable surrender.

That night, Holland lodged at d'Eu's large mansion in the new town, and he dined with the two noble captives, along with the king himself, the prince and Daniels, as well as the Earls of Warwick and Northampton. Preston and his men were quartered in the tavern next door. The innkeeper and his family had already been slaughtered, so the wine was free, and Preston made no attempt to encourage his men to stint themselves. 'You fought well,' the serjeant admitted grudgingly. 'Sir Thomas is pleased with you. He's promised to give each of you a *regard* of twenty shillings for your work this day.' His seamed features cracked into a grin. 'And since we'll be staying in Caen for a few days to lick our wounds, as it were, you don't have to worry about getting up in the morning.'

The men greeted this news with a half-hearted cheer. Once they would have viewed twenty shillings as a small fortune; but now it was a fraction of the money most of them had taken in booty, let alone compared to the small fortune they knew Holland himself would receive for taking the Constable of France captive. Two of their number had died that day, and Robin Wighton, who had lost a hand, was in bed with a severe fever and not expected to last the night.

They helped themselves to food and wine, some of the younger ones boasting of the feats of arms they had performed in the assault. 'I killed five men on the bridge!' Tate asserted proudly, and turned to Preston. 'Am I a soldier now?' he asked with a grin, pleased to be able to turn Conyers' mockery on its head.

Preston glanced across to Martin, who stood alone by the counter, his head tilted back as he poured a flagon of wine down his throat: he had not forgotten his vow never to touch wine again, but there was no ale to be found, and he needed to get drunk. He allowed much of the wine to splash over his face: it was cold and refreshing, and cleaner than the blood that already smeared his features.

'How many men did *you* kill today, Kemp?' asked Preston.

Martin shrugged, and made a dismissive gesture. 'I lost count,' he said bleakly.

Preston pointed him out to the others. 'Now that's what I call a real God-damned soldier.'

Such praise coming from Preston might once have warmed Martin's heart, but that night he was not feeling proud of anything he had done that day. He desperately wanted to get drunk, but no amount of alcohol seemed to be able to blot out his terrible feelings of remorse. As the others sank steadily deeper into a state of complete drunkenness, Martin slipped out of the inn and wandered through the streets of the new town in the dark. He wanted to confess his sins, he realised. Nor did he want to talk about how he had murdered Lefthand and Murray at Cormolain; now, he considered that the least of his crimes.

He found Brother Ambrose sitting outside the mansion next door to the tavern, sharing a flagon of wine with Villiers. 'Hullo, Martin,' said the squire. 'A good day's work, eh?'

Martin nodded, although he did not consider any of his own deeds that day to have been good. 'Pardon me, Master Adam, but I were wondering if I could talk to Brother Ambrose? In private, like?'

Villiers grinned, and made as if to rise to his feet. 'Don't mind me. I can take a hint.'

But the young friar was on his feet first. 'It's all right, Master Adam, you stay put. Young Martin and I can go for a stroll. I need to stretch my legs anyway.'

Villiers nodded, and Martin and Ambrose began to walk down the street, side by side. 'Well then, young Martin, what can I do for you?'

Martin hesitated. 'Do you hear confession?' he asked uncertainly, feeling guilty that after having served in Holland's company for so long, he still had no idea whether or not Holland's chaplain took the men's confessions.

'Rarely, with such benighted, ungodly lost sheep for my flock,' Ambrose replied, gesturing at the tavern with a smile. 'You wish to confess, I take it?' Martin nodded. 'Splendid. Just when I was beginning to think you were beyond salvation. Not,' he added hurriedly, 'that any of the Lord's children ever fall so far that they are entirely beyond redemption.'

They were wandering through the darkened streets illuminated by the moon and stars, and the ruddy glow of the houses that still blazed in the old town.

'Well, what are you waiting for?' asked Ambrose, when Martin did not reply. 'We're neither of us getting any younger.'

'Should we not find a church? A chapel?' asked Martin.

Ambrose shrugged. 'God is everywhere. He hears all and sees all. This is as good a place as any.'

Martin bowed his head. 'Forgive me, Father, for I have sinned. It has been twelve weeks since my last confession.' That had been the Sunday before he had been arrested, accused of rape. It seemed more like twelve months had gone by since then.

'Twelve weeks?' echoed Ambrose. 'Hold your horses. This isn't going to take all night, is it? I rather got the impression that there was one sin in particular that you wanted to confess.' Ambrose seemed to have a very different approach to moral guidance than the curate of Saint Margaret's.

Martin nodded. 'I dishonoured a woman against her will,' he whispered.

Ambrose received this information with equanimity. 'I see. When was this?'

'Today.'

'Immediately after the battle?'

'Aye.'

Ambrose nodded. 'It happens. It's a dangerously short step from blood lust to carnal lust. Well, you can say a few *Ave Marias* if it will make you feel better.'

Martin stared at him incredulously. 'Is that all? Should I not undertake some kind of penance?'

'Such as? A pilgrimage, perhaps? Believe me, boy, if everyone guilty of rape in this army were ordered to go on a pilgrimage to Jerusalem, we might as well abandon this war here and now and go on a crusade to the Holy Land instead,' Ambrose said with a chuckle.

Martin was astonished by the chaplain's attitude. 'But surely . . . '

'Listen, lad. There are those who say that we pay for our sins in this life rather than the next. From the look on your face, I'd say that you're paying already. At least you have the decency to feel guilty about what you've done. That's more than most of the king's men ever do – aye, and the king himself, as some do say. There's more rejoicing in Heaven over one sinner who repents than over ninety-nine righteous people who do not need to repent. The harm you've done to that girl cannot be undone. But perhaps in time she'll come to realise that what you did to her is no true stain on her honour, for it happened through no fault of her own, and with God's guidance she'll be able to draw some comfort from that. You, on the other hand, will have to bear the burden of your guilt until your dying day, and perhaps beyond it.'

'I truly feel better for knowing that,' Martin replied sarcastically.

'If you want me to wave a magic wand to make you feel better, then I'm afraid I can't help you. It's a pardoner you're wanting, not a confessor. All I can do is make you face up to the things I think you already realised, deep down in your heart, if you did but know it. Perhaps that is punishment enough; I don't know, so I can't say. Only God can judge us.'

Martin took his leave of Ambrose. He did not feel any better.

Rudcock was awoken in the small hours of the morning by the overwhelming need to relieve himself. He had bedded down for the night in the main room of the tavern, all of the rooms upstairs having been claimed by knights, squires or men-at-arms. There was no pot handy, and not wanting to foul the room he was likely to be sleeping in for the next few nights he stumbled towards the door, tripping over only half his companions in his drunken stupor. Curses and imprecations followed him as he staggered out into the cool night air.

The city was far from silent, even at that late hour. The men who had marched with the rearguard – and consequently had not started their revels until a few hours after those who were first into the city – were still going strong. The houses burning in the old town still lit up the skyline and the noise of raucous singing and shouting filled the night, along with the occasional burst of laughter and one or two screams.

Rudcock lifted the hem of his tunic and unfastened his breech-cloth to urinate into the gutter that ran down the middle of the street, sighing with relief. He could hear someone singing nearby, the voice slurred with drink but vaguely familiar.

' . . . I've tram'led the folk in wrath and ire, An' cast 'em down into . . . their sh . . . shameful mire.'

Rudcock shook off the drips and readjusted his clothing, turning to search for the singer. A dark figure was walking along the apex of the tavern's tiled roof, swaying drunkenly, arms outstretched to maintain his balance, a flagon in his right hand. Every few steps, he would pause in his song and tilt the flagon to his lips.

Rudcock furrowed his brow in disbelief. He had never seen his friend so drunk before. '*Martin?*'

Martin halted, swaying alarmingly, and peered into the gloom below. 'Hullo, Hodge,' he said, recognising his friend at last.

'For Holy Charity, Martin! What in the name of God are you doing up there?' hissed Rudcock.

'Singing,' Martin replied absently, and glanced at the flagon in his hand. 'And drinking,' he added. 'Why don't you come up and join me, and we can sink a couple of flagons of this French horse-piss they call wine?'

'You're drunk!'

'Aye – not that it's done me any good.'

'Are you trying to get yourself killed?'

'Summat o' that, aye and like.'

'Hold still while I fetch a ladder.'

'There's one round the back.' Martin gestured with his right hand and swayed wildly on one foot, inadvertently dropping the flagon as he struggled to maintain his balance. It rattled noisily down the tiles and sailed out into space, smashing against the cobbles. 'God-damn it! Bring up another couple of flagons on your way, would you, Hodge?'

'I'd say you've had enough,' Rudcock muttered under his breath, making his way round to the yard at the back of the tavern.

One of the dormer windows opened, and a man thrust his head out. 'Will you keep the God-damned noise down? There's decent folk trying to sleep in here!'

'Decent folk?' sneered Martin. 'There's no such thing!'

'Shut up, by Saint Paul's thumb, before I come out there and shut you up!'

'Kiss my arse,' suggested Martin, unfastening his breech-cloth to bare his buttocks at the man, who scowled, withdrawing his head and slamming the shutters on the window.

Rudcock found a sturdy ladder propped up against the eaves, probably the same one Martin had used to climb up there in the first place. 'For Gods sake, Martin, will you come down?'

'Aye, like as not – one way or another.'

Rudcock sighed heavily, and began to climb the ladder. He hauled himself up on to the tiles to find Martin seated on the apex of the roof, his elbows on his knees and his chin resting on his fists as he stared across the rooftops of Caen. Rudcock crawled up to join him. 'I'm asking you nicely,' he panted. 'Will you ... please ... come ... *down*?'

'It's a bonny view from up here,' said Martin, gazing across to where the fires raged in the old town.

'Christ's tears and wounds! What is *wrong* with you, Martin? There's more to this than too much to drink.'

'Don't you think it's a bonny view?'

'Martin!' Rudcock snapped.

'What?'

'Why all this? You hardly touched wine before, and now you're as pissed as a lord and dancing with death like there's no tomorrow. What's got into you? Apart from several dozen flagons of wine, that is?'

'Hodge. Roger. You're my companion-in-arms, aren't you?'

'I try to be,' Rudcock replied evenly. 'You aren't going to turn all maudlin on me, are you?' he asked nervously.

Martin shook his head. 'If I asked you to do me a favour, you would, wouldn't you?'

'Aye, I reckon so.'

'I want you to take me to the king.'

'Take you to the king! What makes you reckon his Majesty wants to see a disgusting drunk like you?'

'He'll pay you forty shillings to take me to him. Someone's going to get that forty shillings, and I'd rather it were my old friend Roger Rudcock.'

'Forty shillings? Martin, what in Christ's name are you . . . ?' Then the penny dropped. 'Oh-ho, so that's what happened to you when I left you in that house. I were wondering how you got that shiner. Crack you one, did she?'

'Christ's blood, Hodge, this is serious.'

'What's the matter? Are you feeling guilty about it?'

'Aye, God damn you!'

'Did you kill her afterwards?'

'Kill her? No!'

'Then she's the lucky one, I reckon. There can't be many women in this city between the ages of twelve and sixty who weren't raped and murdered today. She can count herself lucky she's still alive; if someone else hasn't come along and raped her after you, and slit her throat into the bargain. The king's edict doesn't apply here in Caen. They tried to resist, so now they have to pay the penalty. That's the rules of war, that is.'

'Aye? And what about the rules of God?'

'God closes his eyes when men go to war,' Rudcock opined philosophically. He tried to shift into a more comfortable position, and slipped. He might have fallen from the edge of the roof had not Martin swiftly caught him by the wrist and hauled him back to safety. Rudcock clung to the roof in silence for a few moments, sick with shock and gasping for breath. 'Martin?' he said at last.

'Aye?'

'Can we get down now?'

Martin considered the proposition ruminatively for a moment. 'Aye,' he agreed finally.

In spite of the amount of alcohol he had consumed, Martin still had difficulty in getting to sleep that night. Even when he finally nodded off shortly before cock-crow, he was tormented by nightmares. He dreamed that he had been condemned to suffer for eternity in the fiery pits of Hell. The infernal regions looked remarkably like a burning Norman village, and the Devil who presided over the domain of the damned wore a patch of white silk over one eye.

Sir Thomas Holland rose late the following morning and dressed briskly, picking up a clean towel before making his way downstairs. Like his men, he had made a heavy night of it, drinking hard to keep up with his king. He blinked at the bright sunlight as he stepped out of d'Eu's town-house, making his way to the stone horse-trough that stood in front of the tavern next door. Removing his eye patch, he doused his head in the cool water, before straightening and towelling his hair and face dry. He was replacing the patch when Norwich rode up on a palfrey, looking bright and fresh. Norwich was not a renowned drinker, and had been one of the few who had abstained the previous night.

'Good day to you, Sir Thomas,' Norwich greeted Holland.

'Aye; and a fine one it is, too.' The events of the previous day had been more or less satisfactory, and Holland was in good spirits despite his hangover. 'What news do you bring?'

'And what makes you think I have any news?'

Holland smiled thinly. 'Well, I doubt even you would come solely to gloat over a knight with a thick head.'

Norwich chuckled and nodded. 'Five men tried to sneak out of the castle earlier this morning,' he said. 'We managed to capture two of them alive.'

'And the other three?'

'God rest their souls,' said Norwich, crossing himself piously. 'According to one of the men we captured, the garrison of the castle is ready to surrender.'

'That is good news indeed,' remarked Holland, mopping his neck with the towel. 'What is stopping them?'

'The Bishop of Bayeux,' explained Norwich. 'He still commands the garrison.'

'He is a brave man, then.'

'Or a stubborn one.'

'Does his Majesty intend to assault the castle?'

Norwich shook his head. 'You've seen for yourself how impregnable it is. In addition to that, it has a garrison of one hundred men-at-arms and two hundred Genoese crossbowmen. Yet by the same token, that is a great many mouths to feed, and I do not believe that the bishop had much time to stock the castle with victuals. If morale is as low as they say, I doubt they will hold out for long, even with our stubborn friend the bishop to hold them together.'

'I thought that his Majesty desired to avoid a protracted siege?'

'He does. The word is that Valois went to fetch the Oriflamme from Saint-Denys six days ago.' The Oriflamme was the sacred banner of scarlet silk kept in the crypt of the Abbey of Saint-Denys, and given to the kings of France by the abbot when they intended to lead an army to war.

'Then he intends to raise a fresh army here in the north, without waiting for his son to return from Gascony with his troops.'

*

317

Norwich nodded. 'Valois could be here with a fresh army within two weeks, if he acts swiftly.

Holland snorted derisively. 'I have never associated the name of Valois with swift action,' he sneered.

Norwich shrugged. 'Be that as it may, his Majesty is resolute in his intention that we should leave Caen before the month is out.'

'Within four days,' deduced Holland. 'And if the castle has not surrendered by then?'

'A token force will remain behind to garrison the city and maintain the siege of the castle. But I did not come here to tell you this.' He took a parchment scroll from one of his saddle bags and handed it down to Holland. 'This is a copy of a letter that we found last night in the mayor of Caen's house. His Majesty feels it should be read out to the men, to remind them of why we are at war with Valois.'

'I think my men are happy enough to serve their king without concerning themselves with the whys and where-fores,' replied Holland, unrolling the scroll and casting an eye over the writing within. It was an English translation of a letter from Valois to the burghers of Caen, enjoining them to prepare for an invasion of England. Holland tapped at the date with a forefinger. 'This letter is eight years old.'

Norwich shrugged again. 'It takes a great deal of time to prepare an invasion. You will have it read to your men? They saw the French warships at Saint-Vaast-la-Hougue. Let them draw their own conclusions.'

Holland nodded. He could see through the king's propaganda, but he approved of its intention, and had never been a man to shrink from using unscrupulous methods to achieve what he believed in.

'You may keep that copy,' Norwich told him, guiding his horse on down the street. 'Plenty more are being made.'

*

English and Welsh troops roamed the surrounding countryside during the four days the army lingered at Caen, setting alight the crops that were ripening in the July sun. When they were not sent out foraging for victuals, Martin and his companions had their time more or less to themselves. They spent it wandering the streets of the city. They visited the great abbey to the west of the old town, where they found the tomb of William the Conqueror. Inglewood had to explain the Conqueror's significance to some of the less well-educated members of the platoon. Newbolt remained resolutely unimpressed by the fact that they were standing by the tomb of one of England's most famous kings. Martin, on the other hand, was more inclined to revere the bones of a warrior than a saint. Although he did not doubt for a moment that his family was of Saxon rather than Norman origin, he had always been an admirer of the Norman duke who had conquered England with a relatively small band of followers. But then, as Conyers was quick to point out, history had a habit of heaping praise on victors as much as it cast odium on the defeated.

As they returned to the new town, they encountered Ieuan ap Morgan and Madog Fychan by the church of St Peter. Martin performed the introductions, while his English companions regarded the two Welshmen with a certain degree of suspicion.

'I knew a Welshman once,' said Newbolt. 'They hanged him for thieving.'

'Oh aye?' Ieuan was unperturbed. 'Well, that's English justice for you.'

'Martin's been telling us you reckon yourselves to be bonny archers,' said Rudcock.

'Better than you English, that's for certain,' said Madog.

'Have you ever seen any of our platoon shoot?'

'We saw you lot shooting on the beach at Saint-Vaast.

319

It's a wonder Bertrand and his men didn't sweep us back into the sea.'

'The best man in our platoon can outshoot the best man in yours any day.'

'Is tomorrow soon enough for you?'

'Tomorrow?' Rudcock was caught off guard.

Ieuan nodded. 'At noon, on the common to the southwest of the Île Saint-Jean: an archery contest. Our best man against yours.'

'You're on,' said Rudcock. 'The stake?'

'Our respective reputations as archers,' Ieuan said with a grin. 'Although you're welcome to make a wager on the side if you want.'

'I'll give you two-to-one on Ieuan,' said Madog.

'I'll take it,' Rudcock said eagerly. 'Ten shillings.' He spat into his palm, and they shook on it.

They went their separate ways, the Englishmen returning to the tavern.

'Who is our best archer?' asked Martin.

'You are,' Brewster told him dryly.

News of the impending contest spread rapidly throughout the army. By the time Martin and his friends arrived at the appointed place the following day, there was already a small crowd of soldiers, as well as one or two knights and nobles. Martin had shot well in front of crowds before now, and was determined not to let them put his aim off; but as the appointed hour drew near, he was astonished to see the young prince arrive with Holland. As Martin was taking his longbow from his bow-bag, Preston approached him.

'Sir Thomas has enough faith in your skill to wager twenty marks on you, so don't you dare muff it,' he growled.

A herald had agreed to adjudicate the match with the consent of both sides, and he called the rival archers to join him in the centre of the common, accompanied by their seconds. Martin had chosen Rudcock to be his second.

'So you're the best man your platoon could field,' observed Ieuan, with a smile. Inevitably, he had chosen Madog to be his second.

Martin nodded. 'What are we to use as targets?'

Ieuan waved to Dafydd, who approached leading a mule with a closed-top wicker pannier strapped to its back. The sound of doves cooing was clearly audible.

'Birds in flight?' Rudcock exclaimed in horror. 'That's impossible! I'm sorry, all wagers are off.'

Ieuan shrugged. 'It's no more impossible for Martin than it is for me,' he pointed out evenly.

'He's right,' said Martin. 'Besides, I'm not going to back down now. Not in front of this crowd.'

'If you're ready?' asked the herald. 'I'll release the first dove. When I give the command, you may both loose one arrow each. If either party lets fly before I give the word, then they will be disqualified.'

'What if both parties let fly before you give the word?' demanded Conyers, who had wagered five shillings on Martin, and wanted to be sure that everyone had the rules straight.

'Then it's a draw,' the herald told him with a grimace. 'We replay.'

'Shut up, John,' Rudcock suggested irritably.

Conyers looked put out, but for once said nothing.

The herald ordered Martin and Ieuan to stand at their marks, large, round, smooth, flat pebbles found on the river-bank, spaced ten yards apart. They nocked arrows to their bows and braced their legs.

'Draw . . . ' ordered the herald, and released the first dove. It fluttered up into the air, silhouetted black against the pale blue sky. 'Loose!'

The two archers let fly simultaneously. Martin's shot came close, but it was Ieuan's arrow that pierced the dove's breast. Martin did not question the result, but Conyers insisted that they checked the feathered shaft that impaled the bird, just to be sure, much to everyone else's exasperation.

'Best out of three?' Martin asked wryly.

Ieuan grinned. 'What did you think we'd brought more than one bird for?'

The herald reached for the second dove, and the two archers nocked fresh arrows to their bows. Chafing at his initial defeat, Martin realised that he had not used his longbow in over two weeks, the longest he had ever gone without practising since he had taken up the sport as a young boy; he had grown over-confident.

The second dove winged its way heavenwards. Martin took careful aim, trying to gauge where the bird would be by the time his arrow reached it.

'Loose!'

This time, no one could be sure whose arrow had brought down the dove until its body was retrieved from the marshes nearby, its white feathers stained with crimson blood. The feathered shaft was examined, and Ieuan ap Morgan was proclaimed to be the winner. A groan of disappointment went up from the English ranks.

'Never mind, boy,' Ieuan told Martin. 'You shot well. It takes years of practice to master something like this. Stick at it.'

Martin nodded, accepting his defeat phlegmatically. He had never been a bad loser. 'No time like the present. How about that third dove? I wouldn't mind one more go at it.'

Ieuan shrugged. 'Fine by me, boy.' He turned to the herald, who took out the final dove. Ieuan nocked another arrow to his bow, while Martin surreptitiously took out two more arrows, planting one in the ground at his feet.

The dove lifted skywards. 'Loose!'

Martin's first shot skewered the dove before Ieuan even had a chance to let fly; his second struck home before the bird had hit the earth. Ieuan pushed his cap back on his head and puffed out his cheeks in astonishment.

'I reckon I'm getting the hang of it now,' Martin remarked laconically, as he unstrung his bow before replacing it in its cover and walking slowly away.

Rudcock was grinning as he handed his money to Madog. 'Can *you* do that?' he asked Ieuan gleefully. The English might have lost, but at least some of their pride had been restored.

The English fleet – at least, those ships that had not disobeyed the king's orders by abandoning the army in order to return to the more profitable business of trade – had been sailing parallel with the march of the king's army, ravaging the coast of Normandy until it reached the port of Ouistreham at the mouth of the River Orne. From there it had turned inland and sailed up the river, reaching Caen on the same day that the city fell to the English and seizing all the French vessels it found on the river. All the French captives taken for ransom so far during the campaign were placed on board the ships, along with all the booty.

The fleet left Caen the day after the archery contest, sailing back down the Orne. In addition to booty and prisoners, the ships also carried men too sick or badly wounded to continue with the army, from the Earl of Huntingdon, who was one of the many who had contracted dysentery, to the ashen-faced Robin Wighton, who managed a wan grin as he waved the stump of his left arm from the deck of a small cog. Standing on the south bank of the river, his companions waved back to him. He was expecting a hero's welcome when he returned to his village in the County of Leicester; it would be some time before he realised that an uneducated man with only one hand was fit for nothing but begging for alms.

The army resumed its advance the next day, leaving behind a small garrison to continue the siege of the castle. The countryside around Caen had been laid waste by the depredations of the English troops. The huge column – still about thirteen thousand men strong – made poor time, ravaging the villages and countryside on either side of its route as it passed. In the next three days it covered only twenty-seven miles, reaching the town of Lisieux, which was promptly occupied and put to the sack.

The change in Martin had become more noticeable in the past week. Never garrulous at the best of time, now he had become taciturn and withdrawn. Whenever his companions addressed him, he generally replied in monosyllables, or made a cynical and sarcastic reply. He grew short-tempered.

Most of his friends had no patience with Martin's introspective behaviour. They began to shun him, without making any real attempt to establish the cause of the change that had been wrought within him.

Martin was not the only one who found himself set apart from the camaraderie of the platoon. Following the deaths of Lefthand and Murray, Caynard found himself friendless. None of the others had ever particularly liked him. Now that he sought to spend more time in their company, they became increasingly irritated by his weaselly behaviour, and ignored him all the more. Unlike Martin, who now seemed to prefer his own company, Caynard was desperate for friends and was increasingly ostracised because of it. Occasionally he would glance up from whatever it was he was doing to find Martin glaring at him malevolently, forcing him to look away. The reckless courage and ruthlessness Martin had displayed in the assault on Caen made it clear that he was not a young man to get on the wrong side of; but for Caynard it was too late. In addition to sleeping with his hand on the haft of his dagger, Caynard took his short sword with him whenever he went to answer the call of nature.

He let his guard drop only once.

Preston's men camped just outside Lisieux on the morrow of the Feast of Saint Peter in Chains, the second day of August. As they were bedding down for the night, Caynard glanced across to where Martin sat, leaning with his back against the bole of a tree. Like many of the archers, Martin had helped himself to a 'kettle' helmet from amongst the dead at Caen, and now he wore it tipped forward over his eyes as his chest rose and fell rhythmically. Reassured that the young man was fast asleep, Caynard slipped away from the camp-fire and made his way through the darkness towards the town. As soon as he had disappeared into the gloom, Martin pushed back his helmet and rose to his feet, checking that he had his rondel in its sheath before heading after Caynard. No one asked him where he was going; everyone needed a little privacy from time to time.

Martin followed Caynard into the streets of Lisieux. He had already had a chance to familiarise himself with the town when they had put it to the sack earlier that day, although all the towns and villages they had passed through in Normandy were beginning to merge together in Martin's mind.

Caynard seemed to know where he was going, however. He made his way around the side of one of the larger houses and hammered on the back door. It was answered by a young serving wench, one of the town's many inhabitants who had been naïve enough to stay behind in spite of the approaching English army. It was a miracle she had not already been raped and mutilated. She regarded Caynard in puzzlement, but he pushed her back inside and followed her in, closing the door behind him.

Martin hesitated in the shadows outside. What if this were some kind of trap? There was only one way to find out. He crept silently up to the house, his rondel tightly clenched in hs fist, and pressed his ear to the door.

He heard a woman scream, the sound of a slap, and then Caynard's voice: 'Shut up, bitch, or I'll cut you. I'm not going to hurt you,' he added, and then guffawed nastily. 'Not much, anyhow.'

Martin suddenly felt sick. He did not need this reminder of that afternoon in Caen. Then he realised that this was his chance not only to end his quarrel with Caynard, but also to redeem himself. He took a step back, and kicked at the door with the sole of his shoe, the way he had seen Preston do it. The door sprang open with a snap, and he stepped inside.

The room was a small kitchen, illuminated by the flames that crackled in the hearth at the centre of the floor and by a few rush torches that had been positioned around its sides. The wench was flat on her back on the flagstones, Caynard crouched over her with his dagger in one hand. It was the same dagger he had used to stab Martin, and the very sight of it was enough to make Martin's wound itch painfully.

Caynard leapt away from the girl and whirled around to face the newcomer. 'I were here first,' he hissed. 'If you know what's good for you, you'll . . . ' He broke off, his eyes widening with fear as he recognised Martin. 'You!'

Martin grinned savagely. 'Aye, me.'

Caynard's lips twisted into a cruel leer. 'It had to come sooner or later. You're still worth ten pounds to me, and this time you haven't got any friends to save you.'

'And neither have you.'

Caynard snarled, and suddenly lunged at Martin's stomach with his dagger. Martin leapt back, and then moved in close again. The two of them circled warily in the dim light cast by the flickering flames in the hearth.

Caynard feinted at Martin's belly, before darting the blade of his dagger towards his throat. Martin moved swiftly aside, and stepped in close in an attempt to drive the blade of his rondel into Caynard's stomach. Caynard caught Martin's wrist in his left hand and forced the blade aside, at the same time tossing his dagger a few inches into the air and catching it by the haft with the blade inverted. He tried to plunge it into Martin's heart, but Martin caught him by the wrist.

The two of them struggled chest to chest, each striving to plunge his blade into the other. Martin was the stronger of the two, and he smashed Caynard's right hand against the edge of a table in an effort to break his grip on the dagger. Caynard reacted in desperation, trying to lift his knee into Martin's crotch. Martin twisted at the hips, catching the blow on his thigh. Then he butted Caynard on the bridge of the nose with his forehead. Caynard broke free, staggering back. He slashed at Martin's face with the dagger. Martin jumped back, but he was too slow. He raised the back of his hand to his chin, and it came away with a few drops of blood. He altered his grip on his rondel, holding it with the tip of the blade pinched between thumb and forefinger. He flung it at Caynard, the way he had seen Madog kill a Genoese on the boats at Caen.

The rondel missed Caynard's throat by several feet, the haft clanging against a pot hanging from an overhead beam before it clattered into the far corner of the room. Martin reached for his broadsword, only to find that he had left it at the camp.

Caynard grinned wolfishly. 'Jackass!' he sneered. 'You should have stayed in England.' He advanced slowly, relishing his moment of triumph.

Martin glanced about the kitchen in desperation. A carving knife lay on the table, but it was too far away. The girl was cowering in a corner, gibbering with terror; he could expect no help from that direction.

There was a cauldron of water suspended over the central hearth by a wrought-iron tripod. Martin kicked away one of the legs so that the cauldron was up-ended, sending a tidal wave of boiling water surging across the floor. The girl scrambled clear with a squeal, but Caynard, who stood immediately in its path, was not so lucky. He screamed as the scalding-hot water splashed his legs. Martin dived across to the table at the far side of the room, snatching up the carving knife. With a howl of pain and rage, Caynard closed in for the kill. Martin slashed upwards with the knife, catching Caynard under the jaw with the tip of the triangular blade. All his strength was behind the blow, driving the blade in up to the haft. Caynard was dead before he even had a chance to scream.

The water rolled back across the floor, extinguishing the fire with a hiss so that the only remaining illumination was a couple of rush torches that guttered fitfully in the smoky room. Martin released his grip on the handle of the carving knife, and Caynard's body crumpled in a heap on the floor.

He glanced at the girl who was still cowering, as terrified of him as she had been of Caynard, and he realised that having preserved her honour did not make him feel any better about what he had done in Caen.

But at least he no longer had to worry about Caynard.

He picked up his rondel and returned it to its sheath. He was turning to the door when Preston suddenly entered, followed by Villiers. The two of them took in the scene – Will's corpse, the frightened girl – before turning their gaze on Martin.

'I think you'd best come with us, lad,' Preston said quietly.

Martin made no attempt to resist. If they decided to hang him for murdering Caynard, it was probably no more than he deserved.

CHAPTER THIRTEEN

Martin spent the night in an upper-storey room in one of the houses in Lisieux, watched almost unblinkingly by two tough-looking men-at-arms. But escape was the last thing on his mind: for the first time in a week, he slept soundly, untroubled by nightmares.

Preston entered the room half an hour before dawn, and signalled for the two men-at-arms to leave. Once they had closed the door behind them, he glanced across to where Martin still slept, seated in a chair, his chin resting on his chest, snoring softly. Preston positioned another chair directly facing him, and sat down. He coughed loudly.

Martin snorted and raised his head, blinking his eyes open to peer blearily at the serjeant. Preston waited for him to say something; but as had been the case the previous evening, Martin had nothing to say for himself.

'You deserve to be hanged, if you ask me,' Preston said finally. He spoke conversationally, without malice.

Martin rubbed his right cheek with the heel of his palm, still saying nothing.

'Don't you want to tell your side of the story?' Preston demanded in exasperation.

Martin shrugged. 'Would it make any difference?'

'Not at this stage. We've already questioned the girl. She tells us that you arrived just in time to preserve her honour. We're giving her the benefit of the doubt, of course, and assuming that she had any honour to preserve in the first place.' He chuckled. 'Ironic, really, when you remember that the only reason you're here now is because you're supposed to have raped a woman back in England.'

Martin smiled thinly, without humour. 'Aye, very ironic.'

'I suppose you're going to tell me that you were trying to redeem yourself?'

Martin hung his head, staring fixedly at his knees. 'Summat o' that,' he muttered.

'The Earl Marshal was annoyed that you killed Caynard, of course, or so I'm told,' Preston continued evenly. 'He would have preferred to have taken him alive, so that an example could have been made of him – string him up in front of the townsfolk, let them think the king's serious about punishing anyone who mistreats the locals, all that sort of thing – but since the girl gave the impression that you killed him in self-defence, he doesn't see any reason why you shouldn't receive the forty shillings reward for bringing a transgressor to justice.'

The full implications of Preston's words finally dawned on Martin. 'You mean, I'm free to go?' he asked, stunned.

'Wait a moment, I'm not finished yet!' snapped Preston. 'His lordship may choose to believe that cock-and-bull story about you protecting the lass's honour but, by God's two arms, I'll be damned if I do. First you and Edritch disappear on the same day. You turn up a day later with a wound in your side and a face covered in bruises, but that's the last we see of Edritch. Coincidence, I says to myself. Then Lefthand and Murray, friends of Edritch, burn to death accidentally on purpose, like. At the time, I was ready to believe that it was the French that murdered them, but now that you've killed Caynard I'm inclined to think different. All four of them as thick as thieves, all four of them dead. Concidence again? Just what were you doing following Caynard

330

into that house anyway? You and him never did see eye to eye, did you?'

'You can't prove any of this,' sneered Martin.

'Maybe. Maybe not,' admitted Preston. 'But Sir Thomas certainly believed me when I told him of my suspicions.'

Martin hung his head once more. 'What did he say?'

Preston scratched the underside of his jaw, and grimaced. 'He laughed. Then he said as how someday you'd make a fine serjeant-at-arms. I resent that. To tell the truth, I don't reckon he thought much of Caynard and his cronies, either.' He pushed himself to his feet. 'Come on – time you and I were getting back to the platoon.'

Holland was waiting in the street outside. 'I'll see you back at the camp,' he told Preston, who nodded, taking the hint. Holland began to stride down the street, Martin trotting along beside him uncertainly. Martin did not know what to say, or even if he was expected to say anything, so he kept quiet.

Holland said nothing until the two of them reached the town gate, emerging into the countryside beyond where the rest of the army was encamped outside the walls. 'You cost me twenty marks last Saturday,' he remarked, as they walked between the tents. He did not seem angry, but then he did not seem overjoyed, either. It was often difficult to tell with him.

'Sir Thomas?' ventured Martin, not understanding.

'In that archery contest with the Welshman.'

'I'm sorry, sir . . .'

Holland chuckled. 'Mark you, it was worth it to see you hit the same bird twice before it hit the ground! Perhaps one day we'll see you kill two birds with the same arrow, eh, Kemp? That would be rare archery indeed!' He chuckled again, and fell silent for a few moments before continuing.' Tell me, Kemp, Why *did* you kill Caynard and the others?'

The sudden change of subject caught Martin off guard. 'They . . . they tried to kill me, sir,' he stammered.

'For any particular reason?'

'None that I know of, sir.'

'You're a God-damned liar, Kemp. I ought to have you flogged.'

'Aye, sir.'

Holland shook his head in disbelief. Martin could play the role of the obtuse peasant to the hilt when he chose to, but Holland was no longer convinced. 'It will go ill for you if you persist in trying to take the law into your own hands, Kemp. We have laws in England, and since this land is rightfully the king's, those laws must be applied here, too. You've got away with it this time, but don't think it will always be so. Do you understand me?'

'Aye, Sir Thomas,' replied Martin, chastened. He felt no guilt at having killed Caynard and his friends – that had been necessary, and he did not doubt that they deserved it – but somehow he felt chagrin at having displeased Holland.

Two papal envoys arrived at the camp that morning, and the army lingered around Lisieux for the rest of the day while the envoys negotiated with the king. They were received courteously enough, but the king made it clear that, while he was prepared to treat for peace, any negotiations would have to be based on firm proposals from Valois. The Pope was a Frenchman, and it was widely believed – not without some justification – that he favoured Valois' side of the quarrel; with the papal court in Avignon, exiled from Rome, the Pope was very much dependent on maintaining the good will of the *de facto* king of France.

The envoys were sent to Valois, who was rumoured to be marching to Rouen with an army. The next day the English army set out before dawn, the king apparently eager to make up for time wasted in the negotiations. The English marched thirty-five miles in two days, reaching the town of Neubourg, only twenty-three miles from Rouen. The following day was spent resting at Neubourg, while a reconnaissance party was sent to Rouen under d'Harcourt's command. It returned to the English camp that night, bloodied by combat, to confirm the rumours that Valois had indeed gathered an army, one vastly superior to the king's in numbers.

A pitched battle between the two armies would almost certainly prove catastrophic for the English. Any hopes that the king might have had of marching on Paris to claim the throne of France were now dashed. The best hopes of the English lay in a march to the north-east, to meet with an Anglo-Flemish force under the command of Sir Hugh Hastings that was supposed to have invaded north-eastern France from Flanders about three weeks previously. If the two armies combined, then they might stand a chance against the overwhelming numerical superiority of the French. But no one could be sure how far the Anglo-Flemish army had penetrated, or even if it had set out at all; and between that force and the king's army lay the River Seine. The lowest possible crossing place was at Rouen itself, and d'Harcourt reported that the French were too heavily entrenched there to make a crossing viable.

The English army left Neubourg the following day, marching north-east until it reached the Seine at Elbeuf, eleven miles away, only to find the bridge there destroyed. The Seine was far greater than any of the other rivers it had crossed, being several hundred yards broad at that point, so there was no hope of repairing the bridge in the course of a single night. The army spent the rest of the day at Elbeuf, many of the troops spreading out across the surrounding countryside, setting fire to villages and laying waste to crops.

The next day the army began to march along the south bank of the Seine in search of a crossing, heading upstream towards Paris, now less than sixty-five miles away. It was met on the road by the two papal envoys again, this time accompanied by a French archbishop. The clergymen claimed to have firm proposals from Valois, but the king was not convinced and sent them on their way, determined not to lose another day's march in fruitless negotiations. With Valois' army closing in for the kill, time was not on the side of the English.

The next bridge the army came to lay about eight miles upstream, and was still intact; but a walled town stood on the south bank between the bridge and the English army, and the walls were heavily defended by French troops. The Earl of Northampton ordered those companies of archers marching in the vanguard to take up position facing the walls, while several companies of men-at-arms prepared to assault the town, the siege engineers hurriedly bringing up scaling ladders from the baggage train.

As Holland's company lined up and began to advance, Martin felt the now-familiar stirrings in the pit of his stomach; but now he realised that this was not fear, but excitement. The company halted when it was only two hundred yards from the foot of the town wall, and Preston gave the signal for his men to loose, while Holland paced up and down behind the ranks, ordering them to pick their targets carefully to conserve arrows. Martin recalled Preston telling them at Portsmouth that a few bowshots that found their targets with lethal accuracy could be far more unnerving than a general hail of arrows that bounced harmlessly off the parapet. A few crossbowmen on the battlements loosed a desultory smattering of bolts, but this soon dried up when the English began to shoot. Martin saw a figure peer over the parapet, and took careful but nonetheless swift aim before letting fly. He was rewarded with the sight of the man falling back out of sight without even so much as a scream.

Once the enemy were pinned down behind the parapet, the men-at-arms charged towards the walls on foot, led by the Earl of Warwick and several dismounted knights. Martin recognised Beaumont's jupon, and found himself casually wondering if he could pick the knight off from where he stood without anyone noticing. Then the scaling ladders were thrown up against the walls. As the English troops began to climb up towards the battlements, Holland ordered his men to cease shooting, for fear that they might inadvertently hit their compatriots. Martin was disgusted: if he were to hit a compatriot with a bowshot, he would certainly not do so inadvertently. But perhaps it was for the best, he reflected; he had been lucky to get away with the murders of Caynard, Lefthand and Murray, but if an English nobleman were found dead with an English arrow in him, it was highly unlikely that Holland would be prepared to turn his blind eye a second time.

With the hail of arrows ended, the Frenchmen on the battlements reappeared over the parapet, hurling rocks down at the men-at-arms who swarmed at the foot of the walls. Other defenders attempted to push away the scaling ladders using long forked poles. Martin watched grimly as one ladder was pushed past the point of no return, the men who clung to it screaming as it toppled away from the wall to smash them against the ground. Those who had been near the bottom of the ladder were only bruised, but those at the top ... Martin felt little pity for the men who died in such a manner: they were soldiers, like him, and like him they had a duty to risk their lives for the king. But it angered him to see the lives of good men wasted so uselessly. The town walls had been constructed with the specific intention of repelling such an attack, and it seemed foolish to pretend otherwise. The English might vastly outnumber the men on the battlements, but it was the defenders who had the advantage.

Martin speculated as to how he would have handled the assault if he had been in command. He decided he would have ordered the walls to be attacked at several points simultaneously, so that the defenders would be forced to spread their forces more thinly. Perhaps a three-pronged attack, commencing with a feint attack that would draw defenders away from other parts of the wall, leaving them weak and ill-protected against a surprise assault. It occurred to him that this might be what the Earls of Warwick and Northampton had in mind, but as the slaughter stretched into hours without any sign of the English gaining a foothold on the battlements, he realised that this escalade had not been that well-planned. It was too late now. All Martin could do was watch impotently from a distance as more lives were wasted in a hopeless conflict, and thank God, or the Devil – whichever was responsible – that his life was not to be one of the many so senselessly wasted that day.

The battle had been raging for nearly three hours when Villiers rode up on his rouncy towards mid-afternoon, gesturing frantically beyond the town and across the river towards the north bank. 'Sir Thomas! Look yonder!'

They all looked, and this time it was pure fear that gripped Martin's innards. Hundreds – no, wait, thousands – of armed men were coming into view over the crest of the ridge beyond the river: armoured knights and men-at-arms on horseback; Genoese crossbowmen marching on foot; peasant levies, ill-equipped with farming implements for weapons. The banners that fluttered above this mighty host could just be made out by the English: the arms of France, golden fleurs-de-lys on an azure background; the arms of Godemar du Fay, commanding the Genoese mercenaries; and a three-tailed banner of scarlet silk with a green fringe and tassels, the Oriflamme – the sacred banner of France that symbolised that no quarter was to be given, no prisoners taken. There could be no doubt that this was the fresh army raised by Valois, come from Rouen to oppose the English crossing of the Seine.

After the initial shock of seeing so many of the enemy in such close proximity, Martin's terror quickly subsided. With the walled town standing immediately below the bridge, there was no way the French could cross the river to charge straight at the unprepared English ranks. But with so many troops come to reinforce the men who stoutly defended the town, any attempt to continue the assault would clearly be futile. The Earl of Warwick immediately called off the attack.

Suffering the jeers of the French, the English vanguard abandoned the assault, forming up into a column with as much dignity as it could muster. The army continued its march along the south bank of the Seine, reaching a large village about an hour before dusk and making camp for the night. Valois' army marched parallel with the English on the north bank, and when darkness fell Martin and his companions could see the lights of the French camp-fires across the river. Even though there was neither bridge nor ford for miles in either direction, it was unnerving to be bedding down with such a mighty host of enemy troops so close by. Martin slept little that night.

It was still dark when they were roused the following morning, not by the usual blare of trumpets, but by the serjeants-at-arms kicking their men awake and then whispering orders to keep the noise down. They skipped breakfast and set out marching before dawn in an effort to slip away from under the noses of the French.

They left the river-bank after a couple of miles, cutting across land where the Seine meandered away to the north in a broad loop. In the distance, they could just make out the chalk cliffs of Les Andelys towering above the river on the north bank. It was impossible to cross there, and the short cut would give them a few hours' march on the French. Behind them, a vast plume of dark smoke began to blossom into the sky as the main body of the army sacked the town of Louviers, famous for its cloth, and put it to the torch.

A large castle loomed up before them, its massive curtain walls frowning over the road ahead. It was surrounded by a deep ditch filled with sharpened stakes, and the drawbridge was raised. Martin could see armed men on the battlements. The river bank became so steep there that the path was forced into a narrow defile, dominated by the castle. Any attempt to give the castle a wide berth would lead the army on a considerable detour. Warwick decided to save time for the main body of the army by taking this fortress by storm.

In a repeat of the previous day's events, the archers of the vanguard were brought up to harry the battlements with arrows, while knights and men-at-arms prepared to charge with scaling ladders. Once the escalade was begun, the archers were once again ordered to cease shooting and became impotent spectators in the battle as the men-at-arms were hard-pressed to gain a foothold on the enemy battlements. Holland paced furiously up and down. He constantly switched his gaze from the men-at-arms being slaughtered at the foot of the castle walls to his archers, idly standing by, while three extra scaling ladders lay unused on the ground nearby. He turned to Preston. 'Are you thinking the same as I, Wat?'

Preston grinned. 'Aye, Sir Thomas.'

Villiers could see what the two old warriors were thinking. 'Should we not get permissiom from my lord of Warwick?' he asked dubiously.

Holland smiled. 'Nervous, Adam? It's not like you to shy from an opportunity to win glory.'

Villiers straightened self-assertively. 'Wherever you go, sir, I'll follow.'

'Then I say we join the attack,' determined Holland.

Preston turned to his men. 'Ready for a fight, lads?'

The men needed no further bidding. They threw down their bows and snatched up the ladders, dashing off after Holland and Villiers. They charged past the castle's barbican, dodging the desultory smattering of crossbow bolts that fell around them. They made their way around the rim of the ditch, closely followed by the rest of Holland's company. Preston split his men into two groups of four and one of three, each team carrying a ladder and led by Holland, Villiers and Preston himself respectively.

They halted at the rear of the castle, on the outer rim of the ditch, to raise their ladders against the wall: that would save them from having to clamber down into the ditch, thread their way between the sharpened stakes and haul themselves out at the other side; besides which, the less steep the angle at which the ladders were propped against the wall, the harder it would be for the defenders to push them away.

The unwieldy ladders were heavier than they looked, and it took the strength of four men to manhandle them into position. They had iron hooks at the top end and spikes at the bottom to hold them in position. All three teams managed to hook the tops of the ladders into embrasures in the parapet. There was no sign of any defenders on the parapet directly above them; presumably they were still engaged in fending off the initial attack on the far side of the castle.

Holland began to climb one of the ladders without hesitation. Martin was right behind him. It was the waiting that Martin hated: he preferred to be in the thick of the action, where he was too busy to have time to be scared. He paused at the foot of the ladder, recalling the terrible screams of the men he had seen plummet to their deaths the day before. In for a penny, in for a pound, he told himself, and began to climb. Yesterday he had told himself that it was a soldier's duty to risk his life; well, now it was his turn.

Holland was about two-thirds of the way to the top when the defenders appeared on the battlements above them. They managed to unhook the top of the ladder, and began to push it away from the wall with a forked pole. Martin's first instinct was to start climbing back down so that he would have less far to fall, but Conyers was immediately below him. Holland continued to climb until he had reached the top. Gripping on to the top rung with his left hand, he drew his broadsword from its scabbard and reached around the ladder to hack at the pole. He suddenly drew in his breath sharply, and Martin glanced up to see the shaft of a crossbow bolt protruding from his left shoulder. Undeterred, Holland maintained his grip and hacked through the pole. Martin clung to the ladder for dear life as it fell back against the wall with a bone-jarring shudder. For a moment he thought the ladder must snap, dropping them all to certain death on the sharpened stakes in the ditch, but it was made of sterner stuff than that.

Badly injured, Holland did not have the strength to pull himself through the embrasure, but he managed to maintain his grip, jabbing with the point of his broadsword at the men on the battlements. Then Villiers and Preston were over the parapet at the top of the other two ladders. While Preston and his team held off the defenders on their right, Villiers and his team pushed the enemy back along the catwalk to the left, until Hal was able to help Holland up on to the battlements. Martin and Conyers climbed up after him, followed by Newbolt and Tate.

They had gained a foothold on the battlements, a feat that Martin would have dismissed as impossible a few moments earlier. From their new vantage point they could see how thinly manned the castle's garrison was: there could not have been more than four dozen armed men in the place altogether. But it did not take many men to hold a well-constructed castle against an entire army. Once the attackers had gained a foothold on the battlements, however, it was a very different story.

The defenders fell back, entering the tower at the end of the catwalk and slamming the heavy oak door behind them. Martin and Drayton worked together, repeatedly throwing their shoulders against the door in unison, until the bar that held it shut snapped. They tumbled through, sprawling on the wooden floorboards inside. The rest of the platoon poured through after them, led by Villiers and Preston now, while a pale-faced but grimly determined Holland brought up the rear. They clattered down the spiral staircase and emerged at the foot of the tower in the outer bailey. The Frenchmen in the bailey outnumbered Preston's platoon, but Villiers led them in a charge anyway, seizing the initiative. Terrified by the warlike shouts of the English archers, the French panicked, scrambling for the safety of the inner bailey.

Holland took advantage of this diversion to lead Martin, Rudcock and Conyers across to the gatehouse. They broke down the door and killed the three guards within before the Frenchmen had a chance to surrender. Then Holland directed them to lower the drawbridge and raise the portcullis, showing them how to operate the system of counterweights and levers.

The drawbridge down, a troop of men-at-arms charged through the gateway on foot. They crossed the outer bailey to where Villiers, Preston and the others had seized control of the gates before the French could seal them. The surviving defenders had pulled back into the keep. A battering ram was swiftly brought in, and within a matter of moments the door to the keep had been smashed in.

Every Frenchman found inside the castle was slain without mercy, regardless of whether or not they were armed. The capture of the castle was complete.

The English made no attempt to garrison the castle, moving on as soon as they had ransacked the place for valuables. Holland's company, by now marching with the rearguard, passed another great fortress that had fallen to other units of the vanguard. They caught up with the rest of the army after nightfall, by which time they had reached another walled town that dominated a bridge over the Seine. The town was too well-defended to be attacked, especially by an army that had marched eighteen miles that day, storming two strong castles on the way. The English troops encamped for the night a short distance to the south of the town's suburbs.

Preston's men were flushed with victory when they sat down to supper that night. For the new recruits, it was the first time they had stormed the walls of a castle, and they had been successful, taking the fortress without losing a single man from their platoon, despite having been in the thick of it.

'We showed 'em, didn't we!' boasted Tate. 'No one can say we aren't soldiers now.'

'I can,' sniffed Preston. 'Beginners' luck, that's what I call it.'

Tate's face fell. He did not understand Preston well enough not to be genuinely hurt by the constant stream of derogatory comments the serjeant poured on his men. 'We faced an enemy charge on the beach at Saint-Vaast, took the city of Caen by storm, and assaulted the walls of Gaillon Castle,' he protested. 'What do we have to do to become real soldiers?'

Preston pointed across the river where the camp-fires of the French sparkled in the night. 'Face that lot in open battle without flinching,' he told Tate.

Valois' army had caught up with them.

*

'It is naught to be ashamed of,' the whore said brightly. Her English was thickly accented. 'It happens to men all the time.'

Martin turned his back on her and tugged his tunic over his head. He had never been preoccupied with appearing manly. No one had ever questioned his manhood when he had lived in Knighton, and certainly no one had found cause to question it since he had joined the army; except Caynard, of course. Martin had never felt the need to prove himself to anyone.

But the sight of the whore's naked flesh had reminded him of the girl he had raped at Caen. There was little physical resemblance, but the prospect of sexual intercourse had suddenly brought the memories of his last sexual encounter into sharp focus, making him feel sick with guilt and self-loathing.

'What do you know of shame?' he demanded angrily, and there was so much bitterness in his voice that she flinched.

It was exactly two weeks since they had taken the Château Gaillon. The king's army had marched to within twenty miles of Paris, crossing the Seine at Poissy and evading Valois' army. They had moved swiftly to steal a march on Valois, heading due north and covering more than seventy miles in five days, reaching the town of Airaines in Picardy. The town was less than six miles from the River Somme, the last major obstacle between the king's army and the Anglo-Flemish force led by Sir Hugh Hastings.

Yet despite the fact that the English had gained a two-day start on the French, news reached the English camp that Valois had already reached Amiens, only sixteen miles away. Warwick had led a large reconnaissance detachment to find a suitable place for the army to cross the Somme. They had scouted three bridges across the river. The first two had been heavily guarded by local militia forces, while at the third they had become involved in a brief but bloody engagement with the men of two of Valois' allies, the King of Bohemia and the Count of Hainault. Warwick's knights and men-at-arms had suffered heavy casualties and had been driven off, returning to the main army to report that no unguarded crossing places could be found.

Holland and his men had not been part of the reconnaissance detachment. The surgeon who examined Holland's shoulder had forbidden him from riding if he wanted his wound to heal. Holland had wanted to ignore the surgeon, dismissing him as a charlatan, but Warwick ordered him to ride in a cart in the baggage train. Marching with Cobham's company in the rearguard, Holland's men had missed out on all the engagements the army had fought since the taking of Château Gaillon. The only action they had seen was when the townsfolk of Poix went back on their promise to pay an indemnity to the king if their town was left unharmed. The army had marched on, for once leaving behind a settlement unburnt. The townsfolk had taken advantage of this by attempting to murder the clerks sent by the king to collect the indemnity. The clerks had been wearing chain-mail hauberks under their fustian habits, and it saved their lives. When they caught up with the rearguard to tell their tale to Holland and Cobham, the two knights were furious at this treachery. They led their men back to the town to exact retribution, ruthlessly massacring the inhabitants and razing the houses to the ground.

That had been the day before Warwick's strong reconnaissance. The following day, the vanguard had marched eight miles due west, away from the Somme, towards the coast. Reaching the fortified town of Oisemont, the chief market town of the district, the vanguard had found a scratch army of local volunteers drawn up in front of the gates. This militia had been quickly dispersed by a cavalry charge, its members butchered as they fled.

The rearguard had left Airaines the following morning, only a couple of hours ahead of Valois' approaching army. When it reached Oisemont that afternoon, it had been Conyers who contrived to find the stewhouse, and it had been his suggestion that he and his companions visit it that evening. Martin had gone along reluctantly, leaving his coverchief behind where they were camped outside the town walls. He had already been unfaithful to Beatrice once, and in the nastiest possible circumstances; he did not want to be wearing her coverchief again when he deliberately set out to betray her. But he was not sure that he would ever be able to face her again; indeed, bearing in mind that the army's advance was blocked by the Somme, and Valois' army was close behind them, he was not sure that he would ever have an opportunity to see her again. It was in this fatalistic frame of mind that he had tried to steel himself for one final fling. The wench was both pretty and willing enough, but the shadow of Martin's recent sins still hung over him.

He finished dressing and left a few silver coins – booty from Poix – on the table. It was probably more money than she would have charged, but he had a feeling that he would never get a chance to spend it otherwise.

'That is not necessary,' she said. 'You did nothing . . .'

He laughed bitterly, and slipped out on to the landing, leaving the coins where they lay.

The next door along opened just as he was passing, and Rudcock stumbled out, ashen-faced, naked except for his breech-cloth. There was an expression of puzzled astonishment on his face.

'Hodge?'

'She's killed me!' gasped Rudcock, and it was then that Martin noticed the haft of a knife protruding from an ugly gash in his chest, crimson blood gushing down his pale

345

skin. He stumbled, but Martin caught him in his arms. Rudcock was coughing blood as Martin lowered him almost tenderly to the floorboards. 'Tell my wife . . . tell her I loved her,' he gasped, his eyes glazing over.

Martin found himself laughing and weeping at the same time. 'Which one?' he asked, the tears coursing down his cheeks.

But Rudcock said nothing more. Another spasm of coughing racked his body, and then his eyes rolled up in his head.

Martin was trembling all over. Rudcock had been the first friend he had made in the army, and it had been Rudcock who stuck by him when the others had felt inclined to shun Martin's company. He could not be dead. It was ridiculous to think that a man who had survived so many battles, assaults and skirmishes could be dead, killed by a wench in a stewhouse.

Martin rose slowly to his feet and let out a roar of anguish so loud and terrible that it silenced the moans of passion emanating from the other rooms. Then he pulled his rondel from his belt and kicked the door wide open.

The whore was trying to climb out of the window, dressed in nothing more than a large cloak wrapped over a muslin shift, one bare leg cocked over the windowsill. She paused, wild-eyed, as Martin burst into the room. He crossed the floor in two short bounds and grabbed her by the upper arm before she could jump to the ground below. She kicked and struggled as he dragged her back into the room, clawing at his face with her fingernails.

'*Cochon anglais*!' she hissed, and spat in his face.

'Murdering bitch!' He threw her on to the floor, pinning her down with his left hand on her throat while his right hand plunged the blade of his rondel into her belly. She screamed, bucking beneath him in agony. He stabbed her repeatedly until she stopped struggling.

Then he went on stabbing her, until Drayton and Brewster burst into the room, dragging him away from her bloody corpse.

Martin struggled wildly. 'She's killed Hodge! The God-damned bitch murdered him!'

'It's all right, Martin,' Brewster said soothingly, as Conyers, Freeman, Newbolt, Oakley and Tate followed him into the room to find out what the shouting was about. 'We know.'

'Well, she's burning in Hell for it now,' Conyers remarked grimly, nudging the mutilated corpse with the toe of his boot.

Oakley gestured to the hysterical Martin. 'For Christ's sake, get him out of here.'

Martin stopped struggling, trying to get a grip on his emotions. 'It's all right,' he said, as calmly as possible. 'I'm all right now.'

Brewster and Drayton released him, and they all carried Rudcock's body downstairs to the main room. 'Is everyone else here?' asked Oakley. 'For all we know, this whole God-damned stewhouse could be an ambush.' He scowled at the whore-mistress, who trembled.

The companions glanced at one another. 'Where are Hick and Pip?' asked Tate.

'They stayed at the camp with Pisspants,' Freeman assured him.

That made twelve, including Preston. Twelve out of the twenty men in the platoon who had landed at Saint-Vaast-la-Hougue.

Tate gestured helplessly at Rudcock's body, which they had laid on one of the tables. 'What should we do with him? Bury him?'

'I'm not staying up all night digging no hole,' protested Newbolt.

'But you'd stay up all night fucking given half a chance, wouldn't you?' Conyers sneered bitterly. 'By the Holy

Cross of Bromholm! That's Hodge lying there, for Christ's sake!'

'There's no need for anyone to dig a hole,' decided Martin. 'We'll give him a funeral pyre. That's a fitting tribute to a good soldier and a good friend.' He picked up a rush-light from one of the tables and carried it outside.

The others glanced at one another in puzzlement. 'Where in Hell is he going with that?' demanded Newbolt.

He was answered by the sudden crackle of burning thatch. The seven of them scrambled out of the door to where Martin stood in the street outside, gazing solemnly up at the roaring flames. The whores came running out of the burning building after them, screaming, but the men paid no heed to them. Conyers made the sign of the cross with uncharacteristic solemnity.

'Someone should say a few words, like,' Freeman muttered awkwardly.

'Lancelot already said them,' replied Oakley. 'A good soldier and a good friend. That's as fine a tribute as the best of us can ever hope for.'

They watched in silence as the fire raged, and eventually what was left of the roof collapsed in a shower of sparks. Martin turned away with tears in his eyes. 'Come on,' murmured Brewster.

The sound of trumpets blared forth from beyond the town walls, and they glanced at one another in bewilderment. 'What was that?' demanded Newbolt.

'Sounded like the order to strike camp to me,' said Conyers, a touch of his more usual sarcasm already creeping back into his voice.

It was barely midnight. 'But I haven't even been abed yet!' Newbolt protested.

'You haven't slept yet is what you mean,' said Conyers.

'Come on, let's get moving,' Freeman said briskly.

They hurried back to the camp to find Perkin helping Pip Herrick and Hick Lowesby dismantle Holland's tent, while Villiers was saddling his master's horse. There was no sign of Holland or Preston. 'What's going on?' Tom asked Herrick.

Villiers answered on Herrick's behalf. 'I'm damned if I know,' he said brightly. 'But the order's been given for us to strike camp, so that's what we're doing.' He started tying Holland's equipment to the packhorse, while the archers gathered up their arms. Martin picked up his coverchief, toying guiltily with it for a few seconds before winding it around his neck.

Presently Holland and Preston returned. 'What's happening, Sir Thomas?' asked Villiers.

'We've been interrogating the prisoners,' explained Holland. 'One of them claims to know of a way across the Somme. There's a ford about four miles below Abbeville, but we can only cross when the tide is out. We have to get there before morning.'

While the rest of the army was still forming up, Holland and his archers met up with Warwick and d'Harcourt at the edge of the camp. Led by Warwick, they set out through the darkness, guided by a French peasant. They marched first to Acheux, just under ten miles away, where they were joined by another knight, Sir Hugh Despenser, and the archers under his command.

They reached the marshes in the half-light of the summer dawn. Before them lay a desolate landscape of water channels, lagoons, reeds and mud-flats, stretching out as far as the eye could penetrate the pale-grey mist that hung over the scene. The guide led them through the thick clumps of reeds to where a mud-churned track led down to the water's edge.

'*Ici!*' said the guide. 'Here it is. The water is too deep now, but when the tide goes out in an hour or two . . .'

349

Warwick nodded, dismounting from his horse. 'We'll have to wait, then.'

'You will give me my money and let me go now, *non*?' the guide suggested hopefully.

Warwick shook his head. '*Non*. I keep you by my side until the army is safely across the river,' he said. 'If I find you've been lying, I'll have your hide flayed from your bones.' He turned to Norwich, telling him to ride back to Acheux and bring up the rest of the vanguard.

Preston was crouching by the mud at the water's edge. He straightened, removing his helmet awkwardly to address the earl. 'My lord? Some soldiers have been through here recently. These footprints were made by boots, not peasants' sabots; and these here are the marks of a well-shod horse – a large one, perhaps a courser.'

'How many men, serjeant?'

'Too many for me to be certain. Well over a hundred, I'd guess.'

The noblemen exchanged glances. 'It could mean nothing,' Despenser said dubiously, not even convinced of his own words. 'There are French troops all over the area at the moment.'

Warwick nodded. 'How fresh would you say those tracks are, serjeant?'

'Hard to say, my lord. There's been so little rain of late . . .'

'We can't take any chances,' Warwick decided. 'As soon as the river is low enough, we'll send some scouts through the marshes.'

The sun was rising by the time Norwich returned with the rest of the vanguard, and they settled down to wait for the tide to ebb while the rest of the army caught up. After a couple of hours the level of the water had dropped sufficiently to make a causeway of white gravel visible on the bottom. It would be at least two more hours before the water would be shallow enough for the wagons to be hauled across, but as soon as the Earl of Northampton arrived with the king at the head of the main body of the army, they sent Cobham into the marshes with a troop of hobelars to scout ahead, the French peasant going with them as a guide. They returned presently to report that the ford was guarded on the north bank by several hundred French men-at-arms and even more foot-soldiers, including a large force of Genoese crossbowmen. 'But I think we may be able to fight our way through,' Cobham concluded in his report to the king. 'The enemy do not seem to have carried out any defensive works on the north bank.'

'It seems we have little choice,' replied the king, who had received word that Valois had heard of the army's early departure from Oisemont, and had set out in pursuit. Now Valois' army was only a few hours behind them. 'We must waste no more time,' he added firmly, and commanded Northampton to lead the attack.

The earl relayed the order of battle to his men. Ten platoons of archers were chosen to lead the attack, including Preston's. Northampton and the two knights mounted their horses, riding into the marshes at the head of the column of archers.

The archers waded into the water with their longbows clasped over their heads to keep the bowstrings dry. The brackish water came up to their chests, but the gravel bottom gave them a firm footing. The ford was wide enough to allow a dozen men to march abreast, and they marched in good order. Several companies of mounted men-at-arms under the Earl of Warwick's command entered the water behind the archers.

The rising sun shone brightly, casting a haze over the scene. The air was humid and oppressive. An unearthly silence hung over the landscape, broken only by the occasional eerie cry of a marsh bird. None of the men felt like talking: they were too busy concentrating on keeping their balance as they waded through the sluggish current of the ebb tide. Martin's arms began to ache from holding his bow aloft. He wondered how much further it was before they could reach the other side. He suddenly noticed that the water had dropped to his waist. At first he put it down to the ebbing tide, but then he thought he detected a distinct incline in the gravel beneath his feet; or perhaps that was just his imagination.

At that moment the pale mists before them seemed to part, revealing the north bank of the Somme about three hundred yards away. Hundreds of French and Genoese troops stood underneath the trees that lined the bank, their brightly polished arms and armour glinting in the morning sun.

The two opposing sides saw each other at precisely the same moment; but the Genoese crossbowmen had been waiting, and they began to shoot. Their bolts wrought havoc amongst the closely packed ranks of the archers, and the entire front rank seemed to melt into the water. The English were as yet unable to reply with their longbows, as they could not use them without dipping their ends in the water, ruining the strings. The English continued to advance doggedly, the bolts splashing into the water around them or falling amongst their ranks. Some of the archers cried out as they were hit, but the rest remained silent, taking their bows from their bags with a workman-like air. The three noblemen riding at the head of the column refused to be hurried, seemingly immune to the swarm of missiles that filled the air, although none of them wore armour.

Northampton signalled the archers to halt when they were about two hundred yards from the shore, the water only coming up to their knees. Oblivious to the continuing hail of bolts, the archers closed ranks and nocked arrows to their bows, taking aim. Martin pushed his helmet back, so the metal brim would not get in the way when he drew his bow. The earl gave the signal to loose.

The effect was devastating. It was as if a huge, invisible fist had punched a hole clean through the Genoese ranks. The crossbowmen struggled to reload their weapons. They wore large shields strapped to their backs to offer them some protection when they turned their backs on the enemy while going through the complicated ritual of reloading. The rate of fire of the English longbowman was far higher, and they shot with mechanical regularity at Northampton's signals. The Genoese continued to create casualties amongst the English ranks, but they were swiftly cut down by the volleys of arrows. This duel of archers continued for several minutes, until the Genoese fire began to slacken off. Realising that they were on a hiding to nothing, the crossbowmen had begun to fall back.

Northampton ordered the archers to stand aside from the ford to allow Warwick's men-at-arms to come through. The French men-at-arms rode into the water to block their way at the head of the ford. The Englishmen charged, their horses surging through the water to meet the Frenchmen in the shallows. Holland led his archers to one side of the confused mêlée of rearing horses and shouting men, from where they could shoot into the flanks of the French formation, harrying the men-at-arms who struggled to push to the fore.

It was not long before Holland's men had exhausted their supplies of arrows. He directed them to draw their swords and charge the foot-soldiers who guarded the bank, while he himself wheeled his courser about to join the troop of mounted knights under Warwick's command, preparing to charge.

Martin replaced his longbow in its bag and slung it across his back, replacing his helmet on his head. Drawing his broadsword, he splashed through the shallows after Preston. The men who waited on the river-bank had the advantage of height. They thrust their spears down at the archers struggling to scramble out on to dry land. Martin swung his sword at one of the men standing above him. The blade sheared through the man's calf just below the knee, biting deep into his leg. He fell, screaming, his blood pumping out on to the churned mud at the water's edge. The men on either side of him were already occupied with Martin's companions, giving Martin a chance to climb out of the reeds. He closed with a dismounted man-at-arms, hacking at his shoulder. The man-at-arms fell back, his arm hanging uselessly at his side, the other hand clamped over the bloody gash.

Then three frenchmen came towards Martin from the rear. He seized the initiative, whirling around and lunging forward to stab one in the face. He barely withdrew his blade in time to parry a blow from the second. Then the third arched his back and dropped his sword, the point of Brewster's sword emerging from his chest. Martin thrust the point of his sword in the second man's heart, finishing him off. Grinning, he nodded acknowledgment of gratitude in Brewster's direction.

Tate was struggling to defend himself against two Genoese who had abandoned their crossbows in favour of short swords. As Brewster turned away to go to Tate's aid, Martin glanced about in search of his next victim. He saw an unhorsed English knight being attacked by three men-at-arms. The knight managed to kill one of his opponents, but was hard-pressed to defend himself against the other two. Martin attacked them from behind, stabbing one in the base of the spine before swinging his sword at the other's waist, the blade biting deep into the man's side.

Gasping, the knight pushed himself up from where he had been forced to his knees and turned to face his saviour. Seeing Martin, his face twisted into a snarl of hatred. Martin did not recognise those contorted features, framed by a mail coif and a bascinet, but he recognised the arms on the knights shield: a crimson wyvern on a white background; the arms of Sir John Beaumont.

Martin realised with a pang of regret that if he had recognised Beaumont sooner he would not have gone to his aid. His attitude was immediately proved to be justified when Beaumont suddenly lunged at him with his broadsword. Astonished, Martin was caught completely off guard, and was barely able to parry the thrust. Beaumont swung at him. Martin raised his sword to ward off the stroke, but such was the strength behind it that his sword was dashed from his grip. Disarmed, he backed away as Beaumont closed in for the kill.

Martin tripped over a tree root and fell flat on his back. He reached out in desperation to grip the hilt of his fallen sword, but Beaumont kicked it beyond his grasp. Grinning triumphantly, the knight raised his sword above his head, aiming to decapitate him.

The next few moments seem to last forever. Martin found that his limbs refused to obey him. Images flashed through his mind's eye: the great hall of Leicester Castle during his trial; the day he had been saved from hanging by the Earl of Warick; and that shameful afternoon in Caen . . .

Beaumont began to bring his sword down. The shining blade caught the sun, dazzling Martin.

He remembered the rondel at his belt. But it was too late for that now. Even if he had been able to grab it, it would have been little use against a man in armour.

Beaumont's blade arced downwards. Martin heard a loud clang, and then everything seemed to go dark.

CHAPTER FOURTEEN

'Jackass! He's one of ours!'

Martin recognised Holland's voice. It came as no surprise to him that the ruthless knight had intercepted his progress to the gates of Heaven, claiming him for the fires of Hell. Had Holland also died in the battle, then?

Holland lowered his left arm, and Martin found himself still gazing up at Beaumont, who scowled at them both before stalking away. Martin realised that the darkness that had fallen over him had been the shadow of Holland's shield, and felt very foolish.

Holland returned his broadsword to its scabbard and leaned over Martin, seizing him by the arm and hauling him to his feet. 'Are you injured?'

Martin shook his head numbly, too shaken by his narrow escape to find his tongue.

The two of them gazed across to where the battle was turning in favour of the English. The French ranks had broken, and were fleeing east along the north edge of the marshes, towards the sanctuary of Abbeville. They were pursued by several companies of men-at-arms led by Sir Reginald Cobham. Even as the laggards tried to escape, the men-at-arms would overtake them, cutting them down with a back-handed slash of a broadsword or plunging the tip of a spear between their shoulder blades. Bloody corpses were sprawled on the river-bank or floating face-down amongst the reeds.

Holland chuckled with satisfaction. It was clear that he and his men had done all that could be expected of them that day. 'Perhaps you archers should wear special livery, such as the Welsh do,' he suggested to Martin. 'Warfare is dangerous enough without the added risk of being killed accidentally by your own side. Eh, Kemp?' He hooked the toe of one boot under the hilt of Martin's sword and flicked it into the air with a sudden jerk of his leg, catching it by the grip.

'It would prevent accidents, Sir Thomas,' agreed Martin.

Holland regarded him curiously. Holding the sword in his right hand, just below the hilt, he offered it back to Martin.

'Thank you, sir.' Martin grasped the hilt, wiping the blade clean with a rag before returning it to its scabbard. 'For saving my life, I mean.'

Holland shrugged, turning away to gaze across to the rest of the army, which was emerging from the marshes as it began to straggle across the ford. 'I acted only for selfish reasons,' he said, without turning back. 'I've lost nearly a quarter of my company since we landed at Saint-Vaast, one way or another; your private war against Caynard and his friends has not improved the situation.' He winced, and massaged his wounded shoulder; the sword-stroke meant for Martin that he had caught on his shield had jarred his arm quite badly. 'I may need every man I have before this campaign is out.'

'Then you acted not for selfish reasons, but for his Majesty, sir,' Martin pointed out stoutly, with the stoicism of blind loyalty.

'Aye . . . ' Holland acknowledge vaguely. 'Yes, I suppose I did.' He turned back to face Martin. 'Tell me, Kemp. What will you do when you have served out your twelve months?'

Martin shrugged. He had not really thought about it. 'I don't know. Return to my family in Knighton, I suppose.'

'Return to a life of tilling the soil?' Holland was contemptuous of the suggestion. 'Could you really go back to that, after tasting the joys of war?'

'Joys of war' was not exactly the phrase Martin himself would have chosen to sum up his career in the king's service so far, but he had to admit to himself that the prospect of a life of servitude on Beaumont's manor did not exactly appeal to him. 'What else could I do?' he asked.

'You fought well this day, Kemp. Today, and at Caen. You lack experience, of course, but I doubt that will still be the case in nine months' time, when you've earned your pardon. You could work for me.'

Martin was overwhelmed. 'Sir Thomas?'

'I shall be a wealthy man when I receive the ransom for the Comte d'Eu. I'll be able to employ my own retinue of armed men. Not a large one, perhaps, but I think I can see a place for you in its ranks. I'd pay you thruppence a day during peacetime, plus board and lodging, of course. That would increase to half a shilling when we are indentured to serve the king in his next campaign.'

It was a generous offer. On Stone Gate Manor, Martin earned the equivalent of a shilling a month, and he rarely got to see any of that. He badly wanted to say yes, but he knew he was not in a position to accept the offer. He hung his head disconsolately. 'I am but a villein, Sir Thomas. I could not leave my lord's manor without his consent.'

Holland smiled. 'I'm sure that if I spoke to him . . . offered him a small recompense . . . '

Martin shook his head. 'Sir John hates me. He would never give his consent.'

'This Sir John . . . would his coat of arms be argent, a wyvern gules?'

Martin bit his tongue.

Holland chuckled. 'And you truly desire to go back to slave for this whoreson in a knight's armour who wages private war against his own bondsmen?'

'Desire? No.' Martin shrugged. 'But what choice have I?'

'You have plenty of choices,' Holland told him. 'You could go and live in a borough town for a year and a day: that confers freedom on any villein, by law.'

'A town like Leicester, you mean?'

'Somewhere further from your home would be better, unless you want to be dragged back to the manor in chains and flogged to within an inch of your life. London would be best. I have friends in London. After you have served out your twelve months fighting for the king and earned your pardon, I might be able to get you a temporary post in some rich burgher's household.'

'It all seems like a long time in the future,' Martin said dubiously.

'Aye, and so it is,' agreed Holland. 'But you are young; you have your whole life ahead of you. What do you say, Kemp?'

'We'll have to wait and see, sir,' Martin said pragmatically.

'Wait and see?' Holland was astounded that a churl such as Martin could even contemplate rejecting such a generous offer. 'What is there that remains to be seen?' he demanded irritably.

'Whether or not I live that long.'

Holland stared at him for a moment and then laughed, clapping him heartily on the back. 'Aye, right enough,' he admitted. 'We may yet both be dead before this week is out.' A sudden gust of cold wind blew a thick tuft of cloud in front of the sun, and Holland shivered. 'You'd best get back to your platoon now,' he told Martin.

'Aye, sir.' Martin began to walk along the river-bank towards Holland's company, which was rallying around Villiers and the banner.

'I always thought poaching was against the law, Sir Thomas,' a voice said dryly behind Holland. He whirled around and saw Preston sitting on the trunk of a fallen tree, industriously wiping the blade of his sword clean.

'He has potential, Wat,' said Holland. 'You've as much as admitted it yourself. He would be wasted behind a plough.'

'Like enough,' agreed Preston, rising to his feet and ramming his sword home into its scabbard. 'As you say, he lacks experience, but he's one of the best archers I've ever had under my command, and he's beginning to handle that broadsword as if he was born to it. He'll make a good soldier. My only concern is that deep down inside he may still have some traces of a conscience.'

'So may I, Wat,' Holland said softly. 'It's something you have to learn to live with.'

When the rearguard finally made it through the marshes, it reported that it had been attacked on the south bank by the vanguard of Valois' army, and had lost several wagons from the baggage train. The rearguard had been able to hold off the French until the rest of the baggage train had made it across the ford. By then the tide was coming in again and the French, unable to pursue the English, turned in to Abbeville for the night.

The king's army halted on the north bank of the river for the rest of that day, while Sir Hugh Despenser led a large detachment of mounted troops on a foraging raid towards the coast, burning a nearby port along with the ships he found in the harbour there. He returned to the main body of the army to report that there was no sign of the English fleet which, it had been hoped, would be waiting off the coast with reinforcements and supplies.

The army was in a bad way. True enough, it had successfully evaded Valois' army a second time, and had put the last major obstacle between itself and the Anglo-Flemish force behind it. By now it was barely twelve thousand men strong, while Valois was said to have five times that number. The men were exhausted and footsore from having marched so far so quickly, and many of the foot-soldiers found that their shoes were worn out. They had moved so swiftly since they had crossed the Seine that there had been little time for foraging supplies along the way, and now the victuals carried in the baggage train were almost completely exhausted. There was no more bread left, and hunger had reduced many of the men to eating unripened fruit picked off the trees along the way. Martin knew better than to eat such fruit, but the hunger that gnawed at the pit of his stomach sharpened the temptation. He recognised the irony in having wanted to become a soldier so that he would become rich, and never have to go hungry again. Now his purse bulged with gold and silver, but there was no food to be bought or foraged for miles around.

They set out again the following morning, marching north-east through thick woodland for nine miles until they came to a small valley. A stream shallow enough to be forded ran through the valley beyond the tree line, and a village stood on the north bank. They halted before they reached the village, the king sending out orders for his men to rest while they were hidden amongst the trees. At the same time, he sent out scouting parties: some riding south towards Abbeville, searching for signs of Valois' army to see if it was still in pursuit; others riding to the north-east, hoping for contact with the Anglo-Flemish force. Both sets returned that evening to report in the negative. It was the Feast of Saint Denys, the patron saint of France, and Valois was using the holy day to rest his army at Abbeville while the rearguard caught up. There was no sign of the Anglo-Flemish force led by Sir Hugh Hastings.

That night, Martin dreamed.

He dreamed that his twelve months in the king's army were over, and that he had been granted a pardon. He dreamed that he had lived in London for a year and a day, and had been granted the status of a freeman. He dreamed that he had returned to Knighton, where he confessed everything to Beatrice, how he had raped a girl in Caen. And she told him that it did not matter, she forgave him, she loved him, and she still wanted to marry him. And suddenly he knew that everything was going to be all right.

And then the trumpets sounded reveille, shattering his dream.

'How I love to be woken by the dawn chorus first thing in the morning,' groaned Conyers.

Martin sat up, and slowly realised that he was in a forest somewhere in France. He did not know it, but he was the closest to home he had been since he had landed at Saint-Vaast-la-Hougue, though home was still a long way away. About twenty-one months away, and nine of those yet to be spent fighting for the king. And before those nine months were up he could easily be killed, as easily as he had killed . . . God alone knew how many men he had killed since he had arrived in France.

He pushed himself to his feet. His stomach ached with hunger, and his feet, clad in shoes with almost worn-out soles, were sore; but on the whole he felt good. In fact, he felt a great deal better than he had done for a few weeks now. The previous day's rest had been just what he needed, he decided.

He did not imagine for a moment that today would be the longest day of his entire life.

It was still an hour shy of dawn, the pale grey light of the false dawn visible through the trees overhead. The rest of Martin's companions were beginning to stir.

'Come on, on your feet, sluggards!' growled Preston. 'Mass and communion in half an hour.'

'Mass?' Inglewood was bewildered. 'Is it Sunday already?'

Brewster sat up, rubbing sleep from his eyes. 'Saturday, I think.'

'Mass!' spat Newbolt. 'To Hell with that! A Luxembourg shilling for your mass!' 'Luxembourg shillings' was the name given to the counterfeit coins that were leaching into the markets of Europe.

'You'll all attend mass this morning,' Preston told them firmly. 'King's orders. Do you want to die without absolution?'

'I'd rather not die at all, if I can help it,' said Brewster, smiling.

'There's to be a battle today,' Preston told them simply. 'Four large battalions of French troops have been seen headed this way.'

Martin received this news without much excitement. He had often heard rumours of an impending battle; sometimes there had been one, and sometimes there had not. He would believe it when he saw one side or the other charge. In the meantime, all he felt was a mild irritation: he did not feel like fighting today.

'What's for breakfast, serjeant?' asked Conyers.

'You let the cooks worry about that,' Preston told him gruffly. 'You'll have enough on your trencher as it is.' He chuckled at his own witticism.

Conyers and some of the others groaned. 'I can't fight on an empty stomach!' protested Newbolt.

'You can die on an empty stomach,' Preston replied evenly. 'I don't see why you can't fight on one. If you don't like it, I suggest you take it up with his Majesty.'

Martin shaved himself with his rondel, honed to razor-sharpness with a leather strop; if he were destined to die today, he thought wryly, there was no reason why he should not be well-groomed. Then he polished the blades of his weapons, prompting the others to do likewise. They were subdued but optimistic. The general appearance of things in the camp gave the impression that the king was in earnest about doing battle with Valois. Whether the French would take up this opportunity was another matter entirely, although given that all the scouts' reports implied that Valois had at least four times as many troops at his disposal, it seemed unlikely that he would pass it up.

'Four battalions,' Tate mused out loud, and turned to the others. 'How many men are there in a battalion, anyway?'

'Plenty,' said Conyers.

'Enough,' said Brewster, and shrugged. 'How long is a river?'

'How long is a river?' Newbolt echoed incredulously. 'What in Hell is that supposed to mean? "How long is a river?"!'

Despite the impression given by their constant bickering, they were in good spirits. If the king were ready to give battle, they reasoned, then that must mean he thought they stood a good chance of winning. Like Martin, many of the younger ones were sick of evading any formal confrontation with the enemy. Ever since they had reached the Seine at Elbeuf, it had seemed as if they were running away. Now at last it looked as if they were going to stand and fight.

After mass, the army began to move out of the forest and across the valley. There was a small wood in a hollow about four and a half furlongs to the north of the village, and the baggage train moved around to the far side of this wood. The waggoners formed a leaguer – a large, square-shaped enclosure that had the wagons themselves as its walls – and all the horses were corralled within it. After taking the Earl of Northampton's advice, the king had decided that the knights would fight on foot with their men.

There was a low ridge to the north-east of the village, running for about nine furlongs and facing south-east across a shallow valley. It was on the south-east face of the ridge that the marshals drew up the battle lines, about three hundred yards from the bottom of the valley, where the land had been moulded into terraces for easier cultivation.

There was no confusion. The marshals took their time, working carefully and methodically. If they were going to fight a pitched battle, it was important to get the preparations right. Heralds rode back and forth between the battle lines and the camp, ordering each company in turn to pick up its equipment and directing them to their exact spot on the field.

Holland's company was assigned to the Prince of Wales' division in the vanguard, positioned just below a windmill on the end of the ridge that overlooked the village. When the time came, they would stand facing across the shallow valley in the direction from which the French were expected to approach; but in the meantime the pioneers and sappers handed out a spade to each of the archers, and told them to dig.

Newbolt spat distastefully on the ground, and then spat on his palms with a reluctant shrug, picking up his spade and attacking the soil. 'God's curse! I might've known it! I only joined up because I were sick of working the land. So here I stand, about to face the entire might of Valois' army, and what am I doing? God-damned digging, that's what!'

'Shut your trap, Newbolt,' Preston told him good-naturedly. 'The only reason you're here is that you'd've wound up kicking your heels at the end of a length of hemp otherwise.'

'What are we supposed to be digging, serjeant?' asked Tate, as Preston showed them where to dig.

'Holes,' the serjeant told him succinctly. 'A foot across

and a foot down should do it – just enough to make them stumble when they're approaching our lines.'

Fletchers passed among the archers while they were digging the holes, distributing baskets of arrows so that there would be no danger of them running out. Every archer in Holland's company received at least one sheaf of bodkin-tipped arrows, with steel, pyramidal heads that were specially designed to pierce armour. It was likely that they would be facing armoured knights charging *en masse* for the first time.

Those ugly-looking arrowheads brought the full reality of the situation home to Martin far more than any of the other extensive preparations that were being made. This would not be just another skirmish, it would be a head-on collision between two mighty armies. He began to experience that tight feeling of excitement in his chest and his stomach, but by now it was an old, familiar and trusted friend; like his longbow and his broadsword, the tools of his trade. What happened there that day would either put the king on the throne of France, or cast him into a French dungeon to rot.

It was late morning. The sun shone brightly in a sky that was blue except for a few high-up wisps of cloud. The archers were wet with sweat from the back-breaking toil of digging holes in the hot summer sunshine.

Conyers chuckled nervously. 'I'll laugh if, after all this preparation, the French decide not to fight.'

'Make these holes six feet longer and a few feet deeper, and I reckon they'll make nice graves,' said Freeman.

'Aye and like,' agreed Martin. 'Let's hope it's French corpses that fill them.'

Off to the right they could see the king riding along the front of the lines on a small white palfrey, accompanied by the Earl of Warwick, Sir Thomas Norwich, and Sir John Beauchamp, Warwick's younger brother, the Royal Standard Bearer. Like Holland, none of them had yet donned their armour. Martin found that he could draw strength from their relaxed confidence. The king halted in front of each company to make a short speech.

The archers began to plant their arrows in clusters in the ground at their feet. 'Remember, no one is to loose until the order is given,' said Holland, raising his voice so that the whole company could hear. 'And once battle is joined, on no account is any man to break ranks unless specifically ordered to do so. If anyone does, they'll not only be putting his own life in peril, but also the lives of their companions. If any one of you disobeys either of these commands and lives to tell the tale . . . I'll see to it that he never gets around to finishing it.'

The king rode up with Warwick and Norwich to where Holland stood before his men. He was unarmed but for a white marshal's baton with a gilt head, elegantly dressed in robes of emerald green velvet, his handsome countenance smiling and cheerful. He saluted Holland with his baton. 'Good morning, Sir Thomas. Are you and your men ready for battle?'

Holland bowed low. 'Ready and willing, sire.'

'Excellent.' The king turned to address the archers. 'Well, stout fellows, this is it. We've come a long way since we landed in Normandy nearly seven weeks ago, and in that time you have all fought nobly and bravely for the furtherance of my cause.' He did not need to shout, his strident tones carrying clearly through the ranks. 'I would take issue with any man who claimed that there was one amongst you who had failed in his duty to me. If there were any justice in the world, I could fain send you all home now and ask no more of you, to let others in their turn fulfil the duty that they yet owe to me.'

There was a slight frisson throughout the ranks at the suggestion that they might wish themselves elsewhere that day, but the king raised a hand to calm them, smiling. 'But you all know as well as I that if there is to be any justice in this world then we must make it ourselves,' he continued gravely. Then his features cracked into a grin. 'And if all of you had the opportunity to leave this place at this moment and return to England and safety, I doubt not that each and every one of you would reject it, and in preference stand with me against the usurper Valois.

'Doubt not that our cause is just, and that God the Father, the Son and the Holy Ghost is on our side. And though the enemy may be greater in number, each one of you, armed with the power of God, shall have the strength of ten, and behind you shall stand all the legions of Heaven.

'I speak to you now not as your king, but as your countryman and your companion-in-arms, when I ask you to stand up for my honour and to defend my rights; and that when the time comes for you to do your duty, not one of you shall be found lacking in strength or courage.'

'Three cheers for his Majesty!' said Villiers, and as the archers joined the young squire in his cheers, not one of them suspected that his outburst of boyish loyalty was the result of a strong hint from Holland.

The king waved in acknowledgement, exchanging greetings with one or two men whose faces he was able to put names to. 'Is that old Daw Oakley?' he called.

'Aye, your Majesty,' responded Oakley, grinning with pleasure at being recognised.

'We've come a long way since we fought together on Halidon Hill, have we not?'

'Aye, sire.'

The king spotted Martin in the ranks, recognising him by his coverchief. 'It is Martin Kemp, is it not?'

Martin flushed, overwhelmed at being picked out by the king in front of so many people. 'Aye, your Majesty,' he managed to stammer, bowing clumsily.

'I'm much obliged to you for the loan of your coverchief at Saint-Vaast-la-Hougue. Let us hope that this day it is Valois who gets a bloody nose!'

The men all laughed raucously. The story of the king's accident on landing at Saint-Vaast had spread throughout the army.

The king took the reins of his horse in his left hand and rode on to address the next company. Holland made his way through the press of men as if to speak to one of his serjeants. As he passed Martin, he paused momentarily to murmur in his ear. 'It seems you made quite an impression on his Majesty,' he said humorously. 'Don't let it go to your head.'

'Nay, sir.'

There was still no sign of the enemy by the time the king had completed his inspection of the battle lines at noon. The men were dismissed one unit at a time to make their way to where the cooks were preparing food by the leaguer. While they were awaiting their turn, Holland's men sat down in their positions and began talking amongst themselves. Some played at jacks or dice, while others boasted of the feats they planned to perform that day. Conyers, as enterprising as ever, managed to combine both these activities by arranging a game of jacks and using the French noblemen they hoped to capture as stakes. 'I'll wager the Count of Blois to the Duke of Alençon that you can't pick up all seven on the next throw,' he told Brewster, the platoon's jacks champion.

Brewster grinned. He was on a winning streak. 'Your Count of Blois, and I'll raise you the Count of Hainault.'

'There'll be no taking prisoners this day,' Preston cut in firmly. Taking prisoners usually meant leaving the ranks, and that had already been strictly forbidden. 'You'll leave taking prisoners to your betters and concentrate on your own task: killing Frenchmen'.

Preston's words cast a cloud over his men, reminding them that this was no game they were looking forward to, but a bloody battle. Martin wondered if the tough old veteran could be nervous. If a hardened campaigner like

Preston had cause to be worried, he mused to himself, what hope was there for the rest of them?

Norwich rode up towards mid-afternoon and told Holland that it was time for his men to go and get something to eat. The archers cheered without waiting for the order to be relayed to them through their serjeants, and pushed themselves to their feet, marking their places with their bows, caps and helmets.

'But if you hear the call to arms, you get back here smartish, I don't care what you're doing!' Preston called after them.

A pale-faced Inglewood made no attempt to move. 'Not coming?' asked Tate, replacing his bow in its cover to protect it in his absence.

Inglewood shook his head. 'Not hungry.'

Tate shrugged, and made his way after the others, who were crowding around the field kitchen. 'I hope there's some God-damned food left for us,' shouted Newbolt. 'God's doom, I'm starving!'

Martin skewered a pork chop with his rondel. He did not feel as if he were on a battlefield; the spirits of the men around him were so high that it was more like being at a fair. He washed down the meat with a cup of watered-down wine and strolled into the wood with Conyers.

'You've been in a battle before, haven't you?' said Martin. 'A real battle, I mean.'

Conyers nodded. 'I were at Morlaix four years back. We were commanded by the Earl of Northampton that time. We lined up on a hillside facing the French, just like we're doing today, and we thrashed them hollow. Me and Hodge.' He suddenly fell silent, remembering that he would never again stand side by side with Rudcock facing the enemy.

Martin felt the same way about Rudcock's absence from their ranks, but did not want to dwell on the matter. Rudcock was dead, and no amount of mourning could ever bring him back. 'What were it like?' he pressed Conyers. 'At Morlaix, I mean.'

Conyers chewed his last mouthful of pork ruminatively and swallowed. 'It were like the skirmish at Saint-Vaast, only bigger,' he decided, licking grease from his fingers. 'More men – on both sides, I mean.' He turned his head to glance speculatively at Martin. 'Scared?'

'Aren't you?'

'Aye – scared witless. Don't worry, we'll be all right.'

They crouched on opposite sides of a tree to answer the call of nature. 'If we don't do it now, we'll most likely do it in the heat of battle, and we don't want that,' chuckled Conyers.

It was late afternoon when they got back to their positions. There was still no sign of the enemy. 'Piss-pants reckoned he saw four or five knights at the edge of yonder forest while you were off stuffing your faces, but I'm damned if I could see owt,' said Preston, gesturing vaguely across the valley, to the south-east. 'Mark you, my eyes aren't as strong as they used to be.'

'Five knights do not an army make,' Freeman said in disgust, and hawked loudly before spitting on the ground. 'I'll wager ten to one they don't show.'

'I'm inclined to take you up on that, Freeman,' said Holland, suddenly stepping up behind him. 'Four or five knights could have been a reconnaissance party. Perhaps the rest of Valois' army is not so far behind.'

A dark shadow fell across them, rapidly spreading across the whole valley as dark and gravid clouds suddenly filled the sky. 'Looks like rain,' Villiers said dubiously. Even as he spoke, the first few drops began to patter down. Newbolt swore and unstrung his bow hurriedly. The others did likewise, coiling up their bowstrings and tucking them under their hoods, caps and helmets to keep them dry.

'Can we go and shelter under those trees, serjeant?' asked Conyers, grinning, as the rain rapidly increased in intensity.

'What, and risk missing all the fun?' Preston replied dryly.

The downpour was heavy, and before long they were all soaked to the skin. 'I can't see the French coming out in this,' Hick Lowesby said miserably.

'Not if they've got any sense,' agreed Newbolt. 'They're probably still in Abbeville, sitting warm and snug in front of their fires, and laughing at us stuck out here in the rain.'

'It won't last,' Preston assured them. 'It's just a summer shower.'

As usual he was right. The downpour abated after half an hour, and then died away as suddenly as it had started. The rain-cloud had passed on, and the sun came out once more, low in the sky to the west as it sank towards the horizon, warming their backs. A rainbow appeared across the valley.

'I hope that's a good omen.' said Villiers.

'If we beat the French today, it'll be thanks to English yew, not any omens,' Holland replied cynically.

'If the French show up at all,' grumbled Newbolt.

'What hour do you suppose it is?' wondered Tate.

'It must be nearly vespers,' Inglewood told him.

'The French won't come now, will they?' Tate sounded hopeful. 'It'll be dark soon.'

A couple of black birds winged their way across the battlefield, cawing. They landed in the field near the bottom of the valley, searching the wet grass for earthworms brought to the surface by the downpour. They seemed oblivious to the thousands of armed men massed only a few hundred yards away. Martin wondered if they were some kind of omen ... or was it black cats he was thinking of? No, it was magpies. One for sorrow, two for joy, went the old saying. But these were not magpies.

Tate's mind seemed to be working along similar lines. 'What kind of birds are those?' he asked suddenly just for something to say.

'Crows, I think,' said Lowesby.

'No, rooks.' Inglewood was adamant.

'What difference does it make?' demanded Newbolt. He always got irritable when he was nervous. 'Who cares?'

'How can you tell?' Drayton asked Inglewood.

'My father taught me an old saying,' explained Inglewood. 'If you see a rook standing in a flock of crows, then it's a crow. But if you see a crow standing on its own, then it's a rook.' He frowned. 'Or is it the other way around?' He bit his lip, as if the whole outcome of the battle might depend on his getting it right.

There was a pregnant silence while the whole platoon ingested this titbit of country wisdom. It was Newbolt who broke the silence.

'Ballocks,' he said.

'What?' Inglewood was caught off guard by the vehemence of Newbolt's response.

'Ballocks,' Newbolt repeated succinctly. 'Rooks is just as gregarious as crows.'

Conyers laughed out loud. 'Come again?'

'Gregarious,' repeated Newbolt, self-conscious at his sudden display of erudition. 'It means friendly, like. You know, sociable.'

'There's no such word!' scoffed Conyers. 'You just made it up!'

'There is too! Anyways, how would you know? You can't even spell your own name.'

'And you can, I suppose?'

'All I'm saying is that rooks always hangs around with other rooks,' said Newbolt. 'That's why they always builds rookeries together.'

'Don't talk daft,' cut in Freeman. 'You talk about flocks of crows, don't you? Whoever heard of a flock of rooks?'

'Anyway, whatever those two birds are, they aren't standing in a flock, and they aren't standing on their own, neither,' pointed out Oakley.

A shout went up some distance behind them, and they all broke off their debate on ornithology to glance over their shoulders. A look-out had been stationed on the roof of the windmill, and he was waving frantically towards the king's tent, which had been erected to the rear of the lines, about halfway between the crest of the ridge and the wood behind it. The tent was out of sight to the men in the prince's division, but presently a handful of figures appeared silhouetted on the ridge behind them, gazing over their heads towards the south-east. Holland and his men gazed too. Armour could be seen glinting about a mile and a half away, where troops were emerging from behind the trees that blocked the view of the road to Abbeville. A herald blew the call to arms, a call that was taken up by trumpeters throughout the battle lines. The clamour put the two birds to flight.

Valois had finally arrived with his army.

Martin felt the familiar tightness return to his stomach and chest. He had been so engrossed in his companions' discussion that he had quite forgotten why they were all there. Men who had wandered away from their positions now hurriedly scrambled back into place.

Norwich was standing by Holland. 'The hour is late,' he observed. 'It will be dark anon, and they must be weary from their march. If they have any sense, they will not attack until the morrow.' There were traces of both hope and fear in his voice.

Holland stared at him deprecatingly. He for one had never credited Valois and his vassals with any sense when it came to fighting battles. He made his way unhurriedly to the rear of the line to don his armour with Villiers' help, returning about a quarter of an hour later. He looked invulnerable in his suit of plate armour, chain-mail and reinforced leather, but Martin knew he was no better protected than the knight he himself had slain near Quettehou. Armoured knights were hard to kill, of that there could be no doubt; but it was reassuring to know that they were not invincible. Martin checked his bodkin-tipped arrows. They had parchment fletchings, unlike the feathered fletchings of his ordinary arrows, so it was easy to tell them apart, even by touch.

Then he remembered that he had not yet restrung his bow since the rainstorm. He took the coiled string from under his helmet and fastened it on to the bowstave. But his neglect had made him panicky, and his trembling fingers made a mess of the task. He forced himself to get a grip. The enemy were still over a mile away, and in marching order; it would take them time to form into battle array. He unstrung his bow and started from scratch, forcing himself to take his time.

The archers could see the vanguard of Valois' army more clearly now. There were knights and men-at-arms on horseback, and the usual Genoese crossbowmen with their red and white pennants. There were thousands of the enemy all told, more men than Martin had ever seen at one time before, stretching back along the Abbeville road until they disappeared behind the trees. He could make out the by-now familiar banners of Valois and Saint-Denys.

Holland, Norwich and Villiers were also studying the enemy's banners and pennants. 'There's the famous Oriflamme,' observed Norwich.

'The pennant that signals no quarter is to be given?' Villiers asked nervously.

'The same,' agreed Holland.

'Valois must be with them, then,' said Norwich. 'The Oriflamme is only raised when the French king rides with his army. I can see the banner of Valois' brother, the Duke of Alençon, and the Duke of Lorraine, and our old friend Robert Bertrand . . . ' As he continued, he might have been noting the arrival of contestants at a tournament. 'The Counts of Auxerre, Namur, Blois, Aumâle, d'Harcourt . . . does Sir Godefroi know that his brother rides in the enemy ranks, I wonder?'

'He must be expecting it,' Holland said grimly.

'And look there,' said Norwich, pointing. 'Do you see yonder banner? Gules, a lion rampant *queué fourchée* and passed in saltire argent – the arms of John of Luxembourg, King of Bohemia.'

Holland nodded. 'I'd heard he was allied with Valois. They say it was his men who fell on our vanguard at the ford the day before yesterday.'

'Is it true his Majesty is blind?' asked Villiers.

'So they say,' replied Norwich. 'And there is the banner of King Jaime of Mallorca . . . four kings on a single battlefield, eh?'

'Three kings and a usurper,' corrected Holland.

'Quite so,' Norwich agreed hurriedly. 'A fine array of nobility, nonetheless. Have you ever been the guest of honour at a feast where a stuffed peacock was served, and it almost looked too fine to eat?'

'Today I am feeling extremely hungry, I'm afraid,' said Holland, flexing the articulated fingers of his right gauntlet around the hilt of his scabbarded broadsword.

They could hear the advance of the enemy by now, a cacophony of trumpets, cornets, kettle-drums and war-cries. The vanguard of Valois' army seemed to be in some confusion, but eventually the Genoese crossbowmen began to advance into the valley.

'It seems they wish to take us up on our offer of battle after all,' sneered Holland. 'I was beginning to think they might not have the stomach for a fight.' He raised his voice to address his archers. 'All right, men, this is it. Stand by!'

'Remember, no one is to loose until I give the order!' Preston reminded his platoon.

A herald came riding past at a gallop, reining in his palfrey long enough to murmur briefly in Holland's ear. Holland nodded curtly, and the herald rode on to where Sir Reginald Cobham stood with his men. Holland spoke to Preston, and the serjeant smiled broadly at his master's words before passing them on to his men.

'The first volley is to land sixty yards short! Pass it on!'

'Sixty yards short?' echoed Inglewood. 'You mean, we're to miss on purpose?'

Preston nodded. 'That's right, lad!'

'But what for?' protested Inglewood.

'Never you mind! You just do as I tell you! Any man shoots over two hundred, I'll have his guts for garters!'

'Pisspants is right!' Martin muttered to Brewster. 'What's the point of shooting short? It's just a waste of arrows!'

'Oh, I think the serjeant knows what he's about,' replied Brewster, with a lazy smile.

'You just do as you're told,' agreed Oakley. 'You'll see why soon enough.'

Martin shrugged. He suddenly realised that in spite of all he had been through since landing in France, this was still only the second time he had stood and faced an enemy attack head-on. He remembered how he had panicked and made a mess of things that first time on the beach. This time, his earlier anxiety seemed to have vanished entirely. Now he felt calm and fatalistic. If he was to die, then so be it: it was no worse than he deserved, and death could be no worse than the terror of the mêlée on the bridge at Caen. He selected his first arrow – an ordinary one: the Genoese were poorly armoured compared to the French knights and men-at-arms – and nocked it with practised, workman-like motions. He did not take aim yet: the Genoese were still too far away.

They were advancing in skirmishing order, their cross-bows presented. They crossed the bottom of the valley, three hundred yards away. A great shout suddenly went up from their ranks, doubtless some kind of war-cry intended to intimidate their opponents. Martin and his companions were unperturbed. He idly wondered if it meant anything in Genoese; to him it sounded like a meaningless, animalistic bellow, but that could happen to any word or phrase roared by hundreds of men simultaneously.

Another shout rose from the Genoese as they continued their inexorable advance up the slope towards the English battle lines. The sun was already setting behind the ridge, shining in the eyes of the crossbowmen. Martin recalled what Preston had said on the first day of training about not attacking with the sun in your eyes. It was somehow reassuring, as if the French did not know the first thing about war. Norwich had been right when he said that it would be wiser for the French to postpone their attack until morning, when the sun would be shining in the eyes of the English. Martin smiled to himself, thinking that it was just as well that Valois had not been trained by Wat Preston.

A third shout rose from the Genoese ranks, and at that moment they loosed their first volley.

All the bolts fell short.

Stupid whoresons, thought Martin.

'Steady, lads. Don't loose yet,' cautioned Preston, lest the Genoese volley provoke any of his men into retaliating. He need not have bothered: his men were well-drilled, and knew what was expected of them. 'Remember, sixty yards short!'

The Genoese paused to reload their crossbows. They did not have their large shields strapped to their backs, but they instinctively turned their backs on the English nevertheless. They could not march and reload at the same time anyway. Reloading a crossbow seemed like an awkward and time-consuming process to Martin, and he decided that he was much happier using his longbow. The Genoese resumed their advance. They were only two hundred and fifty yards away now, and Martin knew that at that range he could pick off any one of them; but he also knew better than to disobey orders.

The Genoese were still advancing, loosing the occasional shot towards the English ranks, but they were shooting up-hill, and practically into the sun.

Preston was watching Holland. 'Steady, lads,' he told his men.

Holland drew his broadsword from its scabbard, holding it aloft so it caught the sun's last rays, glinting in the twilight.

'Step up and nock,' ordered Preston. The archers each took one pace forward, nocking their arrows to their bows. 'Mark – sixty yards short, remember! Draw!'

Martin raised his bow, pushing away the bowstave with his left arm, aiming sixty yards short of the advancing Genoese. He reckoned he could easily hit one of them, but if Preston wanted him to shoot short . . .

Holland brought down his sword with a sharp, chopping motion.

'Loose!'

Martin let fly. Suddenly the sky seemed to grow darker as a cloud of arrows filled the air, soughing with eerie menace as they whirred towards their targets. He had never seen anything like it. The arrows – literally thousands of them – seemed to arc downwards as one, like a swarm of bees or a flight of birds flying in formation.

They all fell short of the Genoese, just as had been ordered. To Martin it seemed like a waste of good arrows.

But now the Genoese were running forward, stopping just short of where the English arrows were embedded in the ground. Now Martin could see the reason for shooting short: the Genoese had assumed that was the maximum range of the English archers, and that they would be safe provided they went no further.

'Nock,' ordered Preston. 'Mark to kill this time.'

Martin selected his mark, a crossbowman who was pausing to reload his weapon. The Genoese were targets, just like any other.

'Draw!' ordered Preston, waiting for Holland to give the signal once more. 'And . . . loose!'

Once again the sky was darkened with arrows. They curved down, this time raining amongst the ranks of the Genoese.

The effect was devastating. The crossbowmen were falling dead or wounded on all sides. Martin saw the man he had aimed at go down, and smiled with satisfaction. He was so pleased with the result, so astounded by the impact of the English volley, that for a few moments he forgot to nock another arrow to his bow. Then he remembered where he was and why he was there, and he realised that for every Genoese who had been killed or seriously injured, another ten were still standing.

That's no problem, thought Martin; we'll just have to shoot ten more volleys.

After five more volleys, the Genoese were already beginning to waver. The English and Welsh archers were positioned in wedge-shaped formations on the wings of the prince's division, so that the Genoese found them-selves caught in the crossfire as they advanced to attack the men-at-arms in the centre.

There was a sound like a crack of thunder, but instead of lightning, smoke and flame seemed to fly down towards the Genoese. Astonished, Martin followed the trail of smoke back to where the ribauds he had seen at Port-smouth were positioned beyond the gap between the prince's division and the Earl of Northampton's division on the left flank. Even as he watched, he saw the engineers operating another ribaud. They ran clear of the weapon, and seconds later it belched flame with another crack of thunder. Martin did not know what power lay behind such engines, but he was glad it seemed to be on his side.

Such weapons were known to the French, who had used them long before the English had taken them up, but it was a new experience for the Genoese to come under fire from these engines. At that range, the wide spread of bolts and pellets was largely ineffectual, killing only a handful of the crossbowmen. But the Genoese were terrified by the thunderous noise, the flame-spewing tubes and the trails of smoke. It was as if the English had harnessed the power of thunder and lightning. Did the French not say that the English were demons? Did this not prove that they had the power of Satan on their side? Scared witless by this new and unexpected development, they broke ranks and fled in confusion.

A great cheer went up from the English ranks. 'That'll teach Valois not to hire mercenaries!' shouted someone.

'I hope he demands his money back!' Conyers shouted in reply.

Some of the English archers started to gesticulate at the retreating backs of the Genoese, demonstrating the fact that unlike the archers supposedly captured and mutilated by the French, they still had the first two fingers of their right hands.

Tate was grinning nervously, his face shining. 'Have we won?' he asked.

'Er . . . not yet, lad,' Preston told him dubiously.

They gradually became aware of a rumble like distant thunder, and looked to their front to see several companies of armoured archers and men-at-arms riding into the valley. Even in the failing light they made a brave show in their shining armour, their banners and pennants fluttering. They rode at a trot, lances carried upright.

Then they broke into a canter, callously riding down the fleeing Genoese who got in their way, some of them even aiming sword-strokes at the crossbowmen.

The horsemen were charging in a disorderly mob, and the Genoese who got in their way only served to break up the ranks even further. The hooves of their massive coursers sent tremors through the ground as they charged forward, and it seemed as if nothing could break their impetus.

'Nock!' ordered Preston.

Martin selected a bodkin-tipped arrow and nocked it.

Now the Frenchmen were charging up the slope towards them. It was the kind of slope that looked gentle enough until one tried to run up it. Already the pace of the horses was beginning to slacken, the uneven terraces breaking their rhythm.

'Mark!'

Now Martin felt fear: not the tightness in the pit of his stomach, but a sharper, paralysing fear that turned his limbs to water. It was not the speed of the charging horsemen that frightened him so much as the seemingly implacable power of the charge. Part of him told him he was a fool to stand there, waiting to die, either spitted on one of those long lances or trampled underfoot by the massive horses. Wondering if he was alone in his fears, he glanced briefly left and right. Conyers and Brewster stood on either side of him, their faces pale and taut with fear, but their expressions resolute. Their resolution gave him heart, and he fought back the temptation to turn and flee for his life.

'Draw!'

The serjeant's words snapped Martin out of his paralysing fear. He marked his target, pushing out the bowstave and taking aim.

'Loose!'

Martin loosed his arrow. Horses reared as the volley struck home. Armoured knights fell from their saddles to crash to the ground. Other horses tripped and stumbled over the bodies that had fallen before them, some of them losing their riders. The noise of shouting men, neighing horses and crashing armour was terrific.

But the majority of the knights and men-at-arms rode on. They couched their lances, urging their mounts into a canter. They were less than a hundred and fifty yards away now.

'Loose!' ordered Preston. 'At your own rate.'

Martin had already nocked another arrow to his bow and now he loosed it, reaching for a third arrow and loosing that before his second had yet struck its target. On either side of him his fellow archers did likewise, so that the air was continuously filled with arrows. The horsemen were charging towards the front rank of men-at-arms in the prince's division, so now they found themselves shot at from both sides by the archers in the wings, caught in the same lethal crossfire that had broken the advance of the Genoese. The slaughter was terrible to behold.

Perhaps half the horsemen in this initial charge managed to reach the men-at-arms to the right of where Martin stood, but they could not persuade their horses to charge through the fence of levelled spears that greeted them. They struggled to goad their mounts forward, jabbing at the men-at-arms with their lances or hacking at the spearheads with their swords. A few English men-at-arms were slain, but even more Frenchmen died on those spear-points, and the front rank held firm. The English and Welsh archers continued to pour their arrows into the flanks of the French formation. The ground immediately before the English men-at-arms, between the two wings of archers, had become a killing ground.

Another formation of French knights and men-at-arms was charging across the valley floor towards Northampton's division, further along the ridge. They received a similar reception.

Now the attack on the prince's division began to break, the horsemen wheeling their chargers about and riding back down the slope. The archers continued to shoot after them until they were out of range. The slope was littered with the corpses of men and horses.

Another cheer went up from the English ranks.

Martin felt elated. They had done it! The flower of French chivalry had been routed by a handful of English yeomen armed only with their crooked sticks. He had been told that archers and dismounted men-at-arms could defeat armoured knights on horseback, but he had never really believed it until now.

His elation was short-lived. On the far side of the valley, the survivors of the initial charge were rallying, joined by fresh troops brought up from the rear; and there were plenty more where they had come from.

The battle had only just begun.

CHAPTER FIFTEEN

The French charged again, this time in better order. But in the gloom of dusk, the corpses that now littered the slope presented an even greater obstacle than the holes dug by the archers. The mounted knights and men-at-arms advanced their horses at a walk, breaking into a trot when they were only two hundred yards away and slowly but steadily accelerating into a canter, the powerful haunches of their destriers driving them up the slope.

The archers showered them with repeated volleys of arrows, killing dozens of them.

But dozens were not enough.

The formation of horsemen smashed like a mailed fist into the front rank of men-at-arms. Martin watched in fascinated horror, still shooting arrows as fast as he could nock them to his bow and draw. Swords rose and fell, vaguely silhouetted against the darkening sky. Men shouted and screamed. Horses neighed. The clash of steel against steel rang out.

Then the French were pulling back. The English front rank remained intact, those who had fallen immediately being replaced by the men behind them. It was difficult to see in the thickening gloom if the French were rallying for a third charge. Martin wondered how many more such attacks they could hope to hold off. The French seemed to have no shortage of men in reserve, and Martin had already run out of arrows. Most of his companions were no better off. Preston had sent Inglewood and Tate to the rear to fetch more arrows, but that would take time. In the meantime, he dispatched Martin and Drayton down the slope to recover as many arrows as possible before the French charged again. Men from other platoons of archers were doing likewise.

It had grown so dark that Martin could barely see a few yards in front of him, let alone find any arrows. He skidded and slid over the damp grass, into the mud churned up by the horses, stumbling over corpses in the gloom. He could hear the rallying cries of the French; they sounded uncomfortably close.

If I can live through this battle, he told himself, then God is prepared to give me a chance to make amends for the terrible things I've done; if not . . . then it means that Hell cannot claim me soon enough.

It was easier to find arrows than he had expected. The ground seemed to be carpeted with them. It was impossible not to find them, like looking for corn in a wheat field in August. They were planted in the soil, in horses, in men. Martin plucked them free indifferently. Before long he had as many as he could carry.

He could hear the approach of more horsemen in the distance as the French prepared to charge once more. 'Come on, Hal, let's get out of it.'

'Just let me get a few more arrows,' the big man replied ponderously.

'God-damn it, Hal, there isn't time! We have to get these arrows back to the others.' Martin began to climb back up the slope without waiting to see if Drayton followed.

The ground seemed to tremble beneath his feet. He could hear the thunder of approaching hooves. Panic seized him. Alone out on the side of the ridge in the darkness, he felt exposed. In his mind's eye, he could see the sharp tip of a lance reaching out towards his back as a knight sought to ride him down. Breathing hard, clutching the arrows to his chest, he stumbled through the mud and corpses to where his companions waited. His feet could not seem to get a grip in the churned mud.

Then he was walking on grass, his friends only a few yards away now. He stumbled in one of the shallow pits, but managed to maintain his balance without dropping the arrows. He had only collected enough to give out three or four each; but if two men from each platoon had found that many, it amounted to at least seven devastating volleys.

'Where's Drayton?' demanded Preston, as the men jostled one another – and Martin – in their eagerness to restock their supplies of arrows.

'Right behind me,' panted Martin, hoping it was true.

A gibbous moon was rising over the battlefield, casting its pale light over the scene. Now they could see the French charging across the valley floor. Perhaps it was a trick of the light, but this time there seemed to be more of them than ever. Martin could see Drayton, about fifty yards down the slope, stumbling up through the darkness with perhaps four dozen arrows clutched to his chest, his teeth shining in the moonlight as he grimaced with desperation. The French were riding up the slope perhaps a hundred yards behind him. Once again the steep incline slowed their pace, but they were moving fast nevertheless.

Drayton was not going to make it.

'Loose!' ordered Preston. Another volley of arrows tore into the ranks of the mounted Frenchmen. They came on. This time they were heading not into the death trap between the wings of archers, but were instead driving their horses directly into the hail of arrows that came from the left wing, where Holland's company was positioned. The English formation had worked for as long as the attacking horsemen allowed their instincts to guide them, turning away from the volleys of arrows and riding to their deaths on the spears of the men-at-arms, while the archers continued to shoot at their flanks. Now the French had seen their error, and changed their tactics accordingly. The archers in the left wing could only shoot at the men in the front rank of the charge, and they would not be able to withstand the impetus in the same way that the men-at-arms could fend it off with their spears and lances.

Drayton was only a couple of dozen yards away now. The others shouted encouragement at him. 'Come on, Hal!'

'You can do it!'

'Shift your arse, lad!'

Drayton stumbled and fell. A groan went up from Preston's platoon.

The horsemen were only fifty yards away now. The archers continued to shoot at them desperately.

'Come on, Hal, they're right behind you!' screamed Martin. He had already used up two of his four recovered arrows.

Drayton picked himself up, and to Martin's horror he began to collect the arrows he had dropped.

'For Christ's love! Leave them!'

A horseman had seen Drayton now, and was charging directly towards him, lance couched. Martin let fly, his shaft catching the knight's mount in the chest. It reared up, throwing its rider from the saddle, and then stumbled and fell.

Drayton was moving again now, but the front rank of horses was right behind him. They did not even seem to notice him in the darkness, they were so intent on charging the formation of archers. One moment he was there, and the next he had disappeared, stampeded beneath a hundred hooves. He did not even have a chance to cry out.

'Whoresons!' screamed Martin, nocking his last arrow to his bow. The French were so close now it seemed as if nothing could stop them. Their lances were couched, the tips promising imminent death to any archer who stood in their way.

Martin saw one French knight riding at the centre of the formation. He wore a dark-coloured jupon patterned with fleurs-de-lys. The same design decorated his shield. In the moonlight, Martin could see that his bascinet was encircled by what might have been a jewelled crown.

Valois, thought Martin.

'I'll give you a bloody nose, you pox-ridden whoreson!' he screamed, taking careful aim at the man's head and letting fly.

The man clapped a gauntleted hand to his cheek and seemed to slump in his saddle.

'Got you, you bastard!' Martin roared triumphantly.

Then the mounted knights smashed into the formation of archers. Freeman screamed horribly as a lance pierced his chest and emerged from his back. A horse reared up, striking Pip Herrick a glancing blow on the head with one of its hooves. Herrick staggered back, bumping into Martin, who fell against the side of another horse that was ploughing into the crush of bodies. The horse's rider tried to swipe at him with his broadsword. Martin ducked beneath the blow. He reached for the hilt of his own sword, but then another horse cannoned into him. He fell, sprawling in the mud, his sword trapped beneath his body.

Holland plunged into the thick of it, bringing the blade of his sword down on the head of a horse whose rider tried to skewer him with a lance. The horse slumped forward, its brains exposed, glistening in the moonlight. Men struggled to get clear as the massive beast keeled over. Hick Lowesby slipped in the mud and screamed in agony as the horse fell across his legs, pinning him to the ground.

Martin scrambled clear of another horse's hooves and managed to haul himself up through the crush by holding

389

on to a rider's stirrup. Seeing him, the rider tried to kick him in the face with his spur. Martin jerked his head out of the way. The man tried to reach for his sword. Martin finally managed to draw his own sword, slashing the man's face open on the follow-through. The man reeled back in his saddle, his face a mask of blood, his lacerated jaw hanging slackly.

Martin pushed the man out of the saddle and used the riderless horse as a shield, turning it sideways to the knights who rode up to the breach in the English ranks. He placed one foot in the stirrup, lifting himself up to slash at a knight who rode past. His blade failed to penetrate the knight's coat of mail, but the impact of the blow was enough to knock the knight from his saddle. He crashed to the ground, struggling to lift himself from the mud until a horse put its hoof on his head, crumpling his bascinet and crushing the skull beneath.

Another knight tried to run Martin through with his lance. Martin knocked the lance-point aside with his sword, severing it near the tip. The knight threw away the ruined lance with a roar of outrage, drawing his sword as he goaded his mount to where Martin clung to the side of the riderless horse. He swung his blade at Martin's head. Martin parried the blow, before jabbing his sword-point into the knight's face.

Something struck Martin on the side of the head. Blinding white agony exploded behind his eyes. He lost his grip on the pommel of the saddle and felt himself falling back into the crush. He gripped the hilt of his sword tightly, determined not to lose it.

He sprawled in the mud. A man-at-arms inadvertently put his foot on the blade of the sword, pinning it to the ground. Martin swivelled on his back, lashing out with one foot at the side of the man's knee. He felt rather than heard the bone snap. Then the sword was free, and he pushed himself up on to one knee, parrying another sword-stroke. His helmet had gone. He could feel his own blood coursing warmly down the side of his head. He stabbed one man-at-arms in the stomach and hacked at another, carving himself just enough space to rise to his feet. There was hardly any room to swing his sword. Someone tried to stab him but he squirmed aside, punching the man in the face with his left hand. Another man-at-arms was thrown against him. Martin lifted his knee into the man's crotch, and then kneed him in the face as he doubled up. Someone elbowed Martin in the stomach. He butted his assailant on the bridge of the nose, and managed to get his sword free of the crush, swinging with all his might at another man's neck. The blade sheared through flesh, bone and sinew. Something smashed into the small of Martin's back. He staggered forward, lost his balance and fell face-down in the mud. He tried to crawl out of danger, but it was all around him. Someone kicked him in the side, someone else trod on his left hand. He rolled on to his back and found a knight standing over him, wielding a sword above his head. Martin managed to raise his own sword to parry the blow, but before the two blades could connect, the knight's features contorted as someone stabbed him in the back. Then Preston was there, roughly hauling Martin to his feet.

There was no time for expressions of gratitude. More mounted knights were riding into the breach. Welsh spearmen moved amongst them, cutting their horses' hamstrings with long knives. A dismounted knight was carving a passage through the English ranks. Preston stepped up behind him and seized him in an arm-lock, swinging him around to face Martin. 'Do it, Kemp! In the face!' Martin did not hesitate, drawing his rondel with his left hand to plunge it into the knight's eye.

Brewster ducked beneath another rider, cutting through the belly-strap of his saddle. Conyers and Oakley hurled him to the ground, stabbing him in the face. The enemy pressed in on all sides. A mounted knight hacked at Holland, who caught the blow on his shield before driving the point of his sword up at the man's side. The force of the thrust drove the point through the knight's chain-mail hauberk and up into his ribcage. Newbolt took a sword-thrust in the chest and sank to the ground with a look of annoyance on his face. 'God *damn* it!' he mumbled, and died. His killer followed him to Hell when Preston buried the edge of his sword deep into his left shoulder.

Holland was attacked by three dismounted knights simultaneously. He stabbed one, barely withdrawing his blade in time to parry a blow from the second before a stroke from the third dented his bascinet. He fell on his back, his heavy armour making it almost impossible for him to rise from where he sprawled in the mud. He caught another sword-stroke on his shield, slashed at the second man, the stroke going wide. Then Preston and Oakley stepped in and engaged the third, Oakley seizing the knight from behind while Preston delivered the death-thrust. The second stood over Holland and raised his sword for the killing stroke. Then his body arched grotesquely as a spearhead emerged from his chest. The Frenchmen on either side of him were cut down as a dozen English knights and a platoon of men-at-arms attacked them from the rear. Holland felt a hand grab him by the arm, and recognised the Earl of Warwick peering down at him.

'Are you hurt?'

Holland shook his head, allowing the earl to help him to his feet. He recognised the young prince himself in his darkly burnished armour, charging into the thick of it, hacking and slashing left and right as he carved a passage deep into the enemy ranks. Close behind him, his standard-bearer received a sword-thrust in the face, but no sooner had the prince's banner fallen than Sir Thomas Daniels rushed forward to raise it aloft once more. Sir Reginald Cobham appeared at Holland's side, and the two of them rushed to back up the prince. The French knights and men-at-arms pressed close, determined to win the prize that would assure his captor of the greatest glory of the day: the heir to the throne of England.

Sir Thomas Norwich struggled up the side of the slope to where the king observed the battle from a vantage point on the crest of the ridge, not far from the windmill. In the front line below all was confusion, and in the moonlight it was impossible to tell which side was gaining the upper hand. A fresh wave of French men-at-arms could just be made out charging towards the breach in the English ranks. His face streaked with dirt and dried blood, Norwich went down on one knee before the king, breathing hard, struggling to remember the exact wording of the message Sir Godefroi d'Harcourt had asked him to deliver.

'Your Majesty. My lord of Warwick, Sir Reginald Cobham, and the others who are with your son are hard-pressed on all sides by the French, and they beg that you send in the reserves before more reinforcements arrive for the French.'

The king could not imagine Warwick or Cobham begging for assistance if their lives depended on it. But if the prince's life were threatened . . . ? 'Is my son dead, or so badly wounded that he cannot support himself?' he asked, without taking his gaze from the battle-scene to meet Norwich's eyes. To the left of the position, he could see a troop of men-at-arms led by the Earl of Arundel, charging from Northampton's division to counter-attack the right flank of the French.

'Nothing of the sort, God be thanked, but he is in so . . .'

The king raised a hand to silence Norwich. 'Now, Sir Thomas, return to those who sent you and tell them not to send for me again, nor expect me to come to their aid, come what may, so long as my son lives,' he said sternly. 'Say that I command them to let the boy win his spurs. I want all the glory of this day to go to him, and to those into whose care I have entrusted him.'

If John Conyers had had time to reflect, he might have been overwhelmed with awe at the noble company in which he fought: the Earl of Warwick, Sir Reginald Cobham, and Sir John Chandos, not to mention the prince himself. But there was no time for standing around open-mouthed. Their only significance in his mind at that moment was that they, along with Holland, were five of the greatest warriors in the world; and, more importantly, they were on his side. But chivalric prowess would not be enough against such an overwhelming number of enemies, and their arms were growing tired.

Conyers found himself attacked by an armoured knight. He desperately parried a sword-stroke, and then thrust the blade of his short sword at the knight's chest. But his sword-point only lacerated the fabric of the knight's jupon before glancing off his coat of mail. The knight swung his broadsword at Conyers' head, gripping it two-handed. Conyers raised his own sword to deflect the stroke. The blow broke Conyers' sword near the hilt, jarring his arm. The knight thrust at Conyers, the point of his sword entering Conyers' side. The archer gasped in shock as the steel plunged into his flesh, his legs crumpling beneath him as he sank to his knees. Then the knight withdrew his blade, swinging it back over his shoulder. Conyers raised his arms to protect himself in an instinctive if useless gesture.

A pale figure loomed up behind the knight wielding a broadsword. The blade came arcing down, cleaving through steel, flesh and bone to split the knight's head in two. Conyers felt himself spattered with blood and brains. He wiped the gore from his eyes to recognise Martin standing over him. He had tied his coverchief around his head like a bandana, and the left side of it was dark with blood. His pale face was white in the moonlight but streaked with more blood. He swung the broadsword to his left, hacking off a man's arm near the shoulder, before thrusting the point at a man to his right. He roared savagely as he fought, his teeth bared in a wolfish grin as he swung his sword tirelessly.

Suddenly there were no more French to kill. Arundel's counter-attack had smashed into the French flank, and now the enemy were turning and fleeing into the night. Even if their orders had not strictly demanded that the English troops hold their positions, they were too exhausted to pursue the enemy.

Martin sank to his knees amongst the heaps of bodies and wiped the blade of his broadsword on the hem of a dead man's jupon, returning it to its scabbard. He crawled over to where Conyers lay. 'Are you all right?'

Conyers gestured listlessly at the wound in his side. His ripped tunic was matted with blood. 'I think I'm dying,' he whispered.

'Ballocks,' Martin told him crisply, using his rondel to cut a jupon off a dead knight and wadding up the cloth, pressing it against the wound to stanch the flow of blood. 'Hold this in place,' he said, while searching for some more cloth to make a tourniquet. 'Can you walk?' he asked, when he had finished binding the makeshift dressing in place.

'I'll try.'

Martin helped Conyers to his feet, supporting him as the two of them stumbled through the darkness in search of their companions. 'Why's a miller's cloak the bravest thing in the world?' asked Martin.

Conyers managed a wan smile. 'Because it's the only thing that would clasp a thieving rogue by the neck every day. That's an old one, Martin. How about if I stick to making jests, and you stick to fighting?'

Martin laughed. 'It's a deal.'

They met some Welsh archers moving forward to fill the gaps punched in the left wing by the French attack, and Martin recognised Ieuan ap Morgan. He waved, and the Welshman waved back, grinning. 'Been having fun, boy?'

'Go to Hell,' Martin replied good-naturedly.

'Didn't they tell you? We're already there.'

'I can well believe it,' Martin said grimly. 'Have you seen Sir Thomas Holland's banner around?'

'I've not seen his banner, but the man himself is over yonder in some very exalted company indeed,' Ieuan said, pointing. 'Dafydd's over there, too, looking after some of your countrymen who were too careless to keep their hides intact. Looks to me as if your friend could do with some attention.'

'Thanks,' said Martin. 'Good luck.'

Ieuan chuckled. 'Don't worry about me, boy. A year from now we'll be sitting together in a tavern in Gwent, laughing about all this over a cup of mead.'

'Very well, but you're paying,' Martin told him, smiling.

Martin and Conyers found Holland and Preston seated on the ground amongst the piles of corpses with the prince, the Earls of Warwick and Arundel, d'Harcourt, Cobham and Norwich, and some men-at-arms and a few archers, including Brewster and Oakley. The prince's burnished armour was battered and dented, and covered in blood. He no longer looked as youthful as he had seemed at Saint-Vaast-la-Hougue, but he was smiling, and his princely bearing was unmistakable. The noblemen sat alongside the common soldiers, sharing their gourds of water and chatting as equals. Differences in social status no longer seemed to matter. Dafydd was there, tending to the wounds of the prince's standard bearer.

Martin was unsure how to react to finding himself in such exalted company. He bowed as far as he could, at the same time struggling to support Conyers.

The prince made a dismissive gesture. 'Don't stand on ceremony, man. Sit down before you fall down.'

Martin gently lowered Conyers to the ground before thankfully sinking down beside him. 'Can you see to my friend?' he asked Dafydd.

The Welshman nodded. 'As soon as I've finished with this one.'

'You've got your work cut out for you tonight, eh, Dafydd?' said the prince.

'Indeed, your Highness.'

'What about you, Kemp?' asked Holland. 'That looks like a bad wound you've got there.'

'I'll live.'

'Have you seen Adam?'

Martin shook his head, gratefully taking the gourd of water that the prince handed him.

'What about Pip?' asked Preston.

'He's dead,' Martin said flatly. 'A lance point took him clean in the throat. I don't reckon he felt much,' he added vaguely.

They could hear the rallying cries of the French in the distance, but apart from the moans of the wounded and dying, everything in the immediate vicinity was quiet.

Dressed in full armour and toting a large and vicious-looking mace, the Bishop of Durham suddenly rode out of the night, accompanied by a score of knights and a troop of men-at-arms. He dismounted to kneel before the prince. 'Your father asked us to reinforce your position, your Royal Highness,' he said. 'But it seems our assistance was not required after all.' He sounded morose at having missed out on the opportunity of a fight.

The prince laughed. 'I fear you come too late to make a noble rescue of it, my lord bishop, but I beg you remain with us a while; I fear we have not seen the last of the French for this night,' he said kindly.

Inglewood and Tate arrived at that moment, struggling under the weight of a basket of arrows that they carried between them. 'Did we miss aught?' Tate asked innocently.

Martin found himself laughing helplessly until the tears streamed down his cheeks.

'Not much,' Preston said dryly. 'You might take those arrows down to where those Welsh archers stand. They may be in need of them soon enough, I reckon.'

As if in confirmation, a French trumpet in the distance sounded the charge. The prince pushed himself to his feet, and those around him who could still stand likewise arose. 'Well, gentlemen,' he said. 'Duty can be an insatiable mistress, but one I shall never tire of serving.' He drew his sword and marched back down to the battle line, accompanied by the bishop, the two earls, and all of the knights present except Holland, who lingered, turning to Preston.

'You and your men have done more than enough for a lifetime's service in this one day alone, Wat. No one will hold it against you if you withdraw now.'

Preston looked disgruntled at the very suggestion. 'Will you be withdrawing, Sir Thomas?'

Holland shook his head.

'Well then,' the serjeant said simply.

Holland turned to Martin. 'Kemp? You look as though you're ready to drop.'

Martin stood defiantly with his arms akimbo, his fists balled on his hips, his face implacable. 'I'm not finished yet, sir.'

Holland sighed, and drew his sword. 'Come on, then.'

Afterwards, no one could really be sure how many times the French charged the English positions. Some said eight times, others were adamant that it had been as many as fifteen. Somehow, Martin had expected a battle to build to a decisive climax; but after that third, shattering charge which had barely been repulsed, each subsequent attack seemed more and more lacklustre, until the battle seemed to peter out some time towards midnight. No one was sure if either side had won, or how many of the French were left out there in the darkness. But the bodies of slain French noblemen were heaped on the terraces before the English ranks in their hundreds, and every now and then a handful of disorientated French men-at-arms, deprived of their leaders, would inadvertently stumble into the English lines only to be cut ruthlessly to pieces.

There were no more trumpets, no more battle cries or rallying shouts, only the pitiful moans of the wounded and the dying. Preston and his men sat down where they stood, waiting to see what would happen next. Where once Preston had had nineteen men under his command, now there were only five: Martin, Brewster, Inglewood, Oakley and Tate. Conyers had been taken to the rear, out of the line of battle. Like Villiers, Hick Lowesby seemed to have disappeared, and was presumed dead.

Seated on the ground in a numb daze, Martin found himself staring at the boots of a dead man-at-arms. They were good boots, well-crafted, made of stout black leather, their tops folded down. They were also, he noted, about his size, and in far better condition than the pathetic rags of leather that still clung to his own feet. No harm in trying them on, he told himself.

'Dead men's boots, is it?' cackled Oakley, his voice wheezy from the exertions of the battle. 'There's no good will come of wearing dead men's boots.'

'I'm not superstitious,' Martin replied curtly. The boots were a very good fit indeed.

'It's bad luck, I tell ye.'

'Says who?' demanded Brewster.

Oakley paused to give the question the consideration it deserved. 'Well, they weren't very lucky for him, were they?' he replied, indicating the bare-footed corpse.

'Luck had nothing to do with it,' asserted Martin, stomping around in his new boots to make sure that they would not chafe or pinch his feet.

Brewster rubbed his jaw thoughtfully. 'He had the misfortune to run into you, didn't he?'

Martin grinned.

Tate lay on the ground nearby, pale-faced, the front of his tunic awash with French blood. He might have been mistaken for a corpse had it not been for the rhythmic rising and falling of his chest. He slept with one hand on the hilt of his sword. Preston sat nearby, watching him with almost paternal fondness. 'Well, I reckon he's a soldier now,' he murmured to himself.

The serjeant heard a footfall behind him, and twisted to see Martin standing there. 'Well?' he demanded irritably. 'What do you want?'

'I thought I might go to the river to refill my gourd,' said Martin. He had suddenly realised that his throat was parched, and his tongue felt numb and swollen.

'Not a bad idea,' Preston admitted grudgingly. 'You can take mine while you're at it – my mouth's as barren as Isaac's wife.' He turned to the others. 'Everybody give their gourds to Lancelot –he's kindly volunteered to fetch us all some water.'

'Can I go with him?' asked Inglewood. 'I'd like a chance to stretch my legs.'

Preston shook his head. 'They're quite long enough as it is, Pisspants. You stay here with the rest of us. You never know, those French whoresons may be cooking up

400

another charge for us, and you wouldn't want to miss out on any of the fun, would you?'

Martin started walking along the slope of the ridge towards the village, carrying the empty water bottles so that they hung by their thongs from his hand in a cluster. Torches had been lit throughout the English lines so that they could see if the French attacked again, although that seemed increasingly unlikely. The windmill had been set ablaze, and it burnt fiercely, casting an orange glow far and wide. To his left, Martin could hear the Welsh troops singing *Te Deum*s as part of a thanksgiving mass. He wondered if they were giving thanks for victory, or just because they were still alive. Martin was not yet convinced the English had won, but he was glad he was still living. Did God intend him to have a second chance? The battle might not yet be over; and even if it was, who knew what the next day might bring?

He made his way through the deserted village to the river that lay beyond the cottages along the far side of the road. Compared to the Seine and the Somme it was little more than a stream, really. He crouched down by the water's edge and laid the gourds down on the grass beside him. He splashed water on his face; it was cold and refreshing, reviving him a little. Then he turned his attention to the gourds. He was filling the first of them when he heard a shuffling noise behind him. Reaching instinctively for the hilt of his sword, he rose to his feet and span around, at the same time throwing the half-filled gourd at his assailant's face.

Richard Stamford jerked his head aside with a snarl, and the gourd flew over his shoulder. The element of surprise lost, he lunged forward, his handsome young features twisted in a scowl of hatred, and tried to thrust his broadsword into Martin's chest.

Martin threw himself to one side, rolling on the riverbank and tugging his sword free of its scabbard. Stamford whirled to face him, raising his sword above his head. He tried to bring it down on his opponent. Martin parried the blow before lunging. The squire danced nimbly aside, deflecting the thrust with his blade, before riposting with a swing at Martin's head. Martin leapt back, clear of the blade's arcing tip, only to lose his footing on the grass. He slipped and landed on his backside. Stamford tried to hack at his neck, but Martin was already rolling clear, scrambling away before rising to his feet.

Ever since he had killed Will Caynard, Martin had stopped worrying about the possibility of being caught alone by an enemy; now it looked as if it might cost him his life. Stamford had obviously seen him leaving the battle lines alone, and had followed him, intent on taking the opportunity to settle the score.

The two of them stood facing one another on the river-bank, breathing hard. Martin was the stronger of the two, and in the hard-won experience of the past few weeks he had proved to be a proficient swordsman. But Stamford was nimbler, faster, and he had been trained for warfare since childhood.

The squire lunged, thrusting his sword-point at Martin's midriff. This time Martin held his ground, deflecting the thrust with his blade. He allowed his opponent to move in close before aiming a swipe at his head. Stamford ducked, swinging his sword at Martin's side. Martin tried to parry the blow. Stamford's blade slid down Martin's, jumping over the crossguard, the point scoring a line of blood across the back of Martin's hand. Martin hissed in pain, dropping his sword. He tried to pick it up, but Stamford swung at him again, forcing him to dodge back. Stamford raised his sword above his head, trying to bring it down on Martin with a grunt of effort. Martin dived to one side, rolling in the grass as Stamford's blade bit into the earth. The squire was still trying to tug his blade out of the ground when Martin hurled himself at

402

him, catching him around the waist. The two of them went down, leaving Stamford's sword buried point-first in the ground. They rolled down the bank and into the river.

Martin floundered about in the cold water for a few moments, struggling to regain his footing. He rose to his feet in the waist-deep water, turning to meet Stamford's next attack. Stamford had his dagger in his upheld fist. He tried to plunge it down into Martin's chest but Martin caught his wrist in his left hand, holding the blade at bay above their heads, and drove his fist into Stamford's stomach. Stamford dropped the dagger with a winded gasp, and Martin pushed him over backwards, his hands clutching at the squire's neck as he forced his head underwater. Stamford thrashed about frantically, his hands scrabbling for purchase on the river bed, his lungs filling with water as he gulped for air, Martin's hands squeezing his throat. The squire's fingers curled around a rock, and he lifted it out of the water, smashing it with all his might against the side of Martin's head. Martin's hands released their grip and Stamford managed to swim clear, coughing and spluttering as he gulped air into his lungs on resurfacing.

Martin was sprawled on his back at the river's edge, the upper half of his body out of the water. He lay unmoving. Almost completely drained, Stamford waded to the bank and dragged himself out of the river, crawling over to where his sword stood. Grasping the cross-guard, he pulled himself to his feet. It took him almost his last reserves of energy to tug the sword free of the soil. He dragged it over to where Martin lay at the river's edge, and with a supreme final effort, he managed to raise it above his head.

'Did you truly think yourself worthy of my Beatrice's love?' he panted. 'This will make sure you never trouble her again!'

'Kiss the Devil's arse.' Martin's eyes flicked open, and he thrust his rondel up into Stamford's crotch, burying it to the hilt. Stamford screamed horribly, releasing his grip on the sword. Martin rolled clear a split-second before the massive blade crashed down. Stamford fell to the ground, writhing in agony. Martin was astride him in a moment, grabbing fistfuls of his hair on either side of his head. He smashed the back of the squire's head repeatedly against a rock, grunting savagely with each blow. He did not stop until the back of Stamford's head had been reduced to a pulpy mess, his pale, blood-spattered face staring sightlessly up at the moon.

Martin sank down beside him, breathing hard. After a few minutes he summoned the energy to push himself to his feet, retrieving his sword and rondel. He nudged Stamford's body with the toe of his boot until it rolled down the river-bank and landed face-down in the water. The corpse was caught by the current and whipped away downstream. Martin picked up Stamford's broadsword and hurled it into the centre of the river. Then he calmly finished filling the gourds with water, before walking back to where Preston and the others waited, whistling the tune of 'The Knight Stained From Battle' to himself.

Dawn rose the following morning to reveal the battlefield shrouded in mist. The king, finding himself master of the field, charged Cobham and another knight to make a careful tally of the corpses of the men of quality amongst those strewn across the slope of the ridge. They were assisted by Norwich and two heralds to help identify the coats of arms of the slain, and a couple of clerks whose task it was to make a note of their names. One thing that soon became apparent was that by far the greatest number of them were French. Among the dead were the Kings of Bohemia and Mallorca; Valois' brother, the Duke of Alençon; and d'Harcourt's elder brother, the Count d'Harcourt.

There was no trace of Valois himself, although some Frenchmen captured later claimed that he had escaped the battlefield with the Count of Hainault. Martin was disappointed to learn that he had not slain the king's enemy after all, but was gratified to learn that Valois had indeed been wounded in the face by an arrow. He hoped it had been his own.

Casualties on the English side were astonishingly light. Holland's company had suffered disproportionately high casualties because it had been in the front line where the French had almost broken through; all told, only a few hundred English and Welshmen had been killed. The French dead numbered in thousands.

Hick Lowesby was found beneath a pile of corpses. He was not dead, but his legs had been crushed beneath a horse. He and Conyers were taken with the rest of the wounded to the nearby abbey of Crécy-Grange. Lowesby would never walk again; like Robin Wighton, he too was doomed to a life of beggary.

Adam Villiers was also found. He lay where the heaps of corpses were thickest, the broken-off point of a lance in his stomach, his bloodied sword in his right hand, his left hand clutching Holland's banner to his breast, as if he had died trying to save it from capture. His blue eyes gazed blankly up into the misty sky.

Holland stood with Preston, Martin, Brewster, Oakley, Inglewood and Tate. They had all liked the bold and happy-go-lucky young man, and were grieved at his death, no matter how noble the manner of his passing. Holland's face was stony as he gazed down at his squire's body, but he was silent for a few moments, as if grappling with some inner emotion. Finally he spoke.

'It seems he found his glory, then,' he said bleakly.

EPILOGUE

Two Years Later

The black-clad rider burst out of the swirling autumnal mists like one of the four horsemen of the apocalypse. He was tall and well-built, dressed in a voluminous black cloak with a large, loose-fitting cowl. The hooves of his fleabitten grey hackney clopped against the frozen, compacted earth of the lane as he rode through the gateway into the courtyard, reining in his horse near the foot of the wooden stairway that led up to the entrance of the manor house.

Treroose came down the steps to greet him. 'Good morning. Welcome to Stone Gate Manor.'

The rider ignored him, gazing slowly around the courtyard with a pair of flint-blue eyes. He appeared to be about twenty years of age, with a haggard, careworn, lean-jawed face and close-cropped pale blond hair. A small scar marked his chin, and a large one ran into his hairline on the left side of his head. There was something vaguely familiar about this young man, although Treroose could not at first recall where he had seen him before.

'Sir John is presently at his devotions,' the steward continued. 'If you'll give me your name, I'll let him know you're here as soon as the service is ended. If I can offer you the hospitality of the household in the meantime . . .'

The rider swung himself out of the saddle and handed

the reins to the steward, before striding slowly and deliberately to the small chapel adjoining the manor house.

'Excuse me,' Treroose called after him, rather angrily. 'Sir John does not take kindly to being disturbed when he is at prayer.'

The stranger halted, and then turned back to face him. As he did so, his cloak billowed outwards, affording the steward a brief glimpse of a large broadsword that hung in a leather-bound scabbard at his hip.

'Good.' The stranger's voice had a sepulchral tone to it, as if it had come from the depths of a tomb. It sent a shiver down the steward's spine.

The stranger turned away again, walking to the door of the chapel. He stared contemplatively at the sturdy oak portal for a moment, and then lifted one leg to kick it open with a sharp, practised motion.

Sir John Beaumont was kneeling on the flagstone floor before the altar with Beatrice at his side while his chaplain prepared the sacraments. All three of them looked up sharply as the young man strode in, sweeping his cloak back across his left shoulder so that his broadsword hung in plain view.

'How dare you barge into this house of God bearing that tool of Satan?' the chaplain demanded angrily. 'Do you want to burn in Hell for eternity?'

'Hell holds no terrors for me,' the stranger replied laconically in that sepulchral voice of his. 'I was at Crécy.'

Beatrice stared at him in astonishment. 'Martin?'

Looking at her for the first time in over two years, Martin Kemp felt a lump choking his throat. The thought of her had kept him going through the horror of the campaigning in France, and now he found that she was even more beautiful than he remembered. 'Hello, Beatrice,' he said hoarsely.

Both Beaumont and Beatrice were on their feet now to face the stranger. 'You!' exclaimed Beaumont.

Turning his attention back to Beaumont, Kemp bared his teeth in a cruel sneer. 'Aye.'

'I'd heard you were dead! Killed by the pestilence . . .'

'It takes more than the pestilence to kill me,' Kemp responded simply.

'How dare you burst in here unannounced?' Beaumont struggled to regain his composure. 'You should have returned to Knighton over a year ago. You owe me fifteen months' labour, churl. I shall have you flogged, by God's flesh!'

Kemp reached inside his cloak and produced a scroll of parchment that he unrolled to show to Beaumont. 'Do you see that seal? That is the seal of the Lord Mayor of London. It testifies that I, Martin Kemp of Knighton, having resided in the Borough of London for a year and a day, have been granted the status of freeman in accordance with the laws of this realm.' His broad Leicester accent had gone, lost somewhere in the camp before the besieged walls of Calais and in the streets of London. 'I don't owe you a God-damned thing!' he spat.

Beaumont trembled with rage. 'Get out of here!' he snarled. 'Get out of here at once!'

Kemp shook his head. 'I've come for Beatrice.'

Beatrice blanched. 'What the Devil are you talking about?'

'Come on. We're leaving.'

She stared at him in astonishment. 'Has the moon touched your wits? I'm not going anywhere with you!'

Kemp was confused. Suddenly, the dreams he had built around him, the dreams that had kept him going through so many nightmares, seemed to come crashing down. 'But . . . I thought you loved me!' he protested petulantly.

She stared at him in mute horror for a moment, and then her face softened, and she threw back her head with a peal of laughter. 'Oh, you poor, sweet, naïve churl! How ridiculous you are!'

He frowned. 'How so, my lady?'

'Jackass! Surely you don't believe that I could ever love you?'

'But I thought . . .'

'It's not your place to think,' she sneered. 'Besides, what can a churl like you understand of the nobility of true and genteel love?'

'I'm as good a man as any noble. A better man than Richard Stamford ever was, aye and like.'

Suddenly Beaumont understood everything. 'It was you who slew Richard, wasn't it?'

'Aye,' Kemp admitted freely, absently.

'God's love, I ought to . . . ' Beaumont broke off abruptly, moving close to Kemp, fists clenched to strike him. Kemp was faster, driving a powerful punch into Beaumont's stomach. The knight doubled up, gasping in pain and clutching his midriff. He found himself torn by both anger and fear. This was not the bold but naïve peasant lad he had encountered three years ago; this was a vicious and ruthless killer.

The chaplain moved to intervene. 'How dare you fight in a house of God . . . ?'

Kemp's sword leapt from its scabbard, and he levelled it at the chaplain's chest. 'I've never killed a holy man, father,' he said harshly. 'Do you wish to be the first?'

Ashen-faced, the chaplain backed away hurriedly, and at that moment the door opened and Edith walked in, leading a small, blond-haired, blue-eyed toddler by the hand.

'No!' Beatrice screamed a warning to Edith. 'Don't bring him in here!'

'Bring him in, Edith!' wheezed Beaumont, rising

painfully to his feet. 'Let him see the man who slew his father!'

Kemp stared first at the toddler, and then at Beatrice. 'Your child?'

'Aye, mine and Dickon's,' she said coldly. Then she turned her back on him, scooping the child up in her arms and walking towards the chapel door, followed by Edith.

It was as if the scales had fallen from Kemp's eyes. She had been betraying him all along, telling him she loved him while giving herself equally to him and to Stamford. He felt rage flare up within him. 'You talk of noble love?' he snarled after her, seething with rage and humiliation. 'You're nothing more than a whore! One day I'll be a greater man than your father! When that day comes you'll beg to be my wife! And beg in vain!'

Beatrice's hollow laughter echoed back from outside.

'You can leave now,' Beaumont told him sternly, realising with relish that what Kemp had intended to be a triumphant return was turning into a moment of humiliation.

Kemp shook his head, and seized Beaumont by the mantle, dragging him outside. 'Don't you believe it. I've a score to settle with you.'

'Unhand me, you dog!' protested Beaumont, struggling. But Kemp was eighteen now, and his time in France had hardened him, putting even more muscle on his big bones.

There was no sign of Beatrice, Edith or the child, but the steward was still standing there, unsure of what to do. 'Treroose!' shouted Beaumont. 'For the love of God, aid me!'

'Get the whip, Treroose,' Kemp ordered.

Torn between his loyalty to Beaumont and his fear of this bold, brutal and terrifying stranger, Treroose hesitated.

410

'The whip,' insisted Kemp. He still had his sword in his free hand, and he held the blade against Beaumont's throat. 'Or your master dies.'

Treroose nodded, and hurried into the stable.

Beaumont continued to struggle, so Kemp sheathed his sword and punched him in the stomach. Winded, Beaumont was unable to resist as Kemp tied his wrists to the tailgate of the cart that stood there. Then he tore open Beaumont's robes to bare his back. The steward emerged from the stables, and as soon as Kemp had taken the whip from him he fled into the manor house.

'I'll see you burn in Hell for this, Kemp!' screamed Beaumont.

'Your squire once said exactly the same thing to me,' Kemp replied coolly. 'I dare say his soul awaits mine there even now.' He lashed the whip across Beaumont's back, and as the first bloody weal was raised, the knight howled in agony.

On the seventh lash, Beaumont fainted.

'Stop it!' Beatrice had emerged from the house and was running down the wooden steps into the courtyard. 'For pity's sake, stop it! Can't you see he's suffered enough?'

'No,' Kemp said tightly, lashing Beaumont's back once more. The fact that Beaumont could no longer feel it only angered him further, so that he lashed even harder.

Beatrice tried to grab him by the arm, but he pulled free of her and struck her in the face with his free hand, knocking her to the ground. She lay there, sobbing, and Kemp delivered the last four lashes. Then he coiled up the whip and tossed it down beside Beatrice. He turned away, and then paused, unlooping the coverchief wound around his neck and screwing it up into a tight wad, dropping it on top of her before swinging himself back into his horse's saddle and riding out of the courtyard without a backward glance.

The ride to Knighton from Stone Gate Manor House

411

did not seem half as far as it had done two and a half years earlier. The fields were rich with overripe corn that would soon be killed by frost if it was not harvested, but there was no one working in the fields, just a herd of untended cattle roaming through the ears of wheat. Once such a sight would have filled Kemp with outrage and horror. But after campaigning with the king's army in northern France? The depredations of brutal soldiers soon put a little agricultural neglect into perspective.

This air of neglect extended to the village itself. Pigs and hens roamed loose in the lane, wreaking havoc amongst the vegetable patches, but otherwise the place seemed quiet and deserted. He dismounted outside Simkin Sewell's cottage and knocked on the door. No one answered. He pushed the door open. The place was empty, the floor spattered with bat-droppings. Bewildered, he led his horse down the lane to his mother's cottage. Even though it was over two years since he had last been there, he entered without knocking out of force of habit. There was no one in the main room, but hearing sounds from next door he went straight through to the bower.

Naked, Michael struggled to free himself from the bedclothes, seizing a pitch-fork and stabbing at his youngest brother with it. Kemp snatched it easily from his grip and tossed it into the far corner of the room. He glanced at the bed, where a young woman was trying to cover her nakedness.

He turned to his brother, who was cowering before him. 'Michael! It's me! Your brother, Martin! Don't you recognise me?'

'*Martin?*' Michael peered at him in disbelief. 'By God that sits above, it *is* you! But Beaumont told us you were dead . . .'

'Not yet,' Kemp told him with a bleak smile, and gestured at the girl. 'Who's this?'

412

Michael shifted uncomfortably. 'You remember Lucy Petling, don't you?'

'Lucy Petling?' Kemp was incredulous. The last time he had seen her she had been little more than a girl. Now she was very much a young woman. She nodded and smiled, embarrassed, not really connecting him with the youth that had been Michael's youngest brother. 'So, you married little Lucy, did you?'

Michael shuffled even more uncomfortably, and said nothing.

'I see,' Kemp said dryly.

'Martin, what's happened to you? You look so . . . *old*. And where have you been?'

'London. I've been working for a rich vintner to earn my freedom. Where's our mam?'

Michael's face grew dark. 'Martin, there's something I have to tell you . . . '

Kemp felt sick, suspecting that he already knew the answer to his question. 'Where is she, Michael?'

Marjery Kemp was buried in the graveyard of the church of Saint Mary Magdalen. The markers at other nearby plots showed the last resting places of Thomas Croft, Simkin Sewell, the Foresters, and dozens of other villagers. 'It were a band of brigands,' Michael explained grimly. 'They rampaged through the village, stealing everything they could find of value, raping the women . . . '

'What about Beaumont? Didn't he try to protect you?'

'He were away at the time. Looking for you,' Michael added, glowering significantly at his brother. 'Not that he could have done much if he had been here. They took us by surprise. Simkin, Croft and some of the others tried to put up a defence with their bows, but they were no match for these men. They tortured Hayward Forester to death – they were convinced he must have had a cache of gold

413

somewheres, and nowt anyone could say would convince them otherwise. A few were spared. I only escaped by hiding down by the river . . . '

'I can well imagine,' Kemp snorted contemptuously.

'What would you have had me do?' Michael demanded angrily. 'I'm a farmer, not a warrior. These were hard men, Martin, veterans of Crécy. Trained killers . . . '

'Men like me, you mean,' Kemp observed wryly.

'I didn't say that.'

'You didn't have to.'

The two of them stared at the grave markers in hostile silence for a few moments.

'What about Nicholay?' Kemp asked finally, tonelessly.

'He's well – at least, he were the last time I saw him. He visited the village briefly during the summer. He came top of his class at college and won a bursary to study at the Sorbonne College in Paris. He seemed pleased at the prospect.' Michael tried to put warmth into his voice, to forget the row they had just had.

Kemp said nothing.

'I know the future looks bleak, but things will be different now that you're back,' Michael continued. 'We can start afresh . . . '

Kemp was not listening. He stared down at his mother's grave. He should be feeling something more than this . . . this *emptiness*, he thought to himself. 'I'd like to be alone for a little while,' he told his brother.

'Of course.' Michael moved away, walking to the lych gate where Kemp had tied his horse.

Kemp stared at the various grave markers. The people he had grown up with – all dead. It was as if the world he had left behind all those months ago no longer existed. Could this be God's punishment for raping that girl in Caen? They had been good people, on the whole; why kill them, to make him pay? There was no justice in the world.

He rose to his feet and tilted his face to the heavens, roaring in anguish: 'Why not me?'

He half expected a peal of thunder in reply, but there was nothing, just the cold grey sky and a few spots of rain. He took his rondel from its sheath, gripping it tightly as he pressed the tip of the blade against his chest. His hand was shaking uncontrollably. He tried to grip the dagger in both hands, but he still could not bring himself to plunge the blade into his own heart. Cursing his own weakness, he returned it to its sheath.

He walked sorrowfully back to the lych gate, unfastening the hackney's halter.

Michael looked at him uncertainly. 'Things will be better now, you'll see,' he persisted. 'We must be strong. We have our whole lives ahead of us.'

'Aye,' Kemp agreed grimly. 'That's what I'm afraid of.' He swung himself up into the saddle.

'What are you doing?'

'I'm not staying, Michael. There's nothing for me here now.'

'But where will you go? What will you do?'

Kemp shrugged. 'I'll follow the trade I've learned.' He patted the hilt of his broadsword.

'Fighting?' Michael was disgusted. 'What kind of a life will that be?'

'Life is for living,' Kemp told him softly. 'And I died a long time ago. Maybe it was on a beach in Normandy, maybe it was in a city called Caen, or maybe it was in a field in Picardy. But my last rites are long overdue.'

Michael furrowed his brow. 'What are you talking about? I don't understand.'

'Goodbye, Michael.' Kemp dug his heels into his hackney's flanks, and chucked the reins, riding out of the village and back into the world beyond.

HISTORICAL NOTE

The Hundred Years War never really excited my interest
when I studied it at school. At that level it never seemed
more than a list of peace treaties and battles, each one
accompanied by a date, each battle consisting of the
English archers standing in a line on a hill and shooting at
the French as they charged on horseback. At exam time
one could rely on questions along the lines of: 'Why did
the English win at Crécy/Poitiers/Agincourt?' Whichever
battle it was, the correct answer was always more or less
the same.

I first started writing about Martin Kemp while studying history – specifically, the Italian City Republics of the
Middle Ages – at university. He was originally conceived
as an ageing, cynical, embittered mercenary, fighting in
Italy in the mid 1370s. As I wrote about him, I started
asking myself about his past, the events in his life that had
made him what he had become by that stage. Since he is
loosely based on Sir John Hawkwood, a real-life English
mercenary of the time, I reasoned that he would have had
a similar career: fighting as a young man in the Hundred
Years War. So I went back to study the period once more,
looking not only at the battles, but also the massacres, the
pillage and the destruction waged by the English – an
aspect of the Hundred Years War that is all too often
glossed over. I particularly wanted to understand it from
the point of view of an individual caught up in the events,
rather than a student writing in broad terms with all the
benefit of hindsight.

What I discovered astonished me. Studying the subject in depth for the first time, I found that there was a great deal more to the war than a few battles where the English archers invariably stood in a line on a hill and shot at the charging French horsemen. Now there were men-at-arms rushing to seize bridges before the French; duels between English yeoman archers and Genoese crossbowmen struggling waist-deep in the ford at Blanchetaque; criminals impressed into the king's service for a year and a day in return for pardons (forerunners of the Dirty Dozen?); and knights performing great deeds of valour and generally behaving like outrageous *poseurs*. The knights and earls who fought in those wars ceased to be nothing more than a set of names that cropped up again and again, but instead became personalities who leapt out of the pages of the documents and the chronicles of the time. Here was a collection of characters and tales that were just as exciting as anything I could dream up. Thus this book – hopefully the first in a series – was born.

The Hundred Years War began in 1337 and petered out around 1453, so it was nearer a Hundred and Sixteen Years' War; although if one subtracted all the years in which no fighting took place because there was a truce, or simply because no one could be bothered, I suspect the resulting figure would be rather less than one hundred. Martin Kemp is a relative late-comer to the scene, for the war has already been going on for nine years by the time he lands in France – three years longer than the Second World War in its entirety. The English have already won a decisive sea victory against the French at Sluys (1340), and the Earl of Northampton has already used the new technique of getting the archers to stand in a line on a hill and shoot arrows at the charging French to good effect at Morlaix (1342) – tactics which the English had learned from the Scots the hard way at Bannockburn (1314), subsequently beating them at their own game at Dupplin

Moor (1332) and Halidon Hill (1333). So it was hardly an innovative tactic by the time Northampton advised King Edward III to use it at Crécy.

The impact of the English victory at Crécy was enormous. Previously France had been thought of as Christendom's greatest military power; the fact that the French could be beaten by a considerably smaller force of men from a smaller country considered to be backward and peopled by a race thought to be hardly better than barbarians stunned the Christian world and inflicted a massive blow to French prestige and self-confidence. Perhaps as importantly in terms of the conduct of the war, a large portion of the French nobility was slaughtered in the battle. The nobility being the military elite of the time, this was perhaps equivalent to a modern army having most of its tank regiments and most of its general staff wiped out in a single fell swoop. It was years before the French recovered sufficiently to face the English in battle on the same scale again – just in time for the battle of Poitiers, ten years later.

Why Edward III did not go on to capture Paris and claim the French throne after Crécy is now and will always remain a matter of conjecture. Apparently he did not feel his position was strong enough to make that move; the extent of England's overwhelming victory seeming to have stunned the English themselves as much as anyone. In his defence, it should be pointed out that when he marched to Rheims to have himself crowned King of France in 1359 in a position of perhaps just as much strength, the French were still able to resist him. Even after Henry V was acknowledged heir to the French throne in 1420, the thought of an English king on the throne of France was so abhorrent that most of the French nobility rallied to the Dauphin's cause. In the twelfth century, when Henry II of England ruled more than half of France (and spoke French; indeed, Edward III was the first English king to have more than a smattering of English), it might have been acceptable for an English king to rule France; but the Hundred Years War saw the emergence of nationalism both in England and in France. In the fourteenth century, most of the common people of France hated their nobility, but they probably hated the English nobility even more.

So after Crécy, Edward III continued north, away from Paris, instead besieging the town of Calais, a noted haven for pirates who attacked English shipping and raided the coast of southern England, and a town the capture of which would make future campaining in northern France so much easier for the English. But the siege of Calais is another story.

The song in Chapter 11, 'The Knight Stained From Battle', is my own adaptation of a real one from the early fourteenth century, by William Herebert. The song appears to be a precursor to 'The Battle Hymn of the Republic', both being drawn from the Book of Isaiah, 6:1–7.

Since many of the characters who feature in this book are based on men who actually lived, it seems only fair that I should write briefly of their provenance.

Foremost of these is, of course, Sir Thomas Holland. Although information about him is scanty, I have nevertheless managed to take certain liberties with his characterisation. Any student of the chronicles of the time will find that the chroniclers portray him less as the tough, cynical, hardened campaigner that I have described, and more as what – by modern standards – might be described as a *poseur*, over-imbued with chivalric ideals. During the Crécy campaign, when Edward III's army reached the Seine only to find the nearest bridge broken down, Holland 'and a handful of other exhibitionists'[1] rode up to the edge of the water and shouted 'St George for Edward!' across the water to the Frenchmen standing on

419

the other side. While the famous – if unreliable – chronicler Jean Froissart describes him as having only one eye, at least one historian[2] has suggested that Holland wore his white silk eyepatch as part of a chivalric vow not to uncover that eye until he had performed some deed of valour against the French. But the picture of him having one eye so suited the scarred, experienced campaigner I wanted to portray that I tempered my historical judgement with a little artistic licence and for once went along with Froissart's explanation.

To me, the two different aspects of Holland presented by what little we know of him – the *poseur* and the seasoned campaigner – are not incompatible; in my portrayal, I have merely down-played the former and concentrated on the latter. Indeed, an appreciation of this dichotomy is essential to understanding chivalric society. While the vow described above may seem ludicrous to us today, it was very typical of the nobility of that time; and it did not stop the nobility from winning battles and campaigns through cunning and brutality.

Other characters who merit passing mention are Sir Thomas of Norwich, and Edward of Woodstock, Prince of Wales. References to Sir Thomas of Norwich are even fewer and farther between. He seems to have been a younger brother of Lord Norwich. His only apparent role in history was to carry d'Harcourt's message to Edward III on the field of Crécy, enabling the king to give his famous response concerning his son: 'Let the boy win his spurs.'

As for the 'boy' himself, Edward of Woodstock was to be remembered by future generations as the Black Prince, although there is no evidence that he was ever referred to by this name – which seems to have been a Tudor invention – during his lifetime. Nor is there any evidence to confirm the claim that he wore black armour. A more likely derivation for the nickname is the many 'black' deeds he was later responsible for, such as the sack of Limoges in 1370, a massacre that seems to have been particularly brutal in an age in which slaughter, pillage and wanton destruction were accepted methods of waging war.

Finally, one cannot write either of the Crécy Campaign or of the dichotomy between chivalry and medieval warfare without sparing a few words for Edward III himself. During his own lifetime, Edward III was admired by friends and enemies alike as the epitome of a chivalric ruler. Yet it was Edward who encouraged the use of massed archers to break up charges of mounted knights, a tactic that was considered particularly ignoble and sneaky by the French, who felt that warfare was too noble a pursuit to allow commoners to win any of its glory. He was also expert in the use of espionage, strategic deceit and misdirection, and propaganda: vital weapons in the arsenal of the twentieth-century general, but hardly appropriate – or so one might be forgiven for thinking – in a chivalric milieu. Nevertheless, these weapons contributed to the English victories in the early part of his reign, and thus – indirectly – heightened the glory of his kingship. That he was both an extremely intelligent and an extremely cynical man cannot be denied. According to one story, while he was a guest at one of his noblemen's castles, he is supposed to have raped the nobleman's wife while the nobleman himself was absent. The more one tries to pin down this story, the more ephemeral the evidence becomes; but the very fact that such a story, no matter how unfounded, could gain currency tells us a great deal about the character of Edward III as he was perceived by his contemporaries.

And, yes – if Froissart is to be believed, which is not always the case – Edward III really did trip up and bloody his nose when he first landed at Saint-Vaast-la-Hougue in 1346.

[1]Jonathan Sumption, *The Hundred Years War, Vol. 1: Trial by Battle*, p. 514.
[2]Michael Packe, *Edward III*, p. 114.

A NOTE ON NAMES
AND TERMINOLOGY

As I have updated the dialogue spoken by the characters in this novel from the Middle English, Anglo-Norman and Old French that they would have spoken into modern English and French, I have also up-dated the names into more familiar forms. Thus the names de Holand and Montagu become Holland and Montague, while Martin Kemp, had he not been illiterate, would have spelled his name 'Martyn Kempe'. At the same time, I have used fourteenth-century diminutives rather than their modern equivalents in order to capture the feel of the period: thus Daw rather than Dave for David, and Hal rather than Alf for Alfred (Hal as a diminutive for Henry came at a later date). In the case of non-English characters, I have used the form native to their own country, unless they are so well-known that it would be ludicrous to change their name so much. Thus Godfrey Harcourt becomes Godefroi d'Harcourt, but Philip of Valois does not become Philippe, and Sir Walter Manny, a knight from Hainault, does not become Sir Gautier; as a naturalised Englishman, he would probably have been known by that name anyway. However, since 'Manny' is now widely agreed to be the result of a misreading of 'Mauny', I have made that change, on the assumption that Sir Walter Mauny will remain recognisable to those who have already heard of him, while 'Sir Gautier de Mauny' is so far removed from 'Sir Walter Manny' as to be all but unrecognisable.

To avoid peppering this book with parentheses and footnotes, I have replaced terms in use at the time with terms more readily understood by the modern reader, even when the latter are not strictly accurate. Thus the fourteenth-century term 'arrowstring' has been replaced by its modern equivalent, 'bowstring'. English archers were largely formed into units of one hundred men (*centaines*) subdivided into units of twenty men (*vintaines*), whilst a large formation on the march or on the battlefield was called a 'battle'. These terms I have loosely translated into 'company', 'platoon' and 'battalion', which while not being entirely accurate are more easily recognisable to the modern reader.

To confuse the issue further, I have also used the word 'company' to describe a body of men commanded by a knight, not necessarily one hundred strong, in anticipation of Kemp's future adventures, in which the word 'company' will come to describe a band of mercenaries. The word 'companion' derives ultimately from the Latin word *panis*, 'bread'; literally, a companion is someone with whom one shares bread, and thus a company is a group of men who eat together. This terminology was originally used to describe an association of merchants who worked together for mutual aid and protection; its subsequent application to bands of mercenaries seems particularly apt in view of the fact that both companies of merchants and companies of mercenaries worked together to achieve the same end: making money. One of the most distinguished mercenary captains of the Hundred Years War was Sir Robert Knollys, who openly boasted that he fought neither for the king of England nor for the king of France, but for himself. At a time when professional soldiers were raised under terms of indenture to fight for pay – not dissimilar to the *condotta* system for hiring mercenaries in Italy at that time – the distinction between the men who fought for their kings and the men who fought for themselves was blurred, especially when one remembers the vast profits to be made from booty. Mercenary companies were led by captains, and to this day a company of regular soldiers is commanded by a captain.

A *vintaine* was commanded by a *vintenar* (literally, 'twentieth man'); once again I have exercised a certain amount of artistic licence by translating *vintenar* as 'serjeant-at-arms'. Strictly speaking, by medieval terminology a serjeant-at-arms was any man-at-arms who was not a knight, a concept I have already translated simply as 'man-at-arms'; I have, rather synthetically perhaps, used the term 'serjeant-at-arms' to describe something closer to what we think of as an army serjeant today.

I make no apologies for these and other conscious misusages. This book is intended to be an accurate portrayal of warfare under Edward III in general, and an account of the Crécy campaign in particular; but first and foremost it is a piece of fiction intended to entertain before it educates, and thus my main priority was to create something that would be readily accessible to the general reader without resorting to the use of footnotes or a glossary.